THE MANHATTAN SWINDLE

BOOK 2 OF THE ONE HUNDRED YEARS OF WAR SERIES

JAY PERIN

Publisher's Cataloging-In-Publication Data
(Prepared by The Donohue Group, Inc.)

Names: Perin, Jay, author.
Title: The Manhattan swindle / Jay Perin.
Description: [New York, New York] : [East River Books], [2021] | Series: [One hundred years of war] ; book 2
Identifiers: ISBN 9781736468036 (paperback) | ISBN 9781736468029 (ebook)
Subjects: LCSH: United States--Politics and government--1945-1989--Fiction. | Petroleum industry and trade--History--20th century--Fiction. | Heirs--Fiction. | Nineteen seventies--Fiction. | Conspiracies--Fiction. | LCGFT: Political fiction. | Thrillers (Fiction)
Classification: LCC PS3616.E7443 M36 2021 (print) | LCC PS3616.E7443 (ebook) | DDC 813/.6--dc23

The characters, names, businesses, places, locales, events, and incidents are either the products of the author's imagination or referred to in a fictitious manner. Any resemblance in either the book or the promotional material to actual persons, living or dead, or actual events is purely coincidental.

Editors:
Chase Nottingham
Elizabeth Roderick http://talesfrompurgatory.com/
Cover: www.ebookorprint.com
Maps and illustrations: Murat Bayazit
Video (book trailer): Nauman Gandhi
Special mention: Marcus Jordan https://www.marcusjordanart.com/
Ashley Redbird http://www.redbird-designs.net/

www.EastRiverBooks.com

To the One They Called God;
To the Best of Men;
To That Goddess of Knowledge;
To the Chronicler.

Table of Contents

Part I...1

    Chapter 1.. 1

    Chapter 2.. 6

    Chapter 3.. 9

Part II..20

    Chapter 4.. 20

    Chapter 5.. 26

    Chapter 6.. 46

Part III...49

    Chapter 7.. 49

    Chapter 8.. 59

    Chapter 9.. 70

Part IV...77

    Chapter 10 77

    Chapter 11 88

    Chapter 12 93

Part V.. 102

    Chapter 13 102

    Chapter 14 108

    Chapter 15 119

    Chapter 16 125

Part VI... 133

    Chapter 17 133

    Chapter 18 141

    Chapter 19 155

Part VII..161

    Chapter 20..161

    Chapter 21..171

    Chapter 22..183

    Chapter 23..197

    Chapter 24..202

Part VIII..217

    Chapter 25..217

    Chapter 26..222

Part IX..235

    Chapter 27..235

    Chapter 28..238

    Chapter 29..247

Part X...253

    Chapter 30..253

    Chapter 31..263

    Chapter 32..269

Part XI..279

    Chapter 33..279

    Chapter 34..282

    Chapter 35..289

Part XII...292

    Chapter 36..292

    Chapter 37..297

    Chapter 38..306

Part XIII..313

    Chapter 39..313

Chapter 40 315

Chapter 41 318

Chapter 42 321

Part XIV...325

Chapter 43 325

Chapter 44 327

Part XV 333

Chapter 45 333

Chapter 46 340

Chapter 47 347

Part XVI...352

Chapter 48 352

Chapter 49 358

Chapter 50 363

Part XVII...369

Chapter 51 369

Chapter 52 371

Chapter 53 386

Chapter 54 392

Part XVIII 395

Chapter 55 395

Chapter 56 398

Part XIX...401

Chapter 57 401

Chapter 58 408

Chapter 59 412

Chapter 60 415

Chapter 61...419

Part XX...423

Chapter 62...423

Chapter 63...433

Chapter 64...436

Chapter 65...439

Part XXI...445

Chapter 66...445

Chapter 67...462

Chapter 68...465

Chapter 69...467

Part XXII..471

Chapter 70...471

Chapter 71...475

Part XXIII...484

Chapter 72...484

Chapter 73...487

Chapter 74...489

Chapter 75...491

Chapter 76...493

Chapter 77...494

Chapter 78...501

Part XXIV..507

Chapter 79...507

Chapter 80...527

Chapter 81...530

Afterword..535

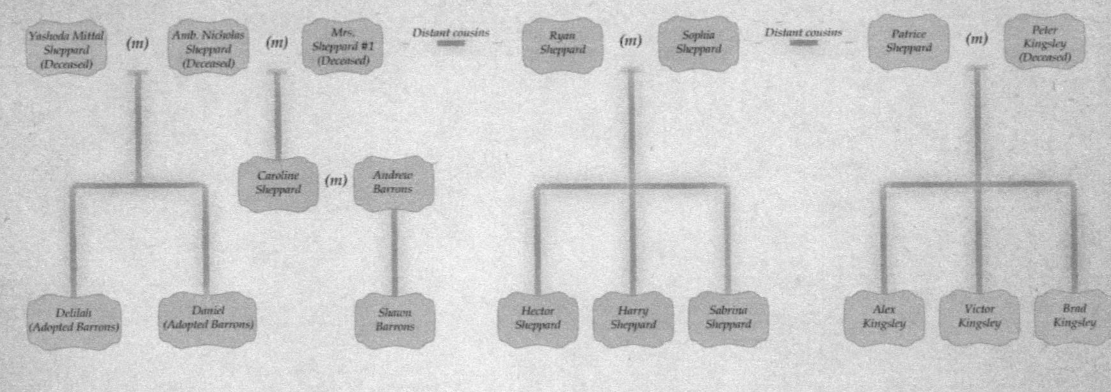

THE SHEPPARDS

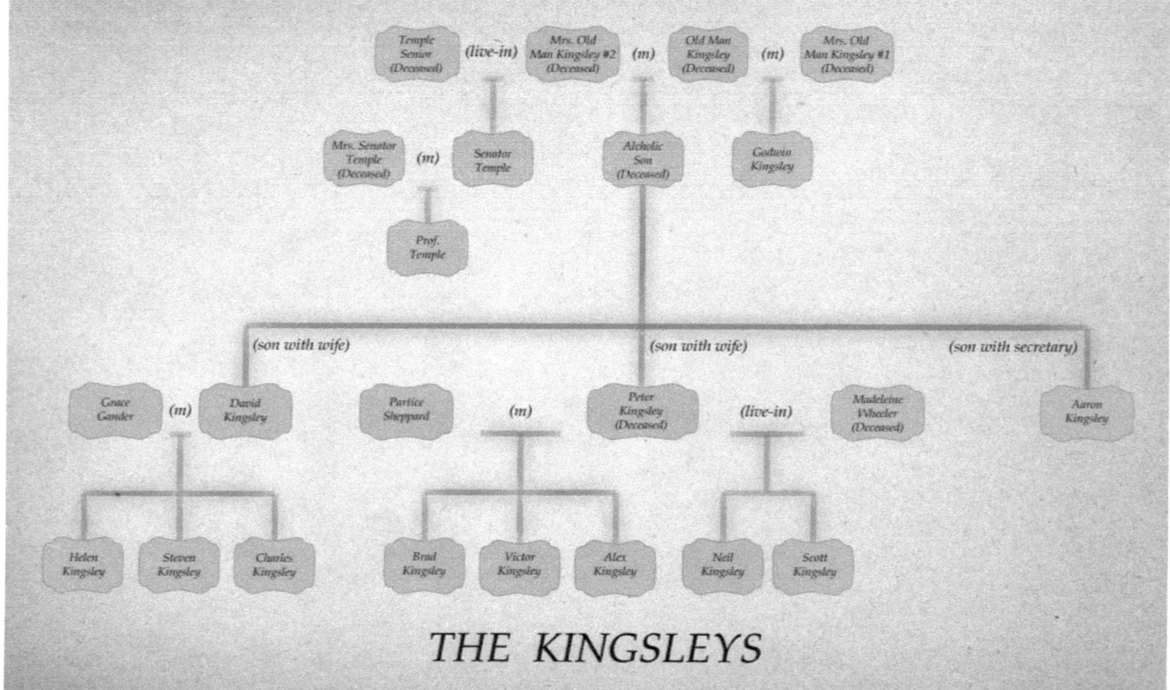

Temple Senior (Deceased)
(live-in)
Mrs. Old Man Kingsley #2 (Deceased)
(m)
Old Man Kingsley (Deceased)
(m)
Mrs. Old Man Kingsley #1 (Deceased)
Mrs. Senator Temple (Deceased)
(m)
Senator Temple
Alcholic Son (Deceased)
Godwin Kingsley
Prof. Temple
(son with wife)
(son with wife)
(son with secretary)
Grace Gander
(m)
David Kingsley
Partice Sheppard
(m)
Peter Kingsley (Deceased)
(live-in)
Madeleine Wheeler (Deceased)
Aaron Kingsley
Helen Kingsley
Steven Kingsley
Charles Kingsley
Brad Kingsley
Victor Kingsley
Alex Kingsley
Neil Kingsley
Scott Kingsley
THE KINGSLEYS

Part I

Chapter 1

May 1974

Washington, DC

In the quiet wood-paneled room on the second floor of the Supreme Court Building, Senator Temple waited for his stepbrother, the judge, to arrive. Shelves lined the walls, books on law and the constitution arranged according to topic, but Temple's attention was on the leather-bound journal in his hands. So many things to jot down, incidents to record... there was an entire collection of such diaries in his library at home, all safely locked in a vault. The secrets contained in those pages were not for another set of eyes... at least not until the people involved were long dead and gone. Still, the tales needed to be recorded for posterity. Then there were those secrets he didn't dare write down, truths which could destroy entire families and alter the existing power structure.

There was a barely audible squeak behind. Someone was at the glass door to the judge's office, pushing it open. Without turning to check the person's identity, Temple tucked the journal inside his blazer and picked up the thick tome from the desk. Casually, he leafed through *Arthashastra*, the discourse on statecraft written centuries ago in India. The author paid gold coins to be granted custody of an impoverished boy and installed him on the throne of an empire. Rumor had it the mentor did the ruling from behind the throne. Temple inhaled the sweet, musky smell of the old pages and smiled on the thought he shared a few traits with the author.

Arrayed in black robes, Supreme Court Justice Godwin

Kingsley strode to the desk and settled into his chair before uttering a crisp "good morning." Like the rest of the Kingsley men, he was tall. The silvery hair drawn back into a low ponytail should've brought comments in a supreme court justice. There was also the white beard, neatly trimmed. Such was his stature in the country's judicial system that no one ever dreamed of castigating him for the eccentricities. Not to mention the powerful position he occupied as president of Kingsley Corp, one of the foremost oil services businesses in the nation. Gray eyes steely, Godwin demanded, "Tell me more about Delilah."

"Lilah," Temple corrected. "Most people call her Lilah. You read the papers I sent over. All the info you need is in the folder. Wait until your grandsons meet her. They'll be fighting—more than they do now—for an introduction."

Blood flowed blue in the veins of the Kingsleys, but they weren't exactly known for their classy conduct or their kindness toward each other. Godwin's grandsons were only in their twenties, and they were already butting heads over eventual control of the family business. The young men were likely to tear each other to pieces over the stunning seventeen-year-old girl Temple would soon introduce to them. Their crude behavior was not going to endear them to Lilah. Plus, there was Harry, the boy she grew up with. Every piece on the chessboard needed to be moved into place. "Beauty's fine," Godwin stated, "but blood and background are more important."

"Which century are you living in?" Temple asked, not bothering to hide his amusement. "My mother came from common stock, and your father had no problem marrying her." Besides, the young lady under discussion might not be aristocracy, but her father was an ambassador. Her mother—an Indian woman—was a United Nations lawyer who met and married the widowed American diplomat in Bombay. Ambassador Sheppard had been retired for a few years by the time he and Lilah's mother died in a plane crash.

"You know the Sheppards well, and Lilah's Indian cousins are all in respectable positions. Military officers, bankers, civil servants... professionals."

"Upper middle class," brooded Godwin. "The same as her father."

"Yes, but she was adopted by *Andrew Barrons*. Not too many men more pedigreed than him." The Barronses were not merely rich; they could trace their ancestry back to the Normans who conquered England. Class hadn't mattered to Andrew when he married the ambassador's daughter with his first wife. In Andrew's rarefied situation, anything out of the ordinary, such as marrying a few rungs below, would merely be thought of as an allowable indulgence. When Ambassador Sheppard and his second wife were killed, their then-fifteen-year-old twins—Lilah and Dan—were adopted by their half-sister and her husband. "Godwin, Lilah is now Delilah Sheppard Barrons. As Andrew's daughter, she *is* aristocracy."

Tugging open a drawer, Godwin brought out a thin folder and flipped it open. "She's also smart... and ambitious." He tossed the folder onto the table and rocked back in the chair, raising an appreciative eyebrow.

Lilah was headed to MIT in the fall for chemical engineering. Her sights were set on law school after undergrad. The senator nodded. "There you go—intelligence and drive along with the Barrons money and lineage."

Godwin appeared slightly mollified, but Temple didn't give a damn about the nobility of Lilah's blood. He'd picked the right person as the intended ruler of their corporate empire. She was perfectly positioned to dethrone the current tyrant ruling the oil and gas business.

Temple's eyes went to the book on his lap, the ancient treatise on politics and governance. Godwin had spotted a copy in the original language and called Temple. This volume completed Temple's collection. It would occupy the empty space in his library next to *The Art of War* and *The Prince*. There was another work, the meditations of an ancient philosopher-king. He once mused the rise and fall of past empires could foretell the future. Temple could not let the mistakes of those who went before be repeated. The new leaders would rule wisely and not let power corrupt them.

"The girl does present us with an extraordinary opportunity," Godwin murmured. Through her and one of his grandsons, the Kingsleys, the Barronses, and the Sheppards would once again be allied against a common enemy. They would defeat the criminal emperor of the energy sector. "Have you mentioned anything to her?"

"No," said Temple, immediately. "We have to give her some time before bringing it up. She needs a couple of years to mature a bit." The delay would give Lilah the break she needed to recover from the trauma of recent events. She would also get a chance to see the world beyond her youthful dreams, to understand what was at stake.

"Not just her." Godwin again tugged open a drawer and took out a small chessboard. "My grandsons, too. You, me... every piece has to be in its place."

Temple wasn't even slightly startled at Godwin echoing his own previous thoughts. When they met as stepbrothers, both were in their teens and bonded over chess. "Lilah likes to decide her own place," Temple mused.

"The arrogance of youth," Godwin said brusquely. "Look at my grandsons. I'm hoping four years in college will be enough to whip them into shape. Even then, we're going to have work to do."

The young men were all at the United States Military Academy in West Point as per family tradition. "Money and arrogance usually go hand in hand," Temple pointed out, laughing. "The army will take care of them. Lilah is... she's unique." She required a different approach. Then there was Harry.

Lilah's biological father—the deceased ambassador—and Harry's were business partners and shared the same last name. The blood connection between the families was extremely remote... an ancestor back in the sixteen-hundreds from what Temple heard. Despite the tenuousness of the link, the men were close, and their kids grew up together. That Harry and Lilah saw a future with each other was clear to anyone who cared to look. Not long after the deaths of Lilah's parents, Harry's family lost the business to the criminal who took over the oil sector, and they were chased out of Libya, where they'd lived for nearly two decades. The seventeen-year-old boy was targeted by the enemy as punishment for his father. Lilah suffered horribly merely for being at Harry's side when he was snatched by hired thugs. The way he and Lilah engineered their escape was nothing short of miraculous.

Two determined young people... it wouldn't be easy to persuade either into cooperating with Temple's plans, but it was the only way to defeat the enemy. The Sheppards wanted payback, but the man responsible for their torments was shrewd, his power and cunning helping him stay beyond the reach of the law. Temple swore he would see justice done. So did the Kingsleys and the Barronses, who finally put greed and old grudges aside, acknowledging the plain fact they wouldn't be too far behind on the criminal's list. Individually, all three clans were sure to lose, but together, they could win the war.

Soon, Harry and Lilah would be told an alliance brought about through Delilah Sheppard Barrons and one of the Kingsley grandsons was needed to take on their common adversary. With the survival of the companies at stake, Lilah's feelings or Harry's couldn't matter.

Godwin pushed the chessboard to the middle of the desk. "Game?"

Temple nodded to himself. It wouldn't be easy, but he knew exactly what moves to make. Oh, yes. Both Harry and Lilah would comply with Temple's instructions. They would help him usher in a new beginning for the world, a new life... a new empire.

Chapter 2

Two weeks later, May 1974

New York, New York

Hefting the two pieces of luggage into the sleeper car of the Amtrak train, Harry tucked the boxes close to the reclining chairs. Thank God he was the only person in the roomette. He didn't feel like company today. Flicking imaginary dust from his jeans and old blue tee, he glanced at his watch. There were a few minutes remaining for him to say his goodbyes. Harry returned to the narrow hallway and winked at a bawling toddler as he squeezed past the kid and his hassled mother to the door of the car.

Indecipherable announcements from the train station's overhead system greeted Harry when he jumped out to join the small group of people on the platform. The whole family was present to see him off to the SEAL training program... his parents, baby sister... Harry's older brother just left to buy himself some soda.

God, Harry was ready to kill for an ice-cold drink. It was so damned hot even his sandaled feet were sweaty. Tugging at his collar, he nodded at his parents. "Mother, Father." He could barely make himself heard over the chatter and laughter of the men and women and children swarming the waiting area next to the railway tracks.

Blue eyes teary, Harry's mother enveloped him in a hug. Ten-year-old Sabrina was a miniature version of their mother with her bright-blonde hair, but her irises were green and quite free of any moisture. She was too busy gawking at the locomotive to pay attention to Harry. Freeing himself from maternal embrace, Harry called, "Hey, Runt."

Before Mother completed her exclamation of annoyance, Sabrina's head swiveled toward him. Nostrils quivering in outrage, she snapped, "I am *not* a runt. Tell him, Mother!"

"Yeah, you are," Harry teased. At six-foot-four, he towered over little Sabrina. Tugging gently at her fat pigtail, he said, "I won't be back for a while, kiddo." First, boot camp in Illinois. Then, the pre-training. Finally, BUD/S training and the rest of it. "Who am I going to pester in the navy?"

The annoyance on her plump face vanished, and with a high-pitched wail, she threw her arms around Harry's waist.

"You two," grumbled their father, combing fingers through dark hair very much like Harry's except for the ample amount of gray. The brown eyes now sported wrinkles all around. Both the Sheppard parents aged rapidly during the ordeal the family went through. More than a year of harassment from Libyan authorities culminated in Harry's abduction, all at the behest of the criminal oilman, Jared Sanders. There was nothing the American government could do to Sanders. No proof, claimed the feds. The Sheppards were told to shut the hell up unless they could hand over irrefutable evidence. Unverifiable accusations thrown at a billion-dollar business like Sanders, Incorporated could destroy the already-tanking stock market while doing nothing to put away the criminal for good.

Their family was only one of many which were devastated by Sanders's hunger for power. Senator Temple vowed he'd do something about it and even promised he'd contact Harry regarding some plans. *Soon,* the seventeen-year-old muttered in his mind. There would be justice for all of Sanders's victims, including Lilah.

He might not have been directly involved in the assault on her, but the kidnapping he arranged led to it.

Concealing the smoldering anger with a grin, Harry patted his sister on her shoulder. "Take care of the old folks."

The two people at the back of the group waited patiently for him to get to them. Bumping fists with Daniel Barrons—Lilah's twin and newly adopted son of Andrew Barrons—Harry asked, "All set for West Point?" Dan was about to start his freshman year at the military academy.

"More or less." Inclining his dark head toward his sister, Dan said, "Got to drop Lilah off at the dorms first."

Harry nodded and turned to the last person. Lilah's hazel eyes were wide and fixed on him, and her teeth bit down hard on her lower lip, leaving it as red as her clothes and shoes.

Awkwardly, he reached out to hold her by her upper arms and pull her into a hug. Lilah's palms landed just as clumsily on his shoulders. Tendrils of slightly wavy, dark hair teased his nostrils, the color of her locks so black it glinted blue under the lights. He breathed deep, trying to imprint his brain with the crazy sexy scent of her perfume.

Within the security of his loose embrace, Lilah palpably relaxed. The edginess would return as soon as he let her go.

Mentally, Harry kicked himself good and hard. He could damned well wait for a kiss. Time... she needed time to heal from wounds both visible and invisible.

Forcing himself to release his hold, Harry managed another smile. "I'll call... and we'll write every week."

Voice raspy even months after the fire they escaped in Libya, Lilah blurted, "I'll send you *baklava*."

"Heh?" Granted, he binged on the sweet every chance he got,

but—

She stuck her tongue out. "I saw this Middle Eastern café near MIT when I visited. I'm gonna be remembering you every time I pass the place."

Injecting comical dismay into his tone, he asked, "Only when you see the café?" As she laughed, the train hissed. A heavyset man in a conductor's uniform trudged up and down the platform with a clipboard in his hands, shouting out a warning for all passengers to climb on board. "Gotta go," Harry murmured.

Without saying a word, Lilah nodded.

A loud whistle blew as Harry leaped in and peered through the window. He continued to stare as the train chugged out, watching the group getting smaller and smaller, watching Lilah stay in the same spot even as the rest moved away.

"I'll be back," he declared, but there was no one around to hear. Three years, and he'd be done with his training.

He returned to his chair and tried to focus on the paperback he bought the day before, but he barely saw the words. The train sped past buildings, factories, and grasslands, tooting the horn when approaching railway crossings. The whistle reverberated in the air, and he imagined the sound echoing down the tracks already traversed, all the way to New York City where Lilah waited.

Chapter 3

Months later, November 1974

Cambridge, Massachusetts

A weight landed on her shoulder and whirled her around. A scream broke, only to be smothered by the hand slamming over her mouth. The obscene name, the order to shut up—or else. The teeth on her lip, biting down. The taste of blood. Tears... screams... a hard slap on her cheek. The ripping sound of her robe tearing.

"*No,*" screamed Lilah, jerking up in bed. Darkness. Pitch-black darkness. The monster was near. Her arms flailed, struggling ineffectually to escape the terrifying night.

"What—who—" shouted the startled voice of her roommate. A click later, yellow light flooded the room. "What's going on?" the girl asked, her eyes darting frantically around.

Lilah panted short, sharp breaths. *Huh? The dorm room? On MIT campus?* She wasn't in Libya. There was no monster, only a scared and confused roommate. "Sorry," she mumbled, her erratic pulse slowly settling into an even rhythm. "Bad dream... didn't mean to wake you."

After a few seconds of gawking in silence, the girl—an architecture major—collapsed back onto the mattress. "Shit... I thought someone was about to murder us. Dreaming! It's all the raw meat you ate. You should've asked for baked kibbeh like I did." She scrambled up and pulled open the side table drawer. "I have some weed if you want... only enough for one joint, but we could share. It will settle your stomach."

"Thanks," Lilah said, mustering a weak smile. "But I'm okay."

Shrugging, the budding architect said, "Suit yourself. *I* need something to calm my nerves... the way you screamed!"

Sweet-smelling smoke swirled around the room as Lilah tugged the comforter up to her chin. Her fingers trembled slightly before she curled them into fists. Every night this week, she woke mere moments before the screams managed to escape the confines of her mind. Every. Single. Darned. Night. This time, she couldn't stop the terror from taking over. She knew why. It was getting closer and closer to the one-year mark of her trip to Libya to celebrate Thanksgiving with Harry and his family, not knowing what awaited her in the country.

In a couple of days, the rest of the students would head to their homes to spend yet another Thanksgiving with their families. Lilah would be one of the few left on campus, fending off horrific memories with only her twin's calls for support. Dan phoned daily the last two weeks to check on her.

Lilah glanced toward the desk calendar. The one person who she believed would've been on the phone with her every day hadn't called at all in five months. They talked right after he got to boot camp, and he said something about waiting for Senator Temple. Since then... zilch.

God, Harry... what is going on with you? Lilah fretted.

Another attempt by Sanders, accident, illness... every calamity that could befall Harry ran through her mind as each week passed without hearing from him.

He did write, his too-short notes claiming the breaks he got weren't long enough even to take a piss. But if she could talk to him at least once... whenever she tried to reach him at the naval training facility, a stern masculine voice always informed her Harry wasn't available at the moment.

Her phone *would* ring over the holidays, Lilah assured herself. Like her, Harry would be remembering what happened this time last year. No way would he not call.

#

"Instant noodles," Lilah muttered, trying to get comfortable in the secondhand rolling chair next to the desk.

"You know you could've gone home," Dan said over the line, making slurping noises. "Turkey and trimmings and apple pie."

"Sure... with Andrew and Caroline. When was the last time they actually wanted me around?" Andrew Barrons and his wife—Lilah's half-sister—were unlikely to remember her existence no matter what day it was. To them, she was merely the girl they adopted out of obligation. "I would've gone if you were there."

"They're not bad people," Dan insisted. "It's just... they look at things differently."

"Not where you're concerned," Lilah retorted. The Barronses would've thrown a huge party if Dan made it home. He was their beloved prince, the heir apparent to Andrew's business holdings.

Not that Lilah was some kind of an ill-treated orphan. She and Dan got the same monthly checks from Andrew's secretary, but Lilah regularly returned hers with a "thank you, but not necessary." She was nearly eighteen, old enough to take care of herself. Almost the entirety of her parents' savings had been invested in Genesis, the Sheppards' oil drilling company. That money was gone, and the stock she got in the family's new business was worth close to nothing at the moment. There were death benefits from her parents' jobs and the small amount of cash in the bank, but those funds were intended as financial cushion for both her and her brother. Didn't matter. Lilah had her scholarship and the part-time job at the campus bookstore. She didn't need Andrew's charity.

Dan chatted with her for a good fifteen minutes. Toward the end of their conversation, his tone turned tense. "You doing okay?" he asked. "I really wish I could've made it home."

Suddenly, acutely, Lilah also wanted to go home. To Brooklyn, that is. To the brownstone she and her twin lived in when their parents were alive. "I miss you, Danny," she whispered, blinking back tears. "You and Papa and Mama."

"We'll go to Green-Wood on Christmas," Dan promised, a small catch in his voice. They'd visit their parents' graves.

"Sorry," said Lilah, sniffing. "Didn't mean to start bawling." They stayed on the line for another minute before hanging up.

All that was left on her agenda for the rest of the day was talking to Harry. Lilah had already managed to connect with Shawn—Andrew's biological son—very early in the morning and for a very short time. Boston to New York rates were much lower before daybreak, and Shawn, too, needed to be careful about cash, having been disinherited for coming out as gay. There were two very dear friends from high school she kept in touch with, but Ginger was vacationing with the flavor of the month, and Vivian was on her way to some hotelier conference with her parents.

Lilah glanced at the alarm clock on the side table, wondering if she should make yet another attempt at calling Harry. No, the staff there was soon going to laugh behind his back about his clingy girlfriend. *Harry* would probably call after eleven at night when rates dropped.

Dragging the thermodynamics textbook out, Lilah flipped it open. Extra classes meant extra hard work, or she'd fail miserably.

Open and closed systems, chemical reaction equilibrium, phase equilibrium... God only knew when she dozed off, but the crick in the back of her neck finally woke her. Lilah massaged her sore muscles and squinted at the clock. After five in the morning? She wouldn't have missed hearing the shrill scream of the phone.

Showering and shoving cereal into her mouth and tidying the appalling mess of a room kept her occupied until it was a reasonable hour in California, where the SEAL training facility was located. The stern-voiced secretary who always answered the main number told her to hang on.

"C'mon," Lilah muttered after a good ten minutes went by. How long did it take to get one of the trainees from the dorm... boot camp... whatever... on a weekend? Also, didn't the office close for the holidays? She could hear sounds of work at the other end of the line—the rapid taka, taka, taka, whirr of a typewriter, masculine laughter.

A clatter came over the line. "Miss Barrons?" asked the same stern man. "Are you still there?"

"Yes," she said before clearing her throat. Her voice was hoarser than usual. The family physician she used to see said it would never return to what it was before the kidnapping. She'd led Melanthios—Sanders's thug who was chasing her and Harry—to a minefield, causing his death. She still needed to run through a burning gate to cross the border to Egypt, resulting in a permanently raspy voice from smoke damage. "I can call back if now's not a good time—"

"That will not be possible. Candidate Sheppard is out on a job."

"A job?" Lilah asked, puzzled. "Harry's only a trainee. What kind of job is he doing?"

"Sorry," said the secretary. "It's confidential."

"But—" The high-pitched dial tone told her the man had hung up.

Huffing in frustration, Lilah set the receiver back. If the SEAL program sent their trainees on fieldwork or something, it could explain his radio silence even on this weekend. Lilah rubbed her temple with fingertips, but the niggle behind her brow refused to be soothed.

#

"No," Lilah screamed, pivoting on her left foot and ramming her right leg into the kick shield held by the instructor, a former marine.

"Keep going," said the instructor.

Sweat-soaked tendrils of hair hanging loose in front of her eyes, she went down the line of students and threw kick after kick at the shields. *"No!"* she shouted with each one.

One, two jabs with her sparring partner... blocking exercises...

every aching muscle in her body meant more power, better endurance. The yellow tank top darkened with perspiration. Under the gray leggings, her thighs itched.

When the instructor called for attention, she jogged to her spot at one end of the row of students and watched the former marine and his assistant demonstrate a move. *Someday*, she vowed. She would be strong enough, skilled enough to spar with the instructor himself.

A couple of hours later, she was shoving her arms into the maroon track jacket. She was lucky the gym was open the day after Thanksgiving. The gun club she'd joined was next door, but they were closed until Monday. Two major expenses every week, but it couldn't be helped. No way would she be a victim ever again.

Harry would learn from the SEAL program how to... what kind of work were they making him do before he even completed his training? And to keep him *sooo* busy he didn't have a minute to spare for his friends?! *Stop*, she ordered herself. Harry was in the military, and his responsibilities to the nation sometimes would take precedence over talking to his girlfriend. Lilah needed to get the idea into her thick head. *She* had her own stuff to do. Unfortunately, the bookstore where she worked part time was also closed until the week after, and none of the extra classes she signed up for were on. A movie, perhaps? But there was nothing she wanted to watch.

Pursing her lips, Lilah blew out a breath and strode to the exit. Chilly air struck her sweaty face, making her teeth chatter. The bus stop... only three people waited there. She shrugged. Maybe a five-mile run back to the residence hall would clear her mind. The backpack was light enough to hang on her shoulders while she jogged.

"Good job today, Lilah," called a voice. The instructor was standing next to his car. "There was more power in your kicks. How are the shooting lessons going?"

Not good enough, Lilah thought. Her bullets now found their way to the middle rings. Better than where she was when she started, but...

They chatted for a couple of minutes before she excused herself and started on her run. The instructor was too professional, too *military*, to show curiosity, but the people at the gym and the range surely knew their students sometimes came with pasts. Only, Lilah's had been buried too deeply for anyone to find out.

Even her friends didn't have a clue she was kidnapped with Harry. No one outside the government and Lilah's immediate family did. The feds warned billionaire oil driller Andrew Barrons not to further damage the already-hurting American economy by throwing accusations of kidnapping at another billion-dollar enterprise like Sanders, Incorporated unless he possessed solid proof. Andrew was only too happy to oblige. He wasn't gonna risk his precious business for anything, especially not when the government assured all concerned another attempt to snatch Lilah was unlikely as long as she stayed safe within U.S. borders. There was also the fact she'd gotten in Sanders's way purely by chance, and the criminal appeared unconcerned by her continued existence.

The Barronses parroted the story crafted by the authorities that Lilah was heading back home from Libya when Harry was kidnapped. And yeah... she caught some kind of exotic illness and ended up quarantined for months. Everyone else involved was forced to go along with the lies.

Small-timers the Sheppards might be, but the news of Harry's abduction and subsequent escape did leak and merited at least one para in the bigger papers. As far as most of the public knew, the Gaddafi government bore the sole responsibility for the crime. The Libyans apparently heartily agreed about not accusing Sanders since it would upset *their* economy as well. None of the restrictions stopped rumors from circulating about Sanders and Genesis, the Sheppards' old oil drilling business. Then there were the couple of accidents Sanders arranged for the boy who escaped his clutches, but Senator Temple forced a police investigation which put a stop to the attempts. Plus, the navy surely wouldn't let anything happen to one of their recruits. Harry was also safe for now.

As Lilah continued her run, a large, colonnaded building came into view. MIT's Great Dome. *Already?* Veering from her path, Lilah jogged toward the entrance. Instead of moping around in her room, she could just as well sit in the library amid other students who didn't get to go home for the holidays.

Weirdly, reading through old editions of the *Journal of the Society of Petroleum Evaluation Engineers* helped her pass the rest of the holidays in peace. Plus, she knew there was a perfectly good explanation for Harry's silence—his job.

No one other than Harry knew *all* the details of what happened to Lilah last Thanksgiving, not even Dan. Certainly not the U.S. government. There was the shrink who counseled her after she returned to the States, but all they talked about was the abduction. The man still tried to push a ton of pills at her. Even if he didn't, Lilah simply couldn't bring herself to tell him about the assault. She couldn't tell *any*one... not until she was ready to confront the monster who did it. *She'd* punish the rapist for his crime. The criminal driller behind the abduction would also pay. Only then could she and Harry erase those horrible months from memory.

Still, Lilah's future plans were back on track. MIT was only the beginning. Chemical engineering, an oil sector job to pay the bills... then, the law degree she'd dreamed of since she was old enough to think of such things. Someday, she'd get herself to the Supreme Court. She *did* put her life back together. So did Harry.

#

Two weeks later

Lilah hurried out of the residence hall into the frigid air and the crowd of noisy students thronging the street. Turning the envelope over, she eyed the air force postal service mark. *Strange.* Harry's letters were usually sent through the fleet post office. She glanced again at the sheet of paper with weird brown patches which looked like spilled soda.

> Sorry I didn't call, but believe me, I think about you every day. It's just been crazy here. Merry Christmas in case I don't get to a phone on time. I swear I'll call on your birthday no matter where I am.
>
> Love, Harry.

Relief. The near-constant tightness in her temples disintegrating with unbelievable suddenness, Lilah glanced heavenward. She'd write back in the evening. The Christmas gift she purchased from the bookstore with her employee discount was still on the desk in her room, ready to be mailed as soon as she got a chance to do a post office run. She'd scoured the entire inventory before deciding on *Tinker, Tailor, Soldier, Spy.* Harry practically *devoured* spy novels. She'd also included a special something inside the front cover—a blurry picture of him with her and Dan and the twins' parents in their Brooklyn home, taken by Harry's sister, Sabrina.

A sharp pang went through Lilah's heart as she tucked the letter and envelope into her jacket. Backpack bouncing against her spine, she sprinted to the chess club meeting and told herself the renewed wetness on her cheeks was from the cold. She was going to remember the happiness of the moment captured on film, not what happened merely days later.

It wasn't as though Harry didn't put effort into *his* gift. A bottle of her favorite perfume was sitting on her desk—Egyptian blue lotus oil. He used to buy it for her at the market in Libya. God only knew where he managed to get it now... and how much it cost. Lilah bit her lip hard. Simply a call every other month would be good enough for her. She could phone him in the months between.

Plucking the letter out of her jacket, she reread the words. All her worry was for nothing. Harry was fine.

Part II

Chapter 4

Three weeks ago (early November 1974)

Coronado, California

"...on your backs!" the instructor barked into the bullhorn. *"On your feet! On your stomachs!"* The commands were shouted so damned fast Harry and the other trainees didn't have a prayer of keeping up.

Jumping buck naked into the freezing bay, back onto the pier with chilly wind blowing over them... into the water, onto the pier... in, out... until dawn. Calisthenics on the beach with full gear on.

"Hit the surf, losers!"

Cold, cold water, rolling around wet on the shore, back to doing whistle drills with sand chafing his crotch and ass until he bled. One blast, two blasts, three blasts... up, down, crawl... up, down, crawl... every bone hurt, every muscle frayed. Hours and days went by without food, without sleep, without even being allowed to sit.

"You *will* make it," Harry said to his swim buddy, keeping on paddling the boat. "All of us will."

"I saw my grandfather," sobbed the Texan cowboy. "He's been dead for three years. I think *I'm* gonna die."

"Hallucinations," said one of the others. "I thought I saw Dolly Parton walking on water."

The crewmates laughed weakly. They relied on each other, kept each other motivated, prayed desperately not to fail.

Harry stared blearily at the shore where an apparition waited. Lilah... *I'm gonna win this thing,* he told her. As long as she stuck around, his mind wouldn't stray from its goal. With her as his anchor, he'd have the resolve to see the shitty week through.

Finally, *finally*... "You guys are secure," said the instructor, his satanic face cracking in a smile for the first time since Hell Week—the six-day stretch of grueling training—started. The students who were still standing would be allowed to continue with their BUD/S training.

Harry vaguely remembered the overwhelming relief, the glorious sense of victory, the group hug of those who made it through. He recalled pulling on the brown tee. There was some recollection of pouncing on pizza and beverage like a rabid dog while waiting his turn at the phone. He needed to talk to Lilah, hear her voice.

"Sheppard!" someone shouted, shaking him awake.

"Huh—what—who—" Harry leaped to his feet and nearly collapsed on his knees. The pizza box slid off his chest and fell on the floor, ants escaping the leftover food. The phone? Was it finally free?

"Your politician is here," said the sailor who woke Harry.

Temple? Harry blinked himself into consciousness.

"*Now,* Sheppard!" said the sailor.

Harry wasn't allowed even a couple of minutes to change out of the filthy clothes and water-logged shoes. And once again, *one more* damned time, he didn't get a chance to call Lilah.

#

Sweat rolled down Harry's chest despite the Pacific breeze hissing in through the window of the small office. Shrill whistle blasts from the last few days echoed between his ears even now, almost prompting him to drop and low-crawl across the ground toward the chairs where the CIA director and Senator Temple were seated.

The politician hadn't been kidding when he promised to involve Harry in the plans to deal with Sanders. From the first weekend in the naval training facility, Temple sent piles of business documents for Harry to study and analyze on top of what he already needed to do as a SEAL candidate. People, places, dollar amounts... he needed to be as familiar with Sanders's holdings as the man himself.

In October, Temple came in person to collect Harry on his way to an urgent NATO meeting in West Germany. Apparently, the world was concerned about Soviet attempts to increase influence through oil. The embargo from OPEC ended months ago, but with the stock market still in bad shape, Americans and their allies could scarcely afford more trouble, this time from the commies. Sanders's friendship with a Russian minister was one of the topics to be discussed. The SEAL candidate accepted the politician's invitation to join the team traveling to Bonn, returning in the early hours of Monday before training resumed for the week. The only thing he did on the trip was listen in while the senator's team gathered crucial intelligence from friendly agencies. He was told to keep his mouth shut... confidential information, etcetera.

Harry never expected a second mission to come now—certainly not one of this magnitude—the morning after Hell Week.

For months, the U.S. Naval Special Warfare Command had been one step behind the terrorists who abducted the fourteen-year-old son of Rear Admiral Benhaim. Finally, the American military got to know of the boy's location before he was moved yet again—a seaside city twelve miles to the south of the Lebanese capital. The window of opportunity to rescue the hostage was small, and there wasn't enough time to plan and execute a foolproof operation. No one in the CIA trusted the Lebanese government's willingness to act against the terrorists. The intelligence agency finally determined the best way forward was a clandestine attack carried out by a small team—one man, two at the most. Petty Officer First Class Eriksson—a SEAL recruited by the CIA—carried the best record in hostage rescue and hot extractions. The petty officer's contact in the area was supposed to assist, but he was killed in the latest skirmish between the Shi'a Muslims and the Palestine Liberation Organization. The morning of his death, he'd sent information about the guards keeping the admiral's son. There were three altogether. One of them—a Sudanese man—used to be a crane operator for the now-defunct oil drilling company, Genesis, owned by Harry's father.

The CIA director personally called the naval training facility to ask for Candidate Sheppard to be loaned to the agency. Before Harry blurted his confusion at the idea of a rookie being sent, the director made it clear the petty officer/senior agent would be in charge of the mission. Harry's part would be quite small. As a former acquaintance of the crane operator-turned-terrorist guard, Harry would show up at the house where the hostage was being held and create a diversion. The operator and the other guards would be kept busy by Harry while the petty officer took care of the actual rescue. Also, with Harry's childhood spent in Tel Aviv and Tripoli, he spoke Arabic and Hebrew like a native, and with some hair on his face, he could actually pass for an Arab. He'd been taught how to point and shoot a gun from the age of ten and was a trained boxer, all of which made him a good fit for the mission.

"I'll be ready in fifteen minutes," Harry swore, standing with his thumbs interlaced at the small of his back. "My family expects to hear from me on Thanksgiving," Harry said out loud. "If I'm not back here by then... lemme call them now and—"

"No," snapped the CIA director, not even bothering to look up from the folder on the desk. In the second chair, Senator Temple stayed silent, his gaze fixed steadily on Harry. The director continued, "No delays. We can't be sure how much longer the boy will be held in that particular safe house. You're flying to Athens as is. The petty officer is already on his way to the air station. Once you both get your ducks in a row, you'll travel to Beirut."

Senator Temple finally spoke, "I'm sure you realize you didn't get into the SEAL program purely on my recommendation. The director was quite clear to the navy brass how the agency wanted you in. There was a reason for it."

Harry inclined his head. "I'm honored by the trust placed in me, sir, and... uhh... hoping I live up to expectations."

"Your only job is to distract the guards," stressed the CIA director. The diversion had to be big enough to draw out the guards but not so much it raised suspicion and got the hostage moved or worse, killed. Anything sizable the military could arrange—like an explosion—would immediately ring alarm bells in the safe house. So Harry it would be. "The actual operation will be carried out by the petty officer. Now, get your ass to the air station." Shoving the chair back, the director stood and nodded at the senator. "I'm going to have a word with one of the instructors."

The politician waited until the director exited the room. "I'm a bit surprised, Harry. You were happy to go with me to Germany last month. I would've thought you'd be jumping at this chance. From what I hear, you have a score to settle with the crane operator fellow."

Harry didn't bother suppressing the vicious snarl. While recuperating from the injuries sustained during his escape, he got plenty of chances to think back to his many, many near-misses since Sanders started putting pressure on the Sheppards. One of them involved the same crane operator having an "accident" with a two-ton load that dropped right where Harry stood less than a minute before. When the Sheppards were forced to abandon their business in Libya, all their former employees dispersed, including the crane operator. Given his current job with radicals, chances were he was paid by Sanders to kill Harry. Oh, yeah. Harry was looking forward to the meeting. "I meant what I said, Senator. I'll be honored to do what I can for the agency. The few minutes I asked for were only so I could shower."

Temple cleared his throat, the blue eyes crinkling in humor. Unlike Harry, the senator didn't look like he'd been rolling around in mud. The gray streaks on his head were actually hair, not sand. "You *are* slightly aromatic."

Sheepishly grinning, Harry continued, "Plus... uhh... my family... the holidays..." He really needed to talk to Lilah. Even if he ignored his own wants, Lilah... what happened this time the year before... he needed to make sure she was all right, to tell her he was there for her.

Temple's eyelids flickered. "Your family might be upset about not hearing from you, but they'll survive. Every minute you waste on contacting them makes it less likely the admiral's son will be rescued. The American government will not do what the terror group wants and release our prisoners. The admiral's son will eventually be killed in retaliation. The time you waste here might make the difference between life and death for the boy. Are you prepared to sacrifice him for a mere phone call, Candidate Sheppard?"

Startled, Harry took half a step rearward. "Of course not, sir."

"I'm relieved to hear you say so." Temple stood from the chair and went to the window to stare out into the night. The senator was somewhat average in height and build, but the force of his personality was such that he staged a presence... when he so chose. "You joined the SEAL program to serve. Many young men dream of doing the same... of being a hero, but most lack the courage to risk their lives for a cause. You claim you're ready to die to stop Sanders from doing any more harm to the rest of the world. But your life's the least of all the sacrifices demanded by the universe.

The love you have within yourself for your family, your friends, even your country—don't let any of it change into attachment which chains you. Love is self*less*, while attachments are centered around what the self desires. So when there's a choice between selfish attachment and selfless duty, true courage requires you to sacrifice. You will need to sacrifice your ego, your *id*, sometimes even your notion of morality. You need to free yourself from conventional ideas of right and wrong. Conditional heroism is no heroism. Do you understand what I'm saying?"

"I think so," Harry murmured hesitantly. Anyone who took on the mission to bring down criminals like Sanders couldn't place terms on what he was prepared to give up for it. The SEAL program demanded the same commitment from its sailors. So would the CIA. "The world needs true and honorable service, but truth without valor to defend it is useless, and valor without sacrifice is meaningless."

With a satisfied murmur, the senator turned to face Harry. "What if the survival of the world someday depends on one small sacrifice on your part? Will you willingly make it? Show me you will. Show me I can trust you."

Clicking to attention, Harry snapped a salute. "Yes, sir!"

Chapter 5

Two weeks later (mid-November 1974)

Damour, Lebanon

Harry had slept all through the flight to Athens and was permitted twenty minutes to shower and change once they landed— the petty officer in charge insisted on it before he'd let Harry in on any pre-mission meetings. They didn't have the luxury of time to put in place an elaborate operation, and Lebanese authorities weren't notified for fear of leaks, but the Israelis came through with crucial assistance. Fake passports took Harry and Petty Officer Eriksson on their supposed road trip through Turkey and Syria to Lebanon. At no point during any of it did Eriksson indulge in any chitchat, limiting conversation to drilling Harry on every step of the rescue plan as it was.

It took two weeks from the day Harry left the States to finally get to Damour, and not one single call was allowed to any lines the CIA hadn't secured. He was told in no uncertain terms phones in MIT dorms were not on the approved list.

From the passenger seat of the Jeep speeding along the highway on the Lebanese coast, Harry watched the mild winter sun glint off the surface of the bright-blue Mediterranean. All around, vehicles honked, and engines rumbled. The black-and-white *kufiya*—Arab headdress—flapped noisily against his face, irritating the hell out of his patchy beard. Memories carried Harry to another place, another time. He was again in a Jeep, racing down another coastal road in a desperate run from the enemies chasing him and Lilah.

Habibti, Harry murmured in his mind, calling her his beloved in Arabic. His girl was strong. With or without him, Lilah would find a way to defeat the nightmares of their past. The admiral's son wouldn't survive to defeat anything if Harry didn't get his act together.

"We have a narrow window of opportunity," came the terse voice of Petty Officer Eriksson from the driver's seat, snapping Harry back to the here and now. Like Harry, the sailor-turned-CIA agent wore a cotton tee over pants as favored by tourists to the beach town. A *kufiya* similar to Harry's was wrapped around the man's blond head now dyed deep brown, but there was no hiding the blue eyes. Back in Athens, he'd tried colored lenses but jettisoned them in a hurry. He reminded Harry of his older brother except the petty officer was somewhat of a giant even for a former SEAL. "I intend to bring the hostage back alive," he continued, "and I don't want to report to your politician I got his protégé killed on my watch, so follow orders, Sheppard."

"Yes, sir," Harry said, absently noting in the rearview mirror the blue van which had been behind them for a few minutes. Word of Temple's visits to the naval training facility had clearly spread to the point it reached the field agents at the CIA. The politician's intense interest in the Sanders saga baffled Harry. As far as he understood, Temple first got involved at Andrew's request during the whole mess with the arrest of the Sheppard parents and the subsequent kidnapping. Sanders was a supporter of Temple's opponent, so it helped the senator's decision. What Harry couldn't see was the point behind the politician's continued involvement. Yeah, there was the humanitarian aspect of it because Sanders was a damned criminal, and the few words from Temple in the SEAL training facility hit Harry hard in the chest. There was powerful commitment in those—

The piercing sound of a police siren startled Harry from his thoughts. Lights blazing, official vehicles sped in the opposite direction. "Right on time," said Petty Officer Eriksson, satisfaction evident in his tone.

The Israeli forces would've begun their airstrikes on the guerilla camps in Mount Hermon. Both official and unofficial authorities in Lebanon would be scrambling, their eyes fixed on the southern part of the country instead of on the prized hostage abducted months ago from a *kibbutz*—the Jewish farm community the boy and his mother lived in after her divorce from the rear admiral.

More police cars raced down the highway in the direction of Mount Hermon. The other vehicles slowed to let the cops pass or to simply gawk. Harry glanced at the cop cars, aimlessly counting how many. Squinting against the rays of the sun, he noted the blue van from before. "We might have a problem," he said.

"I see it," Eriksson said grimly. "Could be coincidence, but...

hold on tight. We're almost where we want to be." Revving up, he shot the Jeep off the highway and onto a side road.

The van followed, keeping a few feet behind as the Jeep weaved through traffic, winding around cars and buses and bikes. "Get in front of the army truck," Harry shouted over the wind whistling past his ears, staring hard at the open cargo area carrying camo-clad soldiers. "If it's Black September, they won't start anything with the military around."

Eriksson's glare clearly told Harry to shut the hell up. The petty officer didn't need a rookie lecturing him about the notorious terror group. After the Jordanian king evicted the *fedayeen*—Palestinian fighters—they arrived in Lebanon and plotted revenge. Black September militants already claimed credit for the assassination of the prime minister of Jordan and for the horrific massacre at the Munich Olympics. The Lebanese government wasn't happy about having them around, but nothing was being done except put out the fires caused by militant presence. Still, the terror group wouldn't risk open confrontation if they could possibly help it... not until they gained enough strength.

Eriksson swung the steering wheel hard to the side and cut into the next lane with barely an inch to spare from the bumper of the car coming up. Ignoring the angry honking, he shot ahead and swung back in front of the truck.

"Nice work!" Harry bellowed, poking his head out for a moment to let the breeze cool his hot and sweaty face. Guffawing despite the tension knotting his belly, he glanced sideways and added, "Sir."

"Stow your 'sirs,' sailor," Eriksson snapped. "I wear stripes and work for a living." He took a hard right to a dirt road next to a small mosque. A short line of men came into view almost immediately, apparently on their way in for prayers. Eriksson couldn't stop the vehicle on time. Cursing foully, he jammed the horn down. Loud screams and curses followed them as people jumped out of the way. Through the shrubs, crushing the undergrowth, spraying reddish dust everywhere, they sped until they came to a grove of banana plants. "We lost the bastard," Eriksson said, slowing the vehicle. "But—"

Harry nodded. "We've been made." If the van were indeed tailing the Jeep, it meant Black September knew a rescue operation was in progress.

Tires squealed as the Jeep stopped not far from a cluster of small clay brick buildings. "Get out," said Eriksson.

"And do what?" Harry asked as Eriksson turned off the engine, eyes scanning the terrain. No blue vans appeared.

"Your only job was to lure out your old pal and his comrades. If the group knows who we are and what we're doing here, the element of surprise is gone. There's nothing else you can do besides somehow get yourself killed. Walk to the main road and hitch a ride to the docks." Eriksson glanced at the field phone in the Jeep. "I'll contact the ship and let them know you're on your way back. They'll send someone else to help. We need to check... if the boy hasn't already been moved, I can get him out. All I need is someone to provide cover."

"We don't *know* it was Black September in the van," Harry pointed out. "Also, Senator Temple knows the risks of what I'm doing. You're not going to get into trouble if anything happens."

Eriksson spat to the side. "I don't give a damn about your politician. I simply don't want to be responsible for getting a rookie killed. Dunno what the agency was thinking. Eighteen years old! It's not as though we couldn't find anyone else to do the same thing."

"Your 'anyone else' wouldn't have the opening *I* would with the guards," argued Harry. At a stern look from Eriksson, Harry raised his hands in acknowledgment. "I get what you're saying, but we're not sure the van belonged to Black September. If it wasn't them, I could still help, right? If it was, you could call for someone else, but I can also assist. Suppose the hostage has been moved. I could help you locate him. The CIA people must've told you something about me. I *know* this region. I lived in Libya most of my life. Hell, I escaped Gaddafi's goons."

A flicker of something passed across Eriksson's face. "I heard." For a moment or two, he stared hard at Harry. "You do speak better Arabic than me."

"There you go." In one quick move, Harry turned off the engine and pocketed the ignition key before leaping out.

"Trusting soul." With a short laugh, Eriksson added, "We need to update the base on the situation. Your replacement will be on standby in case our doubts about the blue van turn out to be correct." A quick phone call later, the petty officer nodded toward the buildings past the banana grove. "Over there."

"Thank you." When the petty officer looked his way, Harry added, "For giving me a choice."

Once more, Eriksson stared hard at Harry. "Follow orders. No ifs, ands, or buts."

Sidling along the backs of sandstone buildings, Harry and Eriksson halted at a gap between walls and surveyed the unpaved lane running across the settlement. A couple of women in long skirts and cotton blouses hurried by with shopping bags overflowing with vegetables, their chatter reaching the duo hidden in the shadows. No men or children... unsurprising since they'd either be at work or in school this time of the day.

This neighborhood was only a few minutes from the tourist haunts in town and the perfect place for the terrorists' safe house. Chances were none of the residents realized there was a hostage hidden in their midst, too drugged to call for help. If the government—or anyone else—tried a direct attack, more hostages were readily available for the militants to hide behind until their mates arrived with additional firepower. In the resulting chaos, the admiral's son could be moved elsewhere or even be killed.

"We need to wait," muttered Eriksson, his eyes fixed on the two-storied building across the lane. There was a single door in front, and the windows were shut. "Give it an hour or so. If our friend in the van was one of the group, we should see some movement soon, and you will return immediately to the Jeep and radio the base. Got it?" When Harry grunted under his breath, Eriksson continued, "If not... remember... there are three guards." Harry would walk in and demand to talk to the former crane operator. The SEAL-in-training needed to create enough ruckus to draw out the traitor and at least one of his buddies. The hostage wouldn't be left completely unattended, so there would be one guard remaining for Eriksson to incapacitate. "They'll all be armed. Use weapons only as last resort." The moment Harry drew the Smith & Wesson 39, a battle would commence, making hostage rescue more difficult. Well... there was a slight possibility Eriksson might still get the hostage out, but Harry would face two or three-to-one odds and was likely to meet his maker before the petty officer returned to help.

Harry jerked his head in agreement and focused on the safe house. The sun wasn't blazing hot this time of the year in Lebanon, but every color around shimmered before sharpening into intense brightness, and every line widened until he could see the infinitesimal cracks in the bark of the date palm next to the building. He shouldn't have been able to tell which of the houses had the radio on, but he could hear every word of the song being played. *Adrenaline*, he thought, sweating profusely under the cotton tee.

A minute passed... ten... thirty... it seemed a lifetime before Eriksson waved his hand even with his head in the standard silent close operations signal to advance. Harry took one step out of the shadows only to have the petty officer's iron grip land on his elbow, dragging him back. "Shit," snarled Eriksson, nodding in the direction of the door of the safe house. A man clad in olive fatigues was walking out, yawning and stretching. "Kanz Panchev... Bulgarian father, Palestinian Christian mother. He and I have run into each other before. Dammit... maybe I could... one bullet..."

"What do you mean?" Harry asked, startled. Of all the dumb ideas! Panchev was outside the house, but the men within could notice him collapsing and pick up on what was going on. "Let's stick with the original plan. So what if Panchev knows you? *You're* not going in the front door; I am."

"Panchev's a bigger monster than most. You might not get a chance to distract anyone. He'll simply toss you into a car and quietly take you someplace else to finish you for the crime of pissing him off. And believe me, he'll make you wish you weren't born."

Harry grinned. "You'll have the diversion you need." At the petty officer's frown, Harry added, "Lemme see what I can do with this Panchev fella. *He's* also not going to open fire at first sight. What if someone hears and calls the cops? He'll wait until he has no choice, right? Or he's gonna try and catch me to do what you said." With his index finger, Harry drew a line across his throat. "Finish me off. All *I* need to do is lead him on a chase and avoid getting caught."

After split-second hesitation, Eriksson said, "He's bad enough the *fedayeen* hate his guts.

"Yeah? Why do they keep him around, then?"

"Oil," said Eriksson. "Panchev has connections to the Soviet oil sector. Means money for Black September."

"Soviet oil?" Harry asked. "How?" Even before the minister was named, Harry knew. "Sanders's man," he stated.

"The Russian minister... yes," said Eriksson, not even bothering to pretend he wasn't aware who Sanders was. "*Panchev* is not simply one of Sanders's troops. Rumor has it they're related. CIA believes Panchev's wife is a distant cousin of the Sanderses. Perhaps a niece. I suppose it makes Kanz Panchev a son-in-law of sorts to Jared."

"The CIA didn't know Panchev was going to be here?"

Eriksson snorted. "I doubt they'd have sent *you* if they did. Dammit, if we got the time to put our men in place, we'd have known Panchev is involved."

"Total bull," Harry retorted. The CIA director surely did, and he'd have told Temple. The agency would never have left Eriksson blind when the operation involved a rear admiral's son. They all knew.

Pieces of info fell rapidly into place in Harry's mind, starting with the surprising involvement of a novice like himself in the task. He was a boxer and knew how to use a gun in addition to speaking the local languages, but agents with all of those skills certainly existed. If any of them could claim acquaintance with the team guarding the hostage, Candidate Sheppard wouldn't have even been told about the mission. The CIA would use his knowledge of the guard if possible but wouldn't gamble the hostage's life on it.

Harry was tested at multiple points to see if he would back out when smacked in the face with imminent danger. The van, the possibility of it belonging to Black September... then, Eriksson bided time until Kanz Panchev came out of the building, until Harry figured out the terrorist's connection to Sanders. There was the weird suggestion from Eriksson about shooting at Panchev. It would blow up any chances of rescue *and* probably get the extraction team killed. If the rookie turned tail... even if he continued but somehow bungled his part... "You have someone else arranged, don't you?" Harry asked. "Just in case I run or botch things. The blue van? I bet it's your backup. You staged the ditching for my benefit."

Eriksson stayed unblinking, not denying the charge, not copping to it.

Incredibly, Harry was hit with the urge to laugh. Shaking his head, he chuckled. "Man, am I a dumbass or what?" Rescue of the kidnapped boy aside, the people in charge were watching to see if Harry proved himself reliable. "Well, I'm here—ready, willing, and able. So let's go. If I screw up, your friends in the van can jump in."

"Not dumb," said Eriksson, stern look still on his face. "A bit too sure of yourself, but the navy will whip you into shape... *if* you live long enough. Panchev won't think twice before shooting the boy merely to stop us from having the satisfaction of getting him out alive. If I drive the Jeep here with the kid inside like we planned..."

"Ahh," said Harry. Eriksson couldn't return for his partner without risking the rear admiral's son. "I'll be on my own."

"I *will* drive by once," Eriksson said. "I can't stop. You'd better be outside, ready to jump in. The... er... blue van won't do anything to raise suspicion unless you screw up or until I'm out. Afterward, the backup team's primary focus will be on getting the hostage to safety which includes following the Jeep to the docks. You'll be expected to take care of yourself."

"Understood." Taking the keys from the pocket, Harry handed them to Eriksson.

"Give me time to get the boy out. Then, do whatever you need to stay alive." Eriksson jerked his head to the side. "Go."

Harry jogged to the end of the row of buildings and taking a deep breath, stepped onto the lane. As soon as he got near the safe house, he raised a hand and shouted, "Hey."

Panchev turned. He was almost as tall as Harry but wirier than bulked up. Up close, Panchev's Slavic features were unmistakable—pale skin, dark coloring, narrow face. A conch shell tattoo covered the left cheek. His right hand adjusted rounded glasses, revealing a metal bracelet with an embedded seashell—another conch. The man eyed Harry up and down, taking in everything from the work boots to the loose tee and pants and the checkered headdress. Something about the stone-hard gaze...

Hair follicles bristled to attention at the back of Harry's neck. The colors around sharpened yet again into a clarity which almost hurt his brain. It was as though his visual field expanded, showing him the shadow of Petty Officer Eriksson slipping behind buildings to the back of the terrorist sanctuary. Harry spoke in fluent Arabic. "I heard the sonuvabitch..." He named the former crane operator. "The bastard and I have business to discuss." Craning his neck to the side, Harry shouted the traitor's name toward the house. "Get out here and face me like a man, you dog."

The once-familiar face of the Sudanese crane operator appeared at the door, his eyes widening in shock. As Panchev silently glanced between his colleague and Harry, the crane operator explained the lad was his former boss's son. "The pest simply wouldn't die," the crane operator finished. "No matter what I did."

"So this is the one who got away." Tone flat, Panchev asked the crane operator, "How did he track you here?"

Harry bared his teeth in a snarl. "I've been keeping in touch with some people back in Libya, the ones who weren't trying to kill me." He could no longer see Eriksson, but the petty officer wouldn't attempt entry until the odds were better. So far, Panchev showed no signs of getting annoyed enough to follow Harry anywhere. Jogging a few feet backward, Harry announced, "I'm gonna get the cops. You need to be arrested for attempted murder."

"Take care of him before he starts trouble," snapped Panchev, talking to the crane operator but keeping his eyes on Harry. "I need to make a call. A few people are going to be interested to hear he showed up here."

Timing was everything. The terrorists wouldn't open fire... not just yet. They wouldn't want to draw attention. Harry needed to pull something drastic to get them away from the safe house while making sure he didn't end up with bullets in his brain. Throwing quick glances to both sides, Harry noted the buildings. The one on the right... the sketch he studied in Greece said it was a church. There was no one outside, no sounds coming from within. The door was open.

He turned and sprinted toward the church. "I know what you are," he taunted as he reached the front entrance. "You work for some kind of crazies... terrorists. The cops are going to get you *and* your friend."

Slipping inside the doorway, Harry drew his gun from the ankle holster and took one step backward to keep himself out of sight. In case there was a gun battle, the lattice windows would give him opportunity to train his weapon on the terrorists from behind the safety of the walls. An eventual escape route Harry could use... there was a trade exit marked on the sketch he studied. He peered through one of the lace-like window frames. *Shit.* The holes were too small to get a good lock on the targets.

"Hello," said a sing-song voice, speaking English.

"Wha—" Startled, Harry wheeled around. A little boy of about three or so years stood at an inner door, sucking his thumb and staring at the intruder in open curiosity. He giggled and said something incomprehensible, and then, a number of children appeared from somewhere behind.

Harry cursed out loud, causing more giggles to erupt from the children. A school? A daycare? The info he got in Athens didn't say anything of the sort went on in the church.

The teacher, a dark-haired woman in a cotton shirt and ankle-length skirt, came to the door, urging her charges outside to play. Her gaze fell on Harry. For a second or two, she simply stared.

Then, her eyes landed on the weapon in his hand. She screamed.

Almost at the same time, the crane operator shouted, "Get out here, you pest!"

Glancing wildly between the killers outside the window and the group of children at the inner door, Harry hissed at the teacher, "Take them back in. Lock the doors."

The teacher seemed immobilized, her horrified gaze fixed on Harry's pistol. She continued screaming. The children who'd been nonchalant mere moments ago bawled and scampered in confusion.

"*Go*," Harry bellowed into the cacophony, readying himself to run out and surrender to the killers. He couldn't even risk looking for the trade exit. The possibility of a shootout in the school... no damned way.

Twin shadows loomed at the door. The little boy who spotted Harry first stood directly in Panchev's way, lips rounded into an O around his thumb. A shot split the air. The boy dropped to the floor. Blood pooled fast under the small body.

Everyone around froze in horror, including the crane operator who stood behind Panchev. Harry opened his mouth to shout, but his throat spasmed hard. No sounds came out. Through a mushroom cloud of red-hot rage, he watched Panchev leap through the door. The crane operator was still outside. For a few moments, there was space around Panchev, giving Harry a clear shot at the monster. Harry raised his arm and fired. Panchev roared as the bullet scorched its way across his temple.

The children resumed running in all directions, and there were several between Harry and the terrorists. The teacher continued screaming. There was one more shot from Panchev. Harry ducked. A second child fell, clutching his leg. Panchev's arm was still raised, his finger still on the trigger.

"Stop!" Harry shouted, shaking head to toe. "I'll go with you. I have things I could tell you... about Sanders." Lowering his gun to the floor, Harry nodded in the direction of the children. "Please," he said to the monster. "Let them leave."

"Get the hell out," Panchev bellowed at the children. "You," he spat in Harry's direction. "Roll up your pants."

Harry gritted his teeth and did as ordered, tossing his backup gun to the floor. The crane operator was gulping, glancing wildly between his colleague and Harry. At least the teacher had stopped screaming and was merely gasping for breath while gathering the crying children, but there was shouting from a distance. Women of the neighborhood were running to the scene—more hostages for the terror group.

"Over here," Panchev ordered, gesturing Harry closer.

Eyes darting around, Harry studied the room as he limped across as slowly as possible. He needed something... an opening.

"Wasting my time," snapped Panchev. He took two steps forward, the crane operator following at his heels. Raising a fist, Panchev drove it hard into Harry's belly. His vision blurred. As he doubled over, a kick landed on his knees, making him fall.

A sharp crack rang out. Harry stilled, waiting for more pain... darkness... some sign of impending death. At the shocked silence around, he looked up and gaped at the blood spurting from Panchev's right shoulder... his shooting arm. When Harry glanced back, the teacher was at the other end of the room, holding a gun. *Harry's* weapon, the one he discarded on Panchev's orders.

Without waiting to think further, Harry straightened and delivered an uppercut to Panchev's chin and used the momentum to shove him onto the crane operator. The men stumbled.

Harry drew the combat knife from the inside-the-waistband sheath. Snarling like a wild animal, he swung the blade.

Blood gushed out of Panchev's neck and spurted onto Harry's

face, his eyes, his open mouth, giving him a taste of warm iron. Thick, red liquid poured over his hand, dripping to the floor. Gaze widening, Panchev clutched his throat and gurgled. His pistol fell to the floor. So did the metal bracelet—the one with the conch shell. Shoving aside his mate, the crane operator raised his gun.

"I'll shoot," screamed the teacher, still holding Harry's weapon. There were more women gathered at the door, all shouting in alarm and weeping. Panting in panic, the crane operator swung a half-circle with his revolver pointed at his audience.

With the back of his hand, Harry wiped off the blood congealing on his eyelids. There was a dark shadow in the periphery of his visual field. Panchev's gun was next to his dead body, the bracelet caught on the trigger guard. Tossing the combat knife to his other hand, Harry dived sideways and grabbed the cocked pistol before springing to his feet. "Down," he shouted in Arabic at the women and children. The crane operator pivoted at the command, and Harry fired into the enemy's forehead.

No one moved for a moment or two. Then, a keening cry came from the door, and a woman rushed in, running to one of the injured children. The rest of the group surged in behind.

A piercing honk blasted over all the noise. With knife and gun still in his hands, Harry shoved through the throng and sprinted out. Churning reddish dust, Eriksson's Jeep was hurtling down the lane. The vehicle slowed barely enough for Harry to vault into the open back and land on top of the rescued hostage, weapons held safely away from his body. The drugged boy made no more sound than a mild hmph as Harry rolled off him. Eriksson drove them out before the neighborhood turned on the people who brought death to their homes.

The Jeep didn't stop until they reached the docks. Eriksson's local contact gawked at the blood on Harry, but one hard stare from the petty officer was enough to stop questions. Quickly and efficiently, the hostage and the two rescuers were loaded onto the waiting chopper. In the cabin, two medics worked on the drugged boy while Eriksson spoke into a radio, giving updates to the team waiting at the air force base in Turkey. The petty officer threw a glance or two at Harry as he washed his face with bottled water, making a goddamned mess on the floor, but there was no opportunity for questions.

It wasn't until they both collapsed into chairs outside the commander's office at the base that Eriksson asked, "Panchev?"

"Dead," Harry said, staring straight ahead. "Him and the crane operator."

With a muffled sound which could've signified anything from mild surprise to abject shock, Eriksson nodded. "How?"

Harry recounted every detail of the encounter, struggling not to remember the innocent curiosity in the eyes of the little boy sucking his thumb. *Be alive,* Harry sent thoughts to the child. *Please... be alive.* Aloud, he ground out, "Tell me you didn't know there was a daycare in the church."

"I didn't," Eriksson said firmly. "No one involved in this operation did. The agency always tries to account for every variable, but something inevitably pops up. All we can do is keep collateral damage to a minimum. There *are* agents who wouldn't give shit about civilian casualties, but even they'd worry about the PR nightmare of what just happened. Children got hurt! Also, you didn't simply kill Panchev. You killed him in full view of the locals. The Lebanese government will not be happy."

The petty officer's words held the ring of truth, and there was no way the CIA could've predicted Harry would choose the church to run into. Praying desperately for the little boy's survival, Harry asked, "How much trouble am I in?"

"The director will fix things... pin it on one of the local militias."

Still staring hard, Eriksson muttered, "You killed Panchev. How?"

Harry frowned. "I just told you."

"You don't get it, do you?" Huffing, Eriksson added, "There are many, many former agents who'll be grateful to you for this."

"You can tell them I got help. Panchev underestimated the teacher. So did I, actually." If not for her, Harry would be dead right now. Instead, two of Sanders's men would answer to a higher power for their crimes. How the teacher reached the conclusion Harry was the good guy in the mess, he didn't quite know. Scratching the back of his neck, he stared at the dried blood coating his nails. "We need to make sure the teacher doesn't get into trouble."

A couple of seconds later, Eriksson said, "As soon as we're done with the debriefing, let's go and get a drink. The first time's always rough."

Harry considered admitting it wasn't the first time. The female guard he killed in Libya... he never meant to, and the woman would've killed him *and* Lilah in a heartbeat. The awareness did nothing to erase the memory. Now, there would be two more faces. Panchev's metal bracelet... the officer who took charge of the dead terrorist's weapon had lobbed the jewelry back at Harry. Vaguely, he remembered tucking the damned thing into his pocket. He needed to hurl it into the closest trash can. "Thanks," he said out loud. "Are we permitted to drink on the base?"

"Not here. A buddy of mine from Athens owns a pub in town." Neither mentioned the fact Harry was under legal drinking age by three years.

#

An hour later

One shot of Russian vodka, a couple of bottles of beer... a pleasant buzz took over Harry's brain, driving away other images. Then, there was poker with Eriksson and the pub owner in the windowless office behind the bar. Outside, drunk men argued loudly over sports.

"You gotta be cheating," the pub owner complained in a mix of Greek and English, glaring at Harry and tossing cards onto the desk. "Royal flush again?"

With an off-balance smirk, Harry responded in the same language, "Not cheating. Magic."

Eriksson guffawed hard on his fourth or fifth shot. "At least you ain't losing any money," he said to the pub owner. Harry had learned a long time ago not to bet anything on card games. Losing even a penny got people all hot under the collar over his tricks. Eriksson soon started belting out some tune about girls waiting for him back home, and Harry joined in, relishing the sweet melancholy of the lyrics.

"Oh, honey," crooned a woman, walking in. There were blonde streaks in her dark hair and a generous amount of pink makeup around her eyes. Apparently, she was the singer for the establishment on a break from entertaining patrons in the bar proper with Turkish versions of American rock. She bent down to plant a kiss on Eriksson before turning to Harry, giving him a glimpse of bountiful cleavage at eye level. "You have a good singing voice, cutie."

Lilah loved to hear him si—before Harry could complete the thought, red-painted nails landed on his cheek, pinching it. He'd barely opened his mouth to protest when warm lips covered his, the flicking tongue giving him a taste of some bitter drink. The smell of tobacco wafted to his nostrils. Harry couldn't see anything beyond the creamy skin of her jaw and the blondish lock dancing around her ear, but there was clear snickering from the other two men in the room.

With a final nip at his lower lip, the singer stood. "Well?" she asked. When Harry didn't respond in the next couple of seconds, she prompted, "What do you say?"

"Wha—" Clearing his throat, Harry said, "Uhh... thank you." Oh, yeah, it was a nice kiss. And he meant *niiice*. His groin was ready to salute in agreement. His mind wandered to the hazel eyes of an American princess. With their first kiss, Lilah wouldn't let him up for air. Not as if he *wanted* air. Breathing was overrated.

The Turkish singer growled, bringing his attention back to the office. Nostrils quivering, she straightened to her full height. Eriksson and his buddy were practically falling off their chairs with laughter.

"What did I say?" Harry asked, baffled. His question once again set the other two off.

Sputtering, Eriksson commented, "You *are* only eighteen." Mirth fading, he mumbled under his breath, "Yet you managed to take out Panchev."

Eyes on the singer, the pub owner taunted, "Face it, Kubra. You're an old hag now. You ain't gonna tempt young fellers like Sheppard."

Eriksson turned to his friend. "C'mon, man. Not cool."

"I didn't mean—" Harry sat up in the chair, his brain finally processing the offer he received from the singer, Kubra. "You're beautiful," he said. "Gorgeous, actually." There was grace in the way she glided into the room, confidence in the manner she declared what she wanted. The lines around the wide mouth showed an inclination to laugh. "I have a girlfriend," Harry blurted.

"Ahh," said Kubra, her gaze softening. "Tell her from me she's a lucky lady." Turning to the pub owner, the singer spat, "Fool." With the same poise she showed when walking in, Kubra returned to her work.

It wasn't long before the petty officer and his friend were snoring in their chairs. Humming along to the Arabic song from the bar, Harry stood to go out and get some fresh air. The room whirled. He gave up his desire for the outdoors and collapsed back into his chair.

Imagining Lilah could be done just as well inside. When Harry returned stateside, he'd see for himself she was all right. The sweet smell of her perfume... the silky skin... her soft lips... in less time than it took some grenades to detonate, he was hard as a rock. Harry shifted, banging his knee against the desk and cursing. He wouldn't be kissing Lilah any time soon. The moment he landed, he'd be marched straight back to Coronado.

There wasn't really another option. Harry *needed* to show his commitment to the cause of taking down Sanders. Lilah would understand... if he could've explained the situation. Sadly, the CIA frowned upon having official secrets shared with girlfriends.

Harry did have the other Lilah for a partner—the combat knife named Ari B'Lilah—now cleaned and tucked in his inside-the-waistband sheath. He'd been tickled when he first heard what it was called, and the moment he actually laid eyes on this prototype developed by the Israeli Counter Terrorism Unit, he was tempted to bow down in worship of the lethal beauty with a slight curve in its grip. The human Lilah would be relieved to know her knifely counterpart saved his skin today.

"Habibti," Harry murmured to himself, grabbing a pen and a sheet of paper from the neatly arranged pile on one side of the small desk. *I killed again. Not sure if I'm sorry...* Harry tossed the pen back onto the desk and slumped in his chair, pinching the bridge of his nose. Nope, the CIA would definitely frown if they found out he wrote to her about it.

He scribbled a short note which said absolutely nothing and was about to fold it when the back of his hand connected with an open beer bottle. The bottle teetered, spilling frothy brew onto the sheet before Harry caught it. Not bothering to rewrite, he tucked the letter into his pocket. He'd mail it when they returned to the base.

Chapter 6

A month later, Christmas Day, 1974

Langley, Virginia

Temple stayed silent as Petty Officer First Class Eriksson gave his personal observations of the lad he was meant to mentor. "Harry was ready to surrender to Panchev to save the children," Eriksson said to the CIA director and Rear Admiral Benhaim. "When the chance came..." The petty officer curled his hand into a fist. "...his survival instinct is extraordinary."

"We already saw it in Libya," said the director, nodding. Which was what told them the boy could be an extraordinary weapon in the hands of the right people. "Thoughts, Admiral?"

"Candidate Sheppard will serve his country well," agreed Benhaim. "I'm thankful he was around to help my boy."

"He's multilingual," enthused Eriksson. "Arabic, Hebrew, French, Italian, Greek... some Spanish. Harry will be an excellent addition to the agency."

"Hindi, too, if I'm not mistaken," contributed Temple. "The young man seems to relish talking to people... perhaps one reason behind his love of learning languages." Smiling slightly, the senator addressed the petty officer, "You call him Harry."

"I like him," Eriksson readily admitted.

"Good," said Temple. "A healthy camaraderie between you and him will definitely help." Harry made plenty of enemies. If Sanders realized the demise of the terrorist he considered a son-in-law happened at Harry's hands, the driller would want to make sure the young man died a painful death. But unlike a certain Brooklyn-born princess, Harry Sheppard also collected friends and admirers.

As far as Temple knew, Lilah stuck to her schedule in MIT—classes, chess club, weekend seminars at Harvard Law School, her job at the bookstore, kickboxing, and shooting lessons. She also seemed to have joined a mountain climbing club, a decision she didn't bother explaining to anyone around. Lilah's strength lay in scholarly pursuits and tactical games. The rest... it was incredible how hard she worked at it. Her sense of commitment to acquiring survival skills so clearly foreign to her natural inclinations was extraordinary. Skills her best friend possessed in abundance, much like his ability to connect with people.

Lilah's social life... negligible was a kind way to put it, but the people she did rub shoulders with were of the same high academic caliber as herself. She didn't realize it at present, but this time in relative seclusion was critical to her continued intellectual growth. It would also instill in her the discipline she'd need in a future bigger than the one she envisioned for herself—much, much bigger than the young man currently being discussed.

"Good," Temple repeated, nodding.

She was not yet eighteen—too young and likely still too traumatized from the events in Libya for Temple to talk to her about the alliance. The delay was immaterial as her destiny was already written. When Temple first encountered Lilah, he'd almost lost hope of ever finding the perfect candidate for his plans. He didn't consider his requirements unrealistic... cerebral and shrewd, strong-willed yet empathetic, fearless but willing to sacrifice... any elite military school would have likely contenders. But opportunity... it didn't come around often. As a girl who was born a Sheppard and was adopted by Andrew Barrons, Lilah actually had a chance to do something with the blessings showered on her by the universe.

Temple would see to her training, molding her into the leader the world deserved. The Sheppard Barrons heiress would then marry one of the grandsons of Temple's stepbrother, Justice Godwin Kingsley, thus putting to rest the resentments of past generations. Three major players in the oil sector would once again be brought under the Kingsley family umbrella. Her stock in the companies would be kept below the level likely to invite trouble under antitrust regulations, but the alliance would cover the entire sector. It would take only a couple of years for the partnership to be big enough to bring down Sanders. He could scream collusion all he wanted, but neither he nor the U.S. government would be able to prove it.

Precedent existed for such American empires. Back in the eighteen-hundreds, wealthy businessmen like Rockefeller, Vanderbilt, and J.P. Morgan were supposed to have colluded to keep money and power in their hands. The robber barons controlled American politics with their cash, ruling the nation from behind the scenes. They could've done much good... they did do a lot of good, building the U.S. into the economic powerhouse it was. Their mistakes—the corrupt practices which led to their downfall—were being repeated by Jared Sanders, amplified by several orders of magnitude. The young ruler of the Kingsley-Barrons-Sheppard empire would be protected from similar blunders. The elders of the businesses would continue to be in charge for a few years. Only with time and enough experience would Lilah take the reins.

Those meant to dethrone tyrant rulers rarely enjoyed the luxury of friendships and certainly couldn't afford to romance lowly sailors no matter how extraordinary. Lilah would soon realize she and Harry were worlds apart. So would he. All they needed was *time* apart to understand. If they didn't... as the ancient political strategists advised: one man's life to save a village, one village to save a nation.

Part III

Chapter 7

A year and a half later, February 1976

Brooklyn, New York

"Something to celebrate, heh?" the dean asked Lilah. "Keep going at this pace, and you could graduate early."

"Thank you for all the support," Lilah said, her inner self doing a victory jig. "I couldn't have managed it without your help." All the extra work she did until falling asleep on top of textbooks was going to pay off! She *wanted* to celebrate. But the people she longed to brag to weren't around. And how in the world was she supposed to do anything normal with the note she got from Harry the day before still burning a hole in her brain?

"Whatever happens, don't give up on me," Harry had scrawled at the end of the message.

Marching out of the dean's office, Lilah first called her twin with the news of her little success before heading to the bus station. It took her four hours to get to the Sheppard residence in City Island. As usual, they were all too busy to even hear what she had to say. Before she finished muttering hello, Harry's older brother picked up his parents, and all of them left for a meeting.

Face it, she told herself. She'd become invisible to the family she once thought of as her own. She didn't understand it. They'd been friends with her papa and mama for decades. Now that the ambassador and his wife were no longer around, Lilah also ceased to exist for the Sheppards.

The only one left in the house was Harry's twelve-year-old sister. Sabrina didn't have any news about Harry and said grumpily he talked more to her father's secretary than any of the family. Well, Lilah knew where to find the secretary, and the trip from the Sheppard home to their place of business in Brooklyn took another hour.

Wintry air gusted into her face, stinging her eyes as she stood at the top of the steps leading to the basement office of Gateway, the Sheppards' new oil trading company. The wind also brought the smell of melted cheese and tomato sauce from the pizzeria next door. Wiping moisture from her cheeks, she took a glance at the street. Slush, strewn garbage, a car with a plastic bag taped over the hole in one of the windows... the Sheppards chose one of the seedier parts of the borough for their office. They lost most of what they owned with the loss of Genesis—their old operation—and the cheap rents in this rough neighborhood were probably all they could afford. Still, Brooklyn used to be home for Lilah.

Shaking her head, she stomped down the short flight of stairs to the matchbox-sized foyer. She was here to figure out what was going on with Harry, not indulge in nostalgia. As she tugged the door open, chimes tinkled overhead. Desks were crammed together in the large hall, papers stacked high on each one, and phones were ringing. A tall, black man carried a pile of folders to a gray-haired lady banging away on a typewriter, grunting when his foot bumped into a table leg.

"Dante," Lilah called. He used to be secretary to Harry's father but was now the chief of operations for Gateway.

Dumping the files next to the typist, Dante exclaimed, "Lilah, what a pleasant surprise!"

In a few minutes, they were toasting the news from MIT with warm, cheesy calzones at the pizzeria next door.

"So what else is going on?" Dante asked, the words muffled by the food. "What brings you here all the way from Cambridge? I'm sure it's not simply to update me on what your dean said."

Hesitantly, Lilah started, "I thought you'd know... is Harry okay?"

Surprise in his eyes, Dante said, "Of course. Why wouldn't he be?"

She flushed. "His letters... he doesn't say much. I got worried about... you don't need me to tell you about Sanders."

"He hasn't tried anything in a couple of years," Dante said.

In Libya, Sanders could get away with hiring a team of mercenaries to abduct two teenagers. He did have a lot of American officials in his pocket, but if he tried such blatant tactics within the borders of the U.S., it would attract intense scrutiny. There would be no camouflaging any of it by pretending a rogue government was behind everything. Markets would crash, and the authorities would be forced to act. The best Sanders could do to his enemies as long as they remained stateside was pick them off under the guise of accidents. That, too, would be impossible if his rivals possessed resources to strike back at least within American borders, and Andrew Barrons did have clout.

The Sheppards, though... they'd lost all their money, and everyone knew Sanders would never give up trying to get the only one to evade his clutches. The seventeen-year-old son of a bankrupt driller like Ryan Sheppard managed the feat, and Sanders wouldn't want anyone else thinking they could do the same. There were a couple of "accidents" Harry escaped after his return to the U.S. The curious coincidences ended when Senator Temple forced the police to investigate potential involvement of Sanders. The criminal would slither out of the case, but he wouldn't try anything else with Harry when it was clear the SEAL trainee had the backing of some powerful people.

Nor could the Sheppards and the Barronses do anything to the criminal oilman. Both sides were limited to attacking each other in the business arena. Stalemate... how and when it would be broken was what worried Lilah, especially with Harry going off on jobs with the SEAL training program.

"But the military *is* serious about security," she mumbled out loud.

"There you go," said Dante. "The navy won't let Sanders—or anyone else—harm one of their trainees. Harry is safe." Eyes crinkling, Dante added, "As far as the letters are concerned... Harry can talk your ear off, but I've never seen him with a pen."

Physical safety was one thing. Psychologically... Lilah knew Harry well enough to feel the pain in the last letter. Something *had* happened, something he didn't want to discuss with her. Unfortunately, like the Sheppards, Dante also appeared ignorant of whatever emotional upheaval Harry was going through.

Dante balled up the paper plate and threw it into the garbage can. "Do you have to return right away?"

"Not really. Why?"

"Let me show you around the office," he invited. "You can see where Harry works. His desk."

"He has a desk here?" Lilah asked, startled. "How often does he come to New York?"

"Once every other month or so." An arm around her shoulders, Dante sighed and hustled her out to the street and the freezing air. "Don't get upset before you hear the whole—"

"I'm not upset." Here she was, worrying herself daily about Harry and thinking her successes in life didn't have quite the same zing without—

"Poor boy really has no free time," said Dante. "I've actually seen Harry walk out the door on his way to Cambridge, but then, his father or Senator Temple comes up with some emergency needing to be dealt with—a meeting they want him to sit in, papers to be handed over in person to a potential buyer. Harry barely manages to breathe."

"Oh," Lilah said, her ruffled feathers unruffling quite quickly. She stepped around the crushed soda can outside the entrance to Gateway's office.

"You first," said Dante, holding open the door. He led the way to the back where there was a small desk next to the restrooms, somewhat isolated from the others. Harry's, she presumed. Waggling his eyebrows, Dante said, "You can snoop while I let the boss know we have a guest."

She laughed. Dante knew very well she'd do nothing of the sort. After he left, though, Lilah eyed the small metal cabinet next to the desk, his parting words tempting her. Muttering irritably at herself, she stood, planning to use the ladies' room.

In a couple of minutes, she dried her hands on paper towels. As she was throwing the damp napkin into the trash can, she heard the familiar voice of her brother-in-law outside the door. "Where's she?" Andrew Barrons boomed. Lilah frowned. Andrew was probably there to keep an eye on his investment. It *was* a pretty big check he wrote to Harry's father so the family could start a new business, but the Sheppards wouldn't appreciate him barging in this way.

"I don't see a purse," said Ryan Sheppard, Harry's father. "Maybe she left. Thank God."

Inside the restroom, Lilah froze. There was no purse outside because it—her backpack—was on her shoulder, but Ryan's words... the tone...

"Three years of planning," exclaimed a third man. Again, it was a familiar voice, but this one only vaguely so. "Everything we did to make sure they see the rest of the world—"

"We didn't know she was going to come looking for Dante," Ryan said. "I'll tell him not to let her back into the office. Too risky."

The Sheppards ignored her when she visited their home and now, this. Lilah didn't get the attitude, but Ryan Sheppard would think twice before insulting her again. Breath vibrating in fury, Lilah shoved the door open. "Why is it risky?" she demanded.

Ryan and Andrew stood next to Harry's desk, with Senator Temple right behind. Andrew's brown hair, blue eyes, and sharp nose screamed New York aristocrat. Except for his short beard, Ryan Sheppard was an older version of Harry. The senator... well, most people who followed politics recognized him, but he'd also been part of the rescue team which brought Harry and Lilah home after they escaped Libya. She would *never* forget the politician. If her elderly papa had lived, he'd have been close to Temple's seventyish years of age. Andrew and Ryan were in their early fifties. The three men couldn't have looked more different from each other, but the expressions of dismay on their faces were comically identical.

"As you said, I came to talk to Dante." Lilah looked Ryan Sheppard in the eye. "But thanks. I got the message. You don't want me here."

Temple pushed his way through. "Ryan simply doesn't want you involved in this business with Sanders. There's no reason to be upset."

When Lilah met the senator before, she'd thought him immensely kind. Palms open, he was currently inviting her to trust him. "Sanders?" she asked, subjecting the politician to steady scrutiny.

Temple's eyes narrowed briefly. Instantly recovering his previous pleasant expression, he patted her shoulder. "Harry's a big part of our plans to deal with that little problem, and he keeps sensitive information here. When Dante said you were sitting at Harry's desk, Ryan got worried. Lilah, you know what happened when you last tangled with Sanders."

Lilah glowered. Did these men take her for a fool? If Ryan Sheppard seriously thought Harry would leave confidential information lying around where anyone could access it, he didn't know his son. And *Sanders?* Tension building, she insisted, "Sanders hasn't shown any interest in attacking *me*. What's really going on? Is Harry all right?"

The senator soothed, "Sanders is not bothered about you partly because he knows you only accidentally got in the way in Libya. Ryan and Andrew are merely trying to keep the impression going."

"C'mon, Delilah," Andrew chided. "Why would Ryan not want you around?"

Temple's summary of the situation was accurate. His warm and open expression... the frown on Harry's father's face, the hand in his pocket, jiggling his keys... then there was Andrew. Something about the tableau put on by the three men simply didn't ring true. Lilah bit her lip, debating whether to probe further.

Dante appeared at the back of the group, red-faced with embarrassment. Poor man. He landed in trouble with his boss because of her. With an awkward smile for him and a terse nod at the rest, Lilah left.

The experience niggled at her brain all the way to MIT, but who could she ask for answers? How could she possibly demand to know from Harry why his parents were such jerks?

#

A month later

New Castle, New York

Spooning creamy lobster bisque into her mouth, Lilah thought of the Styrofoam cups stacked in her dorm room. If it weren't for Dan's visit to the Barrons mansion, she'd have declined Andrew's invitation and spent spring break slurping noodles.

Andrew was booming on about something or the other from the head of the long oak table in the family dining room. His wife, Caroline, was on his left and Dan on the right, with Lilah next to her brother. Shawn, the son disinherited by Andrew for being gay, wasn't present.

"Delilah," Andrew bellowed even though there was only one chair between them. "Daniel says you're going to be done with your degree in three years." The maid backed in through the door, rolling the cart with the next course on it. Andrew dropped the soup spoon into the bowl and waved the maid to them, ready to move on to the next course in the meal and the next topic of conversation.

"Lilah now knows more about oil than any of us," Dan contributed, his tone smug. "Did I tell you she made a killing with stocks?"

Lilah grinned. Her twin hadn't changed in the last few months. West Point might have given him a buzz cut and the erect posture, but he'd always been fussy about his appearance. His clothes were perfectly creased, and Lilah was sure she'd see her reflection if she peeked at his leather shoes. And he still adored his sister.

"Really?" asked Andrew, eyes narrowed. "In *this* market?" The prolonged economic downturn had ended, but stocks still weren't doing as well as hoped, except for oil. "What did you buy?"

"Oil," she admitted, smiling her thanks at the maid for the plate of perfectly grilled salmon. When stock prices crashed toward the beginning of her freshman year in college, she invested in Exxon and Chevron. Her education was covered by scholarships, but it still took her every bit of the nerve she possessed to use a portion of her small inheritance in the market. "There's Pfizer... it's down now, but

I believe it will pick up. I'm also looking at getting gold since the prices went down a bit."

Wiping his mouth with a monogrammed napkin, Andrew leaned forward. "Smart strategy. Who's your advisor?"

"No advisor," Lilah said. "Only me." There was a broker she used, but the decisions were mostly hers.

Andrew blinked. The surprise on his face... Lilah wished she had a camera.

"I took a couple of courses," she explained. Not just that, but she wasn't about to inflate Andrew's already puffed-up ego by telling him she'd paid attention when he was coaching Dan on the possible aftereffects of the oil embargo when it was just beginning. She'd also worked for her friend's grandfather for a few weeks when she was in high school and heard plenty from the old man about the unpegging of gold from the dollar.

"Good," Andrew repeated, this time with grudging respect in his tone.

Lilah preened if only in her mind. The one positive thing about Andrew she ever found—other than his paternal affection for her twin—was his business acumen. All the major newspapers in the world admitted Andrew Barrons knew what he was doing as the chief executive of Barrons O & G. Plus, he never concerned himself with making people feel good, so he wouldn't have bothered with the lukewarm compliment if he didn't mean it.

"Maybe you can hire her, Andrew," Dan suggested. "What do you say? Can she work for the company in the summer?"

Lilah threw a sharp look at her twin. He knew of her plans to apply to Harvard Law School. It would be expensive, and the funds from their deceased parents were not likely to be enough. From what she heard, Barrons O & G paid well. The idea of working for the same brother-in-law she so desperately wanted to be rid of...

"We'll think about it," Andrew said. "I meant to tell you... Senator Temple is also considering asking you to do a summer internship at his office."

It was Lilah's turn to blink. The politician had been on her mind the last few weeks what with the spinning he tried on her. *"I'll* think about it," she said, her chin up.

Andrew's jerk of disbelief was satisfying, but Harry's laughing face popped into her mind.

Be nice, Princess, the memory of her best friend advised between chortles. *Forget your ego for a second and stop pissing people off. You never know when you might need them.*

Temple was related to Supreme Court Justice Godwin Kingsley. An internship with the politician would help her with her application to Harvard, but an introduction to the justice would be invaluable. Lilah planned to be in his place one day—the U.S. Supreme Court. If it were Harry instead of her, he and the justice would probably have been poker buddies already.

Lilah didn't need Dan to get Andrew to call Senator Temple on her behalf. Before she left the Barrons mansion at the end of the week, Andrew brought up the topic again, announcing if she were serious about law school, it would be stupid to decline the offer of internship. The look in her brother-in-law's eyes... he really wanted her to take the position. First, the scene in Gateway's office. Now, this internship.

Something was cooking, something she wasn't going to like. Staring at Andrew, she struggled with sudden unease. If she said no... law school... in the end, Lilah stretched her lips into a grimace of a smile and mumbled her thanks.

Chapter 8

Two months later, May 1976

Washington, DC

At the end of Lilah's first week in the capital city, Temple's chief of staff marched her into the senator's office—a spacious room, brightly lit and smelling faintly of lavender. She squared her shoulders and fixed her gaze on a pencil lying on its side on the desk as the chief launched into a tirade about the intern personally selected by the senator. Arms waving about and nostrils quivering in outrage, the chief complained to Temple about Lilah's "lack of proper deference."

She'd accidentally attended a call from one of the senator's colleagues and used the opportunity to gently suggest a few changes to the gentleman's voting pattern. She *had* tried to be as diplomatic as possible, Lilah thought, feeling intensely cross. The octogenarian politician at the other end of the line still took offense and demanded to speak to "the man in charge."

Senator Temple heard the chief out before pushing off from the desk. Sauntering to Lilah, he flung an arm around her shoulders. "Miss Barrons brings her formidable intellect to our team, and we're lucky to have her on our side."

What?

The chief opened and closed his mouth like a surprised fish. "But—"

"But nothing," said Temple. "The gentleman who complained would've done well to take her advice."

Lilah just about managed to stop herself from saying, "So there!"

Muttering about spoilt princesses, the staffer left. She stiffened.

The senator glanced from his employee's departing back to Lilah's rigid expression. "You expect to be heard, and people are not used to young ladies assuming a position of authority on anything. Your demeanor is one of your strengths. Don't let anyone tell you otherwise. Embrace the royal title people call you and project power. You *are* a princess."

Somehow, coming from him, it didn't sound like mockery. But the idea... Lilah laughed. "I'm no aristocrat, Mr. Temple. My parents were regular people."

"Nobility comes from character," he said. "From what I heard, your father and mother were infinitely qualified to be labeled as such."

Flushing, Lilah said, "I'm very proud of who they were. I only meant—"

"I know what you meant. Society confers such titles on those born into money and power. Even then, *you* are not only the child of your ancestors. You're a fire-borne princess. You took birth from the inferno at the Libyan border." As she giggled at his hyperbole, Temple smiled. "Also, what if you marry a prince?"

A prince? Harry was a regular person like herself. Lilah chided herself. More than two years passed since those childish promises, and neither his occasional letters nor his too-brief calls gave her a clue as to his current romantic inclinations. "Where would *I* meet royalty?"

"You never know," Temple said. "This is Washington. Plenty of rich and handsome young men around. Educated, articulate... I will introduce you—"

"I plan to make it on my own," Lilah said firmly, "and I prefer men who do the same."

Before the politician could respond, his secretary arrived, carrying a message from a donor. On her way out of the office, Lilah noted the fleeting frown on Temple's face but decided it was about the campaign contributor. U.S. senators would hardly be bothered by the marital options of engineering students. Anyway, she was there to work and learn, not meet men.

Work, she did. In fact, she couldn't wait to rush out of the youth hostel each morning and get to the senate office building. The staff was friendly, and the chief's initial annoyance with her notwithstanding, he never minded explaining to her the intricacies of policymaking. Temple's personal secretary, Wilma, taught Lilah the nuts and bolts of what went on in the office. Someone even offered her tickets to a baseball game. Apparently, every last person in the place was a Mets fan, including the senator.

It was Temple himself who was the biggest surprise. Her fears about him conspiring with Andrew and Ryan seemed silly in retrospect. The senator was actually interested in Lilah's plans for her future. He let her use his personal library, a privilege he allowed not even his only son. *Her*, a sophomore in college.

He was also supremely intelligent and very much in touch with what went on in the world. Shrewd, too. Over the next few weeks, the senator tried to tutor Lilah on the fine art of diplomacy.

"It's good to project strength," he said multiple times, "but better to leave the other person feeling he also won something." Temple asked her to accompany him to meetings. Striding toward the senate chamber, he stated, "We're going to seduce them." At Lilah's shocked gasp, the seasoned statesman laughed. "You can always try to state facts and change someone's mind… like you did with my colleague who called. The tactic could fail. Or you could try to understand the motive that drives the other person. His or her innermost desire. Then, use the *possibility* as lure to get what you need."

"In other words, you're a politician." She could've bitten her tongue off the moment she said it.

Temple chuckled. "Pretty sure your father would have said the same. Diplomats need a similar skill set."

Relieved he didn't take offense, Lilah smiled back, but she didn't have her papa's natural talent, and even thinking about attempting Temple's *m.o.* was enough to frustrate her.

The senator stopped at the door to their destination and sighed. "Just don't go out of your way to offend people."

Smile turning into a wide grin, Lilah followed him in.

One afternoon, Temple pointed to the world map hanging in his private office, pins of all colors stabbed into it. "Know what this is?"

Lilah eyed the chart. Of course she did. Chemical engineering might not be where she eventually wanted to end up, but she took it seriously and paid close attention to the petroleum industry. "The major oil discoveries of this century."

The politician shook his head. "Look closer, Lilah. The colors... what do they stand for?"

She hazarded a guess. "The drillers?"

"Yes, the drillers," Temple said. "They're the red pins. The pipeline operators are blue, the traders green, and so on and so forth. The sector is splintered between companies." His nostrils flared. "Now, look at the black pins."

Lilah peered, examining the cluster of tacks. "It's the only color in some regions. One company does it all?" Like Andrew's business. Everyone called him a driller, but he did lots more in the sector besides oil production.

"Clever girl," said Temple. "One company—Sanders, Incorporated. Either on his own or through government contracts."

Lilah drew back, the usual mix of antagonism and dread churning her insides.

"Worried?" asked Temple. "You should be." At the jerky movement of her hands, he added, "No, not about Harry. He is all right. But what about everyone else? For that matter, what about *you?*"

"Me? I thought Sanders believed I was too trivial to bother with."

The senator laughed. "Got to you, did it?"

"Huh?"

"Most people who know about the abduction don't realize you were also involved," Temple remarked. "But even those who do know think it was Harry who engineered the death of Melanthios."

Lilah started. Temple had been flying over the Egypt-Libya border with the search-and-rescue pilot when she and Harry escaped. After she learned the senator was the one to spot her from the chopper, she did wonder if he saw her leading Sanders's thug into the minefield.

"Yes, I saw," Temple answered the unasked question, eyes steady. "It's one of the reasons I believe you're the right person for—Lilah, valor requires shrewd intellect, quick thinking, and a spine of steel much more than physical prowess. You're a brave young lady who was forced to make a split-second decision under extremely trying circumstances, and it was the correct call. Sanders thinks Harry somehow killed Melanthios, and the governments involved believe the death to be an accident brought about by the man's own stupidity. Best to keep your part quiet. We don't need to give Sanders another target."

That had been Harry's reasoning as well. She nodded, grateful for the senator's kindness.

"Does it bother you no one believes you had an active part in your escape?" Temple asked.

"Not really. I never even thought about it that way." She and

Harry survived, and Lilah didn't care who got credit as long as her best friend didn't get into trouble for any of it.

"You shouldn't let what people think distract you," the senator agreed. "But nor should you lose the chance to control the narrative. The obscurity you currently enjoy will help. It is crucial to mythmaking."

Myth— Lilah stared.

Temple elaborated, "In the old days, families used to send their sons to monasteries to be educated. For one, without seclusion and discipline, the students couldn't have sharpened their skills. You're simply following in the same great tradition of learning. Your entire future—perhaps the *nation's* destiny—will one day depend on it."

She'd already told Temple she wanted to be a supreme court justice someday. Lilah let go of terrifying memories and imagined herself writing opinions which would impact the entire country.

"For another," Temple continued, "any mistakes in the learning process of leaders need to be kept secret for the masses to willingly follow him or her into battle. Take ancient literature. Priests—men claiming to represent gods—usually picked promising young people and trained them to be heroes. Their childhoods were erased. According to the stories, most simply sprang into being as fully grown adults with magical powers... as gods... avatars. A hero with a normal upbringing is not easy to hammer into the public imagination as an incarnation. Would take a lot of work to convert mistakes made in the sight of witnesses to some sort of a planned— dare I say, divine—game."

"Propaganda." Discomfited by the idea, Lilah shifted on her feet.

"Yes. Like it or not, such tactics form an essential part of statecraft. Diplomats, politicians, judges, businessmen—all of us need to be keenly aware of how we're seen by the public we serve.

Anything Harry has already done *can* be spun, but not everyone will buy the tales. In your case, my child, we have a lot more room to maneuver. Be glad no one knows you now. Once you're ready for the spotlight, I'll present you myself to the world. There is no doubt you'll be spectacular."

The idea of it... Lilah wasn't sure. Still, she couldn't help but bask in the glow of the senator's obvious approval.

"We must stop Sanders," Temple murmured almost to himself. "Stopping him won't be enough. We'll need to replace him with someone who would actually work *for* the people. A new leader, a hero for the public to follow."

Yanked from her happy space of mind, Lilah exclaimed, "Why would you replace one tyrant with another?"

To her abject confusion, the senator guffawed, holding on to the wall. "Tyrant, eh?" he asked, tears of mirth in his eyes. "Philosophers like Plato and Aristotle defined a tyrant as a corrupt ruler who uses his power to further his own interests instead of working for the common good. What if we choose a leader willing to sacrifice for the sake of humanity? Surely, such a person would be inclined to protect mankind rather than rule over it."

"Plato also said, 'The people have always some champion whom they set over them and nurse into greatness,'" Lilah countered. "'This and no other is the root from which a tyrant springs; when he first appears above ground, he is a protector.' See, Senator? This is the problem with propaganda. It prods the public into acting against its own best interests by choosing some hero—some *super*hero—to rule over them. He could be the entirely wrong sort of fellow to lead, but even if he *were* nearly perfect, it wouldn't be right. Any single person or group, no matter how well-intentioned, should not be given such power. Chances are it will lead to totalitarianism. Democracy might be chaotic and inefficient, but it remains the best route."

The laughter in the senator's eyes faded into a smile which reflected both discomfort and surprise. "I didn't intend to suggest doing away with democracy. We're talking about control of the energy sector, not political authority."

Lilah shrugged. "True. Still, when the world cannot function without oil, leaving one man in charge undermines political democracy."

"Precisely my point." Temple waved a finger in her direction. "Oil and gas form almost two-thirds of the world's energy resources. The sector is critical to humanity's survival. What happens when some lunatic from some corner of the planet decides to use it as a weapon?"

"I'm not sure," Lilah admitted. "But I simply cannot wrap my head around the idea that the answer lies in benevolent dictatorship. No, sir. It would be asking for trouble in my opinion. I mean, it took a lot of effort for the U.S. to rein in the robber barons. Now, we have Sanders. Only, he's worse. We cannot afford to assume a new monarch would be any better."

"But what if—" Temple huffed, adding, "You're not easy to convince, are you?" For the first time since they met, his tone was perturbed... frustrated, even.

Lilah said nothing, wondering what was going on with the politician. He surely wasn't egotistical enough to want everyone around to always chant, "Yes, boss." Leaving her speculating, Temple dropped the topic.

Later, she told herself to be happy the politician was so committed to the cause. Temple was a rarity among his ilk... someone who passionately believed in working for the good of humanity.

There were other parts of the senator's philosophy Lilah found she didn't like at all. After catching her examining the hand-carved chess pieces on his desk, Temple issued a challenge, which she gladly took up. "'To save the family, give up a man,'" Temple quoted from the *Mahabharata*, moving the knight pawn. "'To save the village, give up a family. To save the nation, give up a village.' You've left the black king unprotected."

"Is the value of humanity measured in numbers? And my king will be fine." Lilah moved the queen pawn forward.

"Suit yourself. You'll lose your five bucks." He moved his bishop pawn. Temple sneezed, digging in his pocket and bringing out a snowy-white handkerchief. "Good Lord, child, you wear too much perfume. I could smell it two miles away."

Lilah gave him a bland smile and focused on the pieces. She moved the black queen across the board, no pawns or knights to cover her. Now, the white king was directly in her path. "Checkmate."

The senator rocked back. "Who are you? Minerva?"

The Roman goddess? She was the deity of wisdom and strategy, who sprang from Jupiter's skull fully armed and was prophesied to overthrow her father as the ruler of heaven. Lilah started placing the pieces back in the box. "My interest in politics is mostly in policy and the courts. You don't have to worry about being dethroned, Senator." She noted the pleased expression on Temple but didn't realize until later she'd just claimed him as her intellectual father. It definitely didn't occur to her to worry Jupiter eventually attempted to kill his daughter.

On the last day of her three months in the senate office, she went to thank Temple. He was in his library, examining his collection for damage from humidity.

They ambled along the carpeted room, pausing by shelves when Temple spotted a book he wanted to inspect. "You're still planning on a law degree?" the senator asked, tone casual.

Lilah nodded, telling herself to just blurt it out. She needed his recommendation letter and an introduction to Justice Kingsley. Still, she didn't want it to come across as though she accepted the internship for only those reasons. The experience working for Senator Temple was something she'd always cherish.

"It's not easy to get in," warned Temple. "Especially to places like Harvard. There are applicants with extensive work experience, some of whom have done years of humanitarian service." Eyes twinkling, he added, "Remember our talk about rich young men? They could help. Or the gentleman you told off—the old senator— he's on the governing board. You might have to make nice."

Her face heating, Lilah said, "I'm not going to date anyone just to... about the other thing... I don't mind apologizing, Senator. But only for embarrassing you and your staff. I can't pretend not to have meant what I said. The *gentleman's* policies are clearly meant to benefit his donors, not his voters."

Temple halted. "What if he stops you from getting in?"

"I'm willing to pay the price," she stated.

Staring unblinkingly, Temple asked, "Are you sure?"

"Absolutely certain. I can't sell out my conscience for ambition."

Just for a nanosecond, the senator's expression changed into a sternness which was never there before. "Let's hope you don't come to regret the choice."

The friendly smile returned to his face, but somehow, Lilah knew she'd said something wrong. Did she finally go too far? The recommendation she wanted... she bit her lip in exasperation. She'd have to wait to ask, figure out how to make amends for... what *had* she said that was so offensive?

With careful fingers, Temple pushed a book farther into the bookshelf, aligning it perfectly with its mates on either side. When he continued on his stroll, Lilah followed. There was one more thing she needed from him. Unlike the recommendation, this couldn't wait. For the sake of her peace of mind, she needed to know.

Gathering courage, she asked, "Mr. Temple, I... umm... there's something else. You see Harry when he goes to New York, right? How is he doing? I haven't heard from him in a long time. I mean, he writes, and he does call, but he never says... umm... is he all right?"

Once again, Temple stopped. "Why?"

The quirk in his brow irritated her. "What do you mean 'why?'"

"Harry has responsibilities, child. He's a SEAL, sworn to protect his country. Why do you feel he should place *your* needs ahead of the nation's?"

That wasn't what she asked, but Temple's response made her feel like a petulant, self-centered teenager.

"College is supposed to expose you to the wider world," continued the politician, a thread of exasperation in his tone. A thread so unexpected, so thin that it might have been imaginary. "After two years at MIT, you can't possibly be sticking to the same safe ideas of—" Temple broke off and turned to the bookshelf to tap his finger on an empty spot. "Harry borrowed this one— *Arthashastra*—a second time around. He's got an interest in statecraft. An impressive young man."

Lilah wasn't quite sure how to respond, so she simply nodded.

The politician's eyes softened. "Lilah, there are many things in life beyond the small world you call your own. Among humanity, you're one of the blessed. You have ample intelligence, connections, and yes, looks. Use your gifts well. Think beyond your own needs as Harry is learning to do."

The conversation left her jittery enough that she canceled her bus ride back to Cambridge and made other plans. What Temple said... did it mean Harry no longer cared about his family and old friends? Lilah shook her head. She needed to think clearly. Calling the secretary of the mountain club in upstate New York, she asked to join the weekend's hike across the Adirondack trails.

Stiff branches tore at clothes, and slippery moss-covered boulders lined her path. The sky was hardly visible through the tops of the trees. Blood beaded along a scratch on her cheek as she got to the last cliff. Leaning backward holding on to the cable, Lilah rappelled down the hundred-foot chute.

Conquest... she'd triumphed over yet another peak. *She* was in charge of her own destiny. Win or lose, she would *not* be a victim.

Lilah coiled the rope around herself and thanked her partner for the cold drink. Barefoot and with pants rolled up, the team lounged on the rocks at the bottom of Bushnell Falls.

Nature's awesome strength also brought with it an incredible clarity to her mental workings. In the mountains, thoughts stopped darting around her brain and fell in place. Harry had asked her not to give up on him. She wouldn't.

Chapter 9

A few weeks later, August 1976

Trenton, New Jersey

In the conference room at Temple's local office, the members of the planned presidential exploratory committee excitedly discussed the prospects of their candidate. The senator was seventy-one now and would be three years older when he took office. Age was sure to be one of the negatives hurled by rivals, but at least it meant the tabloids spent less time looking for hints of romance in Temple's life, buying without demur the explanation he remained very much in love with his long-dead wife. Not contributing a word, Temple sat at the end of the table and listened with half an ear as the chief of staff elaborated on potential counters to the opposition's tactics. Not even when the conversation switched from the insanely trivial to electoral college strategies did he bother to contribute.

"More coffee?" asked a pleasant female voice.

"Hmm?" Temple looked up. His secretary stood holding the carafe, her apple cheeks crinkled in a smile. "Thank you, Wilma. I'll take some."

Pouring fragrant coffee into his mug, she muttered, "Cheer up. Or everyone's going to think you're having second thoughts."

"No second thoughts," Temple murmured back. "It's something else. I might have made a mistake."

The laugh lines around her eyes deepened. "You? No way."

Wilma and the chief of staff worked for Temple's father when all of them met. The twenty-eight-year-old son of the politician announced his decision to run for Congress and asked the efficient junior aide and the enthusiastic PR assistant to join him. The duo witnessed Temple's business-like wooing of an older colleague's daughter, his wedding, the birth of his son. The three of them had been a team through every campaign. The chief of staff invariably showed "due deference" as he called it, but in private, Wilma treated Temple the way she would've treated the brother she lost in WWI. She hadn't been silent with her displeasure at how Temple more or less ignored his wife and child except when he needed them for campaign events. But even Wilma wasn't privy to the reason behind Temple's current disquiet. The fewer who knew about the scheme, the better.

With a reassuring half-smile, he asked, "Did Noah get here?"

"Mr. Andersen is waiting in your private office," said the secretary. "He didn't want to interrupt the meeting."

In less than a minute, Temple asked the chief of staff to

continue the discussion, adding, "I have a phone call to make. The Beirut issue."

No one protested. Temple might be on the verge of running for president, but as the chairman of the Committee on Interstate and Foreign Commerce, he already carried heavy responsibilities.

When Temple closed the door to his private office behind him, a man with jet-black hair—dyed to perfection as usual—looked up from the folder in his hands, concern in his green eyes. Noah Andersen, former attorney general, was in Temple's chair behind the desk.

He and Noah met when they were both nervous freshmen at Yale. After law school, Noah joined Kingsley Corp as their attorney but later left to start his own firm. In a few short years, Noah made his practice the nation's foremost securities law firm before going on to be the attorney general. Noah recently accepted the offer from his alma mater to be the dean of the law school. Some called him a mischief-maker for his relentless targeting of his opponents' psychological weaknesses. Noah's ideas on the unexpected snag in the Kingsley-Barrons-Sheppard project would be invaluable.

Temple settled into the chair on the near side and shifted the rotary phone to the top of the binders on the left. This office—unlike the one in DC—was small with metal cabinets on one side and a map on the opposing wall. It used to be his father's when *he'd* been the senator, and Temple moved his operations here after the old man's death. A bit of sentimentality on his part, which his father would probably have snickered at. "Thoughts?" Temple asked.

Noah sighed, his sunken cheeks briefly puffing up. "Just when we got Godwin and Andrew and Ryan to agree." The Sheppards and the Barronses were forced by circumstances to acquiesce to Temple's demands. But the Kingsleys wouldn't have agreed to any alliance which didn't give them the upper hand. When Lilah emerged from the fire at the Egypt-Libya border, Temple was nearly tempted to believe in miracles.

Almost three years passed since the day. MIT, an entire summer at the senate office, no outward signs of lingering emotional damage from the abduction... she should've been ready for their discussion. She should've recognized that destiny put her in a unique place. As the Sheppard-Barrons heiress married to the Kingsley scion, Lilah would have the opportunity to put her gifts to good use.

Temple would've trained her for her eventual role, but they would've had to wait until he was in the White House before making any announcement about the marriage because Sanders would recognize the tactic for what it was. Once he sensed such an existential threat, Barrons clout and American law would no longer be enough to protect Lilah. She would need backing from the most powerful office in the land, from the person who had the might of the U.S. military at his disposal. The planned schedule would've been perfect. By the time the presidential election was done, Lilah would be out of college, and the chosen groom would be of appropriate age. All three clans would have then proclaimed to the world the birth of a new partnership.

Instead, Lilah refused to consider an advantageous marriage, and she was ready to martyr herself over a simple apology to an old politician.

Noah asked, "Do you think her guard was up because of the incident in Ryan's office?"

"Could be," said Temple. "Could be about the young man, too, but I doubt it."

"It would be simple if so," said Noah. "Camouflaging the death of a CIA operative on hostage rescue missions isn't exactly tricky business." They could've cooked up some explanation for the Sheppards so the family would continue cooperating with the alliance. Blamed everything on Sanders, perhaps. Only, it would've been a complete failure as an attempt at controlling Lilah.

"Our difficulty with Lilah has more to do with the girl herself," the senator said. "I *knew* how obstinate she was when Andrew was trying to adopt her and Dan." Andrew wanted the boy for his son, but he wouldn't agree unless his sister did, and she didn't. The billionaire eventually offered a deal: her acquiescence to the adoption in exchange for a very generous investment in the Sheppards' new company. Everyone around reminded Lilah the money and the political backing were needed to keep Harry safe from Sanders, and for a change, she decided to relinquish her pride. When the idea for the new Kingsley-Barrons-Sheppard alliance was first hatched, Temple imagined he could mold her mindset and channel her strong qualities toward their cause. "She rejected the plan before I even brought it up. Lilah's young and idealistic. She might sacrifice herself than do something she doesn't believe in. Right now, her worldview doesn't match with ours."

"We can't afford for it not to," Noah said. The abductions of teenaged Harry and Lilah were the least of Sanders's crimes. There was nothing he wouldn't do to keep tight control over the energy sector—political assassinations, inciting riots, overthrowing regimes.

"Not just because of Sanders and his ilk," brooded Temple. "Even OPEC... look at what they did to us in the last couple of years." As retaliation against the American support of Israelis, an oil embargo was announced, worsening the stock market crash already underway. The unemployment rate climbed to nine percent. Blamed for the global economic downturn, the U.S. was fast losing allies. "Whatever we think of the morality of the Palestinian situation, one of the main reasons Israel pulled back from Sinai and Golan Heights was the blackmail over oil. The West simply cannot keep letting this happen. The rest of the world cannot afford it. A coalition of our own is the only way we're going to be able to protect ourselves from such dirty tricks." Once Jared Sanders was down and the Kingsley-Barrons-Sheppard alliance firmly established, they needed to bring in other businesses to form a network of oil companies. With Sanders out, there would be no one of the same stature left to raise noises on antitrust violations. Objections from other quarters could easily be dealt with either by offering financial incentives or with political pressure. "We've been trying for many years to get it done..."

Noah tossed the folder to one side of the table. "You can continue to work on her."

"I could," Temple muttered. "Unfortunately, we don't have the luxury of time. If things go as planned, I'll be the president in a couple of years, but the office won't magically give me the ability to put an end to the problems over oil. We need the network, and we need it created during my presidency to make sure Sanders doesn't go on the attack."

"Temple, we're not going to win by trying to strong-arm her. If we trick her into things, there's always the risk she'll figure it out. We need her to cooperate."

"There are four billion humans on this planet," Temple said, voice tense. "More than two-hundred million Americans. Lilah is only one of them. A single individual cannot be allowed to upend plans meant to benefit all of mankind."

"Only one way left open. Someone else has to change her mind. Someone she trusts."

Shaking his head, Temple said, "Our 'someone else' is intelligent enough to know something needs to be done, but this idea... hell, no one's dared tell either of them the whole story behind the abduction."

The duo didn't know anything about the old conspiracies or the failures. They didn't know what Sanders wanted was revenge. Andrew and the Sheppards were aware of the dangers waiting in Libya and still let Lilah fly there. Harry believed it was his father's refusal to sell which led to the abduction. If the truth came out, his and Lilah's faith in all those involved would be destroyed.

"Our boy turned out to be useful," Temple continued. "More than we ever imagined. He will be crucial to my campaign. Sanders will support whomever runs against me, and I need Harry to keep the opposition busy. Also, he and Lilah have been apart for a while now. For him to be the one persuading her..."

"We'll have to make sure he does it after the election."

Part IV

Chapter 10

Months later, April 1977

City Island, New York City

Cream lace curtains fluttered as Sabrina—Harry's sister—pushed open the wood-framed windows of her second-floor bedroom. The salty smell of sea breeze rushed in. Sitting cross-legged on the four-poster bed, Lilah had a view of the private beach behind the Sheppard home. Tide was high, and the North Atlantic surf pounded the sandy shore, spraying the wooden steps leading to the large deck. "I like to hear the ocean," Sabrina said, plopping back onto the mattress. "So will you or not?"

"I still don't see why you can't ask your parents to buy you this..." Lilah leafed through Sabrina's copy of *Popular Electronics*, not interested in the articles. "...this computer kit."

"Lilah, they don't get it, and if they tell anyone, the kids at school will call me a geek. I'll die if that happens."

Pursing her lips, Lilah regarded the teen.

Hopeful green eyes stared back. "I don't want anyone to know, okay? Puhlease?"

"How are you going to hide it from your father and mother?"

Sabrina snorted. "*Them?* You think they'll know it's a computer? I'll say it's something I'm building for school. Please, please, please? I'll pay you back from my allowance, I promise."

"Which one do you want?

"Altair 8800." Flipping quickly through the pages of the magazine, Sabrina pointed to a picture.

She'd become Lilah's only connection to the Sheppards since Harry left. Only Sabrina had the time to chat when Lilah visited. Sabrina, in turn, confided in Lilah about her plans to study computers. Lilah heard all about the crush of the month whenever she visited, each time having to pinky-promise never to whisper a word to the rest of the Sheppards.

She eyed the big box with tiny red knobs and circuits and the price mentioned. The cash she had wouldn't be enough. Dan could float her a loan from the ultra-generous checks he got from Andrew as pocket money, but she needed to first make sure Sabrina was not falling for some kind of scam. "Looks cheesy," Lilah commented. "Hollywood surplus."

Breathing in horror, Sabrina repeated, "Cheesy? *Popular Electronics* features the best of..."

What did I start? Lilah's head swam from the technical jargon the kid rattled off at lightning speed. Finally, she held her hands up in surrender. "All right, all right." Sputtering with laughter, Lilah added, "I'll see what I can do."

As the fair-haired girl threw plump arms around her neck, Lilah surreptitiously checked herself in the wall mirror. The flared miniskirt in deep russet and the floral tie-front shirt were a little skimpy for the cool spring weather, but it was the only outfit in her closet that still appeared somewhat new. She wanted to look her best today.

Because this afternoon, Harry would be in New York, moving back home after his first assignment. Nearly three years after he left for his training, they were going to meet.

When guests gathered in the living room for the welcome-home party that afternoon, Sabrina grabbed a photograph from the mantel. "Petty Officer Harry Sheppard," she said, showing Lilah the picture of her brother wearing the coveted SEAL Trident. Lilah smiled and nodded, not mentioning the framed copy which took pride of place on the side table in her dorm room. A car door slammed outside, and Lilah's pulse skittered. She lost track of what Sabrina was saying.

"Here he is," someone shouted when Harry walked in. His steps faltered as though he were surprised to find himself the focus of attention.

Sabrina squealed in excitement and tossed the photograph to the side before elbowing her way through the guests.

Around Lilah, eager chatter and boisterous laughter broke out, but she heard very little of it. Someone bumped into her from the side, but Lilah was hardly aware of anything but Harry's presence. She almost felt... it was weird, this idea that this was their first meeting *ever*.

Gone was the baby fat in his cheeks. His silky, dark hair was tamed in a short, sharp cut. The time with the SEALs had given him the physique to match his six-foot-four frame. Even dressed casually as he was in mustard tee and chinos and scuffed brown loafers, power radiated from Harry. The boy she remembered had become a man—a warrior—tall and muscled and tough.

After returning Sabrina's exuberant hug, Harry shook hands with relatives he likely hadn't seen in years, but his coffee-dark eyes searched the crowd as though looking for something... someone.

Lilah smiled, waiting for him to spot her.

When an old lady in a wheelchair demanded his attention, he dropped to his knees and greeted her with a kiss on the cheek, his gaze still restlessly scanning the gathered guests. Hector, Harry's brother, hauled him up by the collar, welcoming him with backslaps. Then, over Hector's shoulder, Harry's eyes snagged on Lilah.

Sheer, acute delight lit up his face, sending a tidal wave of happiness crashing through her. Harry pushed Hector aside, heading toward her, only to be stopped by his mother. Sophia Sheppard urged him toward their VIP guest, Senator Temple. In the fleeting look Harry threw at Lilah as he was dragged away, she saw his impatience. Silently, he begged her to wait, his frustration evident at being so near to her, yet so far. She debated going after him, but Temple... she wasn't gonna be rude to the man after the kindness he showed when she worked for him.

Harry's conversation with the politician seemed to take forever. Andrew Barrons was also at the party, and he joined them. So did Ryan. Even when Harry extricated himself from the group, there were many people with demands on his time. With each man and woman to accost him, Harry produced a pleased grin, looking each one in the eye as though only he or she mattered in that moment, but Lilah didn't miss the yearning in the sideways glances thrown in her direction.

Settling with Sabrina into seats by the stone fireplace, Lilah primly crossed her ankles under her chair and smoothed the mini over her thighs. She listened to the younger girl chattering about school and out of the corner of her eye, watched Harry make his way toward them. When he finally reached her, she refused to look up and bit her lip to stop the ridiculous smile threatening to explode. First, he'd have to come up with a pretty apology for making her wait no matter what reason.

Harry dropped to one knee next to her and teasingly smiled at his sister. "What have you been up to, Runt?" he asked, his voice deeper than Lilah remembered. The sandalwood scent of his cologne floated to her nostrils. "Getting into trouble at school?"

Still sitting, Sabrina drew herself up, nose in the air. "Don't call me that name."

"Hey, if brothers won't tell you the truth, who will?" he asked.

"You *are* a tiny person." Sabrina was five-foot-one, but Harry's tone made it sound as though she were a Kewpie doll.

Sabrina snorted. "I'm telling Mama."

When she stomped off, Harry exclaimed, "It worked!"

Pursing her lips, Lilah twisted around to eye him.

"What?" he asked, sounding perfectly reasonable. "How else was I supposed to get you alone?"

She couldn't help it. Laughter pealed out. He laughed with her, his dark gaze scanning her face, studying every inch of it. Still kneeling on the polished wood floor, he brushed his fingertips over the flimsy sleeve covering her arm. Her heart thudded.

Lilah attempted a repressive frown. "I prefer your sister's company. She never ditches me for senators."

"Damn it," he said, clenching his fist. "Maybe I should've sent it to Mr. Temple, not you."

She blinked. "Huh?"

His face smugly virtuous, Harry said, "When you get back to Andrew's place, take a look at the fountain outside your room."

Eyes narrowed, she asked, "You didn't leave a snake there, did you?"

He threw his hands in the air. "Oh, God, you still haven't forgotten? It's been six years. And it was a *lizard*."

Lilah sputtered, fingers to her lips.

"Lotuses," he said, tone aggrieved. "As we speak, Andrew's gardener is planting them in the fountain."

Something inside her chest took flight. "What color?" she asked, unwilling to give in so easily.

"Blue, of course." Her favorite kind. Strange, when red was her preferred color for everything else. They grinned absurdly at each other. Three years since they met… so much to say, but she couldn't find the words. "How are you?" he finally asked, his voice barely more than a murmur.

She inclined her head, silently telling him all was well. "You?"

His knuckles came up to graze her cheek. "All good now," he said, a tender smile in his eyes. His gaze drifted down to her mouth. Inside her maroon wedges, her toes curled. Her arms itched to twine around his neck, pulling him down for a kiss.

"Harry," called his father, breaking their absorption in each other. Not paying any mind to Lilah's presence, Ryan Sheppard dragged his son toward Senator Temple and Andrew Barrons.

Even when Harry managed to get away, there were others waiting to talk to him. Temple and Andrew spent a lot of time huddled with Ryan Sheppard. Official announcement had not been made about the senator's run for the American presidency, but everyone who paid attention knew it was happening. Lilah hoped like crazy Temple would win. She didn't think there was a politician currently alive with more genuine concern for the nation. As always, he was pleasant and charming to every guest who approached him. Andrew and Ryan were visibly annoyed at the interruptions. Every now and then, they would glance in Lilah's direction, a faint scowl twisting Ryan's lips. Harry was still continuing his rounds of the room.

Tamping down disappointment, Lilah asked Sabrina to let her brother know she was leaving and headed out. If Harry wanted, he could've invited her along when he talked to—

"Lilah, wait," he called from behind. Her coat draped over an arm, Lilah continued to the front door and with her hand on the knob, glanced behind. Ignoring the protests from the crowd in the room, Harry jogged up. "I'm sorry, I—"

"Harry," called his father.

"Let's go." Not looking back, Harry hustled her out and snapped the door shut behind them.

The voices from the living room receded. Evening had given way to night, and the birds were long gone home to their nests. There was a chill in the air and a full moon in the sky. Standing at the top of the stoop, she breathed in the salty smell of the Atlantic.

"Do you really have to leave?" he asked. "The only person I wanted to see tonight was you, but—"

Lilah said nothing, just arched an eyebrow.

"I have a few days off before the next assignment," he said, voice suddenly diffident. "Maybe we can... you know... hang out somewhere. Uhh... if you don't have anything going on... I'm sure you do, but..."

"Yes," she said. When he blinked, she clarified hurriedly, "I mean... I'd like to hang out. Not that I have nothing else..." She groaned. "Harry, why are we acting weird?"

"Are you?" he murmured teasingly. "I didn't notice anything different."

Curling her fingers into a fist, she punched his shoulder, but he caught her hand in his. Once again, her heart thudded. There was a time when she'd have dragged him into a hug without a second thought, but now... did she dare?

"Harry," his father's voice called again.

She jerked back in mild shock and glanced at the front door. No, still closed.

"Dammit." Harry huffed. "I need some time with *you.*"

"Not happening tonight," she said. "Just show up tomorrow. I'll see if I have a couple of minutes to spare."

He grinned and took her coat from her, helping her shrug into it. When he drew out her hair from inside the collar, his fingers seemed to linger on her nape. Her eyes fluttered closed. She stood there, quivering under his touch, reluctant to move an inch. His breathing was ragged and harsh in the stillness of the night. Ryan Sheppard called a third time, and muttering irritably, Harry shifted away.

In a few minutes as Lilah was starting her car, he yelled her name and took the steps down, two at a time. Leaning into the window, he said, "I forgot to ask. Where are you going to be tomorrow? Andrew's place or Cambridge?"

Wherever you want, Lilah thought, her mouth curving up in a wide smile. "I can skip a couple of classes and stay in New York. But you'd better make it worth my while. Don't bring any senators along."

The next few days passed in a dreamy blur for Lilah. Harry apologized over and over for not being able to visit before and was determined to make up for lost time. The world was apparently willing to give him this brief reprieve before he was due to return to the navy at the end of the week. There was no father asking him to run errands, no senators demanding attention.

Harry rode a brand-new Harley—his first big-ticket purchase with his paycheck—all the way to New Castle each morning and picked Lilah up at the gym. In the parking lot not far from Gedney Pond, he tenderly draped his vehicle in waterproof fabric while she groaned and rolled her eyes. Only when he was absolutely certain no pooping birds or peeing dogs could get anywhere near his beloved bike would he start on their hike along the woods and wetlands of the park.

They talked about everything under the sun—their past, their present, their plans, the people in their lives. Loud arguments erupted over books, movies, the defeat suffered by the U.S. in

Vietnam, and of course, Elvis. In the years Harry spent in training, he seemed to have given up on his saxophone. When Lilah attempted to probe, he simply shrugged and said he didn't have the time. Besides, their tastes had evolved, with Lilah now a huge fan of the Eagles and Harry raving about Led Zeppelin, but the King would forever be part of their childhood. There was rarely a quiet moment, especially at their private contest at the local shooting club when Lilah suffered loss after loss after loss. She mumbled a curse or two, which, of course, set Harry whooping with laughter. Her weekly sessions had turned her marksmanship to decent, but she was no match for a trained SEAL. She got her own back when they played chess in the library at the Barrons mansion, and he went down in ignominious defeat for the third time.

Between nonstop chattering and laughter, there were plenty of whisper-light touches on Lilah's cheek and casual brushes of Harry's mouth against her temple. Even a quick hug or two. She heard the hitches in his breath as loudly as her own, but he always let go and resumed talking.

Harry accompanied her on her climbing trip with the Adirondack Mountain Club that weekend. He chatted with her while she took pictures of the dense green forests of Panther Gorge from the top of the precipice, teasing her about voluntarily jumping off cliffs.

"Tackling my demons," she told him, unwrapping the rope from around her waist. A shadow passed across Harry's face—the memory of their dive into the Mediterranean Sea to escape Sanders's goons. They'd talked about the enemy, about the threat he posed to the rest of the world. Both Harry and Lilah were determined to find a solution, one way or the other. By tacit consent, the specific details of their ordeal in Libya because of him had never been discussed. Even with the shrink she saw after the escape, she'd never talked about the assault. No matter. When turbulent thoughts threatened to attack, Lilah found the peace she craved in the mountains. "Each time I conquer one of these peaks..." she paused, trying to find words to describe the power surging through her. "...I feel... in control."

"Unbeaten," Harry added, his rich, deep voice warm with understanding. He didn't probe further, and Lilah was thankful for it. Oh, she knew he was already looking for the rapist. Harry never said so in actual words, but yes, he was searching. And when the monster was located, *she* would be the one to stare him in the eye as she destroyed him. She needed to be strong enough for it.

That night at the campsite, Harry chatted and joked with the other climbers as they all set up their tents. He charmed the leader of the team—a softball coach from Minnesota—into singing along to an off-color limerick. Even when the rest of the group, tired from the trek, settled in, Harry kept Lilah in splits with his clowning around, pretending not to know how to tie basic knots. By the time the sun plummeted into the hills, cloaking the sky in star-spangled velvet, they were the only two outside. Except for their muted chatter and hushed laughter, the night was silent. She breathed in the earthy smell of spring, carried to them by the cool breeze.

Inside the tent, Harry lit the gas lantern. Under the cover of the shadows in the back, Lilah changed into the much-washed cotton nightshirt which clung so lovingly to her figure. When she turned, he'd already stripped down to flannel pants and was resting on the ground with his head on the rolled-up sleeping gear.

This was it, Lilah told herself. She emerged into the pool of light, and Harry sat up. As he took in the faded yellow tee skimming her mid-thigh, Lilah braided her hair. Through her lashes, she, too, looked her fill of him... the muscled shoulders, his chest... his gaze, sweeping every inch of her. Desire spiraled out from the coffee-dark eyes, heating the air around.

Wildly, she wondered why the tent was not exploding in flames. She bit her lower lip hard to stop it from quivering, but the rest of her body simply wouldn't quit trembling. Her fingers... she kept dropping the strands of the braid. A bead of sweat trickled down her jawline. When her third attempt at taming her mane failed, she heard Harry's sigh, quickly suppressed.

Lilah raised her lashes and surprised a rueful look on his face. His eyes instantly crinkled. "C'mon," he said. "I want to play poker, and you're wasting time."

Say what? She shook her head. "Poker?"

"Yup." Harry dug into his backpack and brought out a deck. "Let me see how you beat me at *this* game."

They played for hours, sitting cross-legged, facing each other. Heat still eddied around her and Harry, but it was a pleasurable burn rather than the overwhelming firestorm she'd sensed approaching. At each sweet smile, each gentle touch, the warmth intensified.

Lilah lost almost every round. "You're cheating," she sulked, throwing down her cards.

"Prove it," he challenged. She glared, and he guffawed.

When they were too drowsy to continue, they curled next to each other in the sleeping bags, cards scattered everywhere. Unsure if she were relieved or disappointed how the day ended, she tumbled into slumber.

The gardens of the Barrons home were quiet as they rode back the next night. Standing under the stars, Lilah continued their argument from the afternoon. She pushed her lip out in a mock-sulk, but Harry wouldn't budge. "Oh, no, once was enough. I'm not letting you drive it into a ditch another time."

"Priorities, Harry! Who's more important? Me or the silly bike?"

"*Shh.*" Straddling the Harley, he kick-started it before leaning toward the windscreen. "Don't listen to the mean girl," he crooned to the bike.

When Lilah rained punches on his shoulders, he laughed and drove off with a shouted promise to be back in the morning. She turned toward the house, smile on her lips, only to jump with a startled squeak as he circled around to stop inches from her feet.

"You, of course. It's always been you." Not giving her a chance to respond, he rode away into the night.

Chapter 11

A few weeks later

Cambridge, Massachusetts

"Imaginary boyfriend," Lilah muttered to herself, pummeling the pillow before collapsing onto it and pulling the comforter over her head. If she chatted about Harry with any of her classmates before, they would've surely thought she made him up. Now... well, the friend part was clear enough to anyone with eyes. The boy prefix? Not so much.

Once she returned to classes the Monday after their climbing trip, Harry had left on assignment. But no matter how hectic his schedule was, he found time to visit Lilah. He drove, flew, and took the bus to Cambridge every chance he got. The staff at Café Pamplona got used to seeing him with Lilah, munching on sandwiches and sipping espresso.

She reveled in the banked heat in his gaze whenever he looked at her. Seemingly accidental touches, fleeting kisses on her earlobe, breezy hugs—they left her aching with a desire she struggled to control. There were even times when a flirtatious remark was enough to set her body on fire. While Harry didn't bother to hide his hunger, he never acted on it. He would scan her face, searching her eyes for something, then withdraw.

If Lilah didn't know him so well, if he weren't spending every spare minute with her with full knowledge of everyone around... no, he wasn't two-timing her. Was that even the correct word to use in their situation? Were they a couple? Were they simply friends? Lilah was ready to pull her hair out in confusion. She debated confronting Harry over it. If she completely, totally, stupidly misread the interest in his eyes... he wouldn't laugh at her, but if he said nothing... if he stared away in awkward silence... she couldn't bear it.

The rest of her life was falling neatly into place, especially her finances. Her shares in Gateway—the Sheppards' oil trading company—were worth something now. They'd won contract after juicy contract lately, growing much bigger than the small-time outfit Genesis—the *old* business—ever was. Harry said the contacts he made while traveling with Senator Temple helped immensely.

His family still didn't seem interested in reconnecting with Lilah. Her graduation was coming up, and she needed a job while applying to law schools. Surely, Gateway could use an engineer with market savvy. In her room at the MIT dorms, she tightened her grip on the phone and silently listened to the awkward apology from Dante, the company's COO. "Uhh... we... Lilah, I really did think we would be okay employing you only for a year, or I wouldn't have given you the interview appointment. But our senior analysts want someone prepared to stay—"

"It's all right," she mumbled. Poor Dante was already being forced to make excuses for the Sheppards, and he didn't need to deal with Lilah's embarrassment on top of it. And thank God she never asked Harry about the position she saw advertised in the paper. He would've pressured his parents into hiring her, and she would've waltzed in, never realizing they didn't want her around even now.

Or perhaps they truly couldn't afford to take on someone who wouldn't stick around for more than a year. Most employers Lilah approached said the same thing, so the Sheppards were not especially to be blamed.

It wasn't as though she didn't have other options. The stock market had been good to her, and the cash would keep her for a few months. The idea of digging into her investments... Lilah couldn't help feeling jittery. Also, she planned to expand her portfolio and needed money for it. Lilah eyed the broker's number for a full five minutes before setting her little phone book aside. Andrew didn't particularly care for her, either, but he'd sign her on to keep her twin happy. And this time, the money she accepted would be in the form of a salary.

There was someone else Lilah could ask—Senator Temple—but he was busy. Newspapers quizzed the politician about the energy policy and the troubles in the Middle East and his likely run for the presidency. All he would say was he was waiting to get to the White House before putting his plans into action. Lilah asked Harry what was expected to happen, and he believed Temple meant collecting evidence against Sanders, something they were already doing. The politician had promised to discuss details once the election was done.

#

Within days of Lilah's graduation, Harry helped her move to Baton Rouge, where she started work as a junior engineer for Barrons O & G in their Louisiana rigs. Her days were busy, and evenings were spent on the threadbare couch, watching television while she filled out law school paperwork. On a warm August day, she wept with millions of fans worldwide as they mourned Elvis Presley's passing. In October, Lilah was on the same couch, listening to Temple officially announcing his bid for the presidency of the United States. His opponent was supported by none other than Jared Sanders. Besides Temple and his team, there was another face Lilah recognized on screen. Dressed in a business suit, Harry stood a few feet behind the politician.

Lilah was appalled the navy let one of their SEALs—uniformed or otherwise—hang around a presidential campaign. It simply seemed wrong, but Harry claimed it was because the senator was the chairman of the commerce committee. Still, it appeared Harry was taunting their enemy, and Temple was letting him do it for reasons she didn't understand.

The spring before the presidential election, Dan made it back to the Barrons mansion for a very brief visit. Setting aside her reluctance to return to the house, Lilah left the tiny apartment she rented and took a bus to New York to meet her twin. The next morning, she sank to the middle of her bed with a copy of *The Washington Post*. Heart quaking in terror, she scanned the story again.

"A non-combat mission... just a day or two," Harry had said, making it seem like he'd land his helicopter on the building's roof and fly back stateside with the rescued envoy.

The newspaper reported an unnamed SEAL landed on the roof of Beirut Hotel but not in a helicopter. He was inserted there, assigned to guard the wounded diplomat while the army negotiated a road evacuation with the militia. Unfortunately, the talks between the American military and Lebanese militia leaders went on for a couple of days, and some other group of insurgents closed in. The SEAL's identity was not revealed, but the paper marveled at how he managed the feat of evacuating his injured charge on foot. Maneuvering his way through street battles and destroyed buildings, the SEAL got the diplomat to a U.S. Army helicopter and piloted them both to safety.

Elsewhere in the paper and apparently unconnected to the rescue mission, there was a short report on a series of explosions in enemy camps located in neighboring Syria, barely five hours from Beirut by road. They occurred within the forty-eight-hour period the SEAL was supposed to be guarding the American diplomat. Strangely, all the destroyed camps were on property belonging to Jared Sanders. The oilman flew to Syria to deal with the fallout, calling a temporary halt to his involvement in the American presidential campaign.

It took Lilah another day to reach Harry. Another day of pacing the bedroom in stark terror, imagining him hurt, bleeding, dying. When she finally heard his voice on the phone, her head swam in relief.

"All right," he teased over the bad connection. "I'll let the navy know you refuse to have me go on any more missions."

"Stop pretending you don't know what I'm talking about," she whispered into the phone, glancing nervously at the closed door. Lilah was alone in her room, but she didn't want to take the chance of the household staff walking by and overhearing. "Look, I agree Sanders needs to be stopped, but what you're up to has nothing to do with stopping him. Temple winning the election is not worth it." She knew it wasn't true as soon as she said it. Sanders could *not* be allowed to be the power behind the throne in the Oval Office. Still, the risks Harry was taking... "Sanders is going to hate you even more. What if he—"

"Lilah," Harry said, tone instantly serious. "We can't discuss such things over unsecure lines. Actually, we can't discuss it... period. I'm not allowed to. I shouldn't have said *any*thing to you before about my work."

"I'm not talking about your *real* work," she howled.

Timbre still even, he said, "The rescue mission was real enough. The rest... I joined the navy to serve. What I do—*everything* I do—is for that purpose. You're right. It's not work; it's my duty. Which is all I'm prepared to say regarding any of it."

"Hardheaded," she snapped.

"*You* should talk."

She bit her lip to smother her frustration. "Just be safe, Harry. Remember, your life is important to some people."

"Some people?" he asked, a husky note in his voice. "I still have the peacock feather you gave me for protection."

It was an old superstition from the Indian side of Lilah's family. Embarrassed at the sudden memory, she scrunched up her face. "Get yourself back home in one piece, will you?" A second later, she added, "The diplomat... I hope he knows... I mean, *I* know... I *am* proud of what you do. Only, I sometimes wish you decided to be an accountant or something. At least you'd be safe."

His surprised guffaw was still ringing in her ears when she hung up in a huff.

Harry's assignments over the next few months seemed to take him to every hotspot in the world. His trips were inevitably followed by disaster striking a rumored ally of Jared Sanders, leaving the criminal businessman no time to devote to American politics.

Lilah had her job, her stock portfolio was humming along nicely, and her application to Harvard Law was being processed. It should've been an exciting time for her, but she could barely focus. *Please... just stay alive,* she murmured to the image in her heart. When Harry called, he flirted madly and teased mercilessly but refused to discuss his activities.

Senator Temple might have been busy, but he knew Lilah was applying to Harvard. He wrote her a glowing recommendation, and at her admission interview, she was told he'd made a personal call to the dean. As a first-year student, she cast her vote in Cambridge and watched on television as Temple won a landslide victory.

Chapter 12

November 1978

Cambridge, Massachusetts

Lilah checked her wristwatch and smiled. Harry had made it on time. As arranged, he picked her up at the law school library, glancing curiously at the new glasses perched on her nose. In his hands were two cups of hot chocolate.

Leaving the Harley safely covered in the parking lot, they walked the short distance to the center of the university campus. He said he needed to go to DC in the evening for a meeting with Temple. Lilah sighed mentally and bit back annoyed questions. She'd take what she could get.

Red and orange and yellow leaves crunched under their shoes as they strolled through Harvard Yard. Students crowded the lawns, taking advantage of the last days of sunshine and warmth before winter set in. Lilah dropped her books to the sparse grass and sat cross-legged on the ground, not too far from the circle of mulch surrounding a tree trunk. The smell of freshly cut bark clung to the air.

Still holding the two cups, Harry collapsed next to her. "You look good," he said, his voice casual.

I'd better be looking like a million bucks! The twenty-five dollars she'd spent on the bow tie blouse in garnet-colored wool and the matching floral bell-bottoms gave her heartburn for a couple of days. She was not the only one who'd taken care with her appearance. Harry looked particularly super in his dark-blue cardigan and gray denims. "You do, too," she said.

With a pleased grin, he handed her the chocolate drink. "When did you start wearing glasses?" he asked, jiggling the earpiece.

"Last week." Lilah swatted his hand away and took a sip of the chocolate, letting the hot, sweet concoction warm her insides. "I need them for reading." Voice tense, she asked, "Are you done with... you know... Temple already won. I hope he's not planning to add to your *duties*."

"No duties today," Harry said, tweaking her nose.

Once again, she swatted away his hand. "Temple should be giving you a job in the White House after what you did for him.

Actually, he should've found a way to win without involving you."

Laughing, Harry said, "I already work for him. He's the commander in chief now. And I've been careful... there's nothing I did thus far that's not morally justified."

That set off a debate on the ethics of corporate and political governance. Harry felt a burning need to bring order to the chaos spread by madmen like Sanders. Order, he contended, was to be created by intellectual power and reasoning applied with dispassion throughout the world.

"You and Mr. Temple," exclaimed Lilah. "The kind of hierarchy you're talking about is simply dictatorship under a softer label. Why can't you see the solution to tyranny is not benevolent tyranny? Humanity is not the military, Harry. The rest of us need the freedom to make mistakes and learn from them... to be less than perfect."

"I'm *not* talking about applying military discipline to the entire world," Harry said stubbornly. "But you cannot deny anarchy breeds corruption. See what happened with Sanders? None of his competitors could agree on rules to live by, and he simply took over. Now, he deliberately feeds the chaos to keep his hold on power. It hurts everyone, but the common man suffers the most. As for what I do... if we insist on playing by the rules while Sanders doesn't... imagine him as the power behind the American presidency! Not a risk the world can afford."

"I never said—oh, God, you *totally* missed my point. *Your* idea is not to simply defeat Sanders. You want your own system in his place. I tell you I'm not sure about it, and all you have to say is Sanders is bad. Temple got to you, didn't he?"

"I don't need Mr. Temple to tell me about my responsibilities *vis-à-vis* Sanders."

Lilah sighed. "Before Temple, you never used to have such a one-track mind. Yes, you have responsibilities, but every argument you make comes back to the same thing. Stop Sanders and other men like him."

Mouth set in a hard line, Harry said, "He *needs* to be stopped. If I could, I wouldn't just be *stopping* him. It was because of him... you..."

As Harry's rant came to a halt, Lilah's pulse pounded. *Please, no,* she begged silently. Five years passed since the horrible, horrible nightmare, and she still didn't want to talk about it. "Look at you," she mumbled. "You used to be... you gave up your plans for college." When Harry murmured a protest, she held a hand up and continued in a stronger tone, "I know. You couldn't spend four years in college with Sanders still out there. I understand sacrifice, and I'm not even saying there are limits, but you're letting your quest control every aspect of your life. You're essentially letting Sanders dictate what you will and will not do. Everything else which used to be important... poof! All gone."

"Not *everything* else. Or I wouldn't be here."

Lilah glowered at him. "You're just saying it so I'd stop arguing."

Harry leaned toward her, mild hurt in his eyes. "I took the first flight home only to see you."

The trace of fatigue in his voice... Lilah took his fingers in hers and peered at the lines of exhaustion on his face she hadn't noticed before. "Harry, did you come here straight from the airport?"

"From JFK. Had my bike waiting for me." With a shrug, he added, "We have only this one afternoon."

"You—" She tugged at him. "C'mon, let's go to my room. You're going to take a nap."

Setting his cup to the side, he circled her wrist with his free hand. "Oh, no. I came here for some quality time with you. Being together like this, listening to you fighting with me... it feels great.

Damned great."

With a hmph, Lilah shook off his light grip and stuck her tongue out. "Debating is not fighting."

"Muhammad Ali," Harry teased, throwing a couple of air punches. "Fighting, hanging out, whatever... I don't even have to talk when we're together. You still get me. And I get where you're coming from."

"You mean I know all your bad habits and still like you," she teased right back. Mock-pouting, she added, "You know all mine, too." When he chortled, she laughed along for a moment.

"What I'm trying to say is you have principles, habibti." He puffed up his chest in naked pride and beamed in the general direction of the universe. "You're gonna be a great judge someday... the best. We'll *partyyy* the day you take the oath. My girl, the supreme court justice!"

Lilah giggled. If she did get to the Supreme Court, he'd probably have both of them dancing the samba at her swearing-in. "I get where you're coming from, too. You want regular people to stand a chance."

Warmth shimmered in his eyes. "Thank you. I don't care if no one else in the world understands, but you... it's important."

Lilah waited for him to continue along the line of thought. When he showed no signs of doing so, she cleared her throat. "Okay, so you don't want any naps. What else do you want to do?"

"I was thinking of watching a movie." Harry threw an exaggerated leer at her. "*Grease*, maybe. We could sit in the back."

And do what? Glance longingly at each other? Biting back the retorts springing to her tongue, Lilah said, "*Grease* has been out of the theaters for weeks. I have another idea."

Later, Harry groaned, and not for the first time. "I can't believe

I'm letting you ride my bike. Again!"

"The military lets you fly an *aircraft*," she argued. According to the papers, the unidentified SEAL used a chopper to get the injured diplomat out of Beirut. She never knew SEALs could fly helicopters. Apparently, Harry asked to be taught at least enough to fly from Point A to Point B.

He shook a finger in her face. "*I* haven't flown into any ditches."

She looked both ways, arching an eyebrow. "You rode around thirty minutes to find this place." An almost deserted residential street with no ditches.

He laughed. "Love is blind, not stupid."

As his words registered, the laughter died. Lilah didn't know how long they stood, leaning against the side of the bike, eyes on each other.

The afternoon was sunny but cool. Brownstones and bare-branched trees lined the quiet road. Save for a cyclist who spared them no more than a cursory glance, they were alone.

"Do you remember Paris?" Harry asked, tone low.

It was the last vacation their families took together before her parents' deaths. Memories came rushing back.

"Lilah," he whispered. Taking her hand in his, he traced the lines on it with a fingertip. Her eyes followed the path of his finger. Her breath hitched, her own fingers curling and trembling. "Habibti," he murmured.

Lilah could barely raise her lashes to meet his gaze. She thrilled helplessly to the caress of his eyes across her face. Slowly, he raised her hand, placing soft, tiny kisses on it, one finger at a time. She whimpered. The touch of his mouth seemed to reach someplace deep inside her.

Harry smoothed up the wool covering her arm. Lips on the

wildly beating pulse at her wrist, he inhaled. His breath trembled on her skin. Lilah wanted his loving to continue forever. She craved his touch all over.

A siren sounded in the distance, but neither could bear to let go. "Habibti," he whispered hoarsely. Grazing her skin with his teeth, he teased them both.

She yearned to touch him, to dig her fingers into the muscles of his shoulders, to run her lips across his collarbone, to torment him the way he was tormenting her.

The siren got louder and closer; an ambulance sped past along the crossroad. Awareness of their surroundings seeped in, and with obvious reluctance, he relinquished her hand.

As they rode out, Lilah sitting behind him, she could feel his entire body thrumming as though in tension. Frustrated, she wondered if he were sentencing them both to live out their lives in this endless agony of unquenched desire. She wanted him every bit as badly as he wanted her. He had to know that. So what was he waiting for?

Not *what* but *who,* she suddenly realized. He wanted *her* to make the first move because of what had happened in her life. Lilah threw her head back and laughed in utter joy.

"What?" he shouted over the roar of the bike.

"Wait," she yelled. She'd tell him. As soon as they stopped, she'd tell him about the nights she'd lain awake dreaming of him, dreaming of having his arms around her, of having his body cover hers.

When they reached the dorms at Harvard, Lilah dismounted, but he remained on the bike, ready to get going. Visor up, he glanced at her to bid goodbye, and his eyes narrowed at whatever he saw in hers.

There was a sweet ache within her chest. "Stay," she said, both a promise and a plea in that one word.

His shoulders bunched. Taking his helmet off, he placed it in front of him. When he turned to her, she smiled at him in sheer joy.

His hand came up to her cheek, thumb caressing the corner of her mouth. Almost as though he couldn't help himself, he leaned toward her and took her lower lip between his.

Lilah's universe shrank to a pair of dark irises. Harry's shuddering breath was warm on her cheek, his five o'clock shadow scraping her skin. The taste and smell of hot chocolate lingered in his kiss. "Harry," she whimpered, yearning for more.

"Oh, God," he murmured brokenly. "So long, so damned long." He kissed her over and over like a starving man finding food, without pretense, without shame. "Lilah," he called her name, his lips swallowing her answering moan. "Need you," he told her, voice raspy. "*Love* you."

Digging her fingers into his silky hair, Lilah yanked him closer. "I love you, Harry," she sobbed in response. "So much." She met him kiss for kiss, whisper for whisper, uncaring of who might see. "Love *me*," she demanded. "*Every*where... all night."

His feverish mouth wandering all over her face, he promised her reckless desire. Harry swore they'd be buried under the sheets in each other's arms until the end of time... kissing, touching, making love until neither could stand. He returned to her lips, his body shaking with barely leashed lust.

Somewhere to the side, someone laughed, but Lilah wasn't bothered. The rest of the world could stay, or it could vanish. All she cared about was Harry... him... them... together. But he groaned and tore his lips from hers, leaving her bereft. His hand stayed, cupping her cheek. His eyes smiled into hers. Lilah mewled in tender complaint and turned her face into his palm, gently nipping his flesh with her teeth.

Visibly struggling to calm his breathing, he murmured, "Bad timing... I'm supposed to be in DC in a few hours. Navy business. Then, Mr. Temple..." Only a little while longer, Harry swore. And they'd be together.

Part V

Chapter 13

Two days later

Washington, DC

The sun shone bright in the blue winter sky when Harry parked his CIA-assigned Chevy in the lot near Union Station and jogged toward the senate office building. Traffic in the capital city was bumper to bumper as usual, and the morning air carried a frigid bite. Inside Temple's office suite, where his staff was preparing for the move to the White House, animated chatter punctuated by excited laughter trickled into the inner room while Harry talked to the president-elect.

"Another antitrust complaint against Gateway." Harry slammed a fist on the papers in front of him before sitting back, his pulse pounding in frustration. The big leather chair across the desk was empty. Temple stood at the draped windows of the large room, hands linked behind his back, eyes on the dome of the U.S. Capitol. It didn't matter that he would soon be sworn in. Sanders and his minions in the government would not let the Sheppards grow big enough to be a threat.

"Gateway's now a big name in oil sector," Temple responded calmly. "But you're limited to brokerage and trading and retail. Andrew Barrons has always been a tremendous force upstream, midstream, and downstream with the drilling, transport, and refining he does. He can help you to some extent. What you don't have control over is energy services."

"Sanders does," Harry said, his tone bitter. "How did *he* get away with all the forced mergers and vertical integration?" Antitrust laws made collaboration between divisions of a sector from beginning to end of the production chain subject to judicial review in the United States.

Temple shook his head. "No one saw him coming. By the time the government noticed what he was doing, he was too big and too powerful. He already had many of the elected representatives in his pocket. Also, his holding company is structured in such a way that illegal behavior is impossible to prove, but he does control majority shares in all the properties."

Pinching the bridge of his nose with his fingers, Harry asked, "How do *we* do it? Gateway gets slapped with lawsuits the minute we try to expand." Somehow, they needed to get bigger than Sanders and take him apart. The tricks they already pulled were nowhere close enough to permanently end the problem. Also, Sanders continued to pursue every legitimate avenue to destroy his enemies.

Temple turned back to face Harry. "If you truly want your insurrection against the enemy, you need an informal alliance with an already established energy services provider. Once you bring Sanders down, I believe the rest of the oil companies will be ready to join your network. With everyone on board, you can formalize a code of conduct for the entire oil sector."

Harry drummed fingers on the table. "By 'energy services provider,' I assume you mean Kingsley Corp? Godwin Kingsley is your stepbrother." At Temple's shrug, Harry added, "I contacted a few of the service providers already. No one will cooperate out of fear of Sanders. Do you think the Kingsleys might be willing to take the risk? We do have a connection there in the form of Patrice Kingsley, Justice Kingsley's daughter-in-law. She was a Sheppard before marriage, but my father says she's not fond of us."

Temple walked back to his chair and stood with his hand on the backrest. "I know Patrice. The Kingsleys and the Sheppards harbored hopes of a business as well as a family alliance with her marriage to Peter, but things didn't work out."

"Would the Kingsleys be willing to consider a new business deal?" Harry asked.

"It's certainly a possibility." Temple huffed. "But Sanders is incredibly powerful now. I'm not certain Godwin will want to directly pit Kingsley Corp against him."

"If *you* talked to the Kingsleys—" Harry suggested. Temple's commitment to the cause was extraordinary. Harry had puzzled over it a time or two, but he was never able to find any reason other than a lawmaker's antipathy toward a criminal. Still, Harry never dared bring up the Kingsleys before today in case it offended Temple. But desperate times, etcetera.

The politician shrugged once again. "Even if they agree, the three companies may be accused of collusion, and the government will have to act. As president, I can't be seen putting my thumb on the scales for you or the Kingsleys." Hands on the table, Temple leaned forward. "Although... perhaps not."

Silently, Harry waited. He'd learned enough about Temple to recognize when he was casting bait.

The president-elect asked, "What about Lilah?"

Harry frowned in confusion. "What about her?"

"If we can't defeat Sanders the usual way, perhaps it's time for a new approach. I just mentioned we'd hoped Patrice's marriage to Peter Kingsley would help us create a business alliance."

It took a couple of seconds for the proposal to register. "What's this, presidential comedy?" Harry asked, chortling.

Temple didn't blink. "I'm not joking."

Laughter died. Harry's disbelieving stare was met by Temple's steady regard. "Hell," Harry hissed. "You're serious. You want Lilah to marry one of the Kingsleys."

"Why not? She's not otherwise attached, is she? For that matter, are *you*?"

Hackles rose. Harry suppressed an angry retort, reminding himself Temple's position entitled him to respect from those under his command. Besides, the idea was dead on arrival. Lilah and Harry had other plans. She'd known even without words how he felt. He'd seen the awareness in her face, the confusion in her hazel eyes whenever he pulled back. He'd debated telling her he wanted her so bad even his teeth hurt. He wanted to carry her off to bed and not let her up for days... but only when she was as wild with need for him as he was for her, crazed enough to pounce on him and claim him as her mate. The kiss and her invitation to stay... if Harry didn't know the CIA brass was waiting with questions about the situation in Lebanon... then, this meeting with Temple. Right on cue, the politician and his vile suggestion... even for one of his kind, the man's audacity was astounding.

Barely able to keep his tone even, Harry said, "At the risk of sounding rude... any plans Lilah and I might have are none of your business."

"Are you sure? Try to imagine the scenario. Barrons O & G is one of the major companies drilling, storing, and refining crude oil. Gateway trades oil and does retail petroleum, too. Lilah's in a unique position here. I'm sure you're aware your father signed over a percentage of Gateway to Delilah and Daniel to pay back *their* father's investment in Genesis. Andrew can be persuaded to give her stock. If she's married to one of the Kingsley grandsons, she'll have an indirect say in oil services, too. Her votes can help us coordinate and control the entire oil sector: upstream, midstream, and downstream. It's the only kind of coalition beyond the reach of Sanders and his cronies in the government. Once we finish him, a system can be put in place to control other rogue actors."

Rage and disgust roiling, Harry said, "I won't let you use Lilah to destroy your opposition."

Temple quirked an eyebrow. "Do you believe I'd use Lilah only to further my career?"

"Why not?" Harry snapped. "You used... you're still using me." Such coalitions were never spur-of-the-moment. Temple damned well planned this. "You didn't dare bring this up directly with Lilah, did you? She'd have told you to... so you decided to tackle me, instead. You needed to wait until now. If I heard this before the election..."

Temple's eyelids flickered, but he didn't look away and didn't deny the charge. "Harry, I'm grateful for whatever you did, yet *you* were just as eager to hit Sanders where it hurt. Also, understand this: even if I discussed it directly with Lilah, we would've had to wait until I won the election before taking any concrete steps toward the partnership. Anyone who heads such an alliance will be at risk of attacks from Sanders. The Barrons name and American law will not be enough to shield Lilah at that point. From the moment the announcement is made, she will need the protection of the highest office in the land, the Office of the President of the United States. It was important for me to be in the White House before we considered putting her in the position because Sanders will not fail to recognize what the marriage will make her: someone with the power to stop him." The politician walked back to the window and pointed to the Capitol. "All those lawmakers, all those statesmen, they can't stop Sanders. I, the president-elect of the United States, can't stop Sanders. You and the rest of the SEALs can't stop Sanders. Only Delilah Kingsley can stop him."

A name not Harry's was intimately entwined with hers. Anger, pure and deadly, rose in a tsunami. Exploding from the chair, Harry stated, "Lilah will not be a Kingsley."

Temple turned back. "Harry, remember the difference between

love and attach—"

"No," Harry snapped. Struggling to silence the roar inside, he held up a hand. "I won't let you... she's not a... Lilah is *not* going to marry any of the Kingsleys."

"Don't you think you should talk to her?" Temple asked, his voice deceptively soft. "Who are *you* to make the decision?"

Harry snarled. "Lilah has already made her choice, and her answer will be the same as mine: no."

Temple shook his head. "Just like that?"

"Change it to 'Hell, no,'" Harry said, stalking out.

The same evening, he was in Langley, listening in confusion as the CIA director gave him his new orders.

"The situation in Iran is not getting any better," said the director, settling into the leather chair across the desk. "The Shah is supposed to go on 'vacation' soon." Which meant he'd be escaping the country to avoid capture by the revolutionaries. "It's not going to be long before Khomeini returns."

"With your permission, sir?" Harry was part of the agency's hostage rescue team, not an assassin. Assigning him to this mission made no sense when there were professionals trained to do the job. Unless, of course, there was a direct order from the incoming commander in chief to send Petty Officer First Class Sheppard to dispatch the ayatollah. "This is not the right time for an intervention. The U.S. has been pro-Shah for years. Anything happening to his enemies will be blamed on us." On the SEAL who was sent on the mission. If the unnamed operative got killed in the process, the obstacle in Temple's path would be permanently removed. "Any attempt to eliminate Khomeini from the picture will need to wait. Now is not the right time with the entire world waiting to see how the U.S. responds."

The CIA director shot a bland look at Harry. "I've been in this position for a good number of years, Sheppard. I don't need to be lectured on the timing of missions." The director slid the folder across the desk. "Saddam Hussein. We need a counterweight to the ayatollah. Cultivate Saddam."

Harry blinked. "Cultivate? Uhh... I'm a hostage rescue specialist."

"The agency wants you to do something else now. Is there a problem, Sheppard?"

Harry smothered a growl. It couldn't be something as idiotic as keeping him apart from Lilah, could it? "No problem, sir," he said, tone steady. As a SEAL, he couldn't disobey a lawful order, but no matter where the CIA stashed him, no matter how long, *Lilah* would tell the president what he could do with his ridiculous suggestion. "I'll be ready in a—"

"Tonight. You'll leave from DC."

Chapter 14

Later that year, October 1979

Baghdad, Iraq

When Harry called Lilah before flying out of DC, he was ready to explode in anger over the whole damned situation. He started with his frustration over the new assignment right after they confessed their feelings. The happiness in her voice immediately gave way to worry. Updating her on the entirety of the Temple problem would need to wait until they met in person, or she'd lose more sleep over Harry's safety. She bought his lie about the navy telling him to get to Jordan. Or at least *seemed* to buy it.

He made arrangements to protect her just in case the damned politician dared... Temple could dare many things. He was the president and possessed the power to arrange the death of a lowly sailor under his command. For the first few weeks in Baghdad, Harry stayed on high alert. Sealed letters addressed to Lilah and his family were sent to a childhood friend from Libya with instructions to hand-deliver them in the event of his death. Even as he put plans in place, Harry knew it wouldn't happen. Temple was too shrewd not to know that alive or dead, Harry would find a way to protect Lilah from a marriage she didn't want. Killing him wouldn't win the president anything, *and* it would cost him support from Lilah and the Sheppards.

The connection between them and Temple was likely at an end, anyway. There was still the problem of Sanders, but if the president withdrew support, the Sheppards were no longer bankrupt and desperate. Harry was no longer a scared seventeen-year-old. He'd already learned enough with the CIA to know how to put a permanent end to the problem. One bullet would be enough to stop the unstoppable Sanders. The assassination would cause turbulence in the market, but a bit of short-term instability was preferable to letting the criminal continue. The operation needed to be carried out without Harry getting himself into trouble. He'd come up with a concrete plan as soon as he was allowed back stateside, as soon as he collected the info needed.

Harry couldn't remember the conversation without seeing red. The intelligence brass took care of debriefings after missions, but he used to give his reports to Temple, as well. Now... since his arrival in Baghdad, Harry routed all communications to the president through the CIA.

Ten damned months in Iraq, and Harry was almost begging for things to happen. His hands itched to teach some would-be assassin a lesson. If he didn't get to do something useful soon, he'd bust a blood vessel from sheer exasperation. Officially, the only diplomatic relationship the Americans had with Iraqis was the U.S. Interests Section the Belgians allowed in their embassy building. Unofficially, Harry was to negotiate with Saddam's bureaucrats on trade and regional security, but all they did at the meetings was go around in circles.

Striding down the hallways of the Belgian embassy, Harry veered right toward the latrine and debated what to do with the rest of the evening. He could go to one of the local markets for dinner, but he badly wanted to talk to Lilah. American personnel working in Iraq were warned of bugged lines, and any contact with those back home carried the potential to be a security risk. An overnight drive to Jordan... there were no meetings scheduled for the next couple of days... his contact in the Jordanian border police always allowed him the use of a field phone to make calls to the States. At some point, the CIA would get to hear of Harry's frequent use of the—

The door opened with a squeak. Rinsing soap from his hands at the sink, Harry threw a quick sideways glance at the bearded man—the Iraqi physicist who was part of the day's meeting.

"Mr. Sheppard?" the physicist called, tone hesitant. "Please... I need to tell you something before they arrest me." Harry already heard from his Jordanian informant about Saddam's sweeping arrests of the scientists in Iraq's atomic energy program. What this bearded fellow was saying went far beyond imprisonment, though. "There's a prison called Abu Ghraib where they take people," said the physicist. "Tell your bosses about it." He detailed for Harry the story of a young engineer on his honeymoon, beaten to death in front of his wife. Elderly academics were electrocuted for their refusal to cooperate. An opposition leader was dissolved in a tub of sulfuric acid, his terrified colleagues and friends made to watch, made to filter out the remaining bits of flesh and bone from the basin.

When the door shut behind the physicist, Harry gripped the edge of the sink and huffed. He didn't know if any of it were true. Still, the information couldn't be ignored. He needed to contact the president. They needed to talk directly, no bureaucratic filters between them.

From an apartment in Riyadh, Harry called Temple. Neither the smell of gasoline pervading the streets nor the sounds of traffic penetrated the luxury home belonging to the Saudi prince sitting in the shadows. The only phone line the president trusted in all Middle East belonged to the prince, but unfortunately, he refused to budge from his position, and Harry had to carry on the entire conversation in the royal's hearing. The Saudis might choose to ally themselves with the Americans, but they wouldn't compromise with security, and an American spy was always considered a threat.

"I have strong objections, Mr. Temple," Harry spoke into the phone, conscious of the need for discretion. "Saddam Hussein is not someone the U.S. can consider a friend. At least, not until we've checked into the rumors."

No amount of persuasion would convince Temple to abandon his plan of working with the Iraqi dictator. In fact, President Temple's tone carried distinct rebuke when he snapped out an order for Harry to shake himself loose of personal morality and get a broader perspective. By the end of the conversation, Harry was certain he'd be reassigned without delay. Muttering a curse under his breath, he hung up and looked through the large windows at the clock tower.

"I could've told you it wouldn't work," said the Saudi prince. He stood and with a hand tucked casually into his pocket, sauntered to Harry. "We need Saddam Hussein. If the ayatollah and his gang extend their rule over more of the Middle East, they could hold the entire world hostage. There could be more famines, wars, death toll in the millions. Saddam will keep Khomeini occupied."

"Countering one threat with another?" Harry asked. "Do you believe Saddam won't eventually turn on us?"

"They always do," admitted the prince. "But in the short term..."

"Yeah, well... short term's not enough. We need to account for what could happen years... decades... from now."

The prince laughed. "No wonder Temple got angry. Young man, the president has been in this game much longer than you. Trust me... he knows what he's doing."

"I'm sure," Harry admitted instantly. "Dammit," he muttered. "I wish there was someone else we could use." A leader whose idea of fun wasn't torture of his own people. "One of the good guys."

"We don't have the luxury of time to wait for a good guy." Eyes softening, the prince added, "Global politics is a strange game, Mr. Sheppard. We pretend to be the good guys, but at the end of the day, there *are* no good guys. We're all looking out for ourselves—including you Americans."

Harry refused to believe it, remembering a girl who insisted on living life on her own terms. Lilah would die of starvation before doing something she didn't believe in. "There's goodness and integrity in this world. Unfortunately, not among those in authority. We need intelligent people in charge, capable of combining humanity with objectivity. Perhaps it's time for a change at the top."

Once again, the Saudi prince laughed. "Change at the top, heh? Careful, Mr. Sheppard. Such talk can get you arrested in some places."

Harry was expected back in Baghdad before morning. He collected his papers and stuffed them into the manila envelope. "If I don't speak up for things I believe in, what kind of a man am I?"

The prince's eyes narrowed. "What if it costs you your life?"

Harry approached the incinerator in the apartment. The security detail accompanying the prince stood by, ready to assist. Harry fed the notes he made about the Iraqi regime into the apparatus. "'The tree of liberty must be refreshed from time to time with the blood of patriots and tyrants,'" he quoted Jefferson.

"You, my friend, are an idealist," said the prince.

"Now, *those* are fighting words, Your Highness," Harry said, grinning.

While the prince was still chuckling over the joke, his men opened the incinerator and showed Harry the ashes. Neither the prince nor his security detail ever saw what was in the papers, but they certainly understood Harry just destroyed all evidence which could condemn world leaders for turning a blind eye to Saddam's atrocities. If it weren't done in front of the men in the apartment, the slip would be reported to Temple, and Harry would rightly be seen as a security threat. Besides, he was a member of the armed forces, and as the commander in chief, Temple was entitled to his loyalty. The oaths Harry swore as a SEAL weren't nullified simply because Temple tried to—Harry suppressed a growl. The president could stick his sick suggestion where the sun didn't shine.

At the exit to the flat, Harry hesitated. "Your Highness, may I make another call? It's personal."

If the Saudi prince was surprised, he didn't show it, but once again, he and his men stayed in the room. Harry could at least discuss vacation plans with Lilah. At some point, he'd get a couple of weeks off, and they would fly someplace where all they did was make love and eat. She was already making a list of honeymoon-type places. Speaking for himself, even Motel 6 in Las Vegas would do.

Unfortunately, they didn't get to discuss anything. Annoyingly cheerful, Lilah's classmate said she was in the library. Harry thanked the classmate and hung up, pausing with his hand on the receiver.

"I take it you were trying to call the, er, 'goodness'?" The prince's voice was amused. "All of us need a little 'goodness' in our lives. I have three of my own."

"Three?" asked Harry.

The expression on the prince's face was nauseatingly smug.

When Harry got back to the Belgian embassy in Iraq, there was a message waiting. *"Monsieur."* Harry halted, letting the clerk catch up. "Telegram for you." The envelope he held was sealed, but the clerk breathlessly advised, "You've been reassigned. They're expecting you in India. A town called Cochin."

#

A day later

Cochin, India

Seething with annoyance, Harry marched out of the tiny airport and waved at the man holding a pickup sign with his name on it. From SEAL-turned-CIA agent, Petty Officer Sheppard's job description seemed to have been altered to include being the president's lackey, dispatched to whichever spot on the world map Temple tossed a dart at. The official line said Harry was sent to assist the Indian government in the investigation of an oil refinery explosion. While the bulk of the work would be done by the local police force, there were rumors of American involvement in the accident, which the U.S. would probe. But there were others in the CIA expressly trained for such jobs. Harry's specialty was hostage rescue, dammit, not diplomatic negotiations and not this... whatever it was he was expected to do.

An hour later, he looked up from the folder in his hands and glanced across what was left of the building and its young occupants. On Temple's special request, the Indian cops had left the scene pretty much undisturbed for Harry to study. His vision grayed. Wiping the sweat off his face with his sleeve, he somehow continued moving forward. All the missions, all the deliberate cruelties he'd witnessed... nothing came close to this.

"Sir?" the local cop assigned to assist called. "Do you want to take a break?"

Harry shook his head. "Let's get this done." He walked past the building and stood under the baking sun, hand shielding his eyes. Unblinking, he studied the refinery with its walls torn apart.

"A school full of children dead from propane tanks rigged to explode at the refinery next door. Who'd do such a thing?" the cop asked.

Sanders... his was the first name listed in the folder. The lives thus lost wouldn't be the only collateral damage from the explosion. India's oil sector was already taking a hit in the stock market. There would be worldwide repercussions. Bankruptcy, worsening poverty, starvation... Sanders would also suffer minor losses, but for him, keeping his brutal grip on every soul on the planet would be more important than a bit of red ink on the balance sheet.

Aloud, Harry said, "We'll find the person responsible and make him pay."

Harry followed the local cop to the refinery and greeted the crime scene technicians at work. "This way, sir," said the officer, leading the American to the other side of the charred building. Harry's gaze traveled up the body hanging from the roof of the office room: the corpse of the refinery owner with his eyes gouged out.

"Whoever did this made certain he wouldn't be caught in the explosion," said the cop. "They wanted him to be found."

"The eyeballs were most likely gone premortem," said a medical technician. "Poor bastard."

The corpse of the dead man's wife was found floating in the canal. Their daughter was missing. The local cop accompanied Harry on his trip to the brothel in search of the child. "This sex-trafficking place is the only lead we have," said the cop. "The proprietor of this hostel was spotted hanging around the refinery owner's house a couple of weeks back. We've been watching him for months, hoping he'd lead us to the higher-ups. If he's involved, he might have brought the girl here."

Broadway in this Indian city was anything but broad, with merchants and their wares spilling into the street. Vehicles honked almost continuously, but there was no moving forward for anyone. Shoppers—unconcerned by the stalled traffic—wound their way around cars and rickshaws. Inside the unmarked car—a model called the Ambassador—Harry muttered a mild curse, perspiration gluing the cotton shirt to his chest.

"It's not far," said the cop. He set off the high-pitched horn, bellowing at the cyclist in front to get out of the way.

They eventually drove through a maze of even narrower streets, turning onto a side road. Paint peeled off the double-story buildings on either side. The lane was quiet. Too quiet. Unlike the street two blocks away, there was not a single soul to be seen outside. A crow cawed, the harsh noise making Harry jump.

The cop parked the Ambassador, its wheels precariously close to the gutter on the left. A wire hung loose from an electric post. "Don't touch," warned the policeman. Rolling up his sleeves, he reminded Harry, "You're a tourist with a taste for—" He grimaced. "—younger ladies. I'm your broker."

"Got it," said Harry. "Your backup?"

"The maid and the guy in the *lungi*," said the cop, nodding at a young man wearing a patterned sarong and a yellowed undershirt. He scurried toward the car. Hushed conversation later, Harry learned the lad was an informant.

"The matron speaks Hindi, but you don't understand it," the cop tutored Harry.

The living room was at most ten by ten, chairs in red plastic arranged around a small coffee table. A strong smell of onions hung in the air, nearly asphyxiating Harry.

A plump woman with a pleasant smile, the matron eyed Harry up and down before turning to fire questions at the cop. Harry knew Hindi, having spent time in India with Lilah's family, and he understood the matron well enough, better than the local policeman who was struggling to answer. The woman wanted to know why a man like Harry was bothering to visit a local brothel. In conspiratorial tones, the policeman told her the American had different tastes. If he "liked" any of the girls, he'd be a repeat customer.

When the first girl was thrust in, Harry started. Dark anger descended. Clenching his fists, he took deep breaths. He'd expected older teenagers resorting to prostitution to feed themselves, not children aged five to nine.

One by one, the matron lined them up. Wearing prim blouses and gaudy long skirts, they clung to the wall, none of them meeting his eyes. "All certified virgins," said the woman.

"These are all the kids you have?" the cop asked, words sharp. "Nothing in the range of ten to fourteen? The American has plenty of money." He named a figure, bringing a glint to the woman's eyes.

"No," she said regretfully. "We don't deal in that age range."

"Well, who might?" asked the policeman.

"I don't know," she said, voice annoyed. "If the American wants, he can pick two of mine for the same price. He'd better hurry, though. I expect most of the merchandise to be sold by the end of the week."

Harry lunged from his chair, unable to see anything but the demon in female form. Thundering in fury, he wrapped a hand around her plump throat. "Merchandise?" he roared.

Her eyes bulged. She gasped for air, long nails scratching his hand.

He dragged her through the inner door. Then, out of sight of the terrified children, Harry slammed her head against the wall.

She slid to the floor, eyelids fluttering closed. A red stain marked the concrete, but she still breathed.

Behind him were the cop and the informant. The cop sighed. "Months of work down the drain."

Harry breathed hard, unable to speak.

"As soon as news reaches the leaders, they'll disappear," the informant agreed.

Shaking a finger in the cop's face, Harry snarled, "You knew."

"Sir," said the annoyed officer. "This is not the only hostel run by the bastards. We've been working to shut the entire operation down, not just this one outfit. I brought you here to get the refinery owner's daughter and leave, not to rescue the rest."

Muffled sobs interrupted the argument. The tallest of the sixteen girls cuddled the child next to her, soothing her with pats on her back.

"Call the shelter," the policeman ordered someone. "They can pick up the kids."

When Harry pivoted, he saw a young woman, a maid—the undercover cop, presumably. "What shelter?" Harry asked. "Can't they go home?" Even as he asked, he knew how naïve the question was.

The maid said, "The girls were smuggled here from Nepal. Most of them are orphans. Some were sold by their families. There are no homes for any of them to go to. Not that the shelters are much different from this place. That's prime hunting ground for sex traffickers."

They'd be preyed on by the same type of vultures who'd brought them to this house. They might be sold again and again. One day, they might even volunteer for a life of prostitution and crime to fill their bellies.

"Ask them," Harry said, "if they want to go to America. If they agree, I'll take them back with me." Even if he needed to personally adopt all sixteen.

"The government won't let you," the cop said, his frustration at Harry's behavior apparently overcome by empathy.

"What if I call a colonel I know in the Indian army?" Harry asked, desperation mounting. "His mother is on the board of an orphanage in Sikkim."

It took a few days for the children to be dropped off at the orphanage. The matron of the brothel was treated at the local hospital, then taken to prison. Her incarceration hardly mattered in the bigger scheme of things. Censure evident in his voice, the cop told Harry the owner of the hostel disappeared. There were no more leads.

Chapter 15

In two weeks' time, November 1979

Washington, DC

Harry reported straight to the Oval Office as ordered. He sat in the chair across Temple's desk, eyes on the flag to the side.

"Tell me," the president instructed, tone impassive.

Small bodies burned to the bones, metal melted into flesh, the charred smell... Harry stared hard at the president. "You sent me there on purpose."

Temple didn't deny the accusation. "The refinery owner who was killed... wasn't he the same one who reported Sanders to the government?"

"Yes."

The president mused, "Rumors say it was the wife's boyfriend who did it."

"There was no boyfriend."

"Of course there wasn't," Temple agreed. "What happened to the owner's family? The wife? And wasn't there a child? A twelve-year-old girl?"

"The body of the wife was found floating in the canal."

"Was she...?" Temple asked.

"Yes."

"Hmm." After a silent moment or two, the president continued, "The daughter?"

Not glancing away from Temple's face, Harry admitted, "I was not able to locate her."

Temple said, "Sanders likes to claim he's a family man, and he is. He keeps his wife and daughters out of limelight, but there was never any gossip of a personal nature attached to him. The people in his hometown in Oklahoma say he was very involved in the girls' education when they were in school. He's also quite the philanthropist. His foundation donates to inner-city schools. Then there's this other side to him. You were already aware the criminals in his pay are not upstanding citizens. They have certain... predilections. You didn't realize Sanders hires them on purpose, did you? He sent the thugs to the refinery owner's house, knowing quite well what they'd do to the child. Who knows where she is by now and in what shape?"

A muscle clenched in Harry's jaw. "I can take care of Sanders. I *will* take care of him."

"Haven't you tried for the last five years? Sanders has his people in the government, but there have been honest men. Don't you think they've tried to bring him down for many, many years prior to you coming into the picture? I'm the president now and can rein him in to some extent, but it won't be forever."

"We always targeted his business activities," Harry said. "Time to rethink our strategy. Dammit, he's allowing his thugs to hurt little children. How can he not be considered a security threat? If you don't want the CIA involved, *I* know how to finish him off. No need to drag anyone else into it." One well-placed bullet would—

"No need to drag Lilah into it, you mean?" the president asked with a sigh. "I, too, have fantasized about sending the CIA after him. About sending *you* after him. You might succeed. We could decide to take the pain of consequences and go ahead with an assassination, but what comes next? For every Sanders you defeat, someone else might... *will* pop up. It's the nature of human society. As soon as a power vacuum is created, other forces rush in. If we don't take control of the situation, there is a high chance the replacement will be worse. More fathers will be killed, more mothers left raped and dead. More children sold into slavery. Without a proper system in place, there's no hope for justice in the world. But the nation has laws designed to prevent collusion between businesses, however well-intentioned they might be. You won't be able to build such an alliance without Lilah. As the Sheppard-Barrons heiress, she has an opportunity here which might not come again any time soon. *We* have an opportunity here."

"Sanders is the one we need to concern ourselves with, and I can do it myself," Harry argued. "How can we expect to stop all the criminal businessmen in the world? It's delusional to think anyone can."

"Is it? Robert Kennedy once said he would 'dream of things that never were and ask why not?' Ask yourself the same question. Why not? Because you're unwilling to sacrifice your own needs?"

"Even so, there *must* be some other way. Once Sanders is gone, we can—"

"Focus carefully on what I'm saying, Harry. See the big picture. Punishing Sanders for his crimes can only be a minor part of the plan. Let's say we succeed in getting rid of him within my time in the White House. I might or might not be able to save you from the electric chair. I might or might not survive politically. We can hope the market will recover sooner rather than later. But the void in the sector... oil and gas form two-thirds of the world's energy resources. Someone else *will* take Sanders's place, and that person will be in control of a critical industry. History shows us such tyrants learn the wrong things from the mistakes of their predecessors, and humanity ends up being worse off than before. You've seen it yourself—the ayatollah in Iran, Saddam in Iraq, communists in Russia. Then there's OPEC and its influence on our foreign policy. The U.S. cannot let it continue. What we need is our own system to keep rivals and rogue elements in check. We need someone we can rely on ready to take charge *before* we consider finishing Sanders off, and the only one in a position to do so is Lilah."

"It's crazy to imagine... how can anyone ask..."

"I didn't reach the conclusions I did easily," said Temple. "How many failures will it take for *you* to understand we won't win by using the same old ideas? How many more will have to die? How many lives are you willing to sacrifice so you and Lilah can be together? A thousand? A hundred? One? What if the one life lost is someone you love? Say... your father. If you were told the only way to keep him from dying was to give up Lilah, what would you do? What would *she* ask you to do? There are millions of other people in this country—men and women you've sworn to protect. Four billion people exist on this planet, those to whom you have a duty as a fellow human. Are you going to tell them their lives are simply not as important?"

An image of his father flashed into Harry's mind. His mother... his baby sister... Sabrina... her mischievous eyes sightless from death, her body charred. Harry gagged before biting back the reflex.

Temple pushed his chair back and went to the side table. Ice tinkled. He set a crystal glass on the desk and poured two fingers of Scotch from the decanter. Handing Harry the glass, he returned to his chair. "Trust me... there is no option except Lilah. Without this sacrifice from you, there *will* be thousands who die. Their blood will be on your conscience. And on hers."

Something... somehow... Harry needed a way out. Frantically, he suggested, "Dan Barrons." Lilah's twin was in the same position as her, sandwiched between the Sheppards and the Barronses. There had to be a girl Dan could marry among the Kingsley lot.

"The only Kingsley granddaughter is already married." Temple took a sip from his glass. "But that's beside the point. Dan's children will be Barronses, and Godwin will not let anyone but a Kingsley inherit the family business. He's old-fashioned about some things. It's got to be Lilah and one of the Kingsley grandsons. Preferably the heir. *Their* children will be Kingsleys."

Lilah married to another man, his child at her breast. Something ripped within Harry's chest. "She won't agree," he insisted, voice cracking.

"*You* will have to get her to agree," Temple said bluntly.

Sharp pain rippled out to Harry's ribs, leaving him shaking.

Temple's eyes softened. "Besides... Lilah and you... she's not for you, Harry. Even without Barrons and his piles of money in the picture, she's the daughter of a former high-ranking diplomat. An Ivy League-educated lawyer. Someone as intelligent and ambitious as her should go far with the right kind of help. Mrs. Harry Sheppard *could* get to the Supreme Court, but she's more likely to live and die as an ordinary lawyer somewhere—perhaps for some civil rights organization. As a *Kingsley*, Lilah will be the leader of a global alliance. Once we defeat Sanders, other companies will be ready to join us, and in a few years, Lilah will be running the oil sector. In effect, she will run the world—with our help. *If* she can be persuaded into it. You know she won't be convinced by anyone but you. When you called me from Saudi Arabia, you were angry at the idea of the United States using a thug like Saddam. You wanted to wait for a good guy... a hero... well, I'm showing you our hero. She can save many families like the Sheppards, many businesses. Hell, many countries if everything goes right. Except she can't do a single thing with you holding her back."

"...if I were in charge of the world, what do you think I'd do?" a voice from his memories asked Harry. Lilah, when they were on the run from Sanders's thugs.

"Love is not always under our control," Temple said. "You can't simply order yourself to stop... but real love comes from a truthful place. It is an emotion so profound you're willing to sacrifice your heart for the object of your affections. You have courage enough to take any amount of pain for her. Attachment is borne out of your senses. It brings the need to shackle the other to you to please your faculties... something inherently selfish. It refuses to see what harm it could cause the loved one or even the world. Attachment essentially destroys love. Free yourself from self-centered desires. Free *her*. Let her reach her full potential. Let her be the leader destiny intends her to be."

No, Harry screamed in silence.

"Imagine," Temple said, "a system which runs to the benefit of humanity. Imagine closing the door on chaos and crime. Imagine collective action to end the ills of the planet. It is certainly ambitious... but not delusional. Dream of things that never were, Harry. None of it will happen unless we make an effort. We can at least try... through Lilah. If you can see beyond selfish attachment to the greater good."

A knock at the door interrupted them. Harry paid no attention to the hushed conversation between Temple and his secretary.

Staring into the amber liquid in the glass, Harry desperately wanted to be drunk out of his mind. He didn't want to hear the voices or see the images. The tormented questions of the parents who'd lost their children in the explosion. The corpse of a battered and bruised woman. Small children, forced into sex slavery. The faces of the dead morphed into the faces of the people he loved.

Lilah... I... we... how can I ask her to...

"Harry," the president called. Temple's countenance was pale, the fine lines sharp with anxiety. "We have a problem. Your contact at Harvard has been trying to get hold of you. Sanders was on campus this afternoon, giving a lecture. Now, they can't find Lilah."

Shoving the chair back, Harry stood. Terror, absolute terror, enveloped him.

Chapter 16

Two hours ago

Cambridge, Massachusetts

"Finally, all three of us together at the same time!" Lilah cradled the phone on her shoulder, stuffing the gym bag with dirty clothes. She was joining the rest of the Barronses for Thanksgiving. Andrew's son, Shawn, was also supposed to be at the family home. "See you soon, Dan."

Zipping the bag, she dropped it on the floor and dialed another number. "Aunt Sophie, it's Lilah. Is Harry coming home for the holidays? I missed his last phone call."

"His time is not his own," Harry's mother said, tone curt. "He works for the president. We're all busy. There's a company to run."

Guilt and its myriad manifestations. The Sheppards—except

for Harry and Sabrina—resented the girl they bartered for the Barrons millions. The sudden insight did nothing to assuage the pain and the anger surging in Lilah's chest. "I understand," she said, voice tight.

The moment she hung up, a thought occurred to Lilah. Though Harry's mother hadn't exactly confirmed it, she never denied it either. Maybe it meant he would be home soon. On her way out of the dorm, the beam on Lilah's face caused a classmate to blink and do an intentional double take. Lilah laughed and sprinted down the steps.

She waved to the security guard, a former marine, on her way out. Apparently, on Temple's insistence, Andrew had contracted a personal security firm to keep an eye on her the last few years— actually, since the escape from Libya. Until Harry mentioned it, she never knew there was a shadow following whenever she ventured outside the dorms or the Barrons residence. Harry installed his own guy after the mission in Beirut just in case Sanders got ideas to do whatever. Now, the men took turns protecting her. Not that anyone believed she was really in danger. "Miss Barrons," the guard called.

"Yes, I know." She hefted the bag over one shoulder. "Sadly, I'll have to miss the pearls of wisdom coming from the great Jared Sanders." She couldn't stand the thought of sitting in the lecture hall, having to listen to him.

"I've been trying to reach Harry," the guard said.

"He's probably on his way stateside." Lilah chatted with the man for a couple of minutes, reminding him that Harvard frequently invited titans of industry to give lectures and that Sanders speaking to a hall full of Ivy-Leaguers would be nothing unusual. Since she was headed straight for the Barrons mansion, the guard didn't need to follow.

Getting into the 1970 Dodge Colt she inherited from her father, Lilah drove sedately. The old car couldn't go fast, but she didn't mind. It gave her time to daydream. Everything would soon come together as she'd hoped—her career, a lifetime of love and laughter and toe-curling passion in Harry's arms.

A loud honk yanked her from her thoughts. There was a shiny red hood in her field of vision, mere inches from the fender of her sedan. Lilah wrenched the steering wheel, bringing her car back into the left lane. Tires squealed. The smell of burnt rubber hit her nostrils. The middle-aged man driving the red Ferrari flipped her the bird. Pretending not to see it, she drove on.

She stopped in Danbury to get gas as she always did. On her way back to the interstate, the lights changed to yellow, and Lilah stepped on the brakes. She frowned at the speed with which the pedal plunged. Had she pushed down too hard? She'd have to be more careful with the car, or she'd end up spending money on a new one.

Evening faded into moonlit night. Once Lilah crossed the state line into New York, there wasn't a single house in sight along the stretch she took. Slipping a mixtape into the cassette player, Lilah smiled in pleasure as the Eagles crooned "Hotel California." It would sound lovely on Harry's saxophone. She'd have to cajole him into once again taking up the instrument. Lilah tried out a couple of lines from the song, biting her tongue when she hit a false note. She laughed in mild embarrassment, thankful no one else was around.

The sheer loneliness of the forest was beautiful. The winding roads under the star-studded sky... simply exhilarating. Lilah rolled the window down and breathed in the crisp, chilly air mingled with the scent of falling leaves and wood smoke. Shivering in the cold, she cranked the glass back up.

A sharp bend in the road was ahead, and Lilah pressed lightly on the brakes. The pedal sank fast. Too fast. The car sped on. She pumped the pedal a second time. Nothing. Her heart started pounding. Breath coming in sharp, shallow bursts, Lilah yanked the emergency brake. The car didn't even slow. Rear wheels skidded. She was losing control. Tires screeched as she managed the curve.

A concrete wall loomed at the next bend. If she hit it at this speed, she wouldn't make it. The opposite lane was empty of traffic. Praying furiously that there were no vehicles coming around the curve, Lilah moved to the wrong side and took a wide turn, avoiding the wall. The car sideswiped the mile marker, sending sparks up.

At least three miles remained to the Barrons residence. She needed to bring the speed down. Lilah tried the brakes again. No pressure at all this time.

No way was she going to die in the car. Not when she had so much waiting for her.

Pulse thundered in her ears. Her muscles tightened. Every object in her field of vision came into sharp focus. To her left, moon glinted on the dark lake past the trees. When she saw the rough trail leading to the water, she yanked the steering wheel in that direction. Crushing the shrubs along the way, the car drove off the path and hurtled into the lake.

With a loud roar, water soared on either side of the vehicle. It gurgled through the floorboards. Heart still pummeling her chest wall, Lilah released the seat belt. The doors wouldn't budge, the pressure differential between the exterior and interior keeping them shut. She tried the window, but the crank swung uselessly. The ice scraper. Lilah reached toward the back seat and grabbed the steel scraper she always kept in the car. Taking a deep breath, she slammed it into the center of the windshield.

No luck. Grunting in panic, she tried again and again. The glass remained intact even after the third try. Lilah gritted her teeth, holding back sobs. Maybe another window. She scrambled to her knees on the seat and with trembling arms, swung the scraper against the side glass. A spiderweb of cracks appeared. The car had already sunk so low she could no longer see the surface of the lake.

The interior light was on, but dark waters surrounded the vehicle. "Mama," Lilah begged her long-dead mother. "Help me."

Something... she needed something heavier than the ice scraper. The things her parents left in the sedan years ago were never removed. The car jack was in the trunk, but the lug wrench... she clambered to the back and got the wrench from the floor. Returning to the driver's seat, Lilah once again knelt. She took a deep breath. With every bit of strength she could summon, Lilah swung the wrench. The glass shattered just enough for her to—

Water rushed in with a terrifying rumble, stinging her eyes, flooding her nostrils. Lilah slid and fell back. Almost blindly, she reached for the steering wheel, but her arms were weighed down— her fingers closed around the rim. Heavy fluid flowed over her, encasing her like a casket. Somehow, she used the steering as crutch to drag herself up and forward. One hand outstretched, she searched for the hole in the window... where was it? A sharp pain cut across her palm. There was just about enough air bubble left near the roof of the car for her to take another deep breath. Screwing her eyes shut, Lilah kicked her way up, her foot connecting with something solid. Her body moved, but she couldn't tell in what direction. More pain... on her left ear, her shoulders, her torso, her legs... but it meant the broken glass was cutting her on her way out. Her lungs were already burning from the air she was holding in. She tried another kick. Fiery agony shot along her heel, worse than any of the prior cuts.

Struggling to the surface, she kept her eyes shut until cool wind struck her wet face. Her wheezy coughs echoed across the water, but there was no one to respond, no one to offer help. The shadowed shore seemed so far away, and her calves were already cramping hard. "Please," she implored unseen gods. It seemed eons before she made it to the grassy bank and heaved herself out. Icy water sluiced down her body, and her teeth chattered in the cold wind. Grimacing against the acute throbbing in her foot, she glanced backward. The lake was calm, no trace of the car to be seen on the surface.

Sanders? Lilah asked the silent universe. Did his attention turn to her as the people around her feared? Or was it simply coincidence that the brakes failed?

With the injured foot, it took her an eternity to limp home along the dark forest roads. Pain shot up her leg with each step, warm blood trickling down. Wind turned water to ice, cementing the clothes to her skin. Every inch of her body burned in the painful cold.

There were police cars along the way, their sirens blasting, but Lilah didn't dare talk to them. She had no way of knowing if the cops were working for Sanders, so she hid in the shadows. She didn't even dare go into any of the houses to seek help. When choppers flew overhead, she crouched behind bushes. She needed to force herself to get up and move and not give in to the temptation to sleep. When she finally reached the iron gates of the Barrons mansion, Lilah found more official vehicles there, and the gardens were flooded with lights.

She couldn't feel her toes. Her legs wobbled. Everything see-sawed. Spotting the blurry form of her twin arguing with an officer, Lilah sank to her knees on the tarred road. "Dan," she croaked. Shouts echoed all around. Lilah didn't remember much else except being bundled into the house.

#

An hour later

Washington, DC

Listening to the list of Lilah's injuries, Harry's hand tightened on the phone.

"She's sleeping," finished Dan, sounding weary. "The doctor gave her a sedative."

"Tell her I'll be there as soon as I can. There's something I have to do before."

"Sanders," said Dan.

"Who else?" Harry said, tone hard.

Dan huffed. "Can't believe he had the gall to show up at the school."

"Believe me, Dan, Sanders has made sure there's nothing to lead the cops back to him. He never cared about Lilah before. He went to Harvard to send me a message."

Harry's constant visits to Cambridge told Sanders she was important to his enemy. A bit of research would've shown the criminal how little Lilah actually mattered to the Barronses. If she were harmed, Andrew would do absolutely nothing in retaliation. Sanders wouldn't know about Temple's plans yet to consider her a threat. Just as it was Harry's selfish longing for her to visit which brought her to Libya at the wrong time, it was he who dragged her into the spotlight now.

Suppressing an angry snarl, he explained, "Sanders thinks he can get at me through her. He needs a reminder Temple is the president."

Harry was asked to cool his heels in DC a couple of days until the FBI director was ready to carry out the orders from President Temple. The SEAL and the director got to the offices of Sanders, Incorporated in the Empire State Building in the same car, but Harry was commanded to stay put in the lobby while the director talked to Jared Sanders.

Whistling a cheery tune, the director returned in little more than thirty minutes. "I've taken care of it," he said as they strode out. "Sanders won't try it again. Not while Temple's still in the White House."

Harry's hands itched to squeeze the breath out of Sanders's

body, but he managed to nod his thanks at the FBI director. The assurance wasn't nearly enough. Lilah couldn't be left unprotected even for a minute until Sanders was destroyed.

Climbing into his black Toyota, the director asked, "Aren't you returning to DC?"

"No, sir," said Harry. "The president asked me to go to New Castle. There's something he wants me to do."

Part VI

Chapter 17

A day later, November 1979

New Castle, New York

Light flurries fell outside the French windows of the library at the Barrons home as Lilah sat on the small couch with her cup of hot chocolate. Her twin lounged beside her. Shawn Barrons—Andrew's son with his deceased first wife—was in a nearby chair, sipping at his own cup.

After graduating from West Point, Dan had opted for a post in West Germany where he could occasionally poke his head into the local offices of Barrons O & G. The society pages resurrected his nickname from boyhood, "Prince Charming." With dark hair and eyes, Dan possessed the same stylish good looks as the twins' half-sister, Caroline. It was perhaps one of the reasons Andrew married her. She made the perfect wife for the billionaire oilman. Like her, Dan also had the class and the wealth. Plus, the near-obsessive fussiness about appearance. There was never even a stray thread to be found anywhere on Dan's clothes.

Very few of the Barrons's social circle mentioned Lilah except in passing. They knew there was a twin... probably. Since she deliberately stayed away from the jet set, it wouldn't be surprising even if her existence came as a complete shocker to most.

Strangely, even the similarity in Dan's appearance to Caroline's never provoked any interest in the twins' antecedents. There was some scattered gossip they were somehow related to Andrew's second wife, but no one seemed to know the teenaged duo who suddenly appeared in the Barrons home were actually Caroline's half-siblings. To the general public, their main identity was that of Andrew Barrons's adopted children.

Unfortunately, while Daniel was accepted as heir presumptive to the Barrons business, Shawn was relegated to the sidelines. Shawn's expulsion from West Point for insubordination and his subsequent refusal to hide his sexuality embarrassed Andrew, and he'd refused further financial support for his son's education. So despite being seven years older than Lilah, Shawn graduated engineering school the same year she did. His interest lay in computers, though, not rocks and oil. Only Lilah and Dan attended Shawn's graduation from Columbia.

Shawn had sandy hair and brown eyes, the coloring surely inherited from his mother since he looked nothing like Andrew. Watching Shawn roll the beads of his amber necklace, Lilah wondered again what its significance was. The memory of a girl, he'd once told her, laughing at her confused expression.

Andrew's such an idiot, Lilah thought for the millionth time. He couldn't see what a gem Shawn was. The Barronses invited Shawn and Lilah for holidays mostly on Dan's insistence. She usually grabbed the chance to spend quality time with her twin, but Shawn didn't need to put himself through the torture of showing up at the home of the father who clearly preferred he didn't exist. He did so only for Dan and Lilah's sake.

She was relieved both Shawn and Dan stayed beyond the Thanksgiving weekend. The cops had ordered her to remain in the safety of the well-guarded Barrons mansion until further notice, and without her brothers—biological and adopted—the silence in the house would've driven her insane.

Resting her bandaged foot on the coffee table, Lilah carefully wiggled her toes, trying to relieve the cramping. She was lucky to escape with no major injuries. Sanders... even thinking the name was enough to make her nauseous with fear. And angry. Somehow, they needed to put a permanent end to the problem of Sanders. Harry was on his way to New Castle, and they would discuss the incident. It didn't mean Lilah was going to let the enemy consume her existence.

There was Harry's promise of two weeks together. She wasn't about to miss out on it whatever the condition of her foot. Sipping hot, sweet chocolate, she plotted ways to convince her protective twin she'd be safe enough with Harry.

His voice... it was almost as though she could hear him... no, she wasn't imagining things. Harry was at the door to the library, talking to the housekeeper. Heart thudding in excitement, Lilah twisted around. Her stomach dropped. His face... she'd never seen him looking this grim.

As the housekeeper walked away, Harry nodded in the general direction of the occupants of the library. "Dan, Shawn." Harry cleared his throat. "Lilah."

She blinked. *What?* Ten months away, and it was all—

Dan stood. "I'll be in the family room. Harry, before you go, I want to know what else we're doing with Sanders—"

"Stay, please," Harry said. "We can talk right now." He stood next to the window, knee bent and shoe resting against the wall, looking away from her. Focused as she was on his demeanor, Lilah barely heard his words. "...not a single oil service company willing to cooperate... Kingsley Corp..."

Lilah frowned. *Godwin Kingsley's company? What would they gain from going against Sanders?*

"The only way is if Lilah marries one of them."

In the stunned silence which followed, Lilah felt her heart stop, then slam hard against her rib cage. *No, that's not what he said. No way.*

"What the hell!" Daniel got to his feet with balled fists, stopping when Shawn stood and placed a hand on his shoulder.

No, no, no way... why would he... crazy thing to say... a stupid prank. At fourteen, Harry imagined it would be funny to give her a lizard for a birthday gift, but they were adults now. He needed his ears twisted for the thoughtlessness.

"As a Kingsley, she will..."

Harry's words whirled around Lilah, trapping her in a storm of confusion and panic. He was her friend, the man she loved. He wasn't supposed to hurt her with such terrible gags. Trembling violently, she begged, *Harry, please.*

Lilah hadn't spoken, but Harry's voice faltered. He met her eyes, his face set in lines of grim resolve. With shock, she realized he was serious. Completely, horrifyingly serious.

Outraged voices echoed in the large room, her brothers united in their opposition. "No," spat Dan.

Patiently, Harry repeated, "This alliance with the Kingsleys is our last hope for overthrowing Sanders, and Lilah marrying one of them is the only way to get it done. It's not simply me saying so... Mr. Temple agrees. Besides, Sanders is merely the first obstacle; we need to bring some order to the sector to prevent future tyrants."

Daniel ground out, "I don't care what Temple says. My sister is not some kind of sacrificial lamb."

Harry explained, "She's hardly going to be sacrificed; Lilah will *lead* our coalition."

Daniel turned to his twin. "I won't let you do it. This is your whole life we're talking about."

"The car episode should've made it clear Lilah's life is not likely to last long," said Harry. "Not unless we finish Sanders."

Her twin fell into shocked silence.

"There *is* no other way," Harry continued. "I've tried. The president has tried. Believe me we tried. Nothing worked. It's not only about Sanders. We need someone at the top who looks out for the common good and not merely for himself."

"Lilah?" called Shawn, his voice gentle. "What do *you* think?"

She *couldn't* think. Something hard was lodged in her throat. Lilah picked up her cup and sipped the hot beverage, welcoming the burning pain. "Huh? I don't... the Kingsleys..." Her hand shook. Thick brown liquid splashed over the sides of the cup, scalding her skin. "I'm... I don't know..." Setting the drink down with a clatter, she stood.

Pain shot up her injured foot, and her knee buckled. Lilah clutched the backrest of the couch, declining Shawn's offer of help. Harry took an instinctive step toward her but dropped his outstretched arms when she turned away. As she limped out, Dan attempted to follow. "No," she snapped, holding a hand up.

She could hear Dan's voice as she clung to the rails of the ornate staircase outside and waited for the sharp ache in her foot to subside.

Her twin said, "Goddamned cold bastard. I thought you—" Dan broke off. "I'm going... I have to make sure she's all right."

Harry's rich voice responded, "Let *me*, please. The president wants an answer by New Year's Eve."

Andrew's home office was on the way to her room. The gray-haired secretary was at the door, closing it behind him. Limping away as fast as she could, Lilah somehow managed a nod at the man. She heard Harry's voice calling her name and flinched. He materialized next to her elbow.

"I'm waiting for Andrew," she lied, her husky voice hoarser than usual. Lilah didn't want to speak to anyone. Not her brother-in-law and not Harry. She wanted to get her climbing gear and go to the mountains. Shut off from the universe, she wanted to roar at the skies, venting her grief and fury at Harry's betrayal.

"Mr. Barrons is not expected back for half an hour," the secretary said.

A desperate snarl escaped her throat, causing the secretary to gape in alarm.

"We'll both wait in the office if you don't mind," Harry said, and he hustled her inside before she could object.

Giving Lilah one last curious stare, the secretary left.

Lilah refused to look at Harry, praying wildly her limbs would magically become whole and healthy and strong enough to carry her away from this heartbreak. Or for Harry to vanish, to never have existed.

His warm hand cupped her elbow. "Sit, please. I need to talk to you."

She recoiled from his touch, growling like a wounded animal. The backs of her knees hit the leather chair across the desk, and she fell into it. Lilah didn't want to hear what Harry would say. She wanted to shriek at him to get out, but words struggled to escape her chest.

Harry leaned against the edge of the table. "I... it will be worth it."

Lilah couldn't... she would *not* give him the satisfaction of knowing the depth of the wound he inflicted. She bent her head, hair falling forward to hide her face. Through her lashes, she saw Harry's hands tremble a bit, just a bit, before he clenched them into fists. The scar she'd once left on his index finger, the souvenir of a childhood game, was still visible.

Harry muttered, "You won't be safe until—"

Her eyes jerked up to pin his. *Liar,* she spat in silence. Or perhaps he thought she was stupid enough to believe the nonsense he fed her family.

"Lilah, I..." Harry slid off the desk and knelt on one knee in front of her. "You asked me once what the world would be like if you ran it. You can bring logic and reason to the sector. Don't you want to see such a future?"

"What about *my* future?" she asked. The dreams she'd weaved... the joyful tomorrows she greedily counted... red heat suddenly clouded her vision. From her chair, she shoved at him with all her strength, even the pain in her leg eclipsed by the rage in her heart. "Bastard," she said through clenched teeth. "You manipulative, rotten *cheat*." Injured as she was, the push barely had any force behind it, but Harry was already on his knees and lost balance, tumbling to the carpet. When he hauled himself up to a sitting position, she slid off the chair and landed on the floor. Lilah grabbed a fistful of his shirt. "Tell me why," she demanded in a violent whisper, her head throbbing.

"No other way," he gasped. Sudden tears streaming down his cheeks, Harry insisted over and over he needed to do this. He needed to let her go. Lilah was meant for other things... bigger things than life with her childhood friend. She *had* to marry a Kingsley.

"The truth, Harry," she said, her chest hurting in the effort to speak. "The whole truth."

Shudders racked his torso as he struggled to hold back sobs. "There are things I can't discuss—"

She shouted, "I don't care!"

Harry crumpled. Head on her shoulder, he told her the story of the shadowy realm he walked every day. Where the stench of violent death fouled every breath. Where human beings were treated as pieces of property. Where children were sold into sex slavery. The tyrants around the world wrote the same tale again and again. The defenseless were crushed to death by power-mad dictators. The leaders looked away, pretending to see nothing.

His body shook in anguish, pain pouring out of him as he detailed the plan for an alliance. When he slowed to a stop, there was no sound in the office except their breathing. Shifting away on the floor, Harry reminded her, tone low and intense, "No one understands what's at stake here more than you and me, not even Temple. The children—how many more like that? Could we live with ourselves if we could've prevented it but didn't? What if you can protect another person from having to go through what you did in Libya? Someone needs to stand up for the common man, and the only one who is in a position to do so is you, Lilah." Harry's voice broke. "The president probably thinks you'll be his puppet. But *I* know you. You had the courage of your convictions to refuse Andrew until he blackmailed you into the adoption. If it weren't for you, we'd have never escaped Sanders in Libya. You had the strength to face down everything life's thrown at you. There's no one I'd trust more than you to lead our insurrection."

Lilah stayed put on the spot below the leather chair, staring at her hands which lay on her lap. Her fingers flexed almost involuntarily.

He said with a ring of finality, "We talk about taking a principled stance against criminal businessmen like Sanders, but what are we willing to sacrifice for those principles? Without the courage to sacrifice, what's our virtue—our truth—worth? Truth without valor is useless, and valor without sacrifice is meaningless." Taking in an audible gulp of air, he called, "Habibti..."

The grief and the longing in the endearment... the defeat, the surrender to the inevitable... he was bidding goodbye. Her head jerked up to meet his red-rimmed eyes.

"I would've given up my life if it meant we could be together even for a single day," he whispered. "But how can I ask the rest of the world to... *we* can't pursue personal happiness at the expense of everyone else. Lilah, you need to do this."

She heard every word, saw his pain, yet all she could feel was the agony in her own heart. The torment tearing her body apart. "No," she said, violently shaking her head. "I can't." Heaving herself to her feet, she added, "I... I'm going." Someplace where she didn't have to see him, hear him, remember him. "Don't come after me."

Chapter 18

Two months later, January 1980

After limping out of Andrew's study without giving Harry an answer, Lilah shut herself in her room in the Barrons mansion and drifted through the remainder of her convalescence in a fog. She must've eaten, she must've slept, she must've woken. She simply wasn't aware of any of it. It was only when Dan wished her a happy birthday that she realized how much time had passed.

Lilah stumbled to the library, waiting on the couch for Harry's customary call. She'd told him not to come after her, but he'd call, wouldn't he? He always did on her birthday. She wasn't sure what he'd say... what she'd say to him. Lilah spent the entire day and night on the couch with Dan next to her, but the phone didn't ring. When dawn broke, she finally allowed her twin to persuade her back to her room.

In the afternoon, Dan walked in. He didn't utter a word, but Lilah hated the pity she saw on his face. When she stayed put in bed, Dan dropped to the side of the mattress, and with his warm hand covering her fingers, he muttered, "Harry left for Hawaii yesterday. There was someone with him, a woman."

The vacation she was supposed to take with Harry... a primal scream erupted within her mind. Lilah bit her lip hard, not letting a single sound escape. She squeezed her eyes shut, unwilling to let even her twin see her bleed.

"Who?" she asked, voice thick. At Dan's shift of discomfort, she insisted, "I want to know."

"Sabrina said some Turkish singer." After a pause, Dan mumbled, "You're not going to do anything stupid like go look for her, are you?"

"No," Lilah stated. She wasn't sure why she asked for the woman's identity. *Message received,* she said to the memory of Harry. He was taking himself out of the picture, leaving her with a single question: was she prepared to sacrifice herself?

The same night, she dreamed of her mother. The warmth of her father's hug. Desperately needing their guidance, Lilah made the trip to Brooklyn the next afternoon—to Green-Wood Cemetery. The cold tombs gave her no answer even after a long vigil.

Dan stood leaning against the old sassafras tree, its furrowed trunk and leafless branches emitting the aroma of root beer. The sharp, icy gust from the pond whipped hair into her eyes as she shivered in silence at her parents' graves. One glove was missing, lost during the train ride to Brooklyn, and only just able to feel her frozen fingers, Lilah tucked her hand into the pocket of the puffy jacket. The sun was on its way down, shrouding the cemetery with its oblivious residents in rapidly deepening darkness. How could it be this late in the evening? How long did she stand there, unable to reach a decision?

Her twin's voice broke the wintry silence. "The gates close in half an hour."

Another deadline. She'd already missed the one set by the president. Lilah thought of walking away. She wanted to throw it all in the faces of the men around her, to lead an obscure, lonely life on *her* terms—without friends, without family, without Harry. If she once longed for the affection of the people she loved, now she wanted them gone. Wanted memories of her loved and loving past to stop hurting so much. What would've happened had her parents been alive? Would anyone have dared suggest this? She'd been their darling.

Memory intruded. *"The children, how many more like that?"* Harry's voice asked.

The kids in the destroyed school—*they* had parents who were grieving their lost little ones. What would they say to her? The girls in the brothel... would they turn to her, expecting to find empathy only to be rebuffed? What would she do if—when—there were more such girls pleading for help?

Lilah stumbled around to face her twin. "Dan, I need you to track down a couple of people."

He made a movement of surprise with his hands. "Who?"

Chilly wind whistled around tree branches, and its icy fingers penetrated the layers she wore. Shuddering violently, Lilah said, "Refugees from Iraq."

#

A couple of weeks later, March 1980

Frankfurt, West Germany

Lilah and her guards exited the car at Maurice Rose Army Airfield. Already having returned to his military duties, Dan was at the gate to welcome her. Lilah didn't know how she'd have managed this without him. She'd been in no state of mind to deal directly with the president, so Dan talked to Temple to make the arrangements she wanted.

Dan led her into a meeting room in a squat white building, leaving her guards outside the door. She watched through the window as airmen walked between the planes in the hangar. There was snow on the sparse grass, but the runway was kept meticulously clean. A couple of black helicopters were approaching fast, and the roar of their engines penetrated the concrete walls.

Burning warmth radiated from the space heater provided by the staff. Lilah crouched to thaw her hands in front of it. Dan had placed himself as far away from the heater as possible. Watching Lilah pull her cardigan tighter, he rolled his eyes.

"Lieutenant," a young soldier called from the door. "Your guest is here." The short, plump woman he escorted was clothed in a black *burka*. "Er... she won't talk if there are men around."

As soon as the door shut behind Dan and the other soldier, Lilah said, *"As-salāmu alaykum."* She stumbled a bit over the greeting of peace.

"Wa alaykum as-salām," the woman returned the blessing.

They sat on chairs, facing each other. The burka covered the woman top to toe except for her eyes—a pair of tired dark eyes with wrinkles betraying her age.

"You speak my language?" the woman asked in Arabic, her voice distorted by the veil. "Or was that the only phrase you know?"

With a smile, Lilah continued in the same language, "I could haggle with the shopkeepers in Cairo. Does that count?"

The woman laughed. "Cairo, eh? What were you doing there?"

"My father worked for the state department," Lilah explained. "Cairo, Riyadh, Tel Aviv, Tri—" she faltered to a stop.

"Tripoli?" completed the woman. "Ever been to Baghdad? That's where I used to live."

"Tell me." Lilah sat forward. "Why'd you leave?"

"Are you a journalist?" the woman snapped. "The army told me you're from the refugee center."

"No," said Lilah, urgently. "Someone—a friend—was there."

"You had a friend there?" the woman said, placing a gloved hand on Lilah's forearm. "Oh, God. Was he from Kurdistan?"

Biting her lip, Lilah debated whether to correct the woman's misunderstanding but settled for saying, "He got out."

"What did they do to him?" the woman asked. Her covered fingers stayed partly flexed, tight against Lilah's wrist.

"I... ahh... don't know."

"You may not want to," warned the woman. Letting go of Lilah's arm, the woman turned to stare in the direction of the heater. "With my husband, they started with steel rods."

Lilah gasped.

"A retired archeologist had no business getting involved with the guerillas. He thought he could help the rebels with the terrain and all that, but I begged him not to do it. For my sake, he stayed away." She put up a hand to her face as though to muffle sobs, but her eyes remained dry. "It didn't matter. Saddam's men got us, anyway. The soldiers came to our house—"

Covering her mouth with her fingers, Lilah stayed silent.

"My husband didn't know where the rebel camp was," the woman said with only the slightest hint of a tremble in her voice. "He explained this to the soldiers over and over. They wouldn't believe him."

The elderly couple had been taken to a prison complex.

"The interrogation room—" the woman whispered.

First, they tried a beating. It lasted all night. By the time morning came around, her husband's skin peeled off to even the lightest touch. His body was covered in blood. He gave them a location at the end, something he dreamed up to get reprieve from the rods.

When the soldiers returned, angry at being thwarted, they took out their rage on his wife. Lilah thought she knew what was coming and stiffened. She didn't ask, but the woman offered, "No, not rape." They dragged her to a tub of bubbling liquid she thought was boiling water. But it smelled strong and sour. She described screaming for mercy when they forced her hand into the liquid. "It may have been just seconds, but—" Her flesh melted away, leaving the bones exposed. They tore her robes and threw the acid on her chest, some of it splashing on her face. Her left breast dissolved almost immediately with the chemical corroding part of her cheek and ear.

Lilah couldn't cry. Horror tightened her chest, stopping her from weeping, from *feeling*. Her eyes darted to the woman's hands. She'd thought the gloves and the burka were in adherence to cultural traditions.

When it was over, the woman crawled to the darkest corner of the interrogation room and closed her eyes to the monsters in human form. She heard her husband's feeble cries, asking God why this was happening.

The torture didn't stop for him. When electrodes didn't get them the answer they wanted, their captors escalated to the woodchipper. "Feet first," the woman said. "He was lucky; he died before the blades got past his ankles." He'd been eighty-two with heart problems.

Shoving her chair aside, Lilah strode to the window and threw it open. She took in great gulps of cold air, trying to tamp down nausea.

Behind her, the woman continued talking. The soldiers tossed her out to the street like a piece of garbage. No one dared help. She crawled to the side of the road and waited until it was dark. The days following blurred into each other. There was only one aim in her mind: to get out of Iraq.

She walked with beggars, eating what scraps she could find along the way. Even when she got back to her hometown, there was no one willing to help. Then, she crossed over to Turkey with a group of refugees. She had children and grandchildren living in West Germany. They took her home. For a while, they thought she'd die from wound infection, but she survived.

"When they told me I was going to live, I swore to myself I'd never cry again," the woman said. "I'd never scream for mercy. If I'd stayed quiet, he could've died in peace."

Lilah spun to face her. "You can't—"

"What?" the woman asked, her voice hard. "Blame myself? I'm not stupid. I don't hold myself responsible for what the monsters did. But my screams gave my husband more pain."

"Did you let the Germans know? The Americans?"

"Oh, I did," the woman said. "I wanted my revenge. I wanted Saddam chased through the streets like a rabid dog. I still do. But—" The Americans already knew. They'd already met hundreds like her.

Lilah knew the story from newspapers, but now she connected the dots. Saddam wanted the oil in Kurdish territory. To gain control over the Kirkuk and Khanaquin regions, he needed to drive out the minorities. There was no crime he wouldn't commit, no child he wouldn't kill in his pursuit of black gold. The rest of the world refused to intervene. Even the Americans withdrew support for the Kurds when Saddam agreed to a deal with Iran, an ally of the U.S. at the time.

"Oil is not worth the pain and deaths of so many," Lilah said. "I'm going to make your story public. People need to know—"

"Know what?" the woman mocked. "Nothing will change. They're all just like I used to be, unwilling to help. People are too afraid to take action because they fear the outcome, but no one seems to care that inaction is tantamount to taking a side... the wrong side. *I* made the same mistake. I didn't let my husband join the guerillas. We wouldn't have won even if I did, but he could've at least met death with honor. We both would've known in our hearts we did the right thing. My selfishness didn't buy me safety or happiness. Only guilt." Soul-searing guilt.

#

Two days later

Sikkim, India

"You sure you want to do this?" Shawn asked Lilah. He peered through the window of the Ambassador car, studying the white, two-storied building. "Dan said you were in bad shape after Germany."

During the two days she spent in Frankfurt, she'd smiled at the dignitaries Temple arranged for her to meet and made pleasant chitchat with them. But turbulent thoughts refused to leave her alone. The words rang over and over in her mind: *They're all just like I used to be, unwilling to help."* Only a few years ago, Lilah begged the maid in the American Club in Libya for help. The maid turned away, letting Lilah be brutally assaulted. The Iraqi woman also turned away, only to soon find herself in need of help. Now Lilah was the one being asked to risk it all to help people she didn't know.

"I need to see them." Lilah wanted to meet the children Harry rescued. Nestled in a side street in this Himalayan town was the orphanage where he sent the girls. Lilah's aunt—her mother's brother's wife—sat on its board. There were iron gates in front of the building, a large sign on top announcing they were at the Maitri Destitute Home.

A watchman in woolen khaki uniform hurried out from the building, his baton tucked under his arm. *"Salaam, Saab, Memsaab,"* he greeted the guests, dragging the large metal gates open. He barked at their driver to park inside.

Frigid wind slapped Lilah's face when she climbed out of the car. Under the layers of thick wool, she shivered. Winter in New York was cold, but it was nothing compared to the Himalayas. She took a breath, inhaling the crisp pine smell of the air from the mountains. Majestic peaks loomed all around, the snow on their tops glinting under the bright sun.

The reception area was kept warm by heaters, but it was strictly utilitarian with sturdy wooden chairs and a small coffee table. A group of children came by while they were waiting and gawked at the sight of Shawn and the two guards. A little boy bravely ventured close and poked at Shawn's pale, untanned arm with a pudgy, brown finger. With a shriek, he turned and ran as though expecting Shawn to go charging after. The other kids followed him in a stampede.

When the girls were led in, Lilah asked the men to leave. Her heart wept when she saw what Harry had seen. The youngest was a cherub with pigtails and chubby apple-red cheeks. She gave Lilah a grin and pointed to a gap in her teeth. "Lost one," she informed in Hindi.

Lilah gestured the girl to the chair next to hers. "What's your name?" she asked, the syllables coming out thicker than she intended. Many years had passed since she last spoke her mother's language.

"Suthanu," the child said. "I'm five." She held up five fingers and counted one by one.

"Very good, Suthanu," said Lilah.

Instead of sitting in the chair, Suthanu climbed onto Lilah's lap. Arms closing around the girl's tiny form, Lilah inhaled the innocence. She'd never thought of herself as particularly maternal, but the feel of the child against her heart filled her with sweet warmth, a fierce need to protect.

Through the window, Lilah could see Shawn and the guards playing a peculiar and very loud combination of baseball and cricket with the other children. Their shouts echoed into the building, but the sixteen girls paid no mind at all. Waiting in polite order, they introduced themselves to Lilah. The toys and books she'd brought along were eagerly examined. The oldest was ten, a girl called Hema. When it was her turn to choose a toy, she was reluctant.

"Don't you want one?" Lilah asked. Hema stayed quiet, watching Lilah through her lashes. "It's yours to keep, I promise."

"Are you going to send us away?" Hema blurted, voice fearful.

Lilah was confused. "Send you where?"

"Back to that place." The brothel masquerading as a hostel.

Shocked, Lilah reared. "No! Why would you think that?"

"Someone said," the girl broke off, muffling a sob. "Someone said the bad man who brought us to that place works for a big person. Someone who owns petro... petroleum. Is that why no one rescued us? Was everyone scared of the big person? Are you scared of him, too? Mister Harry was not."

Suthanu still on her lap, Lilah reached out and tugged Hema into her arms. The girl stayed stiff as Lilah patted her back, unable to speak. She held on tight to the girls, wanting to shield them from every evil. "I swear to you I won't let anyone take you back there. I won't let anyone hurt you."

Suthanu twisted around. "Are you Mister Harry's friend?"

Lilah smiled through the tears clogging her throat. "Yes."

"I'm going to marry Mister Harry," Suthanu said with a determined nod.

From the crowd around came a chorus of "Me, too." Lilah laughed.

#

A week later

Indo-Tibet border

Being connected to the president of the United States brought many benefits, including special permits for the Americans to go hiking close to the border. The same day Lilah asked the embassy if it would be possible, someone from the Indian government contacted her to okay the trip. She'd bundled up in insulating gear and was a lot warmer than expected. Goggles protected her eyes from the harsh sun reflecting off the ice on the peaks. Trekking pole in hand, she trudged through the snow on the banks of Alaknanda River, mountains towering on either side. There was no path, just uneven ground, and in parts, they had to clamber over the cliff face extending to the edge of the river. Rocks kept sliding down the slopes on either side.

Next to Lilah, Shawn complained, "You. Are. Crazy. Middle of winter!"

Lilah's breath puffed out in white clouds. "You didn't have to go with me. I have the guards." The two burly men were right behind, vigilantly scanning the surroundings as though expecting Sanders's assassins to chase Lilah through the world's tallest mountain ranges. In front were the four guides from the tourist office, two whose jobs were to carry food and equipment. The tour guides had only agreed to take them part-way up the dangerous winter trail.

"Are you kidding?" Shawn asked. "Dan would kill me if anything happened to you. Not to mention Harry and the president. And your relatives. Your *crazy* relatives."

Shawn had met Lilah's mother's family. Since they knew she was in the country, she couldn't leave without visiting. There was an uncle who took up meditation in his old age after having lived a life raising hell and committing general mayhem. Escaping the mothers of his many children by claiming to have found God, Shawn suggested. Uncle Neelkanth had not been amused by the remark.

Respects paid to the old man, Lilah was ready to return, but when he invited her back for the summer—*sans* Shawn—to visit Swargarohini Peak, she decided to do the trek right away.

On the mountains, she'd always found clarity in her thoughts. The peaks had stood for millennia, witnessed the fears and dreams of countless humans, their hopes and desperation. Neither their victory nor defeat mattered to the ranges. Life and death held no meaning to them. The mountains were there, solid in their purpose, whatever that might be. The memories of a parent's love, the agony of a broken heart, none of it mattered to the Himalayas. Here, Lilah would find the dispassion she sought. Here, she'd search her soul for answers.

Shawn halted to take a breath, hands on his knees.

"When we get back," Lilah suggested, "join me when I go kickboxing. You need to build endurance."

The glare Shawn threw in her direction promised retribution for the taunt.

Lilah smirked.

"No stopping," shouted the lead tour guide in a rough tone. "We're in landslide zone."

Sure enough, a boulder rolled down the cliff barely two feet in front, crashing into the frozen river. Cursing, Shawn straightened.

They continued the trek, Lilah, Shawn, and their entourage. Once they got to Vasudhara Falls, they would have to return as previously agreed.

The final ascent to the top of the waterfall was steep. The landscape was austere with little greenery to relieve the monotony of gray boulders and white snow. Water plunged down several hundred feet, crashing over jagged rocks. A chilly mist hovered over the cliff they were on, its tendrils circling the humans. Save for the roar of the cascade and their labored breathing, all was silent.

There was a red clay hut not too far from the fall with the symbol *aum* painted on one side. It looked like the numeral three with squiggles around. She settled on a rock next to the structure, waiting for the lead tour guide to build a fire in the *bukhari*—wood-burning stove made of dark metal—he placed almost at the edge of the cliff.

"What's this?" Shawn asked, tracing the symbol on the hut with his gloved finger.

"A shrine," said the lead tour guide. "This place is called Lakshmiban. A princess died here. Fell from the mountain."

"Royalty get shrines?" asked Shawn.

"Some people say she was an avatar of Shri, the goddess," the tour guide said. "She started the war at Kurukshetra before she died."

"She got a shrine for starting a war?" Shawn asked, tone rising in incredulity.

"No, no," insisted the tour guide, his face earnest. "She made the war happen to destroy evil on earth. That was her mission. Thousands of people died, even her own children. She sacrificed everything."

"This spot is supposed to be holy," Lilah interjected, her eyes on the yellow-orange flames crackling up from the stove. She'd heard the story from her grandmother. "The princess destroyed the corrupt ruling class of the entire subcontinent. Back in the Iron Age."

"Yes," the tour guide said. "The princess got *moksha* after she died."

"Absolution," Lilah clarified. "Moksha is absolution. Kind of."

The tour guide nodded. "The princess went to heaven after her death."

"Poor woman," Shawn muttered.

"She did achieve her objective," Lilah pointed out.

"At the expense of her own life and happiness," Shawn said, dropping to the ground. "I wonder if she thought it was all worth it when she died on these rocks."

"What's one woman's life worth," Lilah asked, "when you compare it to the millions she saved from tyranny?" Scrambling up from her stony seat, she stomped to the fall. Her breathing heavy, she stared at the water, the ice crystals on the rocks. A large rainbow shimmered in the mist. All around, the mountains towered, their peaks piercing the blue-gray canopy above. "What's *my* life worth?" she whispered.

Shawn followed her, but he stayed silent.

"All those people," Lilah said, hot tears streaming down her cold cheeks. The Iraqi archeologist subjected to an inhuman death… his disfigured wife lived with regret as her constant companion. "No one to help." If Lilah chose not to fight for them, would she be able to live with herself? "Those girls," she mumbled. The young souls were collateral damage to Sanders's lust for power. "Is their pain any less than mine?"

The world was in chaos. Truth and untruth were constantly at war, the moral with the immoral, and few were willing to take up arms on behalf of that which was good. Somewhere, the chronicler of humanity's story must've despaired over the selfishness and shameful cowardice, but he didn't possess the power to meddle. Here was Lilah being offered the chance to rewrite a small part of the tale. Did she have the strength in her spine to battle evil, faith enough in her heart to see it through? She'd have to end her life as she knew it. Her dreams of a future filled with love and laughter, her career aspirations, they would die. She'd burn her hopes to ashes and walk out of the pyre as a woman reborn, one with no past to haunt her, defeat of the unjust the only purpose of her existence.

Gray clouds rolled over the sky. A winter storm was brewing. Wind whistled, mimicking the sentimental melody from some faraway flute. From the stove by the cliff's edge, flames shot up with a whoosh and danced madly to nature's symphony. The music notes deepened in tone almost as though the cosmic musician had morphed into a warrior, his flute into a saxophone, the bittersweet song of his lips to a call to war. The storm gathered speed, echoing *aum* across the landscape—the sound of Big Bang, the creation of the universe. Primordial energy once whirled, scattering, creating life. In the cosmic dust thus formed, Lilah was but one speck. In this infinite expanse of space and time, her life didn't hold much meaning, but she could make it meaningful. She could leave her mark as the princess once did.

Lilah roared at the sky, startling her companions. She kept thundering until the tearing hurt in her throat nearly equaled the pain in her heart. The mountains amplified her screams of rage— the death throes of a girl, the battle cry of a woman.

When the echoes died, she turned to Shawn. Voice steely, she said, "When we get back, please call Mr. Temple for me." With a knuckle, Lilah wiped the wetness from her cheeks. "Let him know if the sacrifice of one woman is what it takes to rid the world of Sanders and his ilk, then that's what we shall do." Head held high, she gave Shawn a smile. They would build an empire.

Chapter 19

A month later, March 1980

New Castle, New York

From the Himalayas to the hills of New York, Mother Nature seemed to be in no mood to let up on her wintry hold over the northern hemisphere. Noting the pouring rain outside the windows, Lilah took her place at the conference table in the Barrons home. Temple was in the chair across. He'd arrived the night before, barely beating the nor'easter currently battering the state. There was a chessboard set up in front of him, with the king's pawn already making the opening move. Lilah eyed the pieces, almost automatically calibrating strategy. There was a combative tactic she was developing, designed to wrench victory in a seemingly hopeless battle. One of her rooks would deliver the kill blow. She called it the Manhattan Swindle.

The president smiled and waved a hand over the chessboard. "How are things at Harvard?"

"Things have been fine, sir." She couldn't smile back, not just yet. Nor was she in the mood for a game. Ignoring the board, she scanned the room, noting the projector screen at one end. Andrew and Ryan Sheppard were already in attendance, and so was Shawn. Since Dan couldn't personally show up, he'd insisted on Shawn's presence. Lilah's twin knew she'd need one friendly face at the table, someone whose exclusive concern was her well-being.

Wind slammed at the windows, rattling the glass panes, but Lilah heard the president's sigh clearly enough. "'For unto whomsoever much is given, of him shall be much required,'" Temple quoted from the Bible, tone soft.

Perhaps, but the enormity of what she committed to left Lilah quaking inside. There were times during these last couple of weeks when she found herself praying for numbness.

Harry spoke from the door, greeting the rest of them.

Then there were times she hoped wildly this was a nightmare she'd soon wake from. It took every ounce of the strength Lilah possessed to school her face into impassivity and nod at him. The shadows of pain in his eyes didn't matter to her at the moment, nor did the slight tremor in his tone when he said her name, both of which he masked with his usual mischievous grin. He did this to himself... to her. Under the table, her hands tightened into fists in an effort to stop the trembling.

She'd have to learn to maintain a professional attitude with him. Gateway would form one-third of the alliance, and Harry wasn't going anywhere.

Within minutes, they got to the business at hand. "Justice Godwin Kingsley, the patriarch." Harry presented the first slide. "He retired last year from the Supreme Court."

Lilah leaned forward to study the photograph, and so did everyone else. From what she heard, the former justice and his stepbrother—Temple—were the same age at seventy-five.

Temple explained, "My mother was married to Godwin's father, and we shared a half-brother. He—our brother—died in his early forties. Terrible disease, alcoholism. Had three sons, too." The president grimaced. "The youngest with his secretary. It was a big scandal at the time. Godwin never married and has no children, but he adopted our nephews after their father's death. To all intents and purposes, *Godwin* has been their father."

Harry interjected, "Peter, the middle son, was married to a distant relative of my father's—Patrice Sheppard. He also died while still a young man." Harry smiled. "In the arms of his mistress, no less."

The men guffawed as Lilah concealed a grimace.

The president continued, "Between the three boys, there are seven grandsons and a granddaughter."

"Our candidate should be whoever will eventually inherit the CEO position," stated Andrew.

With a small nod, Temple agreed. "Godwin is inclining toward

Patrice and Peter's oldest son. There's some animosity between the grandchildren, so it will take my brother a few months to arrange the succession plan. Marriage to the Barrons heiress will clearly tilt scales, so we'll need to wait until the company decides on future leadership to let the young man meet Lilah, or the rest will realize something's up and start trouble. She can use the time to get familiar with oil politics."

Lilah wondered why it mattered who was heir. They would have their virtual merger as long as the man she married owned shares in the Kingsley business.

"Patrice will not easily agree," Ryan Sheppard said, drumming his fingers on the arm of his chair.

Oh, yes. Lilah remembered Harry once telling her about some kind of fallout between Patrice and the rest of the Sheppards. However distant the kinship, she might not want a Sheppard for a daughter-in-law.

The president waved away the concern. "Lilah is Andrew Barrons's daughter. Andrew wants an alliance with the Kingsleys... which is all Patrice needs to be told when we bring up the topic. Eventually, we'll have to tell her, but only after her son meets Lilah. One look at her, and his mother's agreement will no longer matter."

Lilah started. Her fingers curled, nails cutting into her palms. Bait. The president considered her bait to draw Patrice Kingsley's son away from her control. Lilah glanced at Harry, but his gaze was firmly fixed on the photograph projected on screen.

Temple leaned forward, elbows on the table. "You do understand our reasons, don't you, Lilah? The Kingsleys, the Barronses, and the Sheppards—the combination will be impossible to beat. Once Sanders is squeezed out, we'll make sure he gets the punishment he deserves. Other companies will then be ready to join us. The network thus formed can decide on a code of conduct for the sector."

The image of a tentacled monster flashed into her mind. Lilah stared hard at the president, her brain grasping the intended reach of the plan for the first time. If their strategy worked, she wouldn't be merely dethroning Sanders; she'd eventually be at the head of a network with authority over the flow of oil to every corner of the world. A *puppet* head with the men around her running the show.

Temple sat back in his chair. "These things aren't as unusual as you might think. Consider the Ford-Firestone marriage... there's gossip it was a business arrangement. Maybe true, maybe not. Same with the Kennedys. In our case, the cause will be much more worthwhile."

Outside the safe confines of the Barrons home, nature continued to pummel New York in its fury. Gale-force winds screeched in monstrous glee as they tore through the maples and oaks in the garden. Lilah stayed silent, frantically trying to take in the implications of this deal she'd signed on to. This... this plan... it was so... she never believed in this philosophy of... *Oh, my God. What did I do? What did I just do?*

She opened her mouth to scream her refusal, ordered her legs to get up and run. She'd return to law school... leave the country... anything to avoid this. Lilah knew... she *knew* what Temple wanted. He'd been blunt enough when she worked for him. Lilah could never condone this. It simply wasn't who she was. Temple might be president, but he couldn't force her into this scheme, could he? It didn't matter. She'd leave the country and go to India. Her mother's family... she'd go to the orphanage and live there... *the girls*. Lilah would have to tell the girls she couldn't protect them, after all. They might be safe within the walls of the children's home, but others like them would continue to suffer.

Harry switched to pictures of other Kingsley family elders. Even as Lilah's brain recorded the names and faces, thoughts whirled. What would happen if she called a halt to this idea? The president would be angry, but he... Harry... what would happen to him? What would Sanders do? Everyone said Harry could take care of himself, but he wasn't indestructible. The rest of Sanders's victims... she needed to figure something out. Time... she needed time.

Harry moved on to the Kingsley grandsons, listing the names of the prospective grooms. "...the eldest of them..."

Her nerve endings bristled to attention. Adrenaline thundered across her psyche as though hundreds of horses were galloping through the stormy terrain, signaling the arrival of new allies, new relationships, new opportunities. New ties which could steel the arms of the challenger to the throne or shackle her in gaol. Her mind shrieked a clarion call, a warning.

"...Aunt Patrice's third and youngest son is a sniper," said Harry. "A highly successful one."

Lilah blinked and sat forward. Dark-brown hair, eyes the color of aged cognac... the full-length snapshot showed him in military fatigues. He was obviously tall and fit, and his stance was that of a warrior, fearless and tough. Life thrummed from him even within the two-dimensional confines of the photograph. She surveyed the picture, then Harry. The resemblance was striking—not in the features, though the coloring was similar. The bearing, the attitude, the expression... something about the two men was extraordinarily similar. She wondered why no one was commenting on it.

"Alex Kingsley," announced Harry.

Part VII

Chapter 20

Months later, September 1980

Washington, DC

In the Oval Office, Lilah watched *CBS Evening News* with Harry and the president. Temple had commanded both to the White House for the state dinner the next night honoring the Israeli prime minister. Lilah was told in blunt terms she needed to start mingling with the movers and shakers of the world, and the reason the chief guest requested Harry's presence was made clear by the president.

Operation Trojan Horse, a mission in Somalia to rescue the passengers of a hijacked Air France flight bound for Tel Aviv... only one American was involved, a former SEAL. Harry let himself be kidnapped by militants and acted as the inside man for the Israeli commando force. Except for the youngest—a teenager—all the militants were killed.

Walter Cronkite, America's most trusted newsman, was currently on television. He didn't mention the rescue in making the announcement about Petty Officer First Class Sheppard, the latest recipient of the Medal of Honor from the United States Congress. The media would never hear about such missions, but there was enough speculation about Harry's work as a SEAL. After all, the reason for his medal was an intriguingly vague "awe-inspiring display of bravery on behalf of the nation and its allies."

The rumors, his frequent visits to the Oval Office, and his role in arranging international business deals fed the immense interest in Harry. Cronkite smiled into the camera. "Mr. Sheppard's dramatic rise in profile as a commodities broker in the oil sector will be chronicled by *60 Minutes* this Sunday."

Temple turned off the TV. Across the desk from him, Lilah swiveled her chair to face Harry. "Reckless," she snapped. The Somalian operation happened more than two years ago, but he never mentioned it to her. "And stupid." With satisfaction, she watched hurt flash in his eyes.

With so many things crowding her psyche at the moment, she sometimes wondered how she managed the luxury of being angry with Harry. Once she agreed to be the linchpin to the network, she was given tons of information on the three companies to study. She needed to be well-versed in the politics of the sector. Any hope of the extra work keeping her thoughts from drifting to Harry faded when he insisted on being involved in every part of the plan. As one of the major players in the proposed network of companies, Gateway would of course demand a say, and Harry seemed to have appointed himself representative.

To Lilah's surprise, it wasn't difficult to work with him. She could still trust him to be truthful no matter how badly it hurt. Not limiting his involvement to the paperwork, Harry took over her training in kickboxing and shooting. They met regularly at Hector's gym and at the range. An intense ache now tainted the familiar joy of their friendship. At times, she found herself wanting to wound Harry as badly as he wounded her. Sometimes, she longed to hold him close and kiss away the grief only she seemed to see.

"But brave," Lilah added, glancing toward the TV where the anchor had moved on from the news of Harry's medal to something else. "Without your help, those hostages might not have made it out alive."

Sitting up with a faint smile, Harry turned back to the documents on the table. They'd arrived at the White House a day before the state dinner only to review some details of the proposed

Kingsley-Barrons-Sheppard alliance.

Temple retrieved a stack of newspapers from the floor and slid it across the desk. "Lilah, are you following the *Wall Street Journal* series on dealmakers?"

She studied the black-and-white picture of Harry with the Saudi prince on the front page. The latest agreement negotiated by the young commodities broker was between a commercial airline and Aramco, the Saudi Arabian oil and gas company.

"All this publicity cost me my job," Harry grumbled. Name and face deemed too recognizable for their missions, the navy offered to promote him to officer rank and appoint him to desk duty, but he declined and opted to go inactive with plans to leave the service after the mandatory two years. He now worked full time for Gateway.

"Let's call it a day," said Temple. "I have some phone calls to make. Lilah, I assume Shawn is escorting you to the dinner tomorrow?"

"Yes," said Lilah. "He'll pick me up at the hotel." The alliance was taking longer than expected to arrange, and the internal politics of the Kingsley family meant the plotters had yet to decide which of the clan's grandsons would eventually marry Lilah. The prospective grooms were still in the dark about it all. Those who did know were asked to maintain perfect secrecy while legalities were being sorted out. Staying out of the limelight was no emotional hardship for Lilah, but she was also expected at the same time to raise her profile in preparation for her entry into elite society.

Andrew Barrons was a rich man, and a hint from him was enough for invitations to the major social affairs around the country to pour in. To defend against potential leaks to the media, access to Lilah was strictly controlled, and she was accompanied by Dan or Shawn to the events. When they were not available, Harry escorted her, but he invariably found a girl to chat up, making it clear to the world he was not romantically involved with Lilah. Andrew's wealth also meant his adopted daughter became the cynosure of all eyes wherever she went. The absence of romance in Lilah's life caused intense speculation in the tabloids. The more she ignored the questions, the more determined the media became to dig into her secrets.

Harry answered every question. He joked with male reporters and flirted outrageously with female correspondents, tossing enough red meat at every impromptu interview to keep the press occupied for weeks. Journalists loved Harry, and their readers couldn't get enough of the stories of his romantic escapades. Lilah's relationship with him was firmly assigned to the friendship zone by the rest of the world. Even those who would've known there was once something more now feigned blissful ignorance. Not that one less girlfriend would make any difference to Harry's reputation. The number of glamorous women linked with him crossed the threshold of probability long ago and was now in the realm of the ludicrous. She wondered with some bitterness which glorious creature was going to grace his arm at the state dinner.

"What about you, Harry?" Temple asked. "Who's the lucky lady this time?"

Lilah started. It was as though Temple read her mind.

"Your staff already has the name of my guest," Harry said. Gathering papers together, he asked Lilah, "I'm going to get in a workout. Join me?"

"Not today." She needed to catch up on sleep.

He handed her a stack of folders. "Go through these this week. It's important."

"What is it?"

"The FBI dossiers on the Kingsley cousins." Temple didn't bother hiding the turmoil within the clan. The sons of his oldest nephew and the sons of Peter Kingsley were brawling over control of the family business. The Kingsley lawyers cautioned against signing any documents until the drama was sorted out, thus causing this delay in executing the marriage alliance.

Making sure the president was already on his phone call, she asked Harry, "Are we doing the right thing?" She needed to set aside her anger with him for the moment and talk about her concerns... maybe brainstorm ideas. "I was thinking... what's the difference between this network and a cartel?" Temple threw a sharp look in their direction. Lilah held back a grimace. He'd heard. Lowering her voice even further, she continued, "Who's actually going to run this show? Temple? Do you believe he has no other motive?"

"Of course not," Harry muttered. "He might spout high-minded stuff, but at the end of the day, we're dealing with a politician. Sanders supports Temple's opposition. Once the president replaces Sanders with you, it will cause a huge shift in power. I'm sure Temple imagines he can get you to do what he asks. Let him think whatever. There's nothing he can do to force you once the stock is yours." Harry added Alex Kingsley's file to the top of her pile.

#

The next evening

Cameras flashed as Lilah exited the car at the designated entrance to the White House event. She walked up the steps on Shawn's arm, lifting the short train of her strapless column gown an inch. The densely sequined crimson silk shimmered under the lights, making her skin glow with warmth. Rubies glinted at her ears and throat, and her hair was held back in an elegant twist by crystal clips.

"You've gone all out tonight," muttered Shawn, patting the hand wrapped around his elbow. He sniffed. "Lots of perfume as usual."

"It's the same one I always use," Lilah murmured, smiling graciously at a congressman she recognized.

Shawn had already lost interest and was gawking at a famous actress with bouffant platinum hair gliding by. He had a thing for stage and screen artists. His boyfriends were almost always from Broadway, and they almost always dumped him when they found out he'd been disinherited. Lilah once tried introducing him to a fellow student from Harvard, but when the three of them met at the Lebanese restaurant in Cambridge's Central Square, Shawn resisted her every attempt to leave... an embarrassing afternoon for all concerned.

Not that she had much luck arranging Dan's love life, either. Her twin seemed to have some kind of sixth sense as far as her matchmaking efforts were concerned and managed to be out of town whenever Lilah showed up with a likely candidate. He was content practicing serial monogamy with the various heiresses paraded in front of him by Andrew and Caroline. Lilah did have high hopes for the redheaded office assistant in the executive suite. There was a spark in her twin's eyes whenever they landed on the girl.

Shawn and Lilah sauntered into the yellow room where the pre-reception was to be held. He asked, "Where'd you get all the sparkly stuff?"

"Caroline's," Lilah said.

Shawn snagged a couple of glasses of wine from a waiter. "Really? Caroline let you borrow her jewelry?"

Lilah sipped the cabernet, tasting black cherry and licorice. "She knew it was for the state dinner."

"Of course." Shawn smirked. "Barrons women are always expected to be appropriately dressed."

The society columnist from the *Washington Star* sidled to them.

"Miss Barrons, I'm trying to figure out if your penchant for wearing red is a fashion statement or if you're just a creature of habit."

"What did you decide?" Lilah asked, amused. "Also, it's crimson, not merely red."

The columnist—a socialite who dabbled in journalism—arched an eyebrow. "The color of blood. Dressed to kill, are you? Who's the intended victim?"

Lilah smiled. "No one. I simply wanted to look good."

The columnist laughed and nodded, her short curls bouncing. "You don't seem to understand the concept of fun, so maybe you're telling me the truth. Miss Barrons, attending state dinners with a gay man shouldn't be your idea of a good time." She added, gesturing toward the door, "You're always with one of your brothers or with *him*."

Even before Lilah turned, she knew who she'd see—Harry, dressed in an immaculately cut jacket in rich midnight blue. The lustrous sheen of the black lapels matched the silk bowtie, bright evening lighting bringing out the warm undertones in his hair.

"Who is she?" asked Shawn.

For a couple of seconds, Lilah was confused. Then, she noticed the statuesque blonde on Harry's arm.

"Ana Eriksson," muttered the columnist. "Olympic skier. Think you can get me an intervi... never mind, they're coming over." The glint in the columnist's eyes was almost comical.

With smooth charm, Harry performed introductions. His rich, deep voice flowed over the group like honey. As usual, he appeared to give undivided attention to each person. Even the jaded socialite had a dazed expression.

The blonde skier's pleasant look faltered slightly as she took in Lilah. Infusing the wattage of thunderbolts into her own smile, Lilah kissed the air by the blonde's cheek. They chatted about mountains. Lips curving delightfully and eyes widening in animation, Lilah reminisced about a childhood trip to the Colorado slopes with Harry's family. She ignored Shawn's look of discomfort at her unusual chattiness. There was a change in Harry's stance, an alertness to a threat he didn't yet understand. Lilah gloated. "How did you two meet?" she asked the skier.

Harry's face darkened, but the blonde didn't notice. She recounted a recent party at her brother's apartment where she met Harry, his former colleague. Apparently, the men had worked together for years, but it was the first time Harry asked to be introduced to his friend's famous sister.

"Your brother's a SEAL?" Lilah asked.

Shawn interjected, "I see some people I know." He offered his arm to the columnist. "Want me to introduce you to a young millionaire? He's newly single and on the prowl."

"Do I smell fresh gossip?" asked the woman. Laughing, she walked off with Shawn.

"I love your perfume," Lilah said to Harry's date.

"Oh, my God," said the skier. "I was dying to ask about yours. What an unusual fragrance."

"It's blue lotus oil," Lilah told her. "Someone used to get it for me from the Middle East, but we... ahh... he doesn't do that, anymore. Luckily, I found a florist in Brooklyn who takes special orders."

"They make it for you?" the skier asked, surprise on her face.

"Pay some people enough, they'll sell you their best friend." Lilah heard Harry's sharp intake of breath, saw the shattered look in his dark gaze. She almost snarled in triumph.

As though aware of the shift in the air, the blonde's eyes

skittered between Harry and Lilah. "Umm... okay."

"We should mingle," Harry said to his date.

He proceeded to dazzle the party from then on. With brilliant smiles and witty remarks, he charmed every attendee. Lilah talked to the gathered statesmen and corporate titans, to self-made millionaires and old money, to journalists and thought leaders. But her eyes followed Harry around the room. Every now and then, she caught the skier's angry gaze on the slashes of red across Harry's otherwise pale face and smiled in satisfaction.

An arm wrapped around his date's stiff shoulders, Harry was chatting to the Israeli prime minister and his wife when Mr. Temple gestured Lilah to the group. The guests were surprised when she greeted them in Hebrew. They were delighted to learn she'd spent her early years in Tel Aviv thanks to her diplomat father. Harry didn't leave his spot by the prime minister. The grin on his face as bright as ever, he accepted a glass of champagne from a waiter.

The prime minister's wife nodded at Harry. "Didn't you also grow up in Israel?"

"Just until I was six," he said, tone amiable. The glass in his hand trembled for a second. "Hey, I have an idea."

Before anyone could ask, he strode to the orchestra, persuading them to play a peppy version of "Hava Nagila" in honor of their chief guests. Then, he prodded the prime minister and his wife into asking the crowd to celebrate with the *horah*, the circle dance.

The staff moved the chairs aside, rolled up carpets. Drums, cymbals, violins, and saxophones pealed out in merriment. Music crashed through the East Room. Under the glittering chandeliers, politicians and businessmen held hands with movie stars and journalists, chanting the words to the song. Stepping right, moving in, moving back. Arms linked, the dancers reveled in the joy of living. Exuberant laughter echoed from every wall.

With Shawn on her right and the prime minister on her left, Lilah grapevined her way across the floor. On the other side of the circle, a feverish glitter flared in Harry's eyes in response to the challenge in hers. The skier shook loose his grip on her hand and stalked off, her face tight. With a quick grin at the dancers next to him, he followed her out.

Harry and his date left early, him claiming a need to work the next day. The skier pretended not to notice the arm he offered and walked ahead. Much later, Lilah exited the White House on Shawn's arm, head held high.

Dropping her off at the Hilton, Shawn asked, "All that effort for another woman, huh?"

Lilah stared through the car window into the dark street, saying nothing. The bodyguards in the back seat would—as always—act blind, deaf, and dumb to the humiliating drama of her personal life. The rest of the world... the tabloids... the entrance to the hotel was brightly lit, but no one was around except the doorman. She prayed to be allowed to get to her room without running into another human being.

"Did it work?" Shawn pushed.

"Yes." Harry was in for an unpleasant night with the skier.

"Was it worth it?"

"No." Lilah didn't know what she'd been trying to accomplish by driving away Harry's girlfriend, by reminding him of what they'd been to each other. All she did was wound them both.

For all the roughness of the evening, Lilah slept well, her slumber dreamless and peaceful for once. Drinking lemon-infused black tea in the morning, she perused the society pages. The White House dinner was deemed a spectacular success. Lilah's presence was noted, and her grace and poise were remarked upon by the columnist. The paper also speculated that Harry Sheppard was single again, having been spotted checking into a hotel not far from his girlfriend's apartment.

There was a numbness within Lilah's chest that was new. A little of her had died in the night.

Chapter 21

Two months later, November 1980

Merida, Venezuela

"Yes, I made the reservation a week back," Lilah said to the man at the hotel reception counter.

As rule-abiding as she'd been, her guards believed her lies about having the flu. The poor men were left dutifully protecting the empty dorm room in Harvard. She was half afraid of being stopped at the airport and almost hyperventilated her way through security checks, but it seemed no one thought her passport needed flagging. Not that Lilah was unaware of the danger, but there was something she needed to do without anyone finding out.

"Señorita," a voice called her back to the present. The manager had arrived and apologizing for the delay, offered her something to drink.

Lilah declined politely. Waiting at the desk, she played with the frustrating puzzle Dan once picked up for her at the Nuremberg toy fair. Something called Magic Cube. It kept her mind occupied in the long flight from New York to Venezuela. But now... she tucked the cube back into her pull-along bag. She didn't fly half a day only to play with the puzzle.

God, she was desperate for her plan to work. Losing Harry had changed her into someone she didn't recognize, much less like. She needed to move on.

The Kingsley men were at the conference in the hotel. They wouldn't be told about the marriage alliance until the succession issue in the family business was sorted out, but Lilah thought she could take a look at them from a safe distance. Once she saw them, she could perhaps pick... stupid, half-baked scheme, but it was the only one which occurred to her.

Almost unseeingly, she leafed through one of the brochures on the reception desk. Something about Ologa Lagoon and lightning storms.

"You need help with your bag?" asked a voice.

With a start, Lilah looked up and smiled at the bellboy hovering by her elbow. "It's just this one piece; I can manage."

Mouth agape, the boy took a step back and collided with someone coming around the corner in a hurry. They both went down in a flurry of papers. The newcomer—a man in a charcoal gray business suit—howled and grabbed the sheets.

The skirts of Lilah's mulberry shirtwaist dress brushed the carpet as she knelt on the floor to help. Standing, she held the bunch out. "I think that's the last of them."

The man heaved a sigh of relief and looked up. "Thank..." Alex Kingsley's cognac eyes widened. Lilah bit back a squeak of dismay. She thought she'd timed her arrival perfectly to when all the conference attendees were huddled over balance sheets in the business center. What was this Kingsley grandson doing in the lobby? Well... he was gaping at her at the moment. As he continued staring, she rustled the papers. "...you," he completed. "Thank you."

Their fingers brushed when he took the sheets. Sparks flew. Literally. They both jolted.

"Static," he explained, clambering up. "From carpet fibers."

"*Señorita,*" the clerk called. "Your room's ready." She pocketed her keys and turned to find Alex rooted to the spot, the stack of papers tucked into the crook of his arm. The bellboy who knocked him down had vanished.

Alex asked her, "American?"

Perhaps she could lie... if he recognized her from the society pages... with a quick nod, she attempted to walk ahead.

Before she could take a step, he asked, "Are you one of the people at the conference?"

Phew. It didn't look like Alex Kingsley perused gossip columns. Well... neither had she paid any mind to the yellow press until *they* started paying mind to her. The tabloids often expressed interest in the younger members of the Kingsley clan, but likely by order of the family patriarch, the grandsons seemed to have steered clear of media trouble thus far. If it weren't for the dossiers she was given, Lilah wouldn't have IDed Alex. After a quick debate with herself, she said, "No. I'm on vacation from school. Traveling through a couple of countries. You?"

"I'm American, too. Here for a conference, not vacation." Alex showed no signs of wanting to end the conversation.

Lilah suppressed a grimace. Even if he never saw her in the tabloids, the longer he gawked, the more likely he was to remember her when they were officially introduced. Everyone, including the president, would know she went spying on the Kingsleys before all the plans were in place. She again attempted to move past with luggage in tow, but Alex jogged around to face her. Lilah halted, hand on the pull-along bag. Strange. She almost wanted him to not leave her alone and go on his way. There was a lightness in her chest... a kind of anticipation.

He had nearly half a foot on her, and she was not exactly short. His dark-brown hair was rumpled and his tie askew, but the dishevelment only added to his attractiveness. Alex Kingsley oozed sex appeal. Eyes darkening with interest he made no effort to conceal, Alex grinned. Her lips curved almost involuntarily in response.

This wouldn't do. "Excuse me," she made herself say, arching an eyebrow at him.

"Will you have a cup of coffee with me?" Alex asked.

Lilah stared. "Do you always approach strange women for coffee dates?"

"Just the beautiful ones. Besides, I figure we should stick together, being Americans and all."

She widened her eyes. "For good old U.S.A.?"

"Sure. Anything for God and country." They laughed. He held out his hand. "Alex Kingsley."

She held hers out, too, wondering why in the world she was prolonging the risky encounter. "Harriet Sheppard," she said. Somehow, her mother and Harry's had found it cute to tag Baby Delilah with a middle name which was the feminine derivative of Harry's moniker. Attacked by a strange fit of mischief, she added, "You can call me Harry."

Leaving reception staff to take her luggage to her room, Alex and Lilah picked up coffee and donuts at the café and went for a stroll in the garden. At the end of the stone pathway was a pool where benches faced the water. There was green growth on the submerged floor, and a step or two appeared to be missing from the ladder leading to the diving board. Still, flowers were growing on either side of the path, spilling over onto the stones in charming disorder, and the sky was blue and bright.

"Who're you with... Petrocorp or Barrons?" Lilah asked, plonking herself onto one of the benches. She noted his look of mild suspicion. "All the local newspapers have been talking about it." Barrons O & G had made a bid for a local company, and some of the shareholders were against it. Negotiations were ongoing.

"Yes. I'm sure it's created some excitement in this place." He took the empty cup of coffee from her hand and tossed it into the trash can along with his own. "Neither, actually."

"So what are you doing at the conference?" Lilah asked, knowing fully well the answer she'd hear.

"I'm here representing one of the interested parties, General Potts. He's our dean from West Point."

"You're a soldier?"

"Veteran," Alex said, sitting next to her. "Now, I work for the family company. We're also in oil... Kingsley Corp."

The report on the soldier had extolled his extraordinary record. As an officer with excellent marksmanship, he went to sniper school for more training and was assigned to lead some kind of unit. The rank, the badges, the family background... there was nary a mention of the electric impact of the man. "What are you doing with the dean in that case?" she asked.

"He owns stock in Petrocorp *and* is a friend of my family," Alex explained. "He doesn't believe they should sell to Barrons. I think they used to know each other or some such. General Potts and Andrew Barrons, I mean. Some bad blood there according to gossip. Not sure exactly what."

"Oh?" Lilah's eyebrows rose almost involuntarily. This was news to her, but she wasn't surprised. Annoying people came naturally to Andrew.

"The general would like to buy it himself but doesn't have the money," continued Alex. "Because of the Kingsley connection with oil, he asked my grandfather if we could argue his case. Grandfather sent all of us—my brothers and I and our cousins. He says win or lose, it will be good experience for us. Our team's doing everything possible to persuade the shareholders to vote against Barrons, but we're not getting anywhere. Barrons and his son are making mincemeat out of us."

Lilah dusted off her hands and swallowed the last piece of the donut. "Why not beat Barrons at his own game?"

"What do you mean?"

Lilah smothered a giggle. If Andrew found out what she was doing... on the other hand, the Kingsleys would know she helped them and would warmly welcome her into the family. She was only helping the plan along. *So there!* "Barrons is offering to buy Petrocorp. Make an offer to the Barrons shareholders to buy their stock, instead."

An arrested expression came over Alex. Later, he offered her his arm as they continued their walk around the grounds, enjoying the sunshine and the warmth. "A bluff," Alex said. "We offer to buy Barrons, setting their plans back until they figure out what's going on. In the meantime, we look for a white knight buyer. Kingsley Corp can perhaps be persuaded to come through."

"I'd call it a ruse, but it's the same principle."

"Harry Sheppard, you're a genius." He missed a step. "I know of someone else with the same name."

Dear Lord. Hoping nothing on her face gave her sudden trepidation away, she mumbled, "Oh?"

"A navy man. They recently awarded him the Medal of Honor. I suppose it's a common enough name."

Double phew. Lilah halted. She'd circled the entire garden with Alex, and they were back at the pool. The reflection in the water startled her. The happy and carefree young woman seemed a memory from months ago. Tendrils of blue-black hair danced about her face, and the smile on her lips was almost joyful. The dashing prince at her side appeared captivated.

Lilah finally freed her hand from the crook of his arm,

regretfully saying, "I have to leave. I'm going to... umm..." She could see the reception desk from where she stood. Other guests were crowded around, looking through brochures. "I'm taking the bus to Ologa Lagoon," she blurted. "To watch the lightning."

Alex raised two fingers, lightly brushing off the powdered sugar at the corner of her mouth. "Are you planning to return here?"

"Just to pick up the luggage. Then, it's back to the States for me." It was stupid to show up at the hotel in the first place, and she simply *had* to make things worse by flirting with Alex. Lilah needed to leave before she ruined everyone's plans. Her return flight was much later, but a trip to the lagoon in the meantime didn't sound half bad. Turning, she found herself stopped by Alex's hand on hers.

"Would you mind company?" he asked. "We could go together to watch the lightning. I'm not due to meet the shareholders again until Monday." With a roll of his eyes, he added, "All of them want to watch *Dallas* tonight, and tomorrow's Saturday."

"*Dallas?*" Lilah laughed. "The TV show? "Who shot J.R.?"

"Yeah," Alex said, grinning. "You're not a fan?"

"Umm... no." There were enough conniving oilmen for her to deal with in real life. "Let's go," she said, throwing caution to the winds.

The road trip was everything the brochure promised with chattering tourists and sandwiches provided by the hotel. Then followed a forty-minute boat ride along the river, winding through tropical forest, laughing at the antics of the capuchin monkeys, and gaping at big-billed toucans. Alex and Lilah howled into the wind with spray blowing onto their faces as the boat raced across the water. It was late afternoon by the time they got to the group of brightly painted corrugated tin houses which sat on stilts on the lake.

The tour guides directed the group to one of the houses, asking them to settle onto the hammocks and on the hard plastic chairs lined along the porch. Alex and Lilah sat facing the lagoon, swinging their hammock back and forth with their feet.

The first notes of an old Spanish song caught her attention. One of the boys from the small fishing village had brought out his guitar and was strumming a tune. A young girl danced around the boy, her fingers snapping and feet tapping to the rhythm. Alex hooked an arm around Lilah as they watched the girl whirl to the tune of long-dead ancestors. When the girl clapped and invited the guests to dance along, Alex jumped up and dragged Lilah with him.

Linking hands, they swayed, gazes on each other. Smoothly, he twirled her into a wrap. Lilah gasped. Her back against his chest, she rocked with him. The tour group applauded.

Music thrummed through her veins. Alex spun her out from his warm embrace. He took her fingers, reckless heat in his touch and enchantment in his eyes. Side-by-side, they strutted forward and backward. The audience clapped in time to the music.

The skirts of her dress flaring to her hips, Lilah whirled once, twice, and she was back in his clasp. He dipped her, his arms holding her close. Whistles and cheers erupted around them.

Lilah gripped his shoulders and threw her head back, laughing in exultation.

"Not too bad," Alex murmured, straightening her. "Did you take lessons?"

"Yes," said Lilah. "Long time ago, though. You?"

"Oh, yeah. My mother sent all three of us to a studio. My brothers stopped after a while, but I continued. Loved every minute of it." Waggling his eyebrows, Alex added, "I was the only male in a class of twenty."

Lilah sputtered. With an answering grin, he gathered her closer. Forehead to forehead, chest to chest, thigh to thigh, they swayed.

From then on, the night was theirs. They danced and laughed together. It seemed as though Alex couldn't help touching Lilah. If his arm wasn't around her, he held her fingers in a light grasp. Or he supported her elbow as she stepped from the hut into the small canoe which took them to the shore. The others in the group smiled indulgently at them.

Over the lake, storm clouds growled. The first jagged bolt of lightning lit the sky. Thunder crashed, making them both jump.

"Come on. It's beginning." He pulled her out to face the water.

They stood a bit apart from the tourist group in the shadows thrown by tall coconut palms. The night sky split under multiple forks of pure white energy. The loud roar of thunder followed.

Alex leaned back against a coconut tree. "It's the wind from the Andes," he explained, voice catching.

"Mmhmm." Her wide eyes never left his as he tugged her closer by her arm. Her heart thumped hard; cheeks heated.

"The warm air from the Caribbean." His hands held her at the hips, lips hovering over the corner of her mouth. His breath mingled with hers.

"Ahh." A tiny flicker of hope came to life within Lilah.

"The winds meet," Alex said huskily, his slightly abrasive jaw grazing the smooth skin of her cheek.

Closing her eyes, she inhaled the woodsy smell of his cologne. "They do?" she whispered, gripping his shirt.

"And lightning strikes," he concluded, sliding an arm around her waist.

Thunder continued to roll. Jagged bolts struck the murky waters of the lake. Nature turned the night into a disco with strobe lights and pulsating music. Kissing her with escalating passion, Alex drew her closer. Lilah savored the feel of his arms, the heat radiating from his body.

Putting a sliver of space between them, he whispered, "Harry, you're beauti—"

Everything blinked out. Terror, unspeakable terror. She couldn't see. "No," she gasped. "No. No," she cried, pushing at the hard chest. She struggled against the arms holding her prisoner. Without warning, the manacles fell away, and she slid, losing her footing.

It was a while before she realized she'd collapsed to her knees. Alex crouched by her side, soothing her with hushed whispers. "Shh. Shh. Are you all right?"

Lilah trembled, inside and out. The continuing electrical storm was triggering nausea. Crossing her arms over her chest, she tried to take deep breaths. Alex was staring in alarm. "I'm sorry," she said, lips quivering.

His brows furrowed at the apology. "You're fine. Didn't intend for it to go this far. I understand."

Lilah nodded jerkily. She wondered wildly what had gone wrong. She'd felt no threat from this man. There was only passion in Alex's embrace, a bone-melting kind of attraction.

"Listen, Harry," he said.

She jumped. Alex called her "Harry." She'd been enjoying it until then. Chin to the chest and eyes closed, she tried to calm herself and in a few seconds, gave him a shaky smile.

Alex said, "I'm going to put an end to this takeover attempt tomorrow. Unfortunately, I have to fly out the week after. Can we meet back in the U.S.?" He groaned. "Damn. I'll probably be working on a plan for General Potts to buy Petrocorp. Then, the vacation at the cabin with the family. You're probably returning to college right away. Maybe on Valentine's Day?"

For someone so enthusiastic, he was quite willing to wait almost three months until their next meeting. Just as well, Lilah told herself. He probably wanted to make sure this thing between them wasn't merely holiday magic, and *she* wasn't supposed to be talking to *any* of the Kingsleys. Crossing her fingers surreptitiously, she hoped Alex wouldn't take offense at the unintended subterfuge. "On Valentine's Day," she agreed.

They traveled back to Merida on a rickety old bus with the rest of the tour group. Alex had to sit with someone else, but whenever she looked up, she found his eyes on her. It was dawn by the time they got close to the hotel, but Lilah was so wired she didn't think she'd be sleeping for days. She'd finally found a partial solution to her ethical dilemma about the planned network.

Her conversation with Alex Kingsley had triggered a thought. If she could come up with an idea to beat a big company like Barrons O & G, would she be able to devise financial strategies for her own outfit? After all, she knew the technical side of the business well, and she already possessed plenty of market savvy. Alex Kingsley as her mate and an executive position in the network as her job. Once Sanders went down, the network... alliance... whatever... would be the king of the ocean, but she could put safeguards in place to make sure it didn't morph into another tyranny.

Feeling more hopeful than she had in months, Lilah glanced at Alex. He was still watching her, with heat in the smile he threw in her direction.

At the hotel, she managed to convince Alex to let her walk to her room on her own, only to spy the Barrons contingent in the lobby. Andrew and her twin were at the elevator, talking with some other men. Lilah hid behind a tall potted plant and peeked through the leaves as she waited for them to leave. When they held the elevator door open and continued talking, she muttered something unladylike. The curse became a muted mutter when Dan waved the rest of them in and stayed outside.

The doors closed, and Dan sauntered in her direction, whistling softly. Lilah tried to make herself invisible. When he stooped to tie his shoelaces next to the plant, she crinkled her nose. *Fussy.*

"You can come out now," his voice came dryly. "They've left."

After calling her guards on the phone to pick her up in Boston, Dan personally escorted her to the airport. Lilah sulked, but he refused to take chances with her safety and threatened her with Temple when she demurred. Sitting in the departure lounge, she admitted, "I wanted to see what they were like, Dan. I hadn't meant to strike up a conversation with Alex or anyone else."

"You lied to your guards and sneaked out. Then, you pretended to be a law student on vacation and introduced yourself to Alex Kingsley—under an alias." Dan shook his head. "Who are you, and what have you done with my sister?"

Lilah laughed. "I just needed... I don't know... to breathe free."

"I understand," he said, voice sympathetic. "But please don't do dangerous shit. And you'd better hope Alex doesn't think you're involved in corporate espionage."

She made a face. "About that... you're going to lose. Big time."

"What?" Dan asked, confused.

"What's Petrocorp to a big company like Barrons O & G, anyway?" She advised, "Think of it as my dowry. It might not even matter in the long run. We're all going to be working together, right?"

"Delilah, you tell me right now what you said to Kingsley," Dan insisted, dark eyes wild.

"Sorry, no time. They're calling the flight." Lilah sprinted away before he could pin her down.

Chapter 22

Two months later, January 1981

Central California

Strobe lights flashed on and off. Music blared from the enormous sound system, and the walls of the room shook. It was only lunchtime, but the club was packed with bodies writhing and gyrating to chartbusters.

"Dude, what are you doing?" Alex hollered over the din. "Don't keep the lady waiting."

Brad, his oldest brother, snagged a booth and continued nursing his drink. He waved a hand in dismissal, indicating his disinterest.

With a mutter, Alex squeezed himself into the seat across. "C'mon, Brad, you're too picky. What the hell is wrong with this one? Cute, smart, and a minister's daughter."

"Would have been the perfect date," Brad agreed, grinning. "If I'd been interested."

"Why not?" asked Alex.

Brad pushed round-rimmed glasses up his nose. "I'm too worried about the situation with the business to think about anything else. You should be, too. God knows what our cousins are up to."

Steven Kingsley was the eldest of said cousins. Brad and Steven had followed Kingsley tradition and attended West Point, but after the mandated service period, both returned to the family business. Their grandfather, Godwin Kingsley, recently announced plans to have Brad eventually take over as CEO. Steven hadn't hidden his unhappiness at the decision and almost threatened Brad at one of the meetings. Then, Brad received a tip Steven was plotting something drastic.

Alex *was* worried, though he didn't often show it. After they got the news, they discussed hiring security for Brad but decided against it. For one, their mother thought the idea of Steven trying to kill his own cousin was ridiculous. For another, the three of them—Brad, Alex, and Victor, the middle Kingsley brother—had been there for each other since they were boys. Not even the best guard on the planet would defend Brad more fiercely than his own siblings. Alex and Victor took turns making sure Brad was never left alone, not even for a moment. But Brad needed to relax, too.

The waitress came by to take their order. Blonde curls bouncing, she smiled at Alex as Brad asked for beer for all of them and some food. When the waitress left, Alex said, "It won't kill you to have some fun, Brad. The minister's daughter looks like just the type to make you forget the business drama." At least for one evening.

Brad was unimpressed. "Forget about it. The kind of woman I want is not going to think of me as second-best."

Alex shifted, feeling uncomfortable. The girl did turn to Brad only after it was clear Alex wasn't interested. With average height and the combination of brown hair and blue eyes inherited from their late father, Brad Kingsley was not a bad looker, and Alex didn't get why—

Brad threw a peanut at him. "Anyway, we came here for food... not to meet women."

"Tell it to him," said Alex, jerking his head toward the dance floor where Victor Kingsley was having the time of his life, grooving to Lipps, Inc.'s "Funkytown" with a group of girls. Despite his size, Victor moved well. He claimed the boxing lessons made him a better dancer. Like Alex and other Kingsley men, Victor also once served in the army. The combination of military background with his training as a chef made Victor highly appealing to the gentler sex. "Yo, Victor," Alex bellowed.

It took a couple of calls for Victor to hear. He held up five fingers and continued dancing.

"He's enjoying himself," said Brad. "A couple of hours of fun won't hurt, I suppose. And *I* do my best unwinding around you two."

True enough. Brad visibly relaxed only when he was in his brothers' company—alone.

"Or do *you* want to talk to Miss Minister?" he asked, eyes twinkling. "Clearly, she was impressed with you."

"She's pretty," Alex remarked. "But not the right girl for me."

Brad laughed out loud. "Not even the right-now girl?"

"No, dude. I didn't get the 'click' with her," said Alex.

"Click?" Victor drew up a chair and combed fingers through his hair, smoothing down the thick mane. Despite the differences in build, most people could tell Brad and Victor were brothers; they both shared the same coloring as their father, Peter Kingsley. Not so Alex, who inherited his features from their mother.

The waitress materialized at their table, bringing more beer and plates piled high with onion rings and Buffalo wings. Chewing on smoky hot chicken, Alex thought back to the dreamy interlude in Venezuela. Harry Sheppard. It was surely an alias. She didn't look like a Harry. Who in the world would have been crazy enough to tag a goddess like her with the name Harry? Alex didn't blame her for being cautious, though. If she showed up on Valentine's Day as planned, he would coax her real name out of her.

Alex prayed fervently she'd show. The hazel eyes, the jet-black hair, the body. Five-foot-eight, he estimated... the perfect height and a figure designed to drive him mad. He couldn't imagine not seeing her again.

Victor and Brad were chugging beer, waiting for his response.

Alex explained, "You know, the click in your mind when you meet someone, and you feel you want to keep her in your life?"

His brothers exchanged glances. Almost at the same second, both burst into laughter, spraying beer all over the food.

"Look what you did," Alex complained.

They howled. Victor fluttered his eyes at Brad, asking, "The 'click,' bro. How can you not know?"

"Of course, the click," Brad said, lips twitching. "Only, I could've sworn he's been hearing the click on a regular basis since he was... seventeen?"

"Something along those lines," Alex admitted sheepishly.

Victor coughed when beer went down the wrong way. The waitress returned to check on them. Alex let his mind drift, leaving his brothers talking to her.

A sudden jolt of pain shot up his leg. "What the hell?" he snapped at Victor. His shin had experienced enough kicks from Victor's giant foot not to recognize it. Victor jerked his head toward their waitress.

With a slight pout, the blonde said, "I was asking if you'd like to come by after dinner. The place is happening at night."

"Ahh," Alex said, rubbing the back of his neck.

At his hesitation, temper sparked in the blonde's eyes, and she turned to Victor. "I saw you on the dance floor. *You* seem to know all the right moves." She scribbled on her notepad and tore off the sheet. "Call me."

Tucking the phone number into his pocket, Victor watched the waitress sashay back to the kitchen. "You're losing your touch, bro," he taunted Alex.

"Ha, you wish," retorted Alex.

Brad interjected, "Let's get back to the cabin. Mother must be wondering what happened to us."

Patrice Kingsley's boys loved her and made sure to include her in their plans, generally. Though she had zero interest in shooting quail, she'd agreed to join her sons on the hunting vacation in Big Sur. But there were times when what the brothers got up to was best not witnessed by their mother. Patrice, being an astute sort, decided to catch up on her reading when her sons raised the idea of lunch at the bar.

When they exited the building, the brightness of the day nearly blinded Alex. The walk back from the town to the Kingsley cabin in the mountains would take a couple of hours. They could've driven to the bar but preferred the scenic route. Something about the mountains and forests called to Alex even though he was city-born and bred.

Sunlight filtered through the green canopy high above them, and wood chips crunched under their boots as they hiked the wide trail. Patches of redwood sorrel lined the path.

"Don't call the girl from the bar," Brad instructed, walking up the dirt road with measured treads. "I don't like it when they play us against each other. Reminds me of *him*."

The "him" needed no further explanation. Peter Kingsley, their late and unlamented father. After his abandonment of their mother, Peter ceased to be father to Alex and his brothers, always referred to as *"him."* Unless they were within their mother's hearing, of course. For reasons known best to herself, Patrice allowed no disrespect of her unfaithful husband. It was especially strange considering the mistress he'd left her for had been a friend of the couple.

Patrice never accused Peter of playing her against his girlfriend, but the slightest hint of infidelity from a partner was enough for Patrice's three sons to be reminded of their father. Especially when a girl tried to pit brother against brother.

"I wasn't going to," Victor said. "Family comes first."

Their mother spent twenty years making sure her boys understood this even if their father didn't. Family first. Always. But she'd taken the three of them and left the Kingsley mansion, choosing to live on the pittance sent by her estranged husband and the tiny amount she made as a typist. She claimed she was trying to avoid Grandfather's attempts to use her sons as weapons to get their father to return. Alex had a feeling a lot of it was plain assumption on his mother's part, given how insecure she must've felt being financially dependent on her disloyal husband's adoptive father. Alex never knew Grandfather to be anything but kind to him and his brothers, but Patrice Kingsley sometimes showed enough pride for a dozen women. She never even asked her own family—the Sheppards, whom she loathed—for help.

Whatever her reasons were, the uncertainty in their world caused the three boys to cling to each other and their mother. Family became the only truth in their lives. This remained the case even after Peter Kingsley's death and the return of his wife and sons to the mansion at Grandfather's request.

Victor continued talking about the waitress from the bar. "Not my type, anyway. I like my women a little more—"

"Needy," Alex supplied.

Victor complained, "I was going to say *substantial*." He sketched a figure in the air.

"Substantially needy," said Brad.

As only brothers could, they traded insults and shoved each other all the way to the rocky waterfall. Crossing the narrow bridge in single file, they started the short, steep climb to the ridge. "I'm glad we did this," Victor shouted over the dull roar of the cascade. "Mother misses having us around."

The view from the top was gorgeous, miles of green valley extending all the way to the blue ocean. Stretching his arms to the heavens, Alex inhaled the air of Big Sur, clean with a touch of moisture. "Yeah, this vacation was a good idea." But hunting season was almost over, and it was nearly time to return to New York. Anticipation filled him at the memory of a certain Miss Sheppard.

As they rounded the dirt path, the cabin came into view. A frog croaked somewhere not too far away, but otherwise, the clearing was silent. Leaves rustled in the trees to their right. A condor rose into the air, its large black wings flapping powerfully, and circled the open space. Shading his eyes from the sunlight, Alex studied the bald vulture.

Something zinged past his ear. A sharp crack sounded. Birds flew into the air, squawking raucously. He barely registered the large form bringing him down as Victor.

Their mother came running out of the lodge, her face white with panic. "Stay inside!" Victor screamed. "Someone's shooting at us!"

They crawled to the cabin, gunfire ringing across the clearing. An electric pain shot across Alex's chest. Grunting, he took a quick look. A large wood chip had torn through his shirt, embedding itself in his skin. The stone next to his ear exploded.

"Keep moving," shouted Victor.

Ribs on fire from pain, Alex continued crawling. Once they were all inside, he crouched and dragged the door shut. Grimacing, he put a hand to his chest. A dark stain had spread across the denim shirt. Motioning his brothers and mother away, he went to the small window and stood by it with his back to the wall, peering outside. As a sniper, he knew where the shooter would be positioned.

Like him, his brothers were covered in reddish-brown dust. Twigs were stuck in their clothes and hair. Brad's glasses were streaked with dirt.

"What's happening?" asked Patrice, eyes wide in alarm. "Who's shooting?"

The window exploded, shattered glass falling to the floor with the shot. They ducked, Victor shielding their mother.

"Stay low," bellowed Alex. "Someone call the cops."

On his hands and knees, Brad scooted to the phone. "Dead." He threw it to the side.

Grabbing his hunting weapon from the cabinet, Alex inched his way to the window. A shadow moved among the trees. His eyes narrowed. Vision tunneled until all he saw was his target. Alex fired.

An angry roar sounded from the trees, followed by a barrage of rounds. Flowerpots shattered outside.

"I got him," Alex snarled. "He's not dead, but I got him."

"Also, he's realized we're armed," offered Victor.

Tracking the movement of every leaf outside, every small animal venturing close to the cabin, Alex muttered, "Hope it's enough to keep him from getting too close."

"How many?" asked Victor.

Alex answered, "Judging from the direction, only one. Who the hell, though?"

"It's Steven. You *know* it's him," Victor ground out. He'd butted heads with their cousin over every trick Steven pulled to undermine Brad in the family business. They'd been warned Steven was up to something. He wanted to run the business and was willing to kill for it.

"Steven's out there, shooting at us?" asked Patrice, rising to her feet to peer out the window. "That's crazy."

"Steven's not crazy," said Victor. "He's a damned criminal. Stay down, Mother!"

"Aahh," she screamed. Red spread across her sleeve the same moment the shooter's weapon roared. She sank to her knees, eyes glazed in pain.

Victor and Brad rushed to her side on their hands and knees.

"Is she okay?" Alex yelled, eyes darting between the forest outside and his wounded mother. "One of you better tell me she's okay."

"It's her arm," said Victor. "Brad, I need something. Gimme your handkerchief." Brad pulled a pristine white square of cloth from his pocket. Victor used it to put pressure on Patrice's arm.

"The bullet?" asked Alex.

"I don't see it," Victor muttered. "Wound looks superficial."

"Thank God," Alex said. The bullet must have nicked the flesh and embedded itself someplace else. The shooter had hit Patrice—a small, skinny woman—from across the clearing, through the window. "It's not Steven," said Alex. "He ain't good enough to make a shot like this."

Victor grunted. "He hired someone. Or it's his buddy." Steven's closest friend was also a sniper like Alex. "The bastard—"

"No," said Patrice. "I refuse to believe it. This is not the Wild West."

"Tell me who else could be trying to kill us," Victor demanded, tone as snappy as he dared make it with her. More than all of them, *he* hated their mother's inclination to give the benefit of the doubt to the cousins.

No one offered a good response. The standoff continued, punctuated by shots in their direction, but every bullet was answered by one from the cabin.

Then, silence. The small clock on the wall ticked away. Minutes stretched into an hour. Tension increased. Nerve endings fraying,

Alex kept his eyes peeled for any movement. Sweat trickled down his back.

"Maybe he left?" asked Brad. "You did get him, right? He's wounded."

Leaves rustled in the bush across the clearing. "No," Alex said. "Still there."

"What's he doing?" asked Victor, edgy and angry.

"Waiting us out," Alex told him. "He can either drive us nuts from the pressure, or we'll simply run out of food."

"We need to get out," said Brad. "But he'll shoot the minute we step outside the door."

"There are four of us," Victor pointed out.

"Can't risk it," said Brad. "Especially not with Mother here." His family didn't disagree.

Alex said, "Hold on until dark. I can take care of him."

They looked at their mother, and she nodded, brown eyes glazed from pain.

Victor and Alex took turns keeping watch until pink twilight faded away into moonless night. The lights in the cabin remained off. Once he was satisfied it was dark enough, Alex groped his way to the weapon cabinet. Handing one of the hunting rifles to Brad, Alex tucked his own gun and suppressor into the holster. Alex and Victor ran, bent double, to the back of the cabin.

The hut was built clinging to the edge of the mountain, with rocky cliff plunging barely two feet from the log wall. The small window overlooking the canyon opened noiselessly. Alex gripped the frame tightly and lowered himself to the narrow ledge. His back plastered to the wall, he groped his way to the far corner of the cabin, trying to ignore the inky blackness right in front of him. The muffled grunts told him Victor was right behind. When he rounded the corner and got to the other side, Alex was drenched in sweat.

The skid of Victor's shoe against loose rock sent stones tumbling down the cliff face. Pulse thundered in Alex's ears. There was a distressed mewl from the cabin, quickly smothered. Victor's low grunt came from the ledge, telling Alex his brother hadn't just tumbled to death. Alex suppressed a sigh of relief.

In the moonless night, he felt rather than saw Victor make his way off the ledge and onto safer ground. They crawled on their hands and knees toward the trees. Once under the cover of the thick foliage, they stood and squeezed their way toward the muted chatter coming from across the clearing. The shooter had company.

A twig cracked under Alex's shoes. He stopped, stifling a curse. Every muscle tightening, Alex and Victor waited to be discovered, but the enemy's jabbering continued. Daring to breathe again, Alex crouched and motioned Victor down. Over the course of a painstaking hour, they moved debris aside with their hands and circled in the direction of the shooter.

A rustle of leaves. The sound of liquid being gulped. Alex halted. He took out his Colt Woodsman semi-automatic and attached the suppressor. The night was pitch black, so he couldn't visually locate the enemy in spite of excellent eyesight, but his hearing was also exceptional. So was his ability to use either arm to shoot, the ambidexterity making him one of the most successful marksmen in the military.

A muffled shot. A high-pitched scream.

"What—" said a voice, and a flashlight turned on. Three figures—two sitting, one on the ground.

Two more shots, both to the head. The upright figures fell. A third shot was aimed at the first downed man, just to be sure.

Gun held ready, Alex approached the bodies. The flashlight was on the ground, casting a yellow glow over the corpses. Blood seeped from the bullet holes in their skulls. One of the assassins had been shot through the eye. Flipping the bodies over, Alex and Victor searched through the clothes. No IDs, of course. Only one was armed.

Victor jogged back to the cabin and brought Brad and Patrice out.

"This is bad," Alex said to Brad. "The bastards had only one gun."

Brad swore. "*We* had three between us. The cops won't buy our story."

"Get rid of the bodies," snapped Patrice, a protective hand on her injury.

"How?" Alex asked.

"I don't know," Brad said, wiping the sweat from his forehead. "The ocean?"

Victor nodded. "Let's get to the boatyard."

A small van was parked along the road leading to the house, presumably belonging to the dead criminals. Alex noted their own truck in front of the cabin, its tires slashed. From the cabin, they took only money, identification, and their hunting equipment. Shooting gloves in place, the Kingsley brothers hauled the corpses into the van. They used clothes stripped from the dead criminals to collect whatever blood and gore they found on the forest floor, storing it all in the vehicle.

Gloved hand on the side of the van, Alex took a couple of deep breaths. He'd killed before. As West Point graduates, Victor and Brad weren't strangers to gunshot deaths, either. Still... seeing the corpses of the criminals... it was somehow different.

"Alex," called Patrice, her eyes on his shirt. He submitted to her inspection, wincing when she pulled out a large shard of wood, its sharp edge coated with bits of clotted blood. She didn't seem at all bothered by the carnage wreaked by her son.

Man! She was their mother. Alex *knew* how hard her life once was, how it taught her to always be practical. Patrice Kingsley did what was needed to protect her brood. Her stout-heartedness should not have surprised him.

Ten minutes later, Victor drove them along the forest roads of Big Sur. Redwoods towered on both sides. The sky was hardly visible. A vehicle honked in the distance, making Alex jump. He watched as the lights moved in a different direction. Midnight passed by the time they got to Highway 1. The rocky shoreline looked ominous in the darkness. Except for the sound of roaring surf, all was silent. As they headed north toward Carmel, Alex kept an eye out for the highway patrol.

They parked close to the private boatyard used by a few of the local families. The doors slamming shut sounded loud in the silence of the night, but there were no guards to hear and no one out on the water. There had never been any need to even lock up the place. Patrice stayed in the back of the truck while her sons jumped out.

"Not the Kingsley boat," she warned.

"This one," said Alex, pointing to a motor launch.

Brad noted the slip number and went in the direction of the boatyard office for the keys. When he returned, Victor and Alex loaded the bodies and the rest of the evidence into the skiff, taking care to wipe the van clean.

"What are we going to do about it?" Brad asked. "The van, I mean."

Alex tucked his gloves into his back pocket, squinting in the night. "Leave it here; it will get impounded in a couple of days."

"Yeah... and we can hide in Monterey 'til we figure out what to do," Brad said. "Mother and I'll start walking; the two of you finish here and catch up."

Alex went back to where Victor was examining the boat. Stripping to their shorts, they stored their clothes and possessions in the Kingsley vessel and returned to the other one. The two crafts appeared to be of the same make. The drain plug was probably in the same spot. Alex swam underwater and unscrewed the plug from below. Feeling his way around the side of the hull, he surfaced as quietly as he could. Clenching his teeth against the wet chill, he said to Victor, "Let's go."

"The tank's almost full, thank God," Victor said, powering up. They drove out from the rocky shore. Alex watched the road until darkness swallowed the forms of his mother and brother. "This is far enough," Victor said fifteen minutes later. "It's already a long way to swim back."

Alex asked, "You think it will keep going all the way out to the sharks?"

"Yeah," Victor said. "Once it runs out of fuel, the pump will stop working. With the drain plug out, it will sink fast. Sharks are going to get to the bodies before the Coast Guard does." Even if the sharks didn't, the boat didn't belong to the Kingsleys, and neither did the van. There was nothing except Steven's word to connect Alex and his brothers with the dead bodies. Steven was not going to tell the police he hired the killers.

Alex slipped into the water, Victor right behind. Victor gasped as the shock of the cold hit him. "Keep moving," Alex said. "Or you're going to cramp."

It was another half hour before they waded onto the beach. They caught up with Brad and Patrice long before they got to Monterey. "Where to?" asked Patrice.

Victor answered, "Downtown. We need food and rest."

Chapter 23

Same night

Upper East Side, New York City

Smiling a little, Temple studied the framed photograph on the damask-covered wall of Godwin's home office. It had been taken in the garden of the Kingsley mansion under a thick-trunked tree. The bouquet in the hands of the bride was huge. There was some kind of net cap on her blonde ringlets with the long veil attached to it trailing several feet behind. The satiny sheen of the long-sleeved gown was evident even in the black-and-white photograph. Amid all the feminine glory, the tuxedoed groom was nearly invisible, but once you spotted him by his bride's side, the devotion in his eyes was unmissable.

A crackle. A sputter. When Temple turned, Godwin was replacing the cast-iron screen in front of the fireplace along the opposite wall.

"This is something I'll never understand about you," said the Kingsley patriarch. "Your mother abandoned you to marry my father. How can you possibly not resent it?"

Temple shrugged. "She was who she was. And she didn't really abandon me. I was already living with my father."

"She abandoned you," Godwin insisted, settling into the leather chair behind the large carved desk. "Before you were even a year old."

Temple strolled to the chair on the other side and sat, glancing quickly at the windows. The blue velvet blinds were drawn, not letting winter sun in. The Secret Service would've secured the premises; there would be no one walking by who could overhear the conversation in the room, but Temple couldn't help but check. They might be discussing family history now, but eventually, they'd get to the point of this meeting.

"Perhaps it's the reason we get along," Godwin mused. "We were both blessed with... how shall I put it... unusual mothers." Godwin's mother—his father's first wife—was committed to a mental asylum a few weeks after his birth.

"My mother's attitudes were shaped by the life she lived." Temple never met her family, but he knew she was a fisherman's daughter from Maine who wanted to be an actress. She had the looks for it. Temple Senior was quite blunt with his son about the arrangement his parents made. He helped her get parts, and she... well... the good people of New Jersey didn't care their senator was shacking up with a movie star. When she eventually became pregnant, Temple Senior was very firm he wanted his child. His mistress was equally firm she didn't want one. They made another deal. She delivered the baby and walked out a completely free woman. A couple of years later, she was at the top of her game and met Godwin's father.

The first Mrs. Kingsley was already in the asylum by then. On account of his wife's insanity, the courts granted Godwin's father a quick divorce, and he married Temple's mother. Not long afterward, the first Mrs. Kingsley died in her sleep at the mental hospital.

"My mother had no reason to inform my father about any of it," Temple continued. "Their agreement was no contact unless she wished it." Her son never realized she got married until she invited him to his half-brother's tenth birthday party. Temple was thirteen at the time. Maybe fourteen. Same age as Godwin. "Honestly, I have no idea why she remembered to invite me to the party that particular year." Actually, Temple did know, but it wasn't something he cared to discuss with Godwin. Who could tell how the Kingsley patriarch would react? Hell, when Temple initially heard the story of his mother's first encounter with Godwin's father, he was disgusted at what he saw as her conniving nature. Still... she'd given birth to him, so he supposed he owed it to her to keep her secrets to some extent.

It took Temple a few years to understand either of his parents.

"Until then, I didn't have a clue you even existed." Godwin brooded. "She never mentioned you. How can you not feel bitter about a woman like her?"

"Would you get angry with a fish because it can't fly? She had a native cunning, to be sure. But she wasn't very clever or capable of deep feeling." Another lie, but once again, this was something Temple wasn't about to share with Godwin. "You can only expect much from people who've been *given* much."

"Like Lilah."

With a small laugh, Temple agreed, "Like Lilah. And like *you.*"

In fact, Godwin gave a lot more than he received. He never married and produced no children but ended up being responsible for the sons spawned by the half-brother before his death from alcoholism. The first two—David and Peter—with his wife and a third—Aaron—with his secretary. The three boys revered Godwin. There were problems with Peter when he decided to leave his wife, Patrice, and their sons, but until the day Peter died, he never lost touch with Godwin. The rest of the Kingsleys still worked for the company.

"You're in a generous mood," Godwin commented. "Things must be looking up for America."

"Not yet." Unemployment and inflation were at historic highs. The minute Temple put out one fire, a few hundred others flamed into life. The ayatollah in Iran and Saddam Hussein in Iraq were only the latest in a long line of problem children. Oil prices shot up in the wake of the war between the two neighbors, drawing the U.S. and the rest of the West into the mess. "A lot of work remains to be done, but there's light at the end of the tunnel."

"You honestly believe you'll fix all the problems in the four to eight years you have?"

"I'd have to be a fool to think it. What I *can* do is set the wheels in motion. Our network will go a long way. Which brings us to our plans. We won't be able to delay things much longer. Both Barrons and Ryan Sheppard are asking questions."

Godwin leaned back in his chair. "I'm more concerned about Lilah's behavior. You thought she'd fall in line."

"She did." The moment Temple heard about her agreement, a heavy weight lifted off his shoulders.

"Yes. But you told me she's already making noises about the alliance becoming a cartel. If it bothers her now, how can we trust her with the keys to the kingdom? Also, what about Harry? They're still friendly." Photographs of the duo at the state dinner made the papers.

The former SEAL was unlikely to vanish quietly from Lilah's life, especially not when he wanted to personally see to it the business alliance succeeded. "They've known each other a long time," Temple said.

"I hope it doesn't turn out to be a problem."

"I wouldn't worry," Temple soothed. "Lilah has too much pride to cheat with a man who threw her over... and ethics." No, infidelity was the least of their fears. Yet... something about it... Temple couldn't help feeling uneasy.

"I'm warning you," said Godwin. "The Kingsley family won't allow it. Also, Harry's a wild card. Sanders discovered the fact the hard way. We already know it. The young man refused a request from the president-elect of the United States. All the tricks you needed to pull to get him into line... Harry is a double-edged sword, Temple. Let me ask again. Why are we still keeping him around?"

"He's useful," Temple insisted. "Also, Ryan Sheppard's main motivation behind agreeing to the plan was his son's safety. If there's no Harry, we'll need to cook up some other reason for his family to cooperate."

"A legitimate concern," Godwin acknowledged.

"Let's focus on our more immediate problem. As I said... Andrew is beginning to get suspicious about the delay."

"Can't be helped. This is the only way to make it work. My grandsons won't disobey my orders, but there's Patrice. Her boys wouldn't dream of going against her wishes even to please me, and we need to first make sure *she* has a reason to cooperate."

"We should've simply let the boys meet Lilah. Afterward, there would've been nothing their mother could do."

"Trust me," Godwin said. "None of them will be meeting any girl their mother doesn't approve of... not with an engagement ring in hand."

"Wait and watch."

"Temple..." Godwin huffed. "I'm sure Lilah is beautiful, but frankly, the way you sometimes go on about her is worrying me. As though she's some kind of mythical creature, able to lure men from the bonds of kinship."

With a grin, Temple said, "She wouldn't have the first idea how to. Lilah is not at her best with people on a personal level. What I meant is your grandsons are young. It's going to take them some time to see past her appearance. Even then, she's not going to lure any of them from your influence."

"She won't." Godwin's tone was even, but there was a stern note to it. "Unless Patrice objects, they will all do as I ask."

"We need them to. Lilah's just turned twenty-four, and your oldest grandson is what? Twenty-nine? Long way to go before they can be left in charge. But she *is* intelligent." Temple scooted deeper into his chair. "Forget her appearance. If we could harness all her intellectual firepower and avoid some of the utopian ideas..."

"I know," said the former justice, tone wry. "You've told me a dozen times. MIT, Harvard Law, chess champion... smart *and* ambitious... the fact has been worrying me more."

"Why, for God's sake?" Godwin was acknowledged as one of the nation's foremost intellectuals, but the younger generation of Kingsleys could certainly use an injection of gray matter into their midst.

"*You* should be worrying, too. About her *and* about Harry. Temple, the best time to deal with a problem is before it becomes one. Twenty years from now, we don't need to be sitting in the same chairs, plotting an alliance against Harry Sheppard instead of Jared Sanders."

Temple laughed. "Neither of us is likely to be above ground twenty years from now. Even if we beat the odds to fight Harry in the future, it would be just another day in the life of the Kingsleys." They were American aristocracy with a penchant for hating virulently, loving unwisely, and plotting incessantly. Like this latest skirmish between cousins, all with their fond grandfather holding the puppet strings.

Chapter 24

Same night

Back in California

The sun was coming up over the streets of Monterey when Alex and his brothers got to the city. A homeless man slept under the awning of a pawn shop, reeking of cheap gin and urine. Even the other street dwellers gave him a wide berth as they, too, took shelter on the sidewalk. Two or three buildings down, raucous laughter echoed faintly from within the walls. As Alex escorted his mother past a seedy-looking bar, a man stumbled out of a doorway at the top of a short flight of steps, helped along by the huge bouncer who followed him. The drunk screamed when the bouncer wrenched his arm backward and flung him to the sidewalk.

Before the bulked-up guard stalked back in, he stopped by a young woman standing next to the open doorway. *"No dejes que entren más gorrones."*

Alex spoke fluent Spanish. The bouncer had just told the girl not to let any more freeloaders in.

Waiting until the man disappeared inside, she walked down the steps, calling to someone in the building. "Take him to the free clinic in the city. Talk to Father Dominic."

She stopped next to the injured fellow and gently kicked his hip with a foot. *"Idiota,"* she muttered, turning back.

Alex and Victor approached the young woman. Before Alex could speak up, Victor said in English, "Excuse me, Miss."

She craned her neck. Alex smiled as she gawked at Victor, the tallest of the three.

"Yes?" she said cautiously.

The injured drunk on the street chose that moment to curse loudly and throw something at her. She hopped awkwardly, trying to avoid the stone, and fell, twisting her ankle. The drunk cackled.

Victor spat out his opinion of the drunk before crouching next to her. "Should I get someone?"

She clutched her ankle. "No, no. I'll be all right."

"Let me look," Victor insisted, gently taking her ankle in his hands until her foot rested on his knee. He removed the shoe and checked her injury, probing for tender spots.

"Hilda!" the bouncer bellowed from the doorway.

She scrambled up and would've fallen had it not been for

Victor's steadying hands on her elbows.

The guard came running down the steps.

Hilda muttered, "He was just helping me, Rafael. I think I twisted my ankle."

The man turned to Victor and barked, *"¿Quién eres?"*

Victor let go of her elbows and shook his head, signaling incomprehension. Alex stayed silent. His knowledge of the language often let him extract info unintended for his ears.

"Who are you?" Rafael repeated.

Victor explained, "I was trying to get directions to the closest motel."

Rafael gave the group a narrow-eyed glare, eyes pausing on Patrice's bloodied shoulder. "You can rent rooms above my bar... just don't do anything to bring cops here."

So Rafael was no hired thug. He owned the place. Patrice joined them and nodded wearily at her sons.

They weren't planning to show IDs, but the only demand was for cold, hard cash, which they handed over. As soon as they were shown to their rooms, Brad muttered, "Let me find a telephone booth and call Grandfather."

"No," said Patrice. "Contact Mr. Temple." At Brad's questioning look, she said, "Steven is also Godwin's grandson. Let the president talk to your grandfather. It will be better."

Brad and Victor soon left in search of a phone booth. It took them thirty minutes to return. "We're to stay hidden for now," Brad reported. "As long as Steven thinks we're dead, no one's going to attack us again. Mr. Temple will do some digging on what our cousins have been up to. I'm supposed to call back in three days for further instructions."

They rented large double rooms with connecting doors. Bathrooms were at the end of the hallway. Fortunately, there were no other residents, and the Kingsleys had relative privacy.

In a couple of days, Patrice was going through the newspaper for any report of the missing Kingsleys, when there was a soft knock at the door. "Must be Hilda," Patrice said. She almost never went out, citing pain from the gunshot wound to her arm as reason, but the injury was superficial and already healing. It seemed to Alex she was content to stay hidden from the world. Whenever she asked for food from the bar, Hilda brought it up.

Alex stayed in the chair, legs stretched in front of him. "Come in," he called.

Keeping his eyes closed, Alex listened absently to the women talking. Victor's booming voice echoed from the room next door, interrupting the conversation.

Patrice said apologetically, "Victor is louder than he realizes. Alex, ask your brother to be more considerate of our hosts."

"Oh, no," Hilda said in a surprised tone. "His voice is unique."

Through half-closed lids, Alex considered Hilda with new interest.

"Yes." Hilda warmed to her theme. "Unique, like his eyes! The lovely blue with little silver flecks!"

Alex bit his cheek, trying to stop from laughing. He wished he could tape this. How close did Hilda get to Victor's "lovely blue" eyes to see the "silver flecks"?

"He does have beautiful eyes, doesn't he?" mused Patrice. She studied Hilda keenly as the door between the rooms opened, and the object of their discussion ambled in.

From his seat, Alex plucked an apple off the tray on the table. As he bit into it, savoring its juicy sweetness, he noted the flush on

Victor's cheeks at the sight of Hilda. Suddenly, the memory of another dark-haired girl rushed in. Alex *had* to show up for their rendezvous. If he didn't make it, he'd have to somehow track her down.

The next morning, Brad called Mr. Temple as instructed. Alex squeezed into the phone booth and ignoring Brad's admonishing frown, tugged at the receiver so they could both hear what the president had to say. Temple was quite blunt. "If you return to New York and accuse your own cousins of attempted murder, it will cause any number of problems for the company. Moreover, there will be questions about what happened to the hired killers. You need to stay hidden while we find a permanent solution to this issue. The stock market will take a dive because of your disappearance, but it can't be helped. I'll talk to Godwin and make certain everyone maintains public silence on your status."

"Do we continue in Monterey?" asked Brad. "In the bar?"

"A safe house is a possibility, but official involvement will be politically risky given the deaths of the assassins. You should be all right on your own for now since Steven thinks you're dead. Try to put some distance between you and the area, though. It's too close to your family's hunting cabin. Keep me updated on your whereabouts. I'm working on a plan. And Brad? Contact no one, not Aaron, not even Godwin. I don't want Steven somehow finding out what happened."

Even with Temple's reassurance the three brothers were safe enough, Patrice was unhappy about the idea of remaining in hiding. Alex soothed her with the reminder they would at least move to a different city. Making arrangements to travel in secrecy took longer than they thought, and they were forced to stay at Rafael's establishment a few more days. One of the waiters at the bar, sworn to silence with a wad of cash, promised to get fake IDs for the Kingsleys.

The same night, Alex watched Victor sauntering up the steps, his arm wrapped around Hilda's waist. Since Rafael didn't waste money on things like hall lights, the landing was lit only by the rays of the moon filtering in through a dusty window. At the top of the stairs, Victor's giant shadow engulfed Hilda's shorter one.

Thumb and finger in his mouth, Alex whistled. "Dude, get in here," he snapped.

In low tones, Victor murmured something to his companion. Hilda pulled his head down to hers for a few moments before scampering away, laughing softly.

Victor entered, warily eyeing his brothers. "What?" he asked, tossing his suede blazer over a chair.

"Are you crazy?" Alex asked through clenched teeth. "Going on a date with Hilda?"

"Nothing wrong in it," Victor said, gaze skittering. "She's nice."

Brad stood from his chair, holding a hand up to silence Alex. "I'm sure she is, Victor. Does she know who you are? Who we are?"

"Of course not," Victor said.

Brad let out a breath. "Good. I won't tell you what to do, but you need to remember... one wrong move, and we'll end up losing Kingsley Corp."

"Bro, I swear—" Victor huffed. "Hilda has no idea who we are, but once we sort this out, I'd like to take her away from this place."

"Are you serious?" Brad asked.

"Dunno," Victor said. "But she's sweet. Her brother is a bully and a criminal."

Alex and Brad exchanged glances. As usual, Victor lost his heart to a woman in need of rescuing, but his romance was likely to put the rest of them in trouble. "Dude, family comes first," snarled Alex.

From the connecting door, Patrice said, "As long as you remember what's at stake, Victor, your love life is your own business."

Alex grimaced. They'd thought Patrice was asleep.

Brad wiped his forehead with a hand. "Victor, all we're saying is we're your family."

"I won't do anything stupid, I swear," Victor said.

The next evening, Rafael accompanied Hilda as she carried in Patrice's dinner tray. From the other room, the brothers kept an eye on their mother.

In rapid-fire Spanish, Rafael spoke to Hilda, clearly believing his guests couldn't understand him. Under their current circumstances, the Kingsleys considered Alex's fluency in the language added security and took care not to give it away.

Rafael said, "It's them. Three men and their mother. You just help me confirm their identity, and I can make a call to their cousin. My man in New York says this cousin wants them dead. It's why they are hiding. There may be money in it for me."

Eyes on the table, Hilda muttered back in the same tongue, "This is wrong, Rafael. I won't help you in it."

"You, my dear sister, are going to do what you're told." Rafael nodded at Patrice and departed.

When Hilda left, Alex sat up.

Half an hour later, Victor helped them pack, his face pale and fingers trembling.

"She didn't want him to do it," Alex consoled Victor, sorting out the fake IDs he'd procured.

"Doesn't matter," Victor said between clenched teeth. "She knew who we were. She could've warned us. You were right; I was an idiot."

An hour later, when the maid came to collect the trays, a piece of paper fell on the floor. Alex picked it up, read it, and handed it to Victor. He scanned the note and passed it to Patrice, Brad reading it over her shoulder.

"A trap?" asked Brad. "Maybe Hilda sent this message to... I don't know..."

Patrice shook her head. "I don't believe it's a trap. Why go to so much trouble with an invitation to the movies? It's a public place. Rafael won't find it easy to attack, which is likely one reason she chose it. Also, her brother won't be able to hear what she says to Victor. Let's give her a chance to explain."

When Victor departed, the rest of them anticipated he'd be away at least a couple of hours. Less than thirty minutes later, Alex opened the door to an urgent knock. Victor entered with Hilda behind him, her breath coming in loud wheezes. Flushed and sweating, Victor faced his mother and brothers. "Rafael's dead," he gasped. "Broken neck. I had to. He cornered us in the parking lot with a knife."

"Oh, God," whimpered Patrice.

"I put his body in his truck," Victor said.

Victor and Alex drove the Chevy pickup with Rafael's corpse inside to San Lorenzo Creek. After carefully wiping down the vehicle, they left it under the highway and returned to Monterey on the Greyhound.

"Damned criminal," Victor muttered on the ride back. "Right?"

Alex merely nodded in silence, knowing exactly how his brother felt.

Hilda was waiting in their rooms. Sadly, she murmured, "I know he was a bad man, but he was my *brother*."

According to her, the employees at the bar were used to Rafael taking frequent trips, leaving no word with anyone. So they'd ask no questions and continue working with their usual diligence, having learned from painful experience he'd demand an accounting of every minute when he returned.

Leaving the bar the same night was impossible. "We need to stay here and talk to the police when they show up," said Patrice. "Otherwise, it's going to look suspicious."

The next few days were nerve-racking. Each knock on the door seemed amplified a thousand times, and each siren on the road was surely meant for the Kingsleys. One week passed before a couple of officers came to announce Rafael's death to his sister. Thankfully, the cops never asked to talk to the staff or the renters. Lifespans of career criminals tended to be short, and the authorities seemed inclined to pin the death on one or more of Rafael's associates.

Watching from the window as the officers' car disappeared down the street, Brad asked, "Where do we go now?"

"Nowhere," said Patrice. "A few more weeks in this town... I don't want to risk any of the staff putting two and two together."

"Good," said Victor. "Hilda's all alone because of me. I can't simply leave her here by herself this soon."

"No family?" Alex asked, leaning against the wall of their room.

"Only a cousin in San Diego," said Victor.

"She can't go with us." Patrice's voice was sympathetic. "There will be too many questions."

"What are we going to tell the president?" Alex asked.

"The truth," Brad said, eyes tired. "He's not going to worry much about one less criminal in the United States."

"Yes," mused Patrice, "but I'm afraid he's going to ask us to stay put here until the police close the case... less risk of anyone connecting us to the death."

Temple's tone made it clear he wasn't happy, and he said exactly what Patrice predicted. The group would remain in Monterey. Temple also assured them he and the Kingsley patriarch would continue to work on a plan to put an end to the family squabbles. The president warned it would take a few weeks... maybe months... legal hurdles, complicated business finances, and such. Perhaps the hiding might last longer than the police investigation into Rafael's death. Temple was kind enough to send a message to Patrice, asking her to hold on. After all, the risk to her boys' lives was minimal as long as Steven didn't get the bright idea of investigating what actually happened to his intended victims.

She was visibly agitated at the possibility of a more extended delay than she imagined, but their best option was to go along with whatever Temple wanted and not risk losing his support. It could turn out to be crucial in an eventual corporate battle.

Valentine's Day came and went. Alex watched the partly visible moon from his window and dreamed about the goddess from Venezuela. *Harry Sheppard.* Alex laughed to himself. He refused to call her by the ridiculous name. Not unless he saw it on her birth certificate.

Had she waited at the planetarium as they planned? He dragged a hand through his hair, wondering what she'd thought when he didn't show. He'd have some groveling to do when he tracked her down. Hopefully, she'd accept "hiding from assassins" as a credible excuse.

Three months passed. Every day of those months, Brad and Patrice scoured the papers for news on Kingsley Corp. There was enough speculation on the disappearance of the Kingsley brothers and their mother, but the company made no announcements. Each time they contacted Mr. Temple, with each reminder he sent to their mother they were safe, the lines of strain on Patrice's face only got deeper and deeper. In fact, the president's reassurances of their safety only seemed to remind her exactly how unsafe they were. It reached the point she wouldn't let any of her sons step out of the bar unless they all agreed to go as a group. Victor sneaked out to Hilda's room every night and remained there until dawn.

In May 1981, the cops closed the file on Rafael's death, attributing it to a drug deal gone wrong. Patrice and her sons could finally leave Monterey without suspicion falling on them. Serendipitously, Temple said it was time to talk in person. The evening before the Kingsleys were supposed to drive to San Diego to meet the president, Victor approached Alex. Under cover of the shadows at the back of the bar, they watched Hilda greet patrons and supervise employees. *Her* employees now.

"She's got a flair for it," Alex remarked.

"Yeah," said Victor. He rubbed the back of his neck. "Alex, are you sure we can't take her with us?"

Alex was annoyed. "Dude, I get it. You like her. You ain't gonna stay here, and if she leaves with you, don't you think people will start digging around? She links us to everything in Monterey."

"There's no proof just like with the thugs who shot at us," argued Victor. "Also, Mr. Temple will help."

Alex said, "Same as with the thugs at the cabin, the minute we're *publicly* accused of Rafael's murder, both Kingsley Corp and the president will drop us like hot potatoes. Brad will never get to be CEO. He'll be fired before we sort things out. Are you going to risk his future for a girl you met only a few weeks ago? Family comes first, Victor."

"Right," said Victor, gulping down whiskey. "Hilda's pregnant."

Watching Victor break the news to their mother, Brad and Alex stayed quiet. Neither even dared breathe. Patrice Kingsley never raised her voice, but the flush on her face betrayed the difficulty she had maintaining composure. Sitting straight-backed in the chair, she asked, "A child? When you have no home, no money, not even an identity?"

Almost cowering, Victor stayed mute.

"How do you propose to take care of the baby? Or do you intend not to go through with it?"

"We want the child," Victor said.

There was silence for a few seconds as his words sank in. Patrice stood. "Was this a planned pregnancy?" she asked, eyes wide in shock.

"Hilda would've been alone," Victor muttered by way of explanation.

Fingers raking his hair, Alex bit back a curse. At his side, Brad groaned, hand to his forehead. A mewl at the door caught their attention. Her dark gaze anxious, Hilda waited for the Kingsley family's response to her news.

Patrice surveyed the young woman top to toe, eyes halting for a few seconds at her midriff. Letting out a breath, Patrice asked, "Are you feeling well?"

Alex didn't get how Victor could've been so irresponsible. He was lucky their mother didn't pound him to pulp. In the end, she asked Hilda to stay in Monterey while the Kingsleys straightened things out with their business.

The next afternoon, Hilda saw them off. She stood with Victor at the bottom of the stoop while Alex loaded necessities into the back of the old pickup truck he secured. Brad and Patrice settled into the cargo area.

Hilda told them, "My cousin in San Diego will be happy to help you for some money. If he knows you killed Rafael, he may help even without payment. Rafael was always trying to get Cousin

Eduardo's son into the drug business."

"Are you sure you can get your family to help when the baby comes?" Victor asked. She nodded, eyes brimming with tears, and he added, "I'll send word. I promise—once we've figured this out. If there's an emergency, you can contact our Uncle Aaron. Be careful you don't run into our cousins or their father. Call me once you've seen the doctor."

Her face tightened, but Patrice managed to nod pleasantly at Hilda. "My first grandchild," Patrice murmured, her voice slightly dreamy. She even managed a smile when Victor kissed Hilda in full view of the people on the street.

The jagged cliff reached toward bright-blue sky as they sped south along Highway 1. Below them, the crashing surf of the Pacific battered the rocky shore. Long hours of driving took them to the impoverished streets of southeast San Diego. Parking in the crowded lot, the Kingsleys got out to stretch their legs.

The buildings were mostly low and painted in garish colors. Several featured metal sheets for roofs. Some of the older structures had peeling white paint and the red-tiled roofs usually seen in the better parts of the city. Graffiti decorated the large billboard poster of Che Guevara proclaiming revolution was at hand.

Brad and Victor returned from the phone call to the president. "I've let Mr. Temple know we're here," said Brad.

A couple of blocks down, they stood outside a blue two-story building tucked between a nail salon and an electronics shop promising unbeatable prices. Across the street was a small restaurant. The smell of spiced meat and warm tamales wafted out. Victor sniffed appreciatively while Brad knocked on the door of the blue-painted building. A young boy of about eleven or twelve answered.

"Pardon us, we're looking for Eduardo Garcia," said Patrice.

The boy called out in Spanish, "Papa! They're here. Aunt Hilda's friends."

A man with mild gray in his temples came to the door. *"Señor Víctor?"* Victor, who had been surveying the goings-on in the street, turned to smile at him. *"You're* the *cabrón* who knocked up Cousin Hilda."

Alex snorted while Victor flushed. Eduardo Garcia's sneer made it clear he'd just called Victor a dumbass.

Three days later, a beige sedan parked in front of the building. The occupants stepped out and stood for a second, studying the neighborhood. Brad had been expecting them, and he quickly opened the door. As they entered, Eduardo Garcia and his wife, Carmen, stared open-mouthed at the man they'd seen only on television.

Salt and pepper hair, blue eyes, square jaw, average height. Charmingly polite, President Temple accepted Carmen's offer of homemade lemonade with bits of sour pulp.

Waving the security detail aside, he asked the Garcias for use of their living room. On either side of the door, Alex and Victor leaned against the walls, while their mother and Brad sat talking to the president.

With Eduardo out of view, Temple didn't waste time on niceties. "I have to return before my unexpected detour is noticed by the press. Let's talk quickly."

"What do you recommend we do?" asked Patrice.

"New York City," he said. "I want you to meet the Barronses. Andrew Barrons, specifically."

Behind Patrice, Alex shifted uneasily, and the president noted it. "I wouldn't worry, Alex. Andrew particularly admires your technique in persuading the Venezuelan company to vote against Barrons O & G. He wants you on his side."

Patrice looked puzzled. "Why would Barrons help us?"

Temple drummed his fingers on the armrests. "Patrice, have you heard of Jared Sanders?"

"Of course," she said. Anyone with connections to the oil and gas industry knew who Sanders was. The owner of the biggest, most powerful of oil companies, he ruled the sector with an iron fist.

The president said, "Sanders is a problem for the rest of us—in fact, for the rest of the world—but he crushes every rebellion before it's conceived. Godwin and Andrew Barrons were working on a plan to join forces when *this* happened. Pity Steven's such a... no matter now. It set us back some, but the delay may work in our favor. We can claim you've been drafting a strategy to divide assets with Kingsley Corp. *And* with Barrons on your side, Steven won't dare attempt any more tricks."

"We have no family backing or money now," said Patrice. "If Andrew Barrons wants an alliance with the Kingsleys, why would he choose us instead of Steven?"

Temple responded, "Steven doesn't need the Barronses. You do—which would make this marriage mutually beneficial."

It was Victor who broke the surprised silence. "Marriage?"

Part VIII

Chapter 25

A couple of weeks later, June 1981

New Castle, New York

Summer night rains had left the hills of Empire State carpeted by lush green grass and nearly every flower known to man. A cobwebby mist hung over the sleepy morning as Harry's motorcycle roared down the tarred roads of the wealthy town.

All the houses in this area were stately homes, surrounded by well-tended grounds. At the end of this stretch of road lay his destination—the Barrons mansion, its entrance marked by sculpted iron gates between limestone pillars topped by marble statues. The Harley idled as the armed guard confirmed Harry's identity. Then, the bike entered the pea-gravel driveway bordered by tall oaks and maples. As it rounded a curve, the majestic manor came into view.

Harry got to the steps leading to the front door and executed a tight turn with flourish. The Harley was only a few years old, and the black chrome was still shiny, the black leather unscratched. It rode like a dream. Kicking the bike to park, he took his helmet off and placed it on the handlebars before swinging his leg out. The nip in the air had dissipated with the rising sun. He shrugged off the black leather jacket and flung it onto the backrest before sketching a salute at the Barrons chauffeur who was waiting by the door. Leaving the meticulous old mechanic to park the bike, Harry jogged in.

"Harry!" Andrew Barrons stood to welcome his guest into the study.

There was planning to do for the upcoming corporate event where important guests were expected. Daniel and Shawn walked in and out of the room as Harry worked with Andrew, going over every detail. Even Caroline, Andrew's wife, passed through a time or two. No Lilah, though. From the family's conversation, Harry knew she was in the house.

Within the well-protected home, she could roam around *sans* her guards. Lilah was completely safe, but Harry couldn't help feeling uneasy. Something had changed since the disastrous state dinner the year before. Months went by with lawyers from the three companies hammering out details of the alliance. He met Lilah many times for many things—review of potential business opportunities, joint sessions at the gym. Harry fully expected more of the same anger she showed at the dinner. Strangely, her fury was replaced by a contained excitement he didn't understand. There was anxiety on her face when she heard about the attempted assassination on Patrice Kingsley's sons. President Temple informed only a few key people of the fact, Lilah and Harry included. The Kingsley patriarch then asked for even more time to solve the complication before they wrapped up paperwork on the alliance.

Temple finally called with the news the Kingsleys were ready to move ahead with the plan, but some modifications were needed. They would soon arrive at the Barrons mansion. Lilah should've been with the rest of the Barronses and Harry, doing last-minute checks on the agreement, but she didn't show.

When Lilah didn't turn up for dinner, either, Harry made his excuses and went for a walk around the estate, the crickets in the shrubbery chirping in rhythm with his footsteps. He knew her favorite spot—the small stone fountain with a conch spouting water and blue lotus plants floating in the basin. She sat on the bench next to the structure, lost in thought. Her fire-engine-red crop top and light denim shorts stood out against the darkness of the night. Taking a deep breath, he inhaled the scent that was uniquely hers.

"I hope you're not getting cold feet," he said.

She looked up. "Just trying to think some things through. This alliance... network... whatever... will take longer to work than we expected."

Harry inclined his head. "Yes, but it can't be helped. If we insisted on keeping Kingsley Corp intact, we would've first needed to deal with the problems in the family. I agree with Temple it's best the two sides split up."

"If the idea is to get Sanders out during Mr. Temple's presidency, I would've thought he'd put pressure on the Kingsleys to work together. As things stand, we'd first need to build up the new business to reasonable financial strength before going against Sanders."

"But the partnership will still cover the entire sector," Harry argued. "And we should be able to get big enough for our purpose in a couple of years while Temple's still in the White House."

"Risk of failure goes up with each delay, Harry. You should know it."

"No matter what Temple said to the Kingsleys, the losing side could have seen *you* as a threat." The family patriarch had already announced Brad Kingsley would be the eventual CEO, and after what Steven did, he was completely ruled out as a potential groom for Lilah. The moment the Barrons heiress walked into the family as a bride, joining her clout to her husband's, she would be seen by the wannabe murderer as an obstacle to be removed. "A division is the safest approach."

"I suppose." Lilah shrugged restlessly. Veering from the topic, she asked, "Did Andrew tell you I asked for the CFO position?"

"Yes," said Harry. "Having a formal title is a good idea."

"There's the pre-nup, of course." Lilah hadn't met her future husband yet, but the marriage they planned would definitely involve an iron-clad contract. In a firm tone, she added, "But if we're going to form a cartel, I want actual say over things. Neither of them objected. Not Mr. Temple, not Andrew."

After a second, Harry asked, "Is it a problem?"

"Don't you think it's odd? I barely have any experience."

Harry laughed. "Are you the same fifteen-year-old girl who said she'd manage fine without Barrons and his help? When did you lose your mojo?"

Lilah ignored his needling. "I can live with the idea of marrying one of the Kingsleys." She smiled, a faraway look in her eyes. "I'm positive I'll do a good job as CFO, but I was expecting to have to fight for it. We're talking about the president of the United States trusting a twenty-four-year-old woman with the finances of an organization intended to be bigger than OPEC. Not to mention Andrew Barrons."

"Andrew offered you a job in his company before you even graduated college, and you interned with Temple," Harry reminded her. "They both understand your capabilities. Plus, you'll have shares in all three companies."

"Shares or not, Temple means for me to be the nominal head," she said. "Nothing else. So why isn't he bothered I asked for an executive position? He must have some sort of a plan to keep control of the network regardless of the title I hold, or he wouldn't have agreed."

"Probably," Harry admitted. "But you forget. Gateway's going to be a part of the network."

An eyebrow raised, she asked, "So?"

"The Sheppards won't let Temple sideline you."

She didn't answer, staring at him in pregnant silence.

Harry huffed. "C'mon, Lilah. I know my family hasn't always

done well by you, but do you honestly believe—" He stopped short at the derision in her eyes. "I'm going to be Gateway's liaison in the alliance, and I will make sure we always back you up." No one else in the family seemed too keen on working with the woman who once saved their skins. "Trust me," Harry pleaded. "I've never lied to you."

"True," she said. "With *me*, you've always been brutally honest." Laughing lightly, she turned back to the fountain. "Anyway, there are more immediate things for me to worry about. I'm going to meet my husband-to-be for the first time. Officially, I mean." She drew a knee up and rested her heel on the edge of the bench. "I'm glad Alex is fine. When I heard he and his brothers had disappeared... thank God they called Mr. Temple, or we might have been making other plans."

Harry shot her a sharp look. "*Alex*? Brad's going to be CEO. Didn't you hear Temple?"

"All I need is an *entrée* into the family, so let me do this *my* way. I met Alex earlier this year." At Harry's mutter of surprise, she told him of her trip to South America. "We'd planned to meet at the planetarium on Valentine's Day. Alex probably believes I waited there and left, thinking I'd been stood up. Instead—" Instead, she knew exactly where the Kingsley brothers were on the day.

Alex Kingsley... all these months, and she never breathed a word to her best friend. The romantic encounter was her secret with her lover. It was none of Harry's business. There would be more such secrets... little things couples did together, hopes and desires they whispered only in each other's ears. Life would take Lilah farther and farther away from the childhood sweetheart who decided he didn't want her. Her memories of their time together as something more than friends would soon fade.

Tucking his hands into his pockets, Harry stared broodingly at the water display and the shrubbery surrounding which was cut to resemble chess pieces. Her eyes followed his gaze. The ghosts of the past laughed and played around them. Spirited voices echoed, arguing over matches won and lost.

Suddenly, the voices turned dark and sinister. *Mine,* some stranger roared within his head. He snapped, "You're supposed to lead this revolt, Lilah. You can't afford to get attached."

"Why not?" Her voice held an edge. "I'm supposed to marry the man and reproduce with him, right?" For long moments, Lilah regarded him, her lips curled in mocking challenge, her eyes daring him to put a name to his emotion.

Harry stared in silence at the topiary, refusing to even acknowledge her question. Wishing him a terse goodnight, she left.

He sat at the fountain the rest of the night, dozing off toward the morning, dreaming disjointed dreams of a past when anything was possible, and the air always shimmered with happiness. In his visions, he watched Lilah run off laughing, gesturing at him to join her, but he couldn't move. Ghosts still danced around him, blocking his way. He screamed for his beloved until he was hoarse, but she didn't hear him.

Chapter 26

Next day

Lilah looped the brown braided belt around her floral maxi with its thigh-high slit. Matching pumps went on her feet, hair was left loose, and perfume dabbed on pulse points. She took one last glance at the floor-length mirror in her room and huffed out a breath of anticipation. Time to *officially* meet Alex.

When she reached the garden, six guards fell into place in assigned spots, dressed in designer casual to blend in. The entire house and the surrounding estate had already been secured, of course. The extra precautions weren't merely for the Barronses' benefit; the VIPs expected today needed protection. Guests were already trickling in for what promised to be a glorious summer afternoon with bright-blue skies and chirping birds and cool breeze. Most of the women were attired according to code in sundresses and maxis and pretty hats, the men in sport coats and khakis and loafers. There were couples dancing to the peppy song played by the live band, but all eyes seemed to turn to Lilah when she entered.

To the gathered elite, she was Andrew Barrons's daughter. Tabloids sang lavish praises of her, indulging in exaggerated descriptions of her from the top of the head to the tips of her toes. One magazine was hyperbolic enough to call her the dream incarnate of men and gods. Her scent was supposedly an aphrodisiac, deluding even bees and butterflies. No one cared to know anything of her childhood. Temple once called her a fire-borne princess, and that's what she was even to the people who did know her parents. Lilah Barrons took birth from the flames at the Libyan border as a girl on the cusp of womanhood.

Stop, Lilah ordered herself. What she was currently on the verge of was defeating a brutal tyrant and starting life with a partner she found immensely appealing. With a polite nod for the guests, she made for the refreshment tent, hoping cold water would soothe her suddenly jittery nerves.

Standing next to the open flap of the tent, Lilah studied the man walking into the gathering, his hair combed back over a slightly balding pate, his build stocky and gait purposeful. Jared Sanders was at the picnic.

All the power brokers of the sector were invited to the event, and Andrew had no way of excluding Sanders without causing talk in the market. *He'd* shown up presumably for the same reason. Lilah had seen pictures of the man, but in the months she worked in oil exploration, she never ran into him. The image she carried in her mind was that of a giant monster, but he resembled every successful businessman she'd met. Except, he held himself like a prizefighter. Only the most important of guests were allowed to bring their own security, and there was a guard who followed closely behind. One single guard… which was all Sanders probably needed. She couldn't imagine anyone daring to get within six feet of him. People simply scurried out of his way as he strode through the gathering, scanning each face.

She swallowed hard, glancing in Harry's direction. Hands tucked into the pockets of his chinos, he stood at the periphery of the crowd. The navy blazer and honey-colored tee should've given him a carefree air. His face was anything but carefree. With flaming eyes, he watched the enemy.

Sanders paused when he saw Ryan Sheppard and family but continued searching the crowd for… the oilman halted, glaring at Harry. Those in the path between the men melted away, uneasily glancing between the adversaries.

"Jared," called a voice.

Andrew strolled toward Sanders with a glass of iced tea in his hand. Dan and Shawn were right behind. Turning to the Barrons men, Sanders sneered. He knew he was in enemy territory. He shook hands with his hosts, apparently exchanging pleasantries, but Dan's face tightened. His smile strained, Andrew walked with Sanders toward the refreshment tent.

"Jared," said her brother-in-law, "this is Delilah." Andrew turned to her, warning light in his eyes. "My dear, this is Jared Sanders. He… ahh… asked to meet you."

"Miss Barrons, a pleasure." Sharp gaze unwaveringly pinned to her face, Sanders shook her hand.

Too close. She could feel the air vibrate with each word. Behind Lilah, two of her guards shifted, but they'd been instructed to do nothing today which could create political waves unless there was clear and present danger. She gritted her teeth and forced herself not to take a step back. Had she thought Sanders looked like your average businessman? Jared Sanders was a predator. Anyone unfortunate enough to meet his eye would realize it.

"I've seen you before—at Temple's inaugural ball," Sanders said conversationally. "Unfortunately, you left before I could introduce myself. Hard to believe it's already been a couple of years."

Jovially, Andrew interjected, "Temple will soon be running for reelection. Time flies."

Sanders didn't take his eyes off Lilah. "Six more years to the Temple presidency," he muttered. "At the most."

Matching him stare for stare, Lilah acknowledged his comment in silence. Over the shoulder of the oilman, she saw Harry watching, his stance coiled.

Taking half a step back, Sanders's eyes swept between her and Harry. Their enemy smiled, the corner of his mouth tightening. The malevolence in the smirk was stunning in its intensity.

Lilah bristled. An angry snarl erupted in her mind. Her fingers curled almost involuntarily, preparing to strike with talons unsheathed, clawing out his eyes.

A car door slammed not too far away, startling her. There was only one person who'd have been allowed to drive straight to the picnic instead of being escorted there by security. The president of the United States had arrived.

If Andrew Barrons had been obliged to invite Sanders to avoid disturbing the market, Sanders was forced into paying respects to the president for the same reason. When the criminal oilman moved away to greet Temple, Lilah released the breath she'd been holding. She needed more water... desperately.

Guzzling ice-cold Perrier straight from the bottle, she took a few steps and waited for Andrew's security guards to follow. Harry stayed within ten feet of her, alert eyes scanning the crowd. Society reporters and business journalists mingled with the guests, enjoying the garden party.

"How's my favorite girl?" a familiar voice shouted.

Laughing in recognition, Lilah hurried to greet the latest arrival. "Dante! How have you been?"

"Great." He drew her into a warm hug before holding her away. "Let me look at you."

"How's Harry doing at Gateway?" she asked. He now worked full time for the family company. Dante was his boss.

"I'm whipping him into shape." They both laughed. Voice turning serious, Dante said, "Lilah, you got pressured into the adoption seven years ago. You're an adult now. If you want to walk away, do it. I'll help however I can."

Unexpected tears pricked her eyes. Blinking them back, she whispered, "If *he'd* made me the same offer..."

She didn't need to specify who *he* was. Dante huffed. "He's an idiot—"

"Hey," yelled someone.

A scuffle broke out in the long line of men and women waiting to greet the president. Secret service personnel restrained a young man whose loud and profane objections suggested he'd hit the open bar more than once. Temple looked irate, turning to mutter something to an aide, who in turn persuaded presidential security to let the drunk go. Lilah recognized him from the photographs she'd been shown. Charles Kingsley—one of the adopted grandsons of Godwin Kingsley.

Jared Sanders stood near Andrew, watching the commotion with drink in hand. Sanders's eyes were on Charles and the man with him: his brother, Steven. Mouth pursing, Sanders contemplated each in turn, and then, his narrowed gaze flew to Lilah. Charles staggered to the back of the crowd, muttering furiously. He bumped into Sanders and stopped to snigger. Sanders barked, "Get out."

Nervous titters rose from those around. Insulted, Charles growled loudly and drew himself up to object. He peered into the face of the human obstacle and froze. Mumbling an apology, he slinked away.

#

Tension churned within Harry, his eyes following Sanders's every move. The oilman made no further attempts to speak with Lilah, but he was stalking her. Every man and woman she talked to invariably collided with Sanders next, and each one hurried away at the end of the conversation with relief marking their features. Lilah's smile was bright as ever as she chatted with a young and upcoming politician, but Harry saw the lines of strain around her eyes, the rigidity of her posture.

Daniel called for everyone's attention, wind ruffling his hair. The guests gathered around. Cameras flashed as the heir to the Barrons business announced the Annual Barrons Olympic Skeet Shooting Contest.

Lilah claimed hostess's privilege and went first. The metallic odor of gunsmoke curled its way across the summer garden. The audience clapped enthusiastically, kind to the young woman. *Five misses,* Harry noted. Not bad, but—

"Let me try," said a voice from the crowd behind Lilah. Steven Kingsley ran appreciative eyes over her as he took the twelve-gauge shotgun.

Harry clapped as Steven hit twenty-one.

"Aren't you Godwin Kingsley's grandson?" Sanders asked, walking to where Lilah stood with Steven.

Face stiff and expressionless, Lilah turned.

Bristling with annoyance, Steven pivoted, but as soon as he recognized who it was, he straightened. "Yes, Mr. Sanders," he stammered, eyes darting sideways. "I'm Steven."

Sanders held out his hand, and flushing, Steven surrendered the weapon. "Move over," Sanders commanded and took aim. Twenty-two clays fell.

"Well done, sir," Steven said eagerly.

At his side, Charles Kingsley giggled and clapped. "Grrreat shooting."

At Sanders's flinty stare, Steven mumbled, "Shut up, Charlie."

Charles wandered away, but other guests lined up to try their hand. Daniel kept score. The security team stuck close to Lilah, and Harry noted with relief that Shawn Barrons was also at her side.

Shawn picked up the gun. With whistles and hoots, his siblings greeted him. He tied Steven.

"You're not joining?" a question sounded next to Harry. Just under six feet in height and with a pugilist's build, Hector Sheppard—Harry's older brother—cut an intimidating figure. In coloring, he'd taken after their mother, with blond hair and blue eyes. "He's my student, you know—Steven." Hector ran a boxing gym, and some of the world's best athletes went there to train.

Sanders was still at the range, with Steven Kingsley hovering deferentially behind and Lilah staring stone-faced into the distance. A blond man sauntered to the group. Steven Kingsley lost the hunch on his back, and he grinned broadly at the newcomer. The man clapped Steven on the back. "I'll have a go," said the man, taking the weapon.

"Hey, that's Richard," Hector said, clapping. "Go, Rich," he hollered and pumped his fist high.

"Who's Rich?" asked Harry.

"Richard Armor," said Hector. "His father is Godwin Kingsley's chauffeur. Steven considers Rich a good friend. He's older than the Kingsley lot, around my age. Rich was at West Point, too. He runs the western offices of Kingsley Corp now."

Dante joined the brothers. They watched as Richard introduced himself to Daniel. "Is this Rich any good?" Harry asked.

Hector puffed. "Hell, yeah. He went to sniper school after he graduated... *asked* to go there."

Surprised, Harry asked, "Really? West Point grads are officers. They don't usually—"

"The dean recommended it," Hector said. "Said it would add to his ability to lead certain specialized units. Rich does have an incredible record. Tours in Vietnam, etcetera, etcetera. Not like the Kingsleys and their cushy postings in Europe. He's a reservist now with the JAG Corps, and they just promoted him to major. And I have no idea how Godwin managed to get Charles in... he's still with the army."

Harry smiled, his mind on snipers. "That makes two."

"Huh?" said Hector.

"Two West Pointers who ended up in sniper school before taking up command positions," Harry explained. "Alex Kingsley was the second one. I believe he never went to 'Nam. Troops withdrew by the time he graduated."

"According to Steven, Alex was in Pakistan," said Hector.

Harry nodded, having seen the same info in the dossier on the Kingsley brothers provided long ago by the president. Captain Alex Kingsley only stayed in active service for the mandatory five years. Army records listed his impressive achievements in the short time. He wanted to continue in the service but ended up joining the family business.

"Wonder what happened to him and his brothers," Hector muttered. "Rumors say they died in some accident."

The president insisted on limiting awareness of the Kingsley situation on a need-to-know basis, updating the rest of the players only over the last few days. Hector had been traveling, returning home just in time for this event, and had yet to hear the latest part of the story. Harry took a quick look around. *No, too many people.* On his other side, Dante huffed. Ignoring him, Harry said, "Yeah... too bad."

#

Lilah stared at Steven Kingsley's friend, the man with the close-cropped blond hair. He was either very brave or very stupid. Or perhaps he didn't recognize Sanders and was intervening because of the oilman's threatening behavior. Well, if Lilah needed help handling Sanders in this public and secure venue, she had no business being the linchpin to Temple's plan.

Before she could push the would-be rescuer aside, he picked up the shotgun and pulverized twenty-three out of twenty-five clay birds. The guests clapped enthusiastically.

Mild mockery on his face, he turned to Lilah. "Looks like there isn't going to be much of a contest here, Miss Barrons."

Sanders stiffened. "Who the hell are you?"

Dismissing Sanders with a glance, the newcomer sneered at Lilah. "Major Richard Armor, U.S. Army."

Weird behavior... as though I did something to him... have I seen him before? Squinting, Lilah tried to place the man.

He smirked. "Not one who can beat me." He gestured at the gathered crowd with his weapon, icy-blue eyes disdainful.

The vague thought taking shape in Lilah's mind blinked out.

"Huh? Think very highly of yourself, don't you?"

"Why not?" Armor asked. "All you bluebloods in one place... useless, most of you."

"We all bleed red, mister," said Lilah, irritated.

The seething antipathy permeating the air around him got thicker. "Major," he corrected through clenched teeth, "I'm *Major* Armor."

Sanders was eyeing Steven's friend, speculatively. "Major, I'm Jared Sanders."

"Sanders, Incorporated?" Armor asked.

"The same. Your skill's remarkable, but Miss Barrons doesn't seem impressed."

"No one's stopping her from trying again." Armor thrust the weapon in her direction, barrel pointing at her chest.

Lilah took a startled step back. "Hey," shouted Shawn and one of the guards, almost at the same moment.

Holding out a firm hand, she took the firearm from the major. Out of the corner of her eye, she saw Harry move forward, ready to intercept the interloper.

A man broke off from the ranks around the president, impeding her view of Harry. "The army would take a dim view of what you just did, Armor," said a smoky voice. Lilah turned, gaze colliding with a pair of cognac eyes as the man removed the sunglasses which—along with the dark suit—had allowed him to melt into the crowd of security officers around the president. "May I?" he asked, gesturing at the gun.

Her smile widening, she handed it over.

"Alex Kingsley," he introduced himself to Sanders.

#

Right on cue. Harry smiled in satisfaction. He couldn't have planned a more dramatic reentry for the sons of Peter Kingsley.

Behind Alex loomed a giant. "Victor Kingsley," he boomed, clearly relishing the shock ricocheting around the group. The bright-red blotches on his face made his anger evident.

At some distance was a bespectacled man, watching the scene—their brother, Brad Kingsley. His eyes were pinned unwaveringly on Lilah.

Victor waved away the second shotgun brought by one of the employees. "Thanks, but this is not my kind of sport."

Steven Kingsley and Richard Armor seemed stupefied, staring in open-mouthed silence at Alex and Victor. Even Sanders was at a loss for words at the unexpected reappearance of the three brothers.

With a derisive glance, Alex dismissed his enemies and turned to Lilah. "How about I shoot in your place?"

"A champion?" On her lips was a vivacious smile, something that had been all-too-rare lately.

"Why not?" Alex inquired.

Victor and Alex positioned themselves, blocking Sanders from Lilah. Alex held the weapon at his hip and called for the release of targets. Twenty-three out of twenty-five. Lilah clapped and cheered.

Curious guests gathered. The next four rounds were shot in quick succession. The sun was on its way down, but the remaining three contestants showed no signs of wanting to retire. Shawn shot twenty-two. With an angry sneer on his face, Richard Armor picked up the gun and called for the release of targets. Twenty-four down.

Fingertips to lips, Lilah seemed to be holding her breath as Alex positioned himself and called for the targets. His eyes narrowed. There it was! The telltale whirr of the delay switch. One, two, three. Raising the shotgun, Alex fired, moved around the half-circle, and fired again. All twenty-five clays shattered. Lilah smiled, her delight obvious.

Turning to Armor, Alex said, "I think the lady knows by now which one of us is better at handling a firearm."

Armor's throat worked, but only a growl escaped. Finally, he shook a finger in Alex's face before wheeling and striding away.

"Hey, wha... whash this? This contest is f... hic... guests only," slurred Charles, lurching forward. He squinted wine-blurred eyes at Alex. "*He's* one of the president's..." Drunk as he was, Charles didn't recognize his cousins. "Not a guest."

Steven called out to him, but Charles wouldn't be stopped. He and the group surrounding him hurled loud insults at Alex. Victor grabbed Charles, twisting his arm behind him to push him away. Steven toppled a table in his rush to get Victor. Lilah was directly in Steven's path.

Harry lunged to get her out of harm's way, but before he could reach her, she was caught around the waist and swung to the side. Alex smiled at Lilah as Steven's fist missed her by inches.

Pivoting quickly to the melee, Harry said, "Stop! You're embarrassing yourselves in front of the press. Pull it together before you collectively crash the stock market."

Steven glared at him for a second or two and snarled before turning away, his brother following. Richard Armor had already left the gathering.

Jared Sanders watched them from the edge of the crowd. His eyes were narrowed as he studied the people clustered together— the Kingsley brothers, Delilah Barrons, and Harry Sheppard.

Sanders stopped by Harry before leaving the venue. "Six years," he said, nostrils flaring.

There were at the most six more years until Temple left office and his allies lost the protection of the American presidency. Sanders had recognized the threat in the group assembled in the garden. He'd recognized the threat in Lilah. Jared Sanders was merely making them a promise. Thanks to Temple's presence in the White House, Sanders might not be able to do anything to Lilah for the next six years, but the day after, her life would be forfeit. They had six years to destroy the enemy or be destroyed.

Part IX

Chapter 27

An hour later

By the time Patrice Kingsley received the phone call she'd been anticipating, the party was long over. As instructed, she took the elevator to the hotel lobby. The Barrons chauffeur, resplendent in his crisp royal-blue uniform, met her there and drove her to the mansion.

From the Louis XVI chair, Patrice sized up the occupants of the family room. The first-born son, Shawn Barrons, was at least thirty. Caroline, stepmom to Shawn and mom to the Barrons twins... the resemblance between her and Dan was striking. Except, everyone knew the twins were adopted. Patrice frowned, trying to remember if she'd ever heard of Caroline's own family.

After the president's startling suggestion about a political marriage, Patrice's sons said they already knew the Barronses... sort of. Alex was a senior when Daniel joined West Point, but Shawn was expelled from the academy long before any of the Kingsleys enrolled. All the Kingsley grandsons met Dan and Andrew in Venezuela, but it was as adversaries. Patrice's three boys were now reacquainting themselves with the Barrons men, crowding around the bar at one end. Daniel poured champagne for the guests.

With a smile of thanks at the uniformed maid, Patrice took the glass of deliciously cold lemonade and sipped. She watched Alex in bemusement. He hardly paid attention to the Barrons brothers; his gaze kept slipping to the antique settee next to Patrice's chair where the president was attempting to converse with Lilah.

The young woman didn't seem inclined to chat, though, sitting stiffly next to the leader of the free world. With an exasperated look, Temple got up and strode to a group of men clustered at the other end of the room. His entourage, probably.

Lilah threw a glance back at Alex, tucking her hair behind her ear. Patrice wondered again what could've prompted a girl like Lilah to agree to such a scheme. She was lovely... blue-black hair, wide, hazel eyes lit from within, attractive face and figure. Educated, too. Family pressure, of course. Someone with her looks and credentials would've been expected to go for an advantageous marriage.

Sauntering casually toward the settee, Alex dropped next to Lilah. "*You're* the one Mr. Temple wanted us to meet, huh?" He waggled his eyebrows over the rim of the champagne flute.

Lilah's lips widened in a sparkling smile, and they both laughed.

Patrice frowned. Did they know each other?

Reaching out with his free hand, Alex rubbed a thumb over the corner of Lilah's mouth. "Champagne," he explained. "What should I call you? Delilah, Lilah, or something else?"

"Lilah. I'm Lilah." She narrowed her eyes. "*Was* there champagne?"

"Sure there was," he insisted, grin playful. "Would have kissed it off, but I didn't want to shock your family."

She sputtered. "Funny how it got there since I haven't taken a single sip."

He pursed his mouth. "Must be my mind playing tricks like the time I ran into this girl called Harry."

"Shh." She put a finger to her lips, eyes rounded in the delicious excitement of a shared secret.

"You mean to say they don't *know*?" He shook with laughter.

Stomach knotting, Patrice watched her youngest son and made

rapid calculations in her mind. Next to the fireplace, Brad stood with his elbow resting on the mantel, fingers playing with the stem of a champagne flute. He was talking to Andrew, but his eyes were on Alex and Lilah, expression one of anticipation.

The president called, "Patrice, I want you to meet someone."

A young man came forward. He was around her sons' ages—tall and handsome, with a roguish grin lighting dark features. Something about the smile... he seemed to be asking, *Will you be my friend?* Patrice couldn't help smiling back. To her surprise, he leaned down and kissed her cheek. "Aunt Patrice, I'm Harry Sheppard. We're distantly related. I think you know my father, Ryan Sheppard."

It took a second for the name to register. *Sheppard?!* Before Patrice could respond, her sons gathered around Harry, introducing themselves to their cousin. Apparently, Harry was famous. Even Alex leaped up after a quick grin at Lilah to excuse himself.

"I've heard a lot about you." Alex pumped Harry's hand. "Everyone in my unit talked about the president's go-to guy."

Harry took the drink offered by Dan. "I've been following your exploits as well—one of the most successful marksmen in U.S. military records. Am I right?"

Confused and more than a little angry, Patrice shot a look at the president. Mr. Temple knew she wanted nothing to do with the Sheppards. So what was Ryan's son doing here? But the president's eyes were on her boys and Harry.

Temple's voice was amused as he interrupted. "Stop congratulating each other and help us make some plans. Phone's already ringing off the hook."

"A press conference has been arranged," said Andrew Barrons. "We will put out a sympathetic version of the events leading to the disappearance of Patrice Kingsley and her sons."

Harry turned to a middle-aged man standing next to the president. "Aunt Patrice, you may know Uncle Grayson."

Patrice never met Grayson Sheppard, but she knew of him. Former chairman of the New York Stock Exchange. Cousin to Harry's father.

"How are you, my dear?" Grayson asked.

Patrice smiled in greeting, hiding her shock. More Sheppards! Why were they here? She should've done some checking before agreeing to the president's plan. She would've if she hadn't been so desperate.

Grayson said, "President Temple has asked me to act as senior adviser to Brad and his brothers. The president can't openly show support, but *I* can. I've already sent word to Godwin, asking him to get the whole lot down here. My presence guarantees the entire Kingsley clan will show up. Before they do, we have arrangements to make."

Chapter 28

Close to twelve, Harry nodded his thanks at the maid who told him where to find the Kingsleys.

The Barrons estate boasted of beautiful gardens, and this section oozed old-world romance lit as it was with black cast-iron lanterns mounted on tall poles. Matching chairs were placed between the rose bushes in a carefully casual arrangement. Black and white mosaic tiles cut through the green grass in a straight path leading to the house. It was a lovely summer night, warm and fragrant.

Strolling up to where Alex was leaning against a lamppost, Harry asked, "Enjoying the weather?"

Alex's face creased into a smile. "Oh, yeah. It's been months since we had a chance to be out and about without worrying where the next attack's coming from."

Harry laughed. As Alex glanced back at the house, Harry inquired, "Are you expecting someone?"

Before Alex could answer, the small side door swung open, and Lilah came outside, steps faltering when she saw Harry.

Harry opened a conversation about the latest *Star Wars* movie, ignoring Lilah's narrowed eyes. With a barely audible huff, she joined the discussion. After about thirty minutes when Harry showed no signs of leaving, she excused herself, giving him a pointed look. He raised a mocking eyebrow in salute.

After she disappeared into the house, Alex said to Harry, "I guess you're Gateway's representative in the alliance the president was talking about, but you also seem to be a friend of the Barronses."

Harry inclined his head, acknowledging nothing.

"About Lilah—" Alex paused. "She's beautiful. I mean, she could have anyone she wanted. Then why... I should probably ask *her*, but whichever way I put the question, it's gonna sound offensive."

"Why did she agree to an arrangement like this?" Harry smiled. "'Duty, honor, country.'"

"The West Point motto?" Alex asked, frowning.

"'The code which those words perpetuate embraces the highest moral laws,'" Harry quoted. "'Its requirements are for the things that are right, and its restraints are from the things that are wrong. The soldier, above all other men, is required to practice the greatest act of religious training—sacrifice.'"

Alex eyed Harry, an arrested look on his face. "General MacArthur's speech. But we're talking about a business merger, not a fight to keep our freedoms."

Harry raised an eyebrow. "A business merger with the potential to defeat the current tyrant ruling our system."

"Sanders? There are rumors he was involved in your kidnapping." Though the attack on Genesis and Harry's subsequent abduction were well known, the blame went mostly to Gaddafi and his goons. While Sanders's role in the events had never been proved, stories abounded.

"It's a fact," Harry said. "I escaped, but having a bully like Sanders essentially in charge of our country's energy supply is a threat to national security. To the security of the entire world. The president must have made it clear to you. He wants all hands on deck."

"Dude," Alex said. "Are you claiming Mr. Temple asked Lilah to sacrifice herself for this cause? You and he need to remember she's no soldier."

"Do you believe," Harry asked, voice soft, "only those in uniform are capable of sacrificing their lives for a set of ideals?"

"Of course not," Alex acknowledged.

"In battles between right and wrong, every citizen—every man and every woman—is called upon to give it all. Lilah understands this."

"But doesn't she want," Alex argued, "I don't know... a husband who *loves* her?"

Ignoring the pang going through him, Harry said, "I assume she and the man she marries will eventually find their way to love."

"He'd be the world's luckiest bastard. I... ahh... I believe she'll pick *me*."

Harry waited a few seconds for the sharp pain in his head to subside. "If Barrons is throwing his support in your direction, he'll want to have a say in what happens. Lilah is his way of ensuring it. Make no mistake, any future you build will need to have her involvement. She's not going to be a nominal partner in any venture."

"As my wife, she'll have a say in things."

Alex's mother and brothers walked out of the shadows at the end of the garden and strolled up the path. It was evident they'd overheard the exchange. "Alex," said Brad. "Remember what the president said about the alliance of oil companies. This is going to be a partnership as well as a marriage. It's the reason Mr. Temple suggested *me*."

"We're talking about a woman, not a Kingsley Corp acquisition," Alex snapped.

Had the Kingsleys asked, Harry might have left, but he needed to know what the brothers decided.

Brad said, "You didn't seem to have a problem with the idea until we got to New York."

Patrice sat in a chair and waved her youngest to the seat next to hers. "Okay, let's put aside what the president said. Andrew has promised he'll help us negotiate a division of assets with your cousins. Lilah becoming part of our family is the key to it all. However, we have to agree to a pre-nuptial contract giving her a significant amount of control and a sizable chunk of our company."

Lilah definitely wanted a pre-nup to make sure she got an actual say in things, but *Harry* was the one who insisted on the inclusion of a couple of details. He wasn't quite certain of the Kingsleys. They'd left a body count on their way from California to New York, self-defense though the president claimed it all to be. Even Lilah took Temple's word for it. Harry was surprised at the time at her quick acceptance of the particular version of events, but he supposed it could easily be verified via investigations. Still, the former sniper and his brothers were not men to be taken lightly. Three dead assassins in the mountains... and Harry harbored doubts about the untimely demise of the owner of the bar the brothers used as hiding place the last few months.

"Also, Lilah herself wants an executive position," Patrice continued. "She wants to be the CFO. Even in the event of separation or divorce, she won't lose the voting rights on the stock or her administrative position in the company. She can't even be fired without proof of gross incompetence, or we'd have to give her more shares as compensation. In the event of her death, her stock won't go to Brad. It will go to whomever she has designated as beneficiary, someone other than her husband and his immediate family. Even if she eventually wills everything to her children, it will be held in trust for them by an executor. Again, outside of her husband's family."

The Kingsleys would know they wouldn't profit from Lilah's death. In fact, they'd have good reason to keep her alive.

"One-sided," Victor grumbled.

"I agree," Patrice said. "But I don't see another way out of this mess. This alliance was suggested by Mr. Temple, and returning to Kingsley Corp after declining it will leave us friendless."

"If... *when* Steven tries to kill us again," Victor added, "there might not be anyone willing to help. Let's say our dear cousin turns over a new leaf... or we hire the best possible protection... we still don't want to make Grandfather and the president angry by rejecting this marriage alliance. Mr. Temple says it's also his best chance to make some necessary changes in the oil sector. We can..." Victor eyed Harry for a moment and continued, "...consider more drastic options, but a marriage is a safer alternative than anything else we might try."

With difficulty, Harry kept the frown from his face. More drastic options? As in doing away with Steven? Yeah, the death beneficiary clause in the pre-nup was a very good idea.

"We don't have a choice but to agree to Andrew Barrons's terms, or there will be no alliance between Lilah and the Kingsleys." Patrice leaned in and patted Alex's arm. "Under the circumstances, it has to be Brad since he's going to be the CEO. We can't hand over so much power to the wife of a junior partner. The situation will cause too much uncertainty about leadership, and a seasoned businessman like Barrons will easily see it. He will not let it happen."

Alex argued, "Let *Lilah* decide who she wants to marry. How can Barrons object if it's her choice?"

Patrice sighed. "Do you really want to take the chance? Alex, even if Barrons doesn't object, *I* will. We can't afford to have that kind of a split between you brothers, and Lilah's presence as your wife will cause exactly that."

"I don't see... I'd never go against—" Alex started.

"I know," Patrice said. "But *Lilah* might. In fact, given the money she'll bring in and her position as CFO, she almost certainly will create another power center within the company. If there's a clash, who will get your backing? If you don't back her, how will she retaliate? No, Alex, it will create too many problems."

Alex pleaded, "Mother, you're asking me to give up..."

"Give up what?" Patrice asked, voice bewildered but not unkind. "You just met the girl."

Harry wondered if Alex would tell his family about the encounter in Venezuela. The former sniper was clearly smitten.

Alex scratched his jaw and glanced at the mansion as though waiting for Lilah to dash out and tell all. "Is the business so goddamned important?" he finally asked. "I mean, we're all educated. Why can't we find our own things to do?"

"Without the business, Lilah has no reason to marry *any* of us,"

Victor pointed out. "How can you think of dumping your family for a girl?"

Through clenched teeth, Alex asked, "What are you talking about, Victor? How am I 'dumping' you?"

Patrice said, "When your father left me, Godwin made it clear: he blamed me for Peter's defection from Kingsley Corp. I took you three and left the family home because I could already see you being treated as second-class citizens." She met each of their eyes in turn. "One of the reasons I agreed to return was that the three of you had as much right to the company as David's children. Our absence made it easier for the Kingsleys to ignore our claims." A look of fear flitted across her face. "I never imagined Steven would try to kill you. Even if we don't return to Kingsley Corp, Brad will be under constant threat from Steven."

Alex leaned back in the chair, stretching his legs out. The indolent pose contrasted starkly with the tight grip he maintained on the armrests.

Victor spelled it out: "As long as we're alive and officially the heirs to our father's stock in Kingsley Corp, Steven will consider us threats to his position. It won't matter if we never return to the business. He'll still send more killers after us. Especially after Brad. Are you willing to sacrifice your brother for a girl?"

With a huff, Alex shoved his fingers through his hair.

Patrice said, her voice firm, "Family first, Alex."

Alex eyed his brothers and mother in turn before exhaling. "Right, family first." He stood. "Congratulations, Brad."

Yes, Harry exulted. It was the best outcome for everyone concerned. Pain-filled hazel eyes glared accusingly at him in his mindscape. Harry blinked. What was the point of any remorse on his part when lover boy himself didn't give a damn?

As the brothers left, Patrice stayed with Harry. She glanced at the black-painted chair Alex vacated. "Do you know why I cut myself off from the Sheppard family?" she asked Harry.

"Not really... simply that you and my father don't get along."

"I'm not going to rehash old stories. Suffice to say that I'm here tonight only for my sons. If I'd known Lilah was a Sheppard..."

Harry didn't respond, having heard how, Brad in tow, Patrice Kingsley confronted Andrew Barrons earlier in the evening. The president safely made his escape before she cornered *him*. Given that the marriage paperwork would reveal the names of Lilah's birth parents, Andrew was compelled to admit the twins were Caroline's siblings, born to her father and his second wife. He left out the part about the abduction as he always did.

Patrice hadn't been happy, but there was nothing she could do about any of it. Harry and Temple had expected Lilah to be the bait that lured Brad Kingsley in, but fate conspired to put him and his mother in a position where they were forced to agree to the marriage. Strangely, Patrice herself asked both Andrew and Brad to continue keeping the information about Lilah's origins quiet. Patrice Kingsley's loathing for the Sheppards certainly ran deep.

Someday, Harry made a note to himself. He would figure out the story behind the lady.

"I assume you're here as the Sheppard representative." Patrice visibly gritted her teeth. "So listen well. If Lilah or any other Sheppard leads my family into trouble, we'll walk away from this alliance. My boys come first. Do we understand each other?"

"Yes, ma'am." The Kingsley family soap opera was something else! Harry swatted away the urge to grab Lilah's hand and run from it all.

Fatigue was all it was. A good night's sleep would get rid of this strange disquiet. When he opened the door to his room, Dante was lounging casually on the bed.

"What are you doing here, old man?" Harry asked. "You need to get some rest. So do I. Andrew's invited almost the entire media for the presser tomorrow."

"This seemed the surest place to catch you. You're busy."

Harry crossed to the bathroom. "Whatever it is, say it quick."

"Lilah's going to marry Brad Kingsley—a man she didn't meet until tonight—a fellow she barely even looked at all evening."

"Oh, for God's—I should've known it wasn't about work." Since the day fourteen-year-old Harry became gofer to the then-secretary, Dante considered it his duty to keep his apprentice on the straight and narrow. Even where his damned love life was concerned! Harry stripped off his shirt and threw it violently into the hamper. "The sector needs someone like Lilah at the top, and Brad's the only one who can get her there."

Dante leaned against the bathroom door. "Harry, you escaped Libya seven years ago, but your mind is still trapped in the place. There must be some other way of dealing with Sanders."

Miniature bottles of toiletries toppled to the floor as Harry pawed through the shelves. "This is not only about Libya, and *Lilah* understands it. I heard you tell her to walk away. She didn't, did she?"

"You want to know what Lilah thinks, ask her yourself. Bet you won't dare because you already know what she's going to say."

"It's too late for a change of mind," snarled Harry, splashing cold water on his face. "All our plans are in place." He glanced pointedly toward the exit.

Shaking his head, Dante left.

Later, staring through the window into the moonlit garden, Harry wondered what she was doing. He needed to let her know about the decision made by the Kingsley family, but the clock said it was after one. They'd talk in the morning.

Chapter 29

The next morning

Peeking into the breakfast room, Lilah found Harry *still* with Alex. With an exasperated huff, she sneaked away, scrunching Andrew's note requesting a meeting in his office. First, toast and orange juice in the kitchen. Then, the press conference. Afterward, she'd drag Alex to Andrew's office and finalize matters. With Alex at her side, there was nothing much Temple or Harry could do to force on her a groom she didn't want.

For the next hour, Lilah hid in her twin's room, claiming a need for some quiet time. She heard Harry's voice outside. Rolling his eyes at her pleading gestures, Dan went out to lie for her and said he hadn't seen her since the night before. Harry asked Dan to give Lilah a message in case he did run into her. Apparently, it was critical for her to talk to Harry before the press conference. When Dan returned to the room, Lilah made a zipping motion across her lips. No way was she giving Harry another chance to badger her about her choice of a husband. Anything he wanted to discuss would have to wait until her engagement with Alex was set in stone.

When there were exactly five minutes to the conference, Lilah sprinted all the way across the mansion to the large hall used as the media room. Cold air blasted her in the face when she opened the door. At her entry, the noisy chatter momentarily dipped before flowing again. The U-shaped table was already occupied, with the reporters seated in rows of chairs in front. Down one limb of the U were the Barrons men and Brad Kingsley along with Grayson Sheppard and Dante. At the other was Godwin Kingsley with his adopted sons, David and Aaron, accompanied by a couple of lawyers. They'd arrived in the morning, just in time for the presser.

Temple had already left for DC, but Lilah knew he talked to the Kingsley elders on the phone without sugar-coating words. Steven brought it upon the family and the company, and they'd all have to live with the consequences.

The single empty chair was between Andrew Barrons and Brad Kingsley, where the occupant would be the focus of attention, but the only attention Lilah wanted today was from Alex.

There he stood in one corner of the room, eyes fixed on the gathered press. Lilah lifted her hand to wave, but he showed no signs of turning toward her. Harry was next to Alex, sticking close as he'd done since the minute they were introduced. Deliberately, of course. He was trying to keep Alex from her. Annoyance rose. She agreed to marry a Kingsley to form this network. Now, Harry needed to respect her choices. She glared at him.

He mouthed her name, asking her to come to his side. Extreme urgency on his face, he added, *Please.*

Nuh-uh. No way. No how. With a final sharp look in his direction, Lilah strode to the empty chair. Best friend or not, she couldn't allow Harry's behavior to continue. If it didn't stop once her engagement was announced, she'd have a firm talk with him.

Brad Kingsley was on her right. She nodded at him and turned her attention to the papers arranged neatly in front of her. She'd barely noticed the man the night before. Even now, sitting next to him, she'd find it difficult to describe him without turning and making a study of his face. And Harry thought she ought to happily marry the fellow! Godwin Kingsley was more recognizable to Lilah than Brad. The former supreme court justice… she once wanted an introduction, hoping for his support and guidance on her way to the position he held. She didn't know at the time he and the president planned other things for her.

Gray Sheppard stood to speak, playing spokesman for Brad. "The last few months, the Kingsleys have been working on a division of assets," he announced. Journalists scribbled furiously.

At the end of the conference, Andrew stood. "You must be wondering what I have to do with this. You see, our daughter told us she wants to marry Brad here."

Lilah started. Her mind froze.

Excited mutters rose in the room. Chairs scraped as the senior Kingsleys stood. Godwin Kingsley led the way to shake Brad's hand. David and Aaron were right behind.

Lilah stayed glued to the chair, her thoughts fragmented. She saw Andrew smiling genially at the room. She saw Brad stand to accept congratulations from his grandfather.

"Miss Barrons," someone shouted. Lilah blinked. The reporter from *The New York Times*. "Where'd you meet your fiancé?" he asked, thrusting a microphone under her nose.

"Huh?" she said, the reporter's question adding to her confusion.

At her side, Brad spoke, "Andrew introduced us."

It was as though she were trapped in some alternate reality. Everyone else seemed to be speaking a language she couldn't comprehend. The words were familiar, but they didn't make any sense. Brad Kingsley was acting as though... did Harry give Brad the idea she'd agreed to marry *him?* Alex... where was Alex? They needed to fix this.

"Lilah," shouted another voice. "Let's have a picture of the two of you." The press surged toward the table, cameras flashing.

Oh, my God! What am I doing? She needed to leave the room before this got worse. Lilah stood, her haste causing the chair to topple. "I'll be back," she said. Protests rose as she turned. Cameras continued to click as she swung to Alex. His eyes were expressionless and pinned on his brother. He had to be in shock.

She needed to fix this. Talk to Andrew… Temple… *some*body. *Oh, God, Brad.* She needed to talk to Brad. Tell him how things really were.

Seeing Alex approaching, Lilah nearly wept in relief. He'd help her get Brad away from the press room and explain. After that, she'd let Harry and his co-conspirators clean up the mess *they* made.

Alex reached them and extended a hand to Brad. "Congratulations," he said.

What?

He turned to Lilah, gaze skittering to the side. "Welcome to the family."

"Alex?" she asked, unable to understand. Wildly, she wondered if he believed she'd been two-timing him.

He kept his eyes fixed on some spot to her left, a guilty flush on his face. Lilah reared back in shock. He *knew?* In the periphery of her vision, she saw journalists watching the tableau, glancing between her and the Kingsley men. Her face burned in humiliation.

While the press continued to take pictures, she looked directly at Harry. *Did* you *know?* she asked silently. *Did you let them ambush me?*

Harry met her eyes, his face stoic. There was no denial to be seen, no excuses.

How could *you?* she cried. He didn't move; he didn't say a word. *Why would he say anything?* Lilah thought in bitter fury. Harry Sheppard had everyone exactly where he wanted them.

Lilah drew herself up, nearly shaking in rage. No, she wasn't about to let this happen. Alex Kingsley didn't have to marry her. But she wouldn't let him or Harry treat her as some *prize* to be handed over to the king-in-the-making. Lilah would make her own choices.

"What about Sanders?" yelled one of the journalists.

Lilah jolted. She pivoted to the press. "What about him?"

"Sanders, Incorporated has filed lawsuits to prevent Barrons O & G from expanding into oil services," said the reporter. "With your engagement to Brad Kingsley... the public will see this arrangement for what it is, Miss Barrons. I'm wondering what Mr. Sanders will say."

Her head swam. News of this engagement would be all over the papers. Whether she broke it or not would be immaterial. Sanders would continue to see her as a threat.

"It's a question best answered by Mr. Sanders," Harry said from the side. "This engagement involves two *people,* not two companies. Congratulate them, sir, instead of making insinuations."

"So this is not a dynastic alliance?" asked the journalist. "An attack on Sanders's control over the sector?"

Brad snapped, "What a rude thing to say. I want to marry Lilah, Sanders or no Sanders."

Lilah glanced at Brad's tight face. The sweat on his brow, the uncertainty in his eyes... *he* was risking the humiliation of a public rejection. No, she couldn't do it to him with the media watching. Later perhaps... when they got a chance to talk... but what was she going to say?

"You, Miss Barrons?" the journalist continued probing.

Lilah straightened. Raising her chin, she treated her new fiancé to a bright smile. "I said yes, didn't I?"

Someone clapped, and the rest of the crowd joined in. Out of the corner of her eye, Lilah saw Dan. He was also cheering, but his puzzled gaze went from her to Alex Kingsley, asking a silent question. With an infinitesimal shrug, Lilah let her twin think she was all right. Poor Dan. Like her, he probably imagined a different groom, but neither of them realized she wouldn't be allowed even this limited freedom. Harry... *he* knew. He knew all along.

Throughout the rest of the day, Lilah didn't get a moment to herself, let alone time to talk to Brad in private. At the evening's celebratory dinner, she forced herself to stay through the entire event, pasting an agreeable expression on her face with painful effort.

Harry offered the engaged couple his congratulations. Leaning forward to kiss her cheek, he whispered, "I was trying to tell you."

Smiling pleasantly at the room, Lilah murmured close to his ear, "Go to hell."

Part X

Chapter 30

Next morning

Laboring at the desk in her room until falling asleep didn't help Lilah avoid disturbing dreams. She woke with a crick in her neck and papers scattered all around, the same questions battering her mind. What were her options? Accept Brad? Walk away? What would Sanders do once she left?

Breakfast was immediately followed by a conference with the other half of the Kingsley clan, negotiating over every customer and every contract. On Brad's request, Andrew and Harry were present to provide support against the might of the Kingsleys. As Brad's future CFO, Lilah also claimed a seat at the talks, and she took the opportunity to study their adversaries, wanting more information before deciding on a plan of attack.

Godwin Kingsley, former justice and chairman of the board of Kingsley Corp, kept his silver mane tied in a low ponytail and sported a neat, white beard. He was seventy-six—same age as his stepbrother, the president—and was quite a commanding presence. It was evident all his grandsons inherited their impressive heights and brown hair through the Kingsley genes. While the eye color of the rest of the Kingsleys tended toward gray, Brad and Victor sported blue irises. Alex Kingsley apparently took after the Sheppard side in both coloring and features.

She noted both Aaron and David addressed Godwin as father, though he was technically their uncle, but Patrice referred to him by name in her reminiscences the day before. The older lady seemed neutral toward Godwin and opted to spend time with Andrew's wife instead of joining the rest of them.

The Kingsley patriarch addressed his family. "Because of Steven, the Kingsley name is being dragged through the mud... every newspaper in the country is speculating on the family situation... my reputation is at stake. I suggest all of you be very quiet and let me clean up this mess."

Teeth grinding, Steven said, "Grandfather, I've been putting in my sweat and blood for Kingsley Corp ever since I was thirteen. Even *before!* You had me sorting your mail at ten. How can you justify giving half of it to Brad?"

Brad cleared his throat. "Like you, I too have been working for the company since I was a child. My father, Peter Kingsley, also put in his sweat and blood into building the business. My brothers and I have a legitimate claim."

"Who's denying your claim?" snapped Steven. "Keep your shares, but you don't have the competence to run it."

"Some people believe you're irresponsible with power," countered Brad.

"Can you point out employees who will agree with your assessment?" Steven challenged. "Or clients?"

"Trying to murder potential threats to your control isn't a sign of irresponsibility?" asked Brad. "You should be in prison."

"Oh, yeah?" snarled Steven. "Do you want to tell the rest of us what happened to the assassins I'm supposed to have sent after you? You'll be in the cell next to mine, cousin dear."

"Neither of you is running anything at this time," Aaron interjected. "So sit down. *Sit down.* Father and I agree splitting the company is the best solution. There are whispers. Customers are disturbed. Under the circumstances, it's best the two of you start afresh. Separately."

With the split, it would be a couple of years before the alliance of the three companies got strong enough to challenge Sanders. *If they managed to do it during the Temple presidency.* Lilah shifted in her seat, wondering why Temple couldn't get *Steven* kicked out instead of Brad... she shook her head. Maybe the president's clout in the family didn't extend to such major decisions. Godwin Kingsley was clearly the man in charge, and he didn't seem to want to renounce either of his grandsons, no matter what crimes they committed. A split was the only option.

It took another day for Steven to accept the reality of the division, even if ungraciously. Unfortunately, anytime progress was made, his friend—Richard Armor—objected, sending them back to square one. Apparently, Major Armor was Steven's most trusted advisor.

In the end, Lilah said, "Let's look at the map, shall we? Kingsley Corp does business in Africa, Asia, the Middle East, Europe, North America, and South America. As of this time, your returns from your Latin American clients are not what you want them to be. Ongoing political problems, unstable business environment. Correct?"

Setting his glasses down, Aaron considered her. The men murmured.

She paused to let them rustle through the reports. "Latin America, Africa, and India are what we want."

Brad gave a start and shook his head.

Harry spoke up. "Kingsley Corp has little to lose by giving up these areas. In fact, this may improve your bottom-line."

As each side withdrew to consider the offer, Brad jerked his chair aside and confronted Lilah. "What are you *doing?*" he asked, his voice refined despite the annoyed tone. Actually, he'd sounded just as polished at the press conference when he was snapping at nosy journos.

Showing him a color-coded chart, Lilah said, "Brad, these regions are rich in unconventional reserves, and there's now the technology to extract it."

The world could not rely on a never-ending supply of oil, and it certainly couldn't afford to dirty the environment indefinitely without expecting adverse results. They would need to take a serious look at renewable fuels, but clean power was not yet financially doable. Shale oil and gas were also expensive but not as bad as solar or wind, currently. Industry expectation was extraction would continue to get cheaper in the coming decades.

"Mexico, Brazil, and Argentina have significant amounts of shale," explained Lilah. "Venezuela has high natural gas reserves. Chile shares the Magallanes Basin with Argentina. We already have a big client like Barrons O & G ready to invest in long-term projects. They'll buy our services. Barrons won't see return on investment for a while, but *we* will still get paid. A percentage of the eventual profits can also be written into the contracts. We can either continue to battle Kingsley Corp over every territory and create delays we don't need, or we can grab this chance at being the main business in the localities they don't particularly want. Not only that... the restrictive covenant limiting competition between the two companies will only be for two years. By then, we'll hopefully have built up a reputation as a reliable provider, and we can cut into Kingsley Corp business in richer territories. Long-term strategy, but with a lot of hard work and a bit of luck, we can make it happen."

The paper crackled as Brad flicked his fingers at it. "And what happens in the near term? Do you know how expensive new drilling technology is? Even Andrew Barrons will draw the line if the costs go beyond limits."

Harry took the chart from Lilah. "You forget something, Brad. Lilah is the only chemical engineer at this table."

Brad wiped imaginary sweat from his forehead with the heel of his hand. "A degree doesn't equal experience. What she's suggesting is not financially viable."

Voice mild, Harry said, "She's worked with the technical crew at the Barrons wells, and *Andrew* will vouch for her financial skills. Look around you, Brad. No one objected when Lilah asked for control of finances in your new company. Mr. Temple and Andrew Barrons have confidence in her abilities."

Brad took off his round, horn-rimmed glasses. "You do, too, obviously."

"Yes," Harry stated. "If she says this is workable, believe it."

"Hmm," Brad said. "What about the cost?"

Lilah said, "Gateway trades oil, which gives them plenty of influence in many of these regions. They can help us with the banks. The Sheppards can convince venture capital firms to consider long-term investments in shale extraction services. Even shipping and construction companies will cooperate if it gets them Gateway's business. We can work something out."

"How can *you* guarantee Gateway's assistance?" Brad asked.

"The Sheppards will back Lilah," said Harry. "Always."

"Why?" Brad asked. "So your family can use this alliance to get your revenge against Sanders?"

Harry smiled. "Not revenge, although none of the Sheppards would be terribly upset to see Sanders go down. We owe Lilah a lot. She'll tell you the story some other time."

Cleaning his glasses with a pristine white handkerchief, Brad studied Harry, calculation in his blue eyes. "This is your way of repaying the debt?"

She interjected, "Most of these nations have significant coastlines, and Mexico is south of the border. Panama has the canal.

Gateway wants exclusive contracts to trade oil from these regions."

Harry added, "You've got to admit the three companies working together will make a formidable entity. All of us benefit."

With a sudden smile at Harry, Brad remarked, "The papers were correct. You *are* a deal maker." He turned to Lilah with grudging respect. "You're... unexpected."

Slapping Brad's back, Harry said, "I'm intruding here. You talk while I have a chat with your brothers."

Sitting back at the table, Lilah noted Godwin Kingsley's eyes on them. The Kingsley patriarch had witnessed the entire exchange. She gave him an awkward smile before turning her attention to Brad. *Funny how I never noticed him. My God! Everyone thinks we're going to be married, and I don't even know him!* Nor did he seem very willing to take her advice. Not until Harry intervened.

"So... you think this is a good deal?" Brad asked, settling into his chair.

"It's the best we can get without going to war with your cousins."

"Sorry I was abrupt before." Smoothing back hair, Brad leaned forward. His torso was angled to keep a gentlemanly distance between them while still suggesting personal connection. "I simply don't want us to end up failing miserably."

It *was* a stressful situation. Poor fellow was as much a pawn in this game as her. His eyes drifted to the table where her hand was resting. Lilah realized her fingers were tapping out a nervous rhythm. With an inward grimace, she made herself stop. "Success depends on a lot of factors coming together, right? We'll do *our* part and work hard."

"I'm a lucky man." With a smile, Brad took her hand in his own cold one.

A dark fog swirled, ensnaring her. The screams of a sixteen-year-old echoed in Lilah's mind. She battled the monster. Escape. She needed to escape the clutches of the demon.

Around Lilah, muted conversations ebbed and flowed like ghostly voices. Her fingers flexed in Brad's hand. She opened her mouth to shout for help, but only a small whimper escaped, nearly inaudible. The blurry image of her fiancé was saying something about her engineering degree. All she wanted to do was run from the room, from him.

Somewhere behind, Dan was chatting with someone. With desperate effort, she focused on her twin's familiar voice, using it to anchor herself. Slowly, the room solidified.

Facing her, Brad was looking expectant, so she nodded. "Thank you." It must have been the right response because he smiled and continued talking.

Giving her fingers one final pat, he let go. *Thank God,* Lilah thought in relief. The air-conditioning was turned low in the conference room, but she was drenched in sweat. Her pulse raced as though she'd just dropped from another cliff.

When Brad's uncle, Aaron, pulled up a chair to talk with them, Lilah was grateful for the respite.

There had been nothing threatening in Brad's behavior. *Nothing at all! Why did I react like that? I thought I was over it.*

Aaron handed her a folder, and their fingers brushed casually. Lilah waited for panic to strike again. It took a few seconds for her to realize nothing was going to happen. Her gaze shifted to Brad. *In Venezuela... with Alex... I didn't have a problem.* At least, not until Alex called her "Harry."

When Aaron left, Brad drew his chair closer. "Lilah?" He coughed nervously. "I thought we could have dinner tonight. Just us, I mean."

An entire evening? The walls seemed to close in, trapping her. Crossing her arms to rub her shoulders, she apologized, "I'm a little tired from all the excitement this week. Maybe another day."

The pleasant look on Brad's face slipped momentarily, but he murmured with good grace, "I understand."

#

Three days later

"The bar exam is coming up," Lilah said to Brad, hoping like crazy he wouldn't think she was running away to Cambridge. Which she was. Everyone at the breakfast table probably knew it, including her fiancé and his family. Godwin Kingsley was next to the three brothers and their mother, with the murderous cousins nowhere in sight. The Sheppards had already left, and the Barronses respected the Kingsleys' need for family time. "Also, I'm clerking for one of my professors," Lilah finished.

If she really intended to defeat Sanders, if she meant the promises she made to the children in the orphanage, she'd have to take wedding vows with Brad Kingsley. Perhaps a shared dream was good enough foundation for a marriage. But how was she going to marry the man if something as inoffensive as a handhold thrust her into a nightmare? She couldn't keep coming up with excuses not to be alone with Brad as she did the last couple of days. Lilah needed to get out of all the chaos and formulate a plan of action.

Through her lashes, she watched Alex flush. He was studiously avoiding looking in her direction, buttering a piece of toast as though his life depended on it. With the snippets she got from Andrew and the Kingsleys, she'd pieced together a picture of what happened to make Alex give up any claims on her. He still hadn't offered the apology he owed for tossing her aside for his family, for not having the *decency* to tell her in person, for turning her life into a B-movie.

Victor asked, "Why are you even bothering with the exam? It's not like you're ever going to work as a lawyer. Heck, you're not even *our* lawyer." That job went to Grayson Sheppard, Harry's father's cousin and former chairman of the New York Stock Exchange. "The CFO position should keep you busy enough."

Before Lilah could respond, Godwin said, "Let her finish the exam and the clerkship. She can't start running the business right away, anyway. You'll need an interim CFO. Maybe when things settle down, Lilah can start working with the more experienced executives and learn the ropes."

"I do want to be involved from the—" Lilah started.

Godwin speared a strawberry with his fork and nodded pleasantly at his eldest grandson. "I've blocked off time in my schedule for you. Please make appropriate arrangements for my stay with you and your brothers. You'll need my help. It won't be easy to build something almost from scratch."

"I'm grateful, Grandfather," Brad said. There "But Lilah and I have started drawing up plans, and Harry's supposed to look over our proposal. Besides, Colón will be our temporary headquarters." Incorporation rules, banking privacy, proximity to the States... there were so many excuses for the new company to be headquartered in Panama, but the underlying reason was the latitude they would have to skirt U.S. law. "The city is not very safe. It's not a place I can invite you to."

Shaking his head in dismissal, Godwin said, "Lilah won't have time. Juggling law school and business will not be possible. If she leaves for Cambridge now, she'll miss the rest of the negotiations, but work has to go on. Also, Lilah... don't you need to prepare for the wedding? Focus on the things which need your personal attention and let your fiancé take care of the company. Safe or not, I'll be in Colón to guide him."

Lilah swallowed the retort springing to her lips and waited for

Brad to speak up. Not only was the family patriarch a respected figure in the oil sector, Justice Kingsley had once been a heroic figure to an aspiring lawyer named Delilah.

There was sudden uncertainty in Brad's eyes. "Ahh..." He smoothed back his hair.

"*I* can take care of the wedding arrangements," Patrice Kingsley said from the far end of the table. Over her coffee cup, she looked the old judge squarely in the eye before glancing at her son.

Lilah smiled warmly at her mother-in-law-to-be. "Company documents can be mailed to Cambridge," she said. "So I won't miss any part of our discussions."

"There you go," said Patrice.

"Problem solved," Victor agreed. Alex continued to be silent, his eyes boring into the food on his plate.

Brad nodded eagerly. "Grandfather, I'll always be grateful for any advice you can give, but it's not necessary for you to travel to a place like Colón. I promise to keep you updated. Harry will be on site, and Lilah and I will continue to discuss plans while she's finishing up law school. It won't be long before she joins us there, anyway. Six, eight months? In fact, since she *is* the chemical engineer in the group, I'm hoping she will consider taking on customer relations, as well. CFO and partner liaison. Harry says it's always good when business associates understand they're talking to someone with technical expertise *and* financial savvy."

Lilah was startled by the suggestion but not as startled as Godwin who was staring at his grandson with an unpleasant mix of shock and outrage on his face. With a nearly involuntary jerk of her head, she looked for... Harry wasn't in the room to notice anything untoward, and Brad was smiling at her. Everyone else's attention also seemed to be on her. When Lilah turned back to the Kingsley patriarch, the angry expression was gone, replaced by benevolent concern.

"We'll make it work," Brad assured her. "I could even bring the documents to you once every other week instead of mailing them."

Lilah picked up her OJ, the juice sloshing when her hand trembled. "I... I was actually hoping to avoid all distractions. Not just *you*. I mean *every*one. Besides the business, I... umm... I really need to hit the books."

Brad's smile faded. He stared at her for a second or two. "As you wish," he finally said.

Across the table, a speculative look flashed across Godwin Kingsley's face.

Chapter 31

Six months later, December 1981

Colón, Panama

Peace... Lilah cherished the feeling. For half a year, there had been no painful reminders of the past around her, only the soothing environs of the courts. She also worked her backside off for the Peter Kingsley Company. It got to the point she was almost seeing balance sheets in her sleep, but Lilah didn't mind. To her surprise, she found herself looking forward to Brad's letters. He sounded really nice in the notes he sent, asking intelligent questions and raising objections only when valid. Lilah found the entire exchange intellectually stimulating. She was even anticipating their eventual meeting with some amount of pleasure.

Lilah waited until Harry returned stateside before joining the Kingsleys in Panama. A week prior to her departure from New York, Temple did a couple of pressers where he warned rogue actors and nations any attempt to harm American citizens on foreign lands would provoke his wrath. The president wouldn't invite political suicide for himself and legal trouble for his friends by singling out certain rivals without proof, but at the first hint of wrongdoing, Temple would crack down.

Besides military action, the financial holdings of the transgressors would be targeted, and the fortunes of many of the world's despots were tied up in the Western banking system. The message would've been heard loud and clear by those who needed to hear, including governments supportive of Sanders. The criminal oilman would know he couldn't strike anywhere on the planet without his former pals turning him in. All he could do was wait and watch and use legitimate business tactics to counter his adversaries. And yeah, count days until the end of the Temple presidency.

The alliance would also be marking off days in the tiny office in Panama. *Very* tiny. Only a couple of clerks could comfortably work in the space. More room was needed, but the division of assets left Brad and his brothers poor in actual cash. The New Washington Hotel in Colón had an air of shabby grandeur and would function as both office and residence until they could afford something of their own. The largest and most comfortable of the rented suites were allotted to Lilah and Patrice.

Brad decided to celebrate Lilah's arrival with wine under the stars. They stood on the balcony, holding glasses. Assured she was safe enough with her fiancé, her bodyguards retired for the night. As far as the Kingsleys knew, the extra protection was because of potential attacks to destroy the fledgling network. They were ignorant of Lilah's abduction as a teenager and the car accident Sanders arranged for her. She wasn't ready yet to share with her fiancé that part of her life.

Still, Brad seemed like a nice man. Lilah studied him, wondering why on earth she reacted so badly to his touch before. He checked off most of the boxes a woman might've hoped for in a husband. Then there were the elegant good looks and manner.

The warm breeze from the Atlantic stirred her hair. She was trying to tug the errant strands behind her ear when Brad put the wine glass on the side table and with a soft murmur, drew her to him. There was a purposeful glint in the blue eyes behind rounded glasses. Lilah smiled uncertainly when he grazed her mouth with his.

Sharp teeth bit into her lips, drawing blood. She screamed. With a filthy curse, he slapped her face hard. "Shut up," he ordered as he pushed her onto the carpet. Lilah screamed again as he tore the front of her robe.

Lilah screamed and shoved Brad away. Everything blurred.

"What?" asked Brad, his face fuzzy around the edges. "What?" His voice echoed.

Something tight was around her chest. Lilah wheezed in air, fighting the darkness threatening to drown her. Brad's brothers... when did they run in? The Kingsley men were asking questions, their voices reverberating. She could hear the words, but she couldn't respond. Couldn't even shake her head.

"Did you see something?" Alex asked, turning around to search the balcony. "What's wrong, Brad?"

"I have no idea," Brad snapped.

The blurry form of Victor went to the railing and looked into the night. "I don't see anyone."

"Why did you scream?" Alex asked, wheeling to face her. His tall figure faded in and out. "Lilah," he shouted.

His loud voice penetrated, snapping her out of the thick fog in her brain. She stumbled and found herself caught from the back before she fell.

With a jerky movement, she freed herself from the hands holding her shoulders, scooting away a couple of feet. Brad dropped his arms, angry embarrassment on his face.

"Sorry," Alex said to his brothers. "I thought she was going to faint."

Wiping the sweat from her temples with her knuckles, Lilah croaked, "I'm okay." She squinted blearily at Brad, wondering what explanation she could give. Finally, she muttered, "It was something... a shadow."

Alex glanced curiously between Brad and Lilah, as did Victor. "Where?" asked Victor.

She shook her head. "Overactive imagination. I just need to rest."

Lilah pivoted and strode inside before anyone could ask any more questions.

Back in her room, she dialed Harry's number with shaking fingers. The phone rang for a while, and she was about to hang up when his voice came over the line. "I thought you were asleep," she said, trying to hide the trembling in her voice.

"Lilah," he exclaimed. A bittersweet pang went through her at the shocked delight in his tone. Oh, they talked on the phone over the last few months, but the calls were always at *his* instigation, and she kept the conversations solely about work. Even that they only discussed in general terms because the secure telephones he wanted were arranged barely a day before he left Panama. "Everything all right?" he asked.

Her eyes filled up. "I miss you... that's all."

There was silence from him for a few seconds. "Thank you," he said, immense relief evident in the simple phrase.

Lilah smiled through the silent tears, feeling something click back into place within her. "Did I wake you?"

"This is Manhattan," he teased. "There's always plenty going on. I was watching the world from my fire escape."

"Your apartment." Lilah remembered the fifth-floor walk-up

on Bowery Street he'd bought many months before they ended things between them. The CBGB was right across the street, country music blasting out. Drunks staggered into the Palace Hotel next door at all kinds of hours. On the sidewalk, preppy young men chatted with drag queens. Boys in mohawks and metal-studded leather jackets paid dealers and tucked small packets of white powder into their pants. Harry loved the chaos of the neighborhood.

"Yup," he said. "How's the view from *your* window?"

"Not bad. I can see the sea." She sank into the pillows, twisting the cord around with a shaking finger. There was comforting silence from the other end as she talked brightly about everything and nothing, but Lilah knew he heard each word.

When she finally trailed off, he asked, "Lilah, did something happen? You sound..."

Her fingers tightened on the phone. "Nothing important, really. New country, new family... like I said, I miss you."

"Whatever it is, it's made you talk to me. All those polite conversations were driving me up the wall. Are you ready to let me explain... the pre-nup and what happened at the press conference?"

"*You* insisted on clauses I never asked for in the pre-nup," she accused.

"Yes," Harry admitted, not a trace of embarrassment or apology in his tone. "How else were we going to guarantee your safety? How would we make sure you got an actual say in the company? Or were you prepared to give it all up for Alex Kingsley?" Harry's voice reverberated, annoyance palpable over the phone.

What would she have done if the Kingsleys offered her a choice? Lilah wasn't sure she wanted to answer the question.

When she didn't respond, Harry hissed, "*Were* you?"

She snapped, "My feelings are my prerogative. I accepted your decision to... you and I..." Swallowing hard, she continued, "I know you were looking out for me with the pre-nup, but you let them ambush me at the press conference. You... you *conspired* with Andrew and Temple... against me!"

"I tried to talk to you before," Harry insisted. "I didn't realize Andrew was going to announce it at the presser."

"So you claim." Resentment clogged her throat. "But things fell into place exactly where *you* wanted, didn't they? From the beginning... everything went just as you planned. The adoption... then you stayed away when I was in college..."

"Lilah—"

Wildly, she accused, "Did you return only so you could sweet-talk me into this, Harry?" Her chest heaving on a painful breath, she raged, "Answer me. Were you in on everything all this time?"

"Do you think I'd have manipulated you the way you say?" he asked, a ton of hurt in his voice.

"Why not? It got you what you wanted."

"No, Lilah," Harry insisted. "You don't seriously believe what you're saying. We've known each other far too long. As for Alex... ask him why—" Harry laughed bitterly. "You obviously *want* me to be the guilty party even when you know it's not true, so what's the damned point of trying to explain anything? I'm done trying to talk to you about it. You have all the details, so *you* put it together at your leisure and come to a conclusion. Meanwhile, remember the window of opportunity to overthrow Sanders is narrow, and before the mission, we need the Peter Kingsley Company to establish itself. You have a job to do, Lilah. Try to focus on it."

What use were all the cutting words when Harry no longer cared about anything except this mission of his? "You don't have to bark orders at me. I know what I'm supposed to do."

"Lilah, please—" Harry sighed.

"Goodnight." She slammed the phone down and turned off the lamp on the side table. Hours later, she was still awake, staring into the darkness.

Chapter 32

Next morning

The Kingsleys were back around the conference table, discussing clients. Alex doodled on the margins of his scratchpad, listening as Lilah talked to Godwin Kingsley on the phone.

"Yes, I'm aware the general can help us in Argentina," she said for the third time. "But his kind of help comes with strings attached."

She listened for a few more seconds.

Lilah's hazel eyes sparked with temper, but her voice was mild enough. "This is not one of the strings we can live with. Rumor is the general's coffee company is a front for gunrunning. Neither Brad nor I will let the Peter Kingsley Company get mixed up in such things."

Flipping through the pages in the folder, Brad nodded agreement.

Lilah thrust the phone under her fiancé's nose. "Here. Godwin would like to discuss it with *you*."

There were loud squawks from the receiver. Then, Brad soothed, "I know you want the best for us, Grandfather. But I don't think you're aware this general has a history with Sanders. Harry told us about it. He agrees it wouldn't be wise to get involved in the scheme."

Alex thought he detected the faintest hint of an eye roll from

Lilah. He hid a grin. Grandfather wouldn't have liked her firm rebuff. Slouching in his chair, Alex was still watching Lilah through half-closed eyes when a thunderbolt of pain shot up his shin. Victor's foot, inflicting punishment. Silently promising payback for the kick, Alex sat up and turned his attention to the lists of clients and their requirements, but his thoughts continued to drift to Lilah.

There had been a surprising phone call in the morning from the Israeli prime minister and his wife, congratulating Lilah on her engagement. Apparently, President Temple once introduced her to the couple, and they'd connected Lilah with the scientists and politicians in the country. There was genuine warmth in Lilah's voice when she talked to the Israeli first lady, and her polite request to consider collaboration between oil and gas researchers in Tel Aviv and the Peter Kingsley Company was met with great enthusiasm. Brad claimed Lilah was equally as polite but firm when handling third-world despots and Washington bureaucrats.

He was leaning toward his fiancée, holding a folder open in front of her, his other hand resting possessively on her upper back. Her mouth trembled slightly, and white teeth peeked out as she bit her lower lip. Alex was arrested by the sight of the surging redness, and he was not the only one. As if in discomfort, Brad shifted.

She cleared her throat, eyes skittering to the side. The wheels of her chair squeaked when Lilah stood to go to the side table for water. She'd barely sat back before Brad moved his chair closer, a hand on her knee. Lilah stood once more, papers fluttering to the floor in her haste, and walked to study the map of South America hanging on the back wall. Between her shoulder blades, the pale-yellow shirt was dark with perspiration.

Alex frowned, remembering the scene she made the night before. He spun his pen on the table, thinking back to his evening with Lilah in Venezuela.

"Lilah," Brad called. "You haven't been to the casinos, have you? Go with me, and we can make a night of it."

She gathered her papers. "I'm not much for gambling, Brad. You should go ahead."

Jiggling a foot, he watched his fiancée leave the room and muttered something under his breath before standing. "I believe I will. Either of you joining me?"

"I'm going to call it a day," Alex announced.

"I'm flying to California tomorrow," said Victor. His girlfriend was nearing her delivery date. She was staying put in the U.S. since she had the bar for income, a doctor she trusted, and her cousin's wife who'd promised to help her through the pregnancy.

"So?" asked Brad.

"Oh, all right," said Victor, following him.

#

Moonlight glinted on the surface of the swimming pool behind the hotel building as Lilah cut through the warm water in clean strokes. The splashes echoed loudly in the stillness of the night but did nothing to drown the thoughts zigzagging through her brain. Reality was she was pushed into this engagement. Her wishes didn't matter, her objections didn't count... like with the rape.

Reaching the wall of the pool, Lilah flipped to breaststroke. Through the droplets of water on her goggles, she saw the full moon hanging in the sky, millions of stars glittering all around. With a pang which never left her, she wondered if her parents were up there somewhere. What advice would they give?

A psychiatrist was the most obvious solution, but Lilah already knew what she'd hear. Accept the fact something dark happened in her past, close the chapter, and move on. It was easy enough for doctors to make recommendations, but the "how" of acceptance was the difficult part, especially when she didn't want meds. It wasn't only the rape. All the personal complications had turned her life into a stupid soap opera.

She swam to the edge of the pool and heaved herself out, water sluicing down her body. Tendrils of wet hair escaped from the bun at her nape and plastered themselves to her face. As she picked up her towel, she heard footsteps and whirled.

Her security guard for the shift was still on the lounge chair, peering into the night with a hand on the butt of his gun. From the shadows, an attractive man emerged into the circle of light around the pool: Alex Kingsley, a broody look on his face.

The unpleasant pounding of Lilah's heart slowed. Not one of Sanders's goons. Willing her muscles to relax, she continued to dry her hair.

"Care for a walk?" Alex asked.

It looked like the former sniper had finally steeled himself to talk to her. Lilah belted her short robe. Forcing idleness she didn't feel, she said, "Why not?" Here was a chapter she *could* close.

Dismissing the guard wasn't easy. Her previous claim of spotting a possible shadow had rattled her security team. Only when Alex showed his ankle holster and gun did the former cop agree to retire for the night.

As soon as he disappeared into the hotel, Alex and Lilah strolled the edges of the large pool, making meaningless small talk. Alex seemed to be wrestling with some dilemma of his own, occasionally glancing uncomfortably between her and the hotel building. After a while, they sat on the loungers in the thatched cabana. "Alex," Lilah called, stretching out her legs and crossing them at the ankles. "I was waiting for a chance to speak with you."

He was seated sideways on one edge of his chair, facing her, but his eyes were on the ground. At her words, he looked up.

Her fingers curled in her lap. "I want to make certain you

haven't misunderstood. About the time in Venezuela, I mean, and in New York. I don't want you to think I'm still..." She stopped, wondering how she could claim she wasn't harboring an attraction without hurting his ego.

Finding a pebble on the ground, he threw it a little violently into the pool. "It's fine, Lilah. We'd barely met. You don't have to try to spare my feelings. But why even bother to meet me in Merida?"

She made a gesture of helplessness. "Have you ever felt someone else was directing your destiny? Someone else was making decisions which should've been yours to make?"

"You wanted some control."

"Yes."

"Why didn't you tell your family Brad was not the one you picked?"

She shot an incredulous look at him. "Why would I when you didn't care enough to fight for *me*? Since I already agreed to this insane idea of a political marriage, it might as well be with someone like Brad who wants it—and me—badly enough. You, on the other hand, didn't even have enough backbone to face me. No, I got the better deal with Brad."

Alex winced. "There were circumstances..."

Silently, Lilah chastised herself. She'd meant to wipe the slate clean, not take digs the first chance she got. Turning her palm up in apology, she said, "I'm sorry. I wasn't trying to insult you."

"Can't say I didn't deserve it, anyway." An ankle hooked over a knee, he turned to face her fully. "You know I was in the military, right?"

Curiosity piqued by the uncertain tone, she eyed him. "Yes."

"There was an army nurse I used to go out for drinks with— friends, nothing more. Wonderful girl." Alex hesitated, then continued, "One of the cadets was dancing with her one evening at a bar and according to what I was told later, put a hand on her hip. She nearly killed the cadet... a reaction out of proportion to a mild flirtation, the brass told her. She wouldn't explain it and was officially reprimanded for the incident. She wouldn't let me speak up, either. As a man who was just a friend, she'd felt free to talk to me, and I knew why she acted the way she did."

Lilah was quiet, listening to him through the growing tumult in her mind.

He said carefully, "We're not friends, you and I. But if you ever need one, I'm here."

Her mind caught on to that one word. Friendship? Lilah stared straight ahead at the pool, at once confused and angry. Did he think her naïve enough to believe the empathy he offered was a prelude to only friendship? Or perhaps *he* was the naïve one. Yet the offer was tempting. Oh, so tempting. God, a speck of her existence to call her own, a fraction of a moment to live as she pleased. After a prolonged silence, she whispered, "I wonder if things will ever get back to normal."

"Takes time, but it will happen." In a noiseless move, Alex shifted from his lounge chair to hers and sat on one edge, facing her. "Besides," he teased, "the energy bottled up in you is going to need an outlet. You work from the crack of dawn to late at night. Now, you're out here swimming. You make the air crackle sometimes."

Without warning, music started somewhere close by, turning their attention. A familiar tune, but she couldn't quite place it.

After a few seconds, Alex murmured, "Strangers in the Night." Frank Sinatra.

"Ahh."

Sudden mischief in his eyes, Alex crooned, "Strangers on a

lake," parodying the original.

Lilah laughed at the sweet memory of their first meeting. She swayed in position, raising her face to the heavens, letting the silvery moonlight bathe her skin. "You sing well," she remarked.

"You dance well," he returned, voice husky.

Smiling in pleasure, Lilah said, "I'm hardly moving."

"I was talking about Venezuela," he said. His eyes pinned hers, a silent question on his face.

They were as close as they could get without touching... so close she could feel the warmth from his body. Lilah knew she should move away, but she couldn't tear her eyes from the attraction in his dark gaze. Drums tattooed away in her chest.

Alex took her hand, raising her wrist to his mouth. Recklessly, he whispered, "You're a goddess. Venus, I think."

Amused by his extravagance, she laughed once more. As he leaned forward to kiss the corner of her mouth, she told herself she was surprised. When he teased and tempted her with butterfly kisses, she closed her eyes and breathed in the woodsy scent of his skin. Lilah let go of the last threads of propriety, letting fierce elation fill her soul.

Alex untied her robe and drew it off. She stretched herself on the lounger, arms curled above her head. His hot eyes roamed all over her body, greedy gaze lingering on the thin, cranberry-colored scraps of her bikini. He grazed his fingertips over her navel, and she mewled. When he covered her mouth with his in a deep kiss, she sank her fingers into his thick hair, holding him close.

His fingers fumbled with the hook of her top. Peeling it off, he straightened. As he panted at the sight of her nearly nude body in the moonlight, she unbuttoned his shirt, revealing a muscular chest. She was free, Lilah exulted. Free to love this man. Free to *live*.

"Where can they be?" Brad sounded really close.

Alex stilled. Lilah bit her lip hard, silencing a gasp. Frantically, she pushed against Alex's shoulders.

"The guard said they were walking around the pool." It was Victor who answered. "Probably went exploring."

"In her bathing suit and robe?" Brad asked skeptically.

"Alex is with her," Victor pointed out. "She'll be safe."

The duo in the cabana separated noiselessly and drew to the shadows in the back corner. They waited until the voices faded away. Without a word to each other, they dressed and returned to the hotel.

Her belly clenched on their way back. Lilah broke into a sprint, wanting to get to her room before she was sick to her stomach. Thought after thought hammered her brain... fear of discovery, guilt of betrayal, regret at her actions. Jogging beside her, Alex kept up, but she couldn't bring herself to look at him.

The hallway was dimly lit, and tall potted plants threw long shadows. Tension coiled her limbs as she turned the knob and pushed open the door. Alex's gentle fingers touched her elbow.

"No!" The rejection exploded from her. Her hands curled into fists; breath hitched. Checking the corridor to make sure no one had overheard, Lilah repeated in a quieter tone, "No."

"At the pool, you..."

Shame surged anew. "It shouldn't have happened. I'm engaged to your brother."

"We have to tell Brad. You can't marry him."

Her pulse pounded in panic. "Don't you dare! I won't let you hurt a decent man unnecessarily."

The dim light hid Alex's expression, but the shocked anger

reverberating off him was palpable. "Unnecessarily? You're going to marry him, anyway?"

"*Now* you find the nerve to object? Yes, I *am* going to marry Brad, and I'll thank you never to bring this up again."

Victor's voice boomed up the ornate staircase at the end of the passage.

Shoving fingers through his hair, Alex hissed. "This isn't over, Lilah. I'm not going away."

Lilah slipped into the dark room and shut the door with a snap. She rested her forehead on the wood panel, trying to mute her breathing. Grimacing, she listened to Brad greet Alex, his voice surprised at finding his brother outside his fiancée's suite. The former sniper made a stumbling, disjointed explanation about going for a walk, ending with a mutter about escorting her back to her room. When the male voices grew more and more muffled, she slid the lock into place.

With bitter regret, Lilah admitted she deliberately let the embrace happen. She wanted to prove... it didn't matter *what* she was trying to prove. Her future was tied to Brad, not Alex. She'd promised herself to a man whose touch she couldn't tolerate. A sudden, sharp cry erupted from her throat before she choked it down. Lilah sat all night at the dressing table, hairbrush in her hand. The image in the mirror stared through the glass at the woman in the room, contempt in her red-rimmed eyes.

The next morning, they got back together around the conference table for one last meeting before Victor's flight to California. Lilah spoke to her fiancé, "I think we should have someone in the U.S., lobbying with policymakers and oil companies."

Brad asked, "What do you suggest?"

Praying the evenness of her tone didn't come across as

unnatural, she said, "Neither you nor I can leave since we're the senior-most of executives, and as our troubleshooter, Victor should keep Panama as home base. Alex is the only one of us who can go."

Sudden pallor marked Alex's face, and his lips thinned. "I'll be happy to."

Lilah didn't dare respond.

"C'mon," Brad protested. "There are other options. Lilah, *your* brothers are already in New York; they can help us, can't they? Also, there's Harry."

Victor had been watching his younger brother and interjected, "I agree with Lilah. Alex should go back… to lobby for our company, I mean."

Part XI

Chapter 33

A week later, January 1982

Upper East Side, New York City

Alex flexed cold fingers inside the pockets of his winter coat and stared up at the Gilded Age mansion with the evergreens circling it. He didn't have a clue if the Kingsley residence graced the list of historical landmarks, but it looked like it should. As a very young boy, Alex never considered such things. The place was simply home, at least until the day his father—the late and unlamented Peter Kingsley—walked out on his wife and sons.

The main path led to Godwin Kingsley's private residence in the mansion. Grimacing, Alex wished he'd picked another day to visit Grandfather. The butler did inform Alex about Steven's visit, but once the former supreme court justice heard another of his grandsons was in the city... Grandfather would be hurt and offended if Alex didn't pay respects in the two short days he spent in New York before flying to DC. Plus, he desperately needed the comfort of... what the hell did he call this place? It certainly wasn't home any longer. The only person currently in the magnificent edifice likely to offer familial warmth was Godwin Kingsley, but it wasn't as if Alex could confess to his grandfather what was going on in his life. The way Lilah tossed him aside, the anger at her heartlessness. Grandfather would *not* approve of Alex's feelings for his brother's fiancée.

Five minutes later, Alex was following the butler to the former justice's home office. Hearing the laughter from the living room suite not far away, Alex frowned. He recognized Steven's guffaw. There was another voice which seemed vaguely familiar... not the sonuvabitch friend of Steven's, Major Armor. Not the idiot drunk—Charles—either. "Who's in there?" Alex asked the butler.

"Mister Steven," said the old retainer, his eyes straight ahead as he creaked down the hallway.

"Besides Steven," Alex prompted.

"Er... a guest he wanted the justice to meet."

Alex chuckled. "When did Steven start bringing his friends to visit Grandfather?" As a matter of fact, Alex couldn't remember *any* of the Kingsley grandsons—himself included—ever doing the inviting. Justice Godwin Kingsley decided if and when he wanted to meet someone.

"It's not my place to answer the question, Mister Alex," said the butler.

Alex was about to ask why the secrecy, but they were at Godwin Kingsley's office door. Leaving the butler to knock, Alex glanced at the decorative mirror on the damask-covered wall and peered in the direction of the living room. The door remained closed, offering no glimpse of Steven's guest.

"Alex!" called Grandfather's voice. He was in the leather chair on the other side of the carved desk. As always, there was a chessboard on top with ivory and ebony pieces ready for a game.

By the time Alex greeted the Kingsley patriarch with a hug, the butler was already out. The thought of asking Godwin about the identity of the visitor occurred fleetingly to Alex before he dismissed it. The former justice would view it as impertinence. After a few minutes of chitchat, Alex said, "I should get going. The flight to DC is in a couple of hours."

It took him ten or fifteen minutes to locate a phone booth not far from the mansion. Apart from Grandfather, the only other person in the whole damned Kingsley clan Alex trusted was Uncle Aaron. He was the one who tipped Brad off on Steven's plan to get rid of competition the old-fashioned way.

Aaron's secretary produced the phone number of the health retreat in Florida he visited this time of the year. Once Alex got Aaron on the phone, guiding the conversation to Steven's standing in the family wasn't difficult. "I'm surprised he's back in Grandfather's good books after the trick he pulled on us," Alex complained. "I mean... I don't remember ever being allowed to invite friends."

"Friends? Oh, you must mean Ryan Sheppard's boy. He's been coming around quite often these days."

Alex started. "Harry?" The Sheppards were supposed to be helping Brad.

"No," said Uncle Aaron. "The other one, Hector. You met him at the Barrons event."

"Ahh." The event was the first *Alex* met Harry or his brother, but Victor used to box at Hector's gym. Hector Sheppard's friendliness with Steven was a major source of annoyance for Victor. "It's still strange. I didn't think Hector was Grandfather's type of company."

Aaron laughed. "Alex, my boy, didn't you hear me? Hector is Ryan Sheppard's son. After his father, Hector is the main man in Gateway. Your grandfather is merely making sure the connections remain strong when the next generation takes control. Business, y'know? Or you *should* know."

"Sure," said Alex.

Why the hell had he felt the need to go to such lengths to ferret out the identity of Steven's guest? The whole mess with Lilah... it's all it was. She'd ordered him away, and here he was, unable to forget her even for a moment... her lovely face, the beautiful form, the need within him, the madness, the anger. With supreme effort, he yanked his mind back to the present.

Dammit, Alex almost wanted Steven to be up to his old tricks. Escaping another attempted murder would give Alex something else to focus on. That was it. Hector Sheppard visiting the Kingsley mansion was—unfortunately—nothing worth worrying about. The Sheppard who mattered to their business—Harry—wasn't playing both sides.

Marching to his seat in the plane, Alex rolled his shoulders. The itch in the middle of his upper back wouldn't subside, the instinct that had saved his life far too many times as a soldier.

Chapter 34

A few hours later

Washington, DC

A hand landed on Alex's shoulder, and he jerked up, blinking at the middle-aged man before him. Grayson Sheppard, attorney for the Peter Kingsley Company, had arrived at Dulles International Airport to pick up the new chief business development officer.

Alex stood. "Hello, sir." At the Barrons mansion, Harry introduced Grayson as a cousin. How many Sheppards were there, anyway? They seemed to breed like rabbits.

"Gray will do."

"Right."

Alex was to work with Gray while in DC. At the end of the first day, Alex's head ached. Wheeling and dealing weren't his ideas of a good time. He could zero in on targets with ease, but business negotiations seemed to involve multiple motives and many decoys. Then, it was a trip to the counter-threats division. A fierce critic of

Manuel Noriega was recently killed in an air crash, and trouble was brewing in Panama; they needed to have an ear to the ground. In between, Alex found time to make a few important calls, all of them to contacts in the navy.

He was in his hotel room one morning when the phone rang yet again with the same answer everyone else gave. Military intelligence was more tight-lipped than usual regarding the activities of Petty Officer First Class Harry Sheppard.

Alex swore. "I simply want to know if my brothers and I need to worry about double-dealing."

The man at the other end of the line said, "Wait, Captain. I have more."

Another West Point grad, William "Liam" Luce, had left the service the month before to take a job at Gateway. He worked in the DC office. But Liam wasn't merely an employee. His father was the largest shareholder in Gateway outside of the Sheppard family.

"You know Captain Luce," said the caller. "Correct?"

"Yeah," said Alex, almost unable to believe his luck. He'd been peripherally aware of Luce involvement in oil trade, of course, but it didn't factor in the solid friendship which developed when Liam arrived at West Point a couple of years after Alex.

On the weekend, Alex was standing in front of his friend's apartment. He'd barely raised his hand to knock when the door was flung open, and he got the stuffing hugged out of him by a young woman with platinum-blonde hair curled in Farrah Fawcett style. Fumes of Chanel Nº 5 drifted around as gray-blue eyes shone up at him.

Alex laughed. "Verity! What are you doing here?"

"My sister decided to check out the shopping scene in DC," Liam said, grinning. "She claims she emptied the stores in New York."

Alex didn't even have to bring up the topic of Gateway. As they caught up on each other's news, Liam asked, "So what's it like working with the Sheppards? *The* Harry Sheppard, no less!"

"You tell me," said Alex.

"They don't pay much," interjected Verity, crinkling her nose.

With a long-suffering sigh, Liam said, "Once again... I'm only a junior analyst. I get paid what I'm worth."

"Papa is a stockholder," Verity argued.

"I make the same as everyone else in my pay scale," maintained Liam.

Alex huffed in his mind. So Liam wasn't high up enough in the hierarchy to know anything about Harry's doings. Even if Liam were privy to such details, it might have been too much to expect him to snitch when his father was involved in the company. Still, he was a friend, and Alex was right now badly in need of one.

"I wish I refused to answer when you asked," Liam continued grumbling. "I should've simply said I make more than enough for my needs. And it's the last time we're going to discuss it."

Liam was blasé about money the way only those who never did without could be. He was happy with his own life, the small apartment in DC, the same old Chevy from five years back. Verity, though... the white-gold, diamond-encrusted watch on her wrist was a Patek Philippe. Since the only work she ever did was some half-hearted dabbling in interior design, her father surely bought it for her.

Verity could never imagine a life in which every shiny bauble in the world couldn't be hers for the asking. From the time Alex met her at one of West Point's events, she'd sulked and whined until he gave in to her demands and taught her how to shoot. She even badgered him into teaching her to ride a bike—a *motorbike*. His wariness gave way to genuine fondness when he realized the pampered princess was not trying to add him to her collection of boyfriends. She was who she was, without an ounce of pretense anywhere.

"Least you can do is take me along when you have some kind of work party," she complained to her brother. Turning to Alex, Verity prattled on in her lilting voice. "Papa says they're too boring for him, but I want to meet Harry. One of my friends met this model who used to date him. Their pictures were everywhere! *You've* met Harry... *and* Delilah Barrons. She looks so gorgeous in the magazines! I heard her father—the real one, not Andrew Barrons— was a cousin of some kind of Harry's father. Is it true? There are so many Sheppards it's impossible to tell how everyone is related."

Were they cousins? Alex was told Lilah was born a Sheppard, but he didn't know any details beyond that. Nor had their conversations ever gotten to any discussion of their respective families. "She's engaged to my brother," he said, keeping his tone steady. "I don't know much else about her."

Later, Liam and Alex got drunk and maudlin. When Alex started belting out sad songs, Verity rolled her eyes and went to bed. "You gonna tell me what happened?" asked Liam.

"Gotta take my mind off things is all." Alex groaned. "I'm supposed to fly to Texas tomorrow. Maybe it will help... new city, new people."

"You know what we can do?"

"What?"

"Tell you when we get there. And bring your blazer... you'll need it."

Sometime later, Alex turned and inquired of his grinning friend, "Eden? The strip club?"

Once they got past the armed security guards, they were greeted by a doorman who addressed Liam by name and showed them to a table close to the bar. No strippers to be seen. There were a few barely clad women walking around, chatting to guests. Some were on the dance floor, discoing with the men to pulsating music. Scattered across the room were more guards—dressed in well-cut suits, but the soldier in Alex easily picked out fellow vets.

"Tight security," Alex remarked.

"Yeah, Lupe doesn't play around," Liam said.

"Where's the show?" Alex asked.

"Inside. We'll go there after a drink or two."

"Liam!" came a high-pitched squeal.

He let himself be dragged away by a Marilyn Monroe lookalike and called over his shoulder, "I'll send someone to you."

Sometime later, Alex watched with a frown as the young girl he'd ejected from his lap disappeared into the horde. He peered into the crowd, trying to locate Liam. A brunette of Amazon-esque proportions glided over and introduced herself in a throaty voice, "Hello. I'm Lupe."

Alex eyed her as she signaled a waiter and ordered him a drink. Slumberous eyes, full lips, and a voluptuous body screaming of sex. *Why not?* he thought. Maybe getting laid was the answer. Sipping Absolut Cranberry, he asked, "What's *your* story? Putting yourself through college or single mom?"

She laughed, a deep-throated sound. "Neither. I own the place."

In fifteen minutes, they were in the apartment upstairs. *"La Paloma"* played as Lupe shoved Alex onto the bed. Lifting himself on his elbows, he watched her straddle him. She pushed his shoulders back and leaned forward to undo his tie. The shimmery fabric of her silver gown made the shadow between her ample breasts even more enticing. Alex breathed in her perfume. Cinnamon. Blood surged to his lower body.

"Move your arms up," Lupe ordered. She looped the silk tie around his wrists and tied it to the headboard.

Lupe then put on a private show, shedding her garments one by one. Her gently curved belly and the lush hips hovered within Alex's reach, but he couldn't move his hands. He was her prisoner. Her plaything. Alex bared his teeth, growling. She unbuttoned his shirt, kissing her way down his chest. Her tongue dipped into his navel. Alex tugged against the restraints and surged up. With a low laugh, Lupe peeled off his pants.

He remained at her mercy all night.

In the morning, she leaned on one elbow, watching from the bed as he dressed. Silk sheets bunched around her hips.

"Stay," she demanded.

He glanced up, buttoning his cuffs. "We both agreed this would be a one-night deal."

Temper snapped in her eyes. "I don't usually sleep with patrons."

"I didn't mean to imply..." Alex sighed. "I'm not in a good place... not a good time to start things. I'm leaving for Texas tonight."

"Her loss," Lupe said. At his questioning look, she added, "Whoever's got you running."

"The loss is all mine." He closed the door behind him.

For his first three weeks in Austin, Alex worked nonstop, meeting clients and regularly connecting with his brothers and Gray on the hotel phone. On the last call to Panama, Patrice announced in great excitement that Victor was in Monterey with Hilda and their newborn son, Baby Gabriel.

Smiling a little at the thought of the youngest Kingsley, Alex drove to the building housing the Military Officers' Association.

General Archer, a former instructor at West Point, sat on the board of one of the drilling companies Alex needed to impress. At the military club, he waited for the general to arrive, watching some of the junior officers crowded around the outdoor shooting range.

"Alex Kingsley," a bright voice said from behind him.

The sparkling brown eyes and chestnut curls were familiar to Alex even if the gawky teen he remembered had morphed into a tanned and toned young woman. "Belle!" he said, grinning. "What a surprise. I came here to meet your dad."

#

A month later, March 1982

Washington, DC

There was something tickling Alex's nose. Hair, a hint of perfume, the smell of coffee. Even through his closed eyes, the light in the room shone through. He shifted on the mattress, trying to get comfortable. A feminine murmur of protest rose, then a second. *What—* Alex grimaced.

Oh, yeah. He returned to the capital city the night before and again took refuge with Liam Luce. An impromptu party, a phone call to Liam's stripper pals from Eden... there was a slow pounding within Alex's skull. He gritted his teeth, trying to figure out how much he imbibed.

The coffee smell was stronger now. He could really use some of it. With a muted groan, he tried to roll over and sit up.

With a sleepy giggle, a female voice said, "Careful."

Blinking his eyes into wakefulness, Alex looked around the room. There were two ladies in the king-sized bed with him, their naked bodies tangled up in white sheets. Asleep on the couch and curled up on the carpet were three more in various stages of undress. No Lupe Valdez, thank God. She hadn't been part of the drunken orgy.

In two minutes, he staggered to the kitchen and accepted the cup Liam offered. For a minute or two, they simply sipped the hot beverage in silence.

"I should leave," Alex finally said. "Tomorrow's a workday, and Gray has a few meetings planned."

Liam nodded. "Don't worry about Belle. She's not going to track you down through me."

"Thanks, man," Alex muttered. "I need to get my act together."

Liam didn't disagree.

Chapter 35

As arranged by Grayson Sheppard, Alex met with counter-threat officials again. Whispers abounded about the presence of Pablo Escobar and his drug cartel in Panama, and there was a second criminal—someone from Burma calling himself Prince—who frequently worked with a couple of Noriega's lieutenants. Victor usually dealt with the whole gang, trying to get what the company needed without letting the criminals invest. Alex would make certain the Peter Kingsley Company was kept out of trouble with the U.S. government.

As Alex strode out of the building, he spotted Harry Sheppard ambling through the front door, accompanied by a tall African-American man—Dante Maro, the COO of Gateway. Hector Sheppard walked in behind. Harry was strolling along as though he knew exactly where he was going and how much time it would take him to get there. Which he probably did.

Alex didn't get much from his investigation of Harry Sheppard, but very often, what sources refused to reveal was telling. There were also the known facts about the former SEAL and his meteoric rise to the top of international oil trade. If Alex were a betting man, he'd put his money on the CIA... perhaps the political action division. Oh, yeah. Harry was likely quite familiar with the state department.

The Sheppard brothers were definitely important contacts to have. Hector, the future leader of the company, was even invited to visit Godwin Kingsley. Hector's chumminess with Steven, the murderous sonuvabitch, predated Harry's alliance with Brad and his brothers. Alex had decided against asking Liam about any of it, but the junior analyst did volunteer a couple of interesting observations. One, save for a few, the Sheppards were indeed a greedy and back-stabbing lot. Liam counted Harry among the good guys. Two, Steven's equation with Hector was personal. It had nothing to do with the alliance or with Harry. Which made the friendship none of Alex's beeswax.

Then there was the rumor Ryan Sheppard and Lilah's biological father were somehow related. Alex winced, wondering how long it would be before the sound of her name stopped inflicting pain.

A state department employee hurried forward to shake hands with Gateway's executives. After a quick nod at the fellow, Harry turned a half-circle and scanned the area, his stance suddenly alert despite the secure surroundings. "Alex," called Harry, the surprise on his face lasting only for a fleeting moment before it was chased away by a friendly grin. "Didn't I leave you in Panama?"

#

Close to midnight

Back in his hotel room, Harry hung up the phone and collapsed onto the couch, staring at the skyline visible through the window. White-hot rage threatened to explode. Lilah had lied to him. She claimed it never occurred to her to let him know Alex was back in the U.S. Not in all these weeks. Not in all the phone conversations after their last argument about the same man.

"They do need someone stateside," soothed Dante. "Lilah certainly wasn't making it up."

"Uncle Gray represents the Peter Kingsley Company in the U.S.," said Harry. "And lobbying for business is not exactly Alex's forte."

"And *you* won't stop poking your nose into things which should no longer concern you," Dante muttered. "I'm going to bed." Smothering a yawn, he walked to the door before halting. "Harry, take my advice and let it be. Yeah, the pre-nup. I'm sure if both Lilah and Alex insist, the rest of the family will find a way to make it work."

"Not possible," snapped Harry. "All the sacrifices... this alliance... it has to be Brad."

"Of course, the alliance." Shaking his head in obvious exasperation, Dante stepped into the hallway. "Good night, Harry."

One second... two... three... striding noiselessly to the door, Harry locked it. Then, he dialed the number to the private line of the CIA director.

Part XII

Chapter 36

A month later, April 1982

Catskill Mountains, New York

Skirting the boulders jutting into his path, Harry hiked up the steep trail to the double waterfalls. Alex was right behind until they entered a clearing. At the sight of the silvery streams crashing down to the rocky ledge, he stopped. The former sniper leaned forward with his hands on his knees, laughing quietly.

Harry peeled off his sweaty shirt and threw it haphazardly to the side. "What's the joke?"

"No joke. Just amazed how beautiful this place is. Thanks for inviting me here, dude."

"The Sheppard family started doing this annual reunion a couple of years ago." Harry bent to skim stones in the pool at the bottom of the cascade. "Thought you might like to join us since we're going to be working together. You've never been here before? Didn't you live most of your life in New York?"

Alex stripped to his shorts and stepped into the pool, yelping about the cold water. He waded to the falls. "When our... ahh... father was living with his girlfriend, we were pretty poor," he shouted over the roar of the water. "No money for extras."

Harry blinked in surprise; he'd known about the estrangement in the Kingsley family, but it somehow never occurred to him Patrice Kingsley and her sons didn't live the lives of the privileged during the time.

"She had two sons." Alex clarified, "The girlfriend. She died soon after he did. The boys went to her brother. Mother did ask to adopt them, but their uncle wanted to as well, and Grandfather thought it best they stay there. They're twins. One of them is in medical school. The younger one's a physicist, already done with his Ph.D."

"You've kept track," Harry commented, amused at the pride in Alex's voice.

"They're family. Mother's been keeping track, too."

Patrice Kingsley was clearly a remarkable woman, her disdain for Ryan Sheppard and the entire Sheppard clan notwithstanding. Curious about her background, Harry had tried asking around. The two families had pushed Patrice and Peter Kingsley into marriage though it was clear they were a mismatch. Once the personal relationship fell apart, the arrangement between the two businesses disintegrated. When Harry heard the story, a thought intruded, sudden and unwelcome: Lilah's situation was not much different. Ruthlessly, he pushed it away.

Even the gossipy Sheppards didn't seem to know the details of the fallout between Patrice Kingsley and Ryan Sheppard, and Harry's father dismissed it as water under the bridge.

Hector, on the other hand, was quite forthcoming about his dislike of her. Patrice was one of the people he tried to contact for help when the senior Sheppards were arrested back in Libya. She never even returned his call. It was young Steven Kingsley who took the initial message, calling back with a promise to have his grandfather look into the situation. Fortunately, Hector's dislike didn't extend to the three men who were critical to the alliance. Nor did the Kingsley brothers seem to have anything against the Sheppards.

Alex stepped out of the pool and wiped himself off with his discarded shirt. He lay back on the ground, hands clasped behind his head. "When our... ahh... father died, Grandfather asked us to move back into the family home. He's been wonderful to us, you know; he tried his best to make up for..." Alex cleared his throat. "...what Father did. The one thing Grandfather insisted we do was follow the Kingsley tradition and go to West Point."

"You're the only one who wanted to stay in the army?" Harry asked. The CIA director had said quite a lot about Alex's actions when he was in active service. The unit led by the West Point graduate with sniper training was not what it seemed on paper, its record not limited to what was public knowledge. Thanks to Captain Alex Kingsley and the troops under his command, the American military had eliminated several problems in the Afghanistan-Pakistan region and surrounding countries. An illicit nuclear plant which went dead without warning, a Nobel Prize-winning scientist who magically escaped Soviet guards and sought asylum in London, precision strikes which took out terrorist leaders... Alex's decision to go on reserve duty before quitting altogether had come as an unpleasant surprise to the army brass. Especially so since he'd frequently expressed interest in a lifetime career as a soldier, unlike his brothers.

"The others weren't interested enough. Brad and Steven wanted to get back to Kingsley Corp. Victor took up boxing, but he left it after a year and went to Paris to study cooking at Cordon Bleu."

"Is he any good?"

"The best," Alex bragged. "But he hasn't cooked for us in a while... maybe he will once we have a home of our own. Consider yourself invited."

Splashing into the pool, Harry dipped under for a few minutes before coming up, freezing water sluicing down his chest and shoulders. "How did you both wind up working in the oil business?"

"Brad asked us to return. The head-butting with Steven was getting to him."

"Neither of you minded?"

"Nah." Alex shrugged. "I was good at what I did in the army, but there's a thrill to building something like this from the ground up. Victor was planning to start a restaurant, but he's always liked to rescue and fix, so he enjoys being the troubleshooter." Alex continued in the same tone, "Lilah is your cousin?"

"Cousin—no." Harry turned to float on his back. "Who said so?"

"I'm good friends with Liam Luce and his sister. Liam was a couple of years behind me at West Point. They told me Lilah's father was one of *your* father's many, many cousins." Alex's mouth quirked. "Exactly how many of you Sheppards are there?"

"When God said, 'Be fruitful and multiply,' we Sheppards took it literally," Harry said mock-solemnly. "For us, everyone's a cousin even if the only connection is taking a piss in the same latrine."

"My mother came from a poor branch of the Sheppard family," said Alex. "According to her, the connection with your father was six or seven generations back." He chuckled. "Hey, does that make *us* cousins?"

"Absolutely." Standing, Harry waded to the fall. "Lilah's father and mine were also only distantly related. *Very* distantly. The ancestor we have in common is a convict who ended up on the banks of the Potomac in the sixteen-hundreds. My father looked up Ambassador Sheppard when our company was in some financial trouble. If Lilah's papa hadn't invested money in Genesis, we'd have sunk without a trace—at least, that's what I'm told; it was around the time I was born. Then, he became Special Envoy to the Middle East. In fact, he advised my father to move the business to Libya when they first found oil there. I even stayed with them in Tel Aviv while Father was setting up wells in Sirtica. When Lilah's father left the state department, they moved to Brooklyn. So yeah, Lilah and I have known each other a long time."

Two more steps, and Harry was under the waterfall. The cascade sluiced through his hair, blurred his vision, pounded his back and shoulders. He relaxed, enjoying nature's massage.

When Alex stayed silent, Harry splashed out to the rocky ground. "Come on... let's get to the top."

The footing was tenuous, and spring was slow in returning greenery to the mountains this year, but the view was still worth it. They sat on the ledge, enjoying the sight of the plateau below.

"Dude," Alex said abruptly. "I need to tell you something. You were the only one around when my family decided Brad would marry Lilah. Also, you grew up with her... I need advice... maybe you can help."

Harry listened while Alex spilled the beans about the interlude in Venezuela. Lilah's reaction to Brad, her moonlight walk with Alex, and the events which followed... staring straight ahead in silence, Harry took in every word. By the end of the confession, he was nearly blinded by white-hot fury. *Betrayal,* roared his mind, uncaring of the truth he was the one who betrayed first.

"I'm in love with her," Alex muttered.

"Love?" Harry mocked, keeping his decibel level normal with almost superhuman effort. "In the three or four times you talked to her?"

"I think she feels the same about me."

A beast thundered within Harry's skull, demanding retribution for her faithlessness no matter it was *he* who first walked away from their promises to each other. "No. Lilah put a stop to it. You confessed; you feel better... the only thing left for you to do is shut the hell up about it all. If you really feel any affection for her, don't talk to anyone else about what she told you. And accept the fact she chose Brad—your *brother.*"

"Yeah, because he's going to be CEO," Alex said.

"Bullcrap," spat Harry. "You think she picked the one with the bigger bank account?"

It took Alex a few seconds, but he admitted, "No. I do know why she agreed to the marriage. Sanders, the oil sector..."

"So why are you acting like a jackass? Did you think all you needed to do was crook a finger, and she'd forget everything else to run off with you?"

"Of course not," Alex said, eyes skittering.

"Even if her decisions were selfish, it was her damned right to say no," Harry said. "To you or anyone else." It was. All he was taking away was her opportunity to say yes to the wrong man.

Chapter 37

An hour later

The trip down the trail was easier and faster. They talked about inconsequential things, but with each step, Alex sifted through thoughts and emotions. Harry's disdain came as a hard punch to the jaw, but surprisingly, the weight lodged within Alex's chest seemed lighter. He *would* get over Lilah. All he needed was time... and a good friend to knock sense into him.

At lunch, they shared a table with Hector Sheppard. "You should've gone with me, Harry," Hector said, talking about an evening he'd spent at the Kingsley family mansion. Popping the cap off, he took a healthy swallow of beer. "Godwin keeps an excellent selection of wine. President Temple was there, too, and Steven. I wish I'd invited Steven here. I want him to meet Sabrina."

Harry stilled for a fraction of a moment, then sat up. "Steven and Sabrina?" he asked, eyes narrowed. "Why?"

Exactly what Alex wanted to know. Perhaps Hector believed

whatever lies Steven fed him about the murder attempt in California, and the friendship survived. But the wannabe criminal as a potential in-law? Hector Sheppard needed his brotherly ass kicked for the suggestion.

"Why not Steven and Sabrina?" retorted Hector. "It's one of the things done by friends and family... introduce people to each other if they think—"

Loud hooting erupted at the next table, momentarily drawing Alex's focus from Harry and Hector and their plans for their sister. A group of Sheppard cousins was squabbling about the baseball season. Hector pushed his chair back with a high-pitched screech and went in search of something, leaving Harry and Alex on their own at the table. Harry was almost glaring at his brother's disappearing back.

Alex was not the only one paying attention to the argument between siblings. The itch between his shoulder blades was back. When he glanced behind, a girl raised a questioning eyebrow at him. *No, not at me... at Harry.*

Hair the color of burnished gold, eyes forest-green... she turned to smile at someone.

Sunbeam, Alex thought. Warmth, light, the promise of happiness.

"Stop checking out my sister, will you?" said Harry. "I'm right here!"

Alex started. "Sis—sister?" he stuttered. *This* was Sabrina? *She* was being set up with Steven? No way!

"Yes, my sister, Runt... Sabrina." With a speculative look, Harry added, "She's nineteen. Ask her out if you like, instead of ogling."

"Heh? Ask her—" Alex cleared his throat.

"You're not a bad fellow, Alex," said Harry. "Or you wouldn't have confessed what happened. Nor are you an idiot. You understand that the past is over and done with. Nice guy like you, educated, someone who knows the value of family... exactly the sort I'd want for my sister."

No more was said about the topic, but Alex simply couldn't help noticing Sabrina afterward.

In the evening, he found more friends at the picnic lodge. William Luce, Sr.—Gateway's biggest shareholder outside of the Sheppards—had finally accepted the standing invitation to join the family vacation. His offspring, Liam and Verity, were with him. With the exception of Harry and Hector, every Sheppard bachelor who imagined himself young enough vied for Verity's attention. She happily held court in one corner of the banquet hall, but the spectacle seemed to annoy the hell out of her brother.

"Greedy lot," Liam muttered when he and Alex were briefly out of earshot of the rest. "None of them give a damn about her. What they want is ownership of a chunk of Gateway through my father."

Liam didn't seem to notice how Verity was low-key angling her position to keep an eye on Harry as he chatted with the other guests. Will Luce, Sr. wasn't paying any mind to either of his children.

With blond hair and gray eyes, Will resembled his son, but his rotund form clearly suggested a fondness for food. He was also an obnoxious drunk.

He sat at the table and loudly mocked the poker being played. "What kind of cheapass folks are you? *Five* dollars?"

Standing by the fireplace in the large hall, not too far from the card players, Alex and Harry were chatting with Liam, enjoying beers. "Dad," Liam called, face red in embarrassment.

Will ignored his son. "Play like a *man*," he said to Ryan Sheppard, Harry's father.

Tone mild, Ryan said, "This is just a friendly game, Will."

Will took another swallow from the vodka glass, clear liquid dribbling from the corner of his mouth. "You need balls to play a good game of poker."

"Please, Dad," Liam begged, voice tight.

Will flung a hand up without looking back. "I'll bet a thousand bucks. C'mon, who wants to join me?"

Ryan muttered something under his breath and stood. "I'm out." So did the other players at the table. A couple of the older men drew up chairs.

"*Two* men?" Will derided.

Hector Sheppard intervened. "Stop, Will. You're not in Atlantic City."

"So?" Will swept his drink to the side, and the crystal glass toppled, spilling vodka on the hardwood floor. "Let me see if I can tempt you, Hector. I'll bet half my shares in Gateway."

"Half your stock?" asked one of the interested players, a short, skinny man, his balding pate shining under the yellow lights.

"Will!" said Ryan. "You need to stop."

"Why should I?" Will demanded. "It's mine, ain't it?"

With more patience than Will Luce deserved, Hector said, "You're too drunk to play. Also, don't you think SEC might have something to say about what you're doing?" The Securities and Exchange Commission regulated sales of even private stock.

"Hector," called Harry. "Let him. I'm sure whoever wins can find a workaround with SEC."

Surprised at Harry's attitude, Alex turned to him. "Don't, please," Liam entreated, covering his mouth with cupped hands.

Verity sidled to them, a couple of her friends trailing. "What's going on?" she asked, eyes confused. Liam flung both hands up. The rest of the guests drew close, gawking at the scene.

Harry added, "Alex and I will join the game."

Alex coughed hard, nearly choking on his beer. *They would?*

"Five-card draw," Harry said, seating himself.

Alex followed, wondering what Harry was up to.

"I prefer Texas hold 'em," said Will.

Harry picked up the deck and arced it in front of him to inspect the backs of the cards. "We've been playing five-card draw all evening," he said. "Take it or leave it."

Will glared at Harry. "Whatever."

Harry scooped up the cards and spread them, face up. Dividing the deck into multiple stacks, he scrambled it. He moved the cards around the table in circular motion and turned to Will Luce. "Are you man enough to put up *all* your stock?"

A collective gasp went through the crowd around. Will snorted. "You willing to put up all yours?"

"Sure thing," said Harry, eyes crinkling.

Heads swiveled between the two high-rollers. "Harry," his father said, voice uneasy.

"Trust me," Harry answered, not looking at Ryan Sheppard.

Alex scooted his chair back. "Are you mad?" he hissed. "Will is *Liam's father.*"

"I'm aware of it," Harry muttered. Turning to Will, he taunted, "Go ahead. Show them you have *balls.*"

"All right, *boy,*" Will snarled. "All my shares in Gateway."

The bald player objected. "What about the rest of us? I can't match your ante."

"We make our own rules," Will said, a manic glint in his gaze. "Every player bets something it would hurt to lose. What are you worth? A couple hundred mil?"

Harry collected the cards and dealt them, five for each player even though the others had yet to agree. Alex couldn't believe the stupidity. "You're out of your mind," he said to Harry, half up from his chair. "I don't have the kind of money you do."

"I'll put up your stake," Harry said. "What do you say, Will? Half my shares as Alex's ante and the other half as mine?"

"Fine," Will snapped, eyes glittering.

"Dude," Alex said. "This is crazy."

Harry mumbled, "Sit in for the hand, okay?"

With a huff, Alex settled back. As chatter rose in the room, he muttered, "I hope you have a plan. Put a pill in everyone's drink or something."

"Who do you think I am?" Harry asked, also under his breath. "James Bond?" He smiled at the rest of the players. "All five in? Good." He gathered the cards, shuffled twice, and passed them to his left to be cut.

With slips of paper noting their antes in the middle of the table, Alex sweated, feeling slightly dizzy. Once more, Harry dealt the cards. Five cards per player, five players at the table. He stacked the rest of the deck to the side.

Alex fanned his cards out between his thumb and fingers. A couple of sevens, a king, a ten, and a three. Not the best hand, but he did have a king kicker to the small pair.

The bald man sitting to the left of Harry bet a thousand. Around the table, the remainder of the four players called. A thousand bucks of Alex's own money! The Peter Kingsley Company was currently short on cash, most of it being tied up in getting the new business off the ground, and Alex's salary was not terribly high. If he lost, he'd have to ask one of his brothers for a loan. Victor perhaps, assuming he had any leftover cash after covering Hilda's pregnancy expenses. Alex couldn't imagine having to approach Brad or Lilah with this particular problem.

The play continued to draw. When it was his turn, Alex stared holes into his cards. The king and the ten were high ranks; he didn't want to lose them. On the other hand, the sevens were a pair. But except for one of the sevens, they were all hearts. Finally, he said, "One," and gave up a seven. *Phew.* Ace of hearts. A flush with ace-king high. Alex settled himself more comfortably in the chair.

The second round of betting began. They were all studying each other with intensity, trying to guess at the hands. Sweat beaded on the bald man's pate, his thin frame somehow sinking even further into his clothes. Will Luce, his eyes bloodshot, smirked at Harry. On his part, Harry took a sweeping glance around the table and signaled the waitress for drinks. When he asked for "Scotch, straight," Alex nearly whimpered in panic. The fifth player, a professorial-looking man with a neat beard, was adeptly maintaining one of the best poker faces Alex ever saw.

The bets remained the same. No one raised. No one folded. No one dared to since the initial antes were this high. It was time for showdown.

Face pale and sweaty, the bald man showed his cards. One jack was all he had.

Will snorted, slapping his own cards onto the table. Four eights and an ace. His four-of-a-kind beat Alex's flush.

Alex swore quietly and succinctly and waited while the third player—the professor type—laid his hand on the table. A pair and nothing else.

When Alex revealed his losing cards, excited chatter went

around the audience. Someone whooped.

"Go ahead, *boy*," Will jeered. "Show us what you've got."

Face bland, Harry drew a card from his hand and placed it face up in front. Ten of spades.

"C'mon," said Will. "Don't waste time."

Milking the moment for drama, Harry placed the rest of the cards, one by one. Jack of spades, queen of spades, king of spades, and ace of spades. A royal flush.

Alex couldn't breathe. The highest possible hand? How the hell—

The audience gasped. Behind the table, Liam turned away, hands covering his ashen face.

Will Luce stood, knocking his chair over. "You *cheated*."

Murmurs of agreement went around the room. None of the Sheppards spoke up for Harry. Anger swirled, punctuated by the sounds of wait staff moving between guests.

Alex tensed, readying himself to drag Harry out before the crowd erupted.

"Whoever wants to can check," Harry said mildly.

Which, of course, the rest of the players did. There wasn't a thing wrong with the cards. None marked, none damaged. None missing, nothing extra. One by one, the losing players conceded, but the air remained thick with resentment. There was no applause for the winner of the game. Looks of disbelief were evident on every face, impotent fury in every hiss. But no one else vocalized the suspicion Harry cheated. Without proof, no one could raise their voice against the son of the CEO.

Except Will Luce.

Mouth open in confusion, Verity looked on as the old man

started a tirade. "What happened?" she asked. No one answered. The fact that her father just lost all their money in a matter of minutes hadn't yet sunk in. Her expensive car, the jewelry, the lavish lifestyle, all gone in an instant of arrogant stupidity.

Harry signaled to a couple of the men. "Take him back to his room and let him sleep it off." As Luce was being tugged out, kicking and screaming, Harry turned to Liam. "If I didn't do this, he'd have lost it to someone else tonight. His stock will be made over to you and your sister but to be held in trust by the board of Gateway." He told the other players, "The rest of you can have your antes back."

Once more, muttering rose among the crowd, some laudatory, some accusatory. Face gray, Liam shook Harry's hand. "Thank you," he said, voice shaking.

Verity marched to Alex and pulled at his sleeve. "What happened?" she asked again, tone plaintive.

"Tell you later, sis," Liam said.

"He cheated," screamed Will Luce as he was hauled out the door.

"*Did* you cheat?" Alex asked in a murmur.

Under his breath, Harry responded, "You'll never know." He winked at Alex and stated loudly, "Anything to impress a pretty girl."

Verity blushed.

Later in the evening, boogieing with Alex to "Electric Slide," she bombarded him with questions about Harry. Moving from one step to the next, Alex laughed at her unabashed interest in his cousin. When the gathered Sheppards clapped appreciatively at the end of the song, Alex caught Sabrina's eyes on him and smiled.

Chapter 38

A week later

City Island, New York City

After the reunion, Alex accompanied Harry to the Sheppard family residence, invited to stay there for the duration of his New York visit. Harry and his brother were also spending time with their parents, and Sabrina—a sophomore at Hunter College—still lived at home.

Life in the household was peaceful... on the outside.

At dinner one night, Hector abruptly announced his engagement to one of the instructors at his gym. The eldest Sheppard son stared hard at Harry and declared there was no point in waiting for other things to fall into place. Hector apparently used to date the woman before and reconnected with her, quickly deciding she would suit. Ryan and Sophia Sheppard's expressions were also odd, their strange coldness directed toward Harry.

After a puzzled glance at the rest, Harry congratulated his brother and left to fetch a bottle of champagne. Sabrina also appeared confused at the behavior, but she didn't probe.

Sabrina *was* lovely, almost vibrating with enjoyment no matter what she was doing. It didn't matter to her whether she won or lost a poker game with her brother. She spent her time watching every move of Harry's fingers with an eagle eye, trying to catch him cheating. The former SEAL was apparently a boxing fan, but he needled his sister on the sorry state of her favorite baseball team, the New York Yankees. Alex's, too. Sabrina dived for the biggest piece of chocolate cake at dinner and sang as loudly as she possibly could on her way up and down the stairs.

Spine straight with pride, she showed Alex the "muscliest" of cars owned by any of the Sheppards—her aqua-colored Mustang.

She was still paying for it by working her butt off at her part-time job with some tech company called CompuServe.

Fate was throwing them together, but somehow, Alex couldn't work up the courage to make a move. With his recent track record, there was every chance of it ending in disaster, and he couldn't afford to anger her. She was a Sheppard, and the Kingsley brothers needed Gateway's support.

He usually just worked in his room while the Sheppards were away in their office, and one beautiful day in May, Sabrina dragged him out for lunch, claiming she was at loose ends. At the restaurant, she ordered the fattest lobster in the tank, telling him if he could play high-stakes poker, he could very well fork out a couple of hundred bucks to feed her. Only, at the end of their meal, she split the bill with him, announcing imperiously she was a feminist. No question she was. When he simply happened to glance down at the locket hanging around her neck, she told him very firmly where to keep his eyes if he wanted to keep his family jewels. Also, there was the reading material he'd seen around the house, from *Sexual Politics* to Wonder Woman comics.

Chatting amicably, they strolled back, and once inside the door, she puckered her lips. There were still a few hours before the Sheppards were expected to return, but beyond a quick brush of her mouth with his, Alex refused to take advantage. Instead of surprise or annoyance, there was comical resignation on her face, followed by mulish determination.

Over the next couple of weeks, they continued to lunch together whenever she got free time. With fluttering eyelashes and pouting lips, she made plenty of advances. Alex was determined not to succumb. First, he needed an opportunity to be honest with her, to tell her of his recent failures and ask if she still wanted to risk it.

On a fine afternoon, Alex sat on the bench facing the waters of Long Island Sound and watched Sabrina chase the neighbor's kid—

a boy of ten or so—down the boat ramp. Seagulls called to each other as they flew into the cloudless summer sky.

"Hey, watch what you're doing," Sabrina yelled.

The lad climbed to stand on the bow of the boat and turned, rolling his eyes at her. He teetered.

"Get down, you little idiot," she shouted.

Alex's eyes drifted shut in preparation for a pleasant nap. A sudden, loud splash had him snap them wide open.

"Oh, God!" Sabrina shrieked, her scream followed by a second splash as she dived in.

Bulleting off the bench, Alex ran to the ramp. Ripples spread through the water. He sprinted up the boat and launched himself over the side. When Alex opened his eyes underwater, he saw Sabrina's shadowy form not too far away, struggling with the child. He swam to them, only to watch the boy kick off upward.

All three surfaced at the same time, the boy laughing. Alex's pulse pounded in fear and anger. "Is this your idea of a joke?" he demanded.

The laughter died. The boy sidled next to Sabrina as they splashed out. "I'm sorry," the boy offered. "I didn't think you'd worry." Sabrina glared at him. "Okay, so I did," he admitted, "but I didn't think you'd be this angry."

"I'm taking you back to your mother," Sabrina said.

The boy wheedled, "Do you have to tell her?"

Sabrina made an inelegant snort and marched the rascal off to face the music.

Alex had already changed into khaki shorts and a polo shirt and was making coffee when she returned to the main house, still dripping water. She hurried to her room, and he watched surreptitiously as her wet form ran up the stairs, the off-shoulder, green blouse clinging to her shapely curves.

Without warning, she whirled, catching him red-handed.

He dragged his gaze back to her face, groping around in his mind for a way to apologize without actually having to admit he'd been staring at the enticingly rounded bottom covered by denim shorts.

Sabrina drew herself up, somehow managing to look down her nose at Alex though she was only half his size.

He bit back a grin. A height of sixty or so inches and a deliciously curvy body didn't exactly scream intimidating.

At his continued silence, she stiffened, her green eyes shooting flames.

Okay. If admiring a beautiful woman were a crime, he'd confess without compunction and cheerfully admit he was likely to be a repeat offender. Alex was ready to apologize for embarrassing her, but he refused to be cowed into feeling guilty about finding her sexy.

Sabrina was now tapping a foot, looking more like an outraged pinup girl than one of her favorite superhero characters.

Hoping he wouldn't explode into laughter, he met her stare without flinching.

A blonde eyebrow shot up. She returned the favor, eyes lewdly sweeping from his face to his biceps and abdomen and thighs, lingering leisurely on his groin.

His back against the kitchen counter, Alex stretched his arms high above his shoulders, silently inviting her to keep admiring his body.

Sabrina tilted her chin, apparently unimpressed. Kicking off her wet Birkenstocks, she leaned casually against the handrail and drew a toe along her calf.

His shorts were instantly tight. Painfully so. Alex gulped.

She didn't miss it, the little tease. Laughing in victory, she pumped her fists in the air. Then, she twirled and boogied up the stairs, singing, "Dancing Queen."

She returned soon, wearing another pair of denim cutoffs and a psychedelic tie-dye shirt in navy, the moisture from her blonde waves leaving a dark patch on the back. Her usual cool grass scent hovered delicately around her. Alex had been all prepared to deliver his apology, but the beatific smile on her face suggested she didn't want any. They sat on lounge chairs on the deck, holding steaming mugs, and chatted about the boy they thought they'd rescued from drowning.

"He's grounded for the rest of his life." Sabrina sighed in satisfaction. "At least for the rest of summer."

"Oh, c'mon," Alex said, laughing. "Bit harsh, doncha think? I did worse things in my time."

She snorted into her coffee.

He raised a hand and swore, "My mother could tell you stories."

"I want to hear your *army* stories," she demanded. "Everyone says you're a genuine military hero."

"Your brother's one," Alex commented.

She waved it off. "Harry doesn't count."

"I'd rather talk about you. Beautiful women are always more interesting."

Her eyes narrowed. "You think I'm beautiful? Not cute or cuddly?"

"You *are* cute. And sexy as hell. I thought you noticed my *feelings* back there."

Peeping over the rim of her mug, Sabrina said, "Your *feelings* were a reflex response. When you got the chance to make a conscious move, you didn't."

"Roger that," Alex muttered, gulping a mouthful of coffee.

"What?" she asked. "Do I remind you of the sister you never had or something?"

Alex choked, sending coffee the wrong way. Coughing, he said, "God, no."

"Because it happens to me all the time," she admitted.

"Let me make it clear," Alex attested, a hand to his heart. "I have no brotherly thoughts about you. None whatsoever."

Waves crashed on the shore, and gulls called to each other on the beach. She huffed. "Words are cheap. They make nothing clear."

"What will?"

In one smooth move, she swiped the coffee from his hands and set both their mugs on the wide arm of her Adirondack chair. "This," she said and climbed onto his lap, straddling him. With mischief in her eyes and the taste of roasted beans on her soft lips, she covered his mouth with hers.

#

The senior Sheppards and Hector were at the Brooklyn offices of Gateway, Incorporated, expected to return late as usual, but Harry took a cab back to City Island with the intention of discussing some plans with Alex. He didn't like to use his Harley there, what with the lack of space to park where it wouldn't get scratched or dented. The bike stayed in its own spot in a garage in Manhattan, safe in the hands of the retired mechanic who managed the place.

The afternoon sun was bright in Harry's eyes, but he could make out two figures on the deck of the Sheppard home. The man was sitting on the chair with the girl astride him. His hands were on her hips, and her fingers were in his hair, holding him close while they kissed. The girl slid off the man's lap and stood. When she sauntered into the house, he followed.

Harry turned to walk to the nearest restaurant and stayed there until the day faded away.

When he returned, Alex's car was still parked outside, and so was Sabrina's Mustang. Harry jogged up the steps to the deck and slid open the glass doors leading to the kitchen. The room was shrouded in shadows. Warm breeze drifted in behind him, ruffling his hair. Complete silence reigned in the house as though there weren't two people upstairs.

Harry picked up the steel-tip dart from the countertop and threw it at the target mounted on the opposite wall, barely visible in the darkness. The dart hit dead-center. The board oscillated from the force and fell to the floor with a thud. He smiled in satisfaction.

Part XIII

Chapter 39

A few weeks later

Fourth of July on City Island was grand with red, white, and blue balloons adorning the stores. Since it was summer, the kid brigade was out in full force, roller-skating where they shouldn't be. Alex scooped deliciously cold Italian ice into his mouth and sauntered down the street, smiling at Sabrina. They nearly got caught the last time they made love, what with all the howling she did. But he was willing to risk discovery for the joy, the incredible enchantment of just being with her.

Memories of his past—of other women—seemed dull in comparison. Even the mental images of his brief time with Lilah faded away day by day. A miracle, considering Sabrina herself brought up Lilah's name several times. Harry's sister adored Lilah. Alex didn't know how the hell he was supposed to come clean with Sabrina under the circumstances. He didn't want to risk losing her, and he definitely couldn't risk her anger when there were bigger things at stake, like his family's future.

Sabrina also asked Alex to keep things quiet for the time being, worried about her parents' reaction to having him under their roof if they knew.

"Alex," she called, kicking a pebble with her shoe. Her voice was unusually moody.

The top of her head reached the middle of his chest when they walked side-by-side, and unless he bent to peer into her face, he couldn't see her expression. "What?"

Her brothers were approaching, jogging across the street with hot dogs in hand. "Later," she said.

Dinner was a quiet affair. Ryan and Sophia Sheppard had gone upstate to visit her family, but the siblings stayed behind. Hector's fiancée was on one final vacation with friends before their upcoming nuptials. "By the way, Alex," Hector said, "I hope you don't mind, but I've invited your cousin Steven to join us tomorrow for dinner."

Pretending indifference, Alex reached for the wine bottle.

Hector continued, "I'm hoping Sabrina and Steven will take a liking to each other."

The wine splashed over the sides of the glass. Alex apologized, grabbing a napkin to soak up the red liquid. A smirk on his face, Harry thrust a kitchen towel under Alex's nose.

Pale and anxious, Sabrina stared at her older brother. "I don't want Steven here."

Harry returned to his food, but Hector was clearly surprised. "Relax, it's only dinner."

Sabrina stood abruptly and ran out of the room, leaving Hector gaping. Harry studiously enjoyed his after-dinner sweet.

"What's wrong with her?" asked Hector.

Alex put the wine-stained towel down. "I'll check."

Sabrina was standing on the deck, arms across her chest. Mindful of her brothers watching through the open glass doors, Alex maintained distance. "Are you all right?" No answer was forthcoming. "Steven coming for dinner doesn't have to mean anything." Gently, he touched her elbow.

She didn't turn. Voice high and loud enough to carry into the house, she said, "I'm pregnant."

Chapter 40

Harry's fork clattered to his plate. *Preg—* He shook his head. Hector appeared equally nonplussed.

Outside, Alex's jaw was almost on the floor. At his continued silence, a muffled sob erupted from Sabrina. She ran into the kitchen and up the stairs.

"Sabrina," Alex called, jogging after her.

Hector stood.

"Where are you—" Shoving his chair back, Harry leaped to block Hector's path. "Let them talk."

"I'm going to kill him," snarled Hector.

"Don't be stupid. What Runt needs from us right now is our support. *Unconditional* support. No matter what she chooses to do. Wait until then to decide how to deal with Alex."

A door slammed upstairs. "Sabrina," bellowed Alex. "Let me in."

"My God," said Hector. "What am I going to tell Steven?"

Harry blinked. After a couple of seconds, he made himself nod. "Yeah... better cancel the dinner invitation." When Hector went to the phone, Harry got busy clearing the table. *Family,* he mused, his heart heavy. He didn't want to believe he was wrong to have faith in their affection. Not that *he* was any better.

Alex's shouts turned to pleas, then to frustrated mutters. Apparently, Sabrina wasn't budging. Hector stayed in the study to call the Sheppard parents. Good thing, since Alex stomped down to the kitchen, face dark and exasperated. "She won't even talk to me," he announced, shoving fingers into his hair.

"She's upset," Harry said. "Give her a couple of hours."

"What do *I* do? Go for a walk?"

Ignoring the angry sarcasm, Harry said, "Whatever clears your mind."

Without another word, Alex wheeled and left the room. In a few seconds, the front door snapped shut.

When their parents got home later, Harry had to forcibly stop his father from going out to look for Alex. Harry grabbed Ryan by his arm and dragged him into the small home office. His worried mother followed them—Hector, too.

"We should've never let the sonuvabitch stay—" Hector fumed. "Your fault, Harry. Dammit, he *knew* I was planning to introduce her to Steven."

Poor Sabrina. Two brothers, and neither of them worthy of the title. Out loud, Harry said, "Sabrina is a grown woman, and it was her choice to go to Alex. Let *her* decide what she wants to do going forward."

Ryan would not be pacified. "Nineteen and pregnant! She's barely an adult. She's not ready for those kinds of responsibilities. Her dreams... her future..."

He was looking at the door and didn't see Harry's face harden as he remembered Lilah at sixteen, stating in a voice devoid of emotion she was not pregnant. He remembered Lilah being asked to give up her dreams for the sake of *his* family.

"My poor baby," said Sophia Sheppard. "I'm going to talk to her."

As the Sheppard parents went to their daughter, Hector stomped his way back to his room. Harry stayed in the kitchen, unable to sleep, mind full of turbulent thoughts. Toward the morning, the phone rang. "Hello?"

"Harry?" Uncle Gray's voice responded. "Good. I was hoping

to get *you* on the phone. I tracked Alex's movements as you asked me to. He *has* worked hard on building his contacts. But remember when he mentioned meeting General Archer in Austin? What he didn't tell us is he asked the general's daughter to marry him. Rumor has it he showed up at the ceremony and told her he couldn't do it."

"Marry—*shit*." Harry pinched the bridge of his nose.

"Belle Archer. She gave me a phone number to pass on to Alex. There's more... when he returned to DC..."

When the morning sun turned the Atlantic sky pink, Alex walked in through the patio doors. Harry was making himself some coffee and handed Alex a bit of paper. "Uncle Gray called with a message for you to get back to someone in Austin."

Alex made the call from the office and came out looking worried.

"Problem?" asked Harry.

"Huh? No. Maybe. I don't know... I need to talk to Sabrina."

"No, you need to talk to us," said Sabrina's father. The Sheppard parents came down the stairs with their daughter. As everyone sat around the kitchen table, Ryan Sheppard continued, "We're not thrilled... but Sabrina wants to keep the baby, so marriage may be the best outcome to this situation."

Hector walked in, glowering at Alex.

With a hesitant smile, Alex reached for Sabrina's hand. "I don't need your parents to tell me what to do, Sabrina. You... you're wonderful, and I think we have something special between us. I'd like to marry you if you'll have me."

The sudden brightness on her face made her answer crystal clear.

"My sweet girl," Sophia sniffled, hugging her youngest child from the side.

"I'll keep her happy," Alex said, nodding at his future in-laws. "I swear."

As Ryan shook hands with his daughter's new fiancé, Harry glanced at the bit of paper sticking out of Alex's pocket, the one with a Texas phone number on it. Hector was also staring hard at Alex. Not with anger or concern or even reluctant acceptance... but with acute resentment at the outcome.

Chapter 41

A few weeks later, August 1982

Upper East Side, New York City

Alex was commanded by his grandfather to make an appearance at the Kingsley residence and to bring Harry along. Leaving Harry to park the car, Alex walked into the home office and was greeted with a warm hug from the patriarch. "Alex, my boy. I miss having you around here... always asking to tag along when I went to the range."

"I was ten years old, Grandfather." Alex slapped the old man's back with affection, surprised to see President Temple a couple of feet behind. "These days, I manage to get myself there."

Arm around Alex's shoulders, Godwin led him to the side table to pour a drink. "To me, you're always going to be the same eager kid, my favorite grandson."

Temple smiled his thanks as Godwin handed him a brandy snifter. "Congratulations on your engagement, Alex. I remember Sabrina—a pretty girl. Didn't realize you knew her."

"We met only a few weeks back." Alex shoved fingers into his hair, hoping his embarrassment didn't show. News of the pregnancy had assuredly reached the president and the family patriarch.

It had been damned awkward announcing it to Patrice, and she was too shocked even to blurt objections at the idea of one more Sheppard for a daughter-in-law. Brad was excited... and disgruntled at the delay in his own wedding. Something always got in the way when he and Lilah tried to set a date. Victor claimed he would get hitched only when the company was financially stable. Alex would thus be the first of the brothers to marry. He and Sabrina would say their vows barely a week after Hector's wedding to his gym instructor fiancée.

"I hear Harry introduced you," Godwin said. "Hector was trying to set her up with Steven. Doesn't matter. Sabrina will still be a part of the Kingsley clan—the Peter Kingsley branch of it. The Sheppards must be happy about both the girls snaring Kingsleys."

Snaring? Bemused, Alex said, "Harry has been supportive."

"I'm sure he has," said Temple. "Alex, *I* asked Godwin to get you both here for a chat."

"Yeah?"

They stood around the large carved desk as Godwin moved the ever-present chessboard to the side and spread a map open. "This is the Argentine-Chile border. East of the Andes is Neuquén. There are tight gas sands there, and I'm told the engineering team of Barrons O & G brought up the idea of experimental wells when Lilah worked for them. She asked them to table it since the native tribes living on the land opposed drilling. What if something happened to move them out?"

"'Move them out?'" Harry echoed from the doorway. The Kingsley butler was right behind and inclined his gray head toward the patriarch before closing the door and creaking off. Harry waited a couple of seconds, then continued, "Mr. President, I thought Lilah made it clear she wasn't about to have the tribespeople bullied out of their homes when the Barrons board discussed this. Also, it would be a long-term project. Not a quick money-maker. Barrons didn't want to invest in the undertaking when there was likely to be political turmoil over the tribe's concerns. The board voted against it."

Temple nodded. "Yes, but circumstances have changed."

"How so, sir?" Harry's voice was pleasant.

"We've already had delays we don't need with our alliance against Sanders," said Temple. "You must know he is the one who supplies the tribe with weapons and money. In return, they block any attempts by other drillers to gain a foothold. This way, Sanders gets to wait until new oil and gas technology becomes more profitable to obtain exclusive access. If we get the tribe to vacate, it will be our first strike against him and the next step in our expansion plan."

Alex was confused. "*We*'re in oil services. Andrew Barrons handles the drilling side of our alliance, and if he's already said no—"

"The Peter Kingsley Company is located outside the U.S.," Godwin interjected. "So are the proposed wells. It won't be easy for Sanders to instigate antitrust lawsuits."

Harry objected, "The Peter Kingsley Company's income comes from payments by drillers for services rendered. Gateway has been helping Lilah reduce costs by asking shipping companies and other vendors to accept a percentage of future profits as part of the payment, but they won't do it when the drilling company itself is new. The Peter Kingsley Company *will* be new to the drilling arena. Banks and venture capitalists will balk at lending money for the same reason. A long-term project with an essentially unknown entity? Few financiers will want to play that game. For Brad and Lilah and the rest to venture into drilling on their own, either the project needs to be something which would yield immediate returns, or they'd need their own cash lying around which they can use to expand."

"What if we help with the money?" Godwin asked.

Startled, Alex said, "Help us... but... I mean, not as if I'm not grateful. But why?"

"Remember the purpose of the alliance," said President Temple, nodding at Harry. "With all the postponements, we can't afford to waste more time. If it doesn't get done while I'm still in office... Sanders is counting days."

Chapter 42

Later in the week

City Island, New York City

The Sheppard home was packed with guests. Harry stood at the periphery and smiled as well-wishers congratulated the engaged couple. Gossip about the bride's pregnancy had spread, and Alex was forced to blush his way through all the raunchy jokes.

Only Grayson was subdued. "Harry, the rumor mill in Austin says Belle threatened to call Alex's fiancée." They watched Alex, now with his arm around his glowing wife-to-be. "I hope he's not going to ditch our Sabrina and run off with strippers," Grayson muttered.

"He wouldn't dare," Harry said. "The Kingsleys need us."

Dante stalked to them, an angry glint in his eyes. "This is too much, Harry," he announced. "I didn't dream you'd go this far. What is *wrong* with you?"

"What are you going on about?" asked Harry.

Grayson made the universal gesture of surrender and walked away.

"Couldn't *stand* to see her happy with someone else, could you?"

Dante asked.

"You think I did this to spite Lilah? There are valid reasons for her to marry Brad, and she knows them."

From among the crowd in the room, a tinkling sound arose. Ignoring it, Dante muttered, "Poor girl. Have you given even a single thought to how she must be feeling now?"

"May I have your attention, please?" Verity stood with a glass and a spoon in hand. "We have all wished the happy couple well. My friend Alex..." A smooch on his cheek. "...and our very own Sabrina." Another smack. "Now, we should have some music and dancing."

Guests cheered and rushed to move chairs back, creating space. Dante was practically dragged onto the makeshift dance floor by one of the older Sheppard ladies.

"*Harry,*" Verity squealed, handing him a saxophone. "Sabrina tells me this is yours."

He blinked in mild surprise. His sax... he'd ignored it since leaving Libya, but someone had kept it polished. Harry took it from Verity, running light fingers over the lacquered finish and the flawless key design. He waited for the old itch to hit, to play a tune guaranteed to tempt a teenaged Lilah into twirling around him. There were times when she forgot her awkwardness enough even to sing along. Bittersweet echoes of those inept renditions lapping at the edges of his mind, he smiled.

Verity's voice broke into his reminiscences. "Tell me you'll play, please, please, *please.*"

"I'm too rusty for a public performance."

She pouted and tried to tug him into the crowd. "I hope you at least remember how to dance."

Harry had to manually unclench her fingers from his elbow

while holding on to the sax. "I have some work to do, but please enjoy the party."

Sounds of revelry filtered into his father's office as Harry placed the sax on the mahogany desk and settled into the rolling chair. He eyed the instrument, the notes of Led Zeppelin's "Stairway to Heaven" flowing through his mind. The image of Lilah danced around in his memory.

His hand went to the phone several times before he made the call. When Lilah answered, he asked without preamble, "Are you all right?"

"You're really concerned about me?" she taunted. "Or are you afraid I might think you're jealous?"

Harry pinched the bridge of his nose. "Dante gave you his version."

"You have your sources, and I have mine." Lilah laughed. "Poor Dante. He doesn't realize Harry Sheppard was merely keeping the puppet leader in line."

He picked up a green glass paperweight. "A puppet? You? C'mon, Lilah. We know each other better."

"*You* know I take my responsibilities seriously. I was the one who asked Alex to return to the U.S. Why would you then imagine I'd risk our plans for him?"

"Uh-huh... things did get to the point you needed to send him away. Why did you lie to me about it?" Harry toyed with the paperweight, tossing it up and down.

"Why did I lie about *my* personal life?" Lilah exclaimed. "You forfeited your right to ask." The paperweight clattered to the desk. Neither spoke for a couple of moments. "Your own sister," she finally muttered. "How *could* you?"

"All I did was remind Alex of the things at stake. Then, Hector tried to set Sabrina up with Steven Kingsley."

"Steven—*what?* Doesn't Hector know Steven tried to kill Brad and his brothers?"

"Of course he does," Harry said. "Two families—two companies—with rivalry enough to prompt a murder attempt. I publicly sided with Brad and his brothers at the Barrons party, so why was Hector trying to set up our sister with Brad's enemy?"

Lilah's sharp intake of breath came through clearly. "So *that* was your reason for pushing her at Alex."

Without confirming or denying, Harry added, "Hector went to dinner at the Kingsleys' before he found out about Alex and Sabrina. Then, Godwin Kingsley called Alex and me for a business meeting. There's a cash offer on the table."

"What's going on, Harry?"

Harry's hand clenched as Lilah articulated the question inflaming the back of his mind. Was it really Hector's idea to marry Runt to Steven? Or was it planted there by someone? Why was Godwin Kingsley involving himself so much in their plans? The cash he was putting up *would* help them achieve their goal, but if the former justice were so concerned about Sanders, why hadn't he allied himself with Brad instead of sticking with Steven? Were the Sheppards—Harry's own family—part of a possible conspiracy? Harry was no longer certain whom he could trust.

Part XIV

Chapter 43

Two months later, October 1982

Colón, Panama

My boys. Patrice watched her three sons around the conference table, talking to Harry and the man sent by Godwin Kingsley. She couldn't believe Alex was married. Her baby. Then there were Peter's children with his girlfriend. All five brothers should've grown up together, but Godwin decreed the younger two would stay with their uncle. With a pang, she pushed away the thought of the sixth, her deepest, darkest secret, her private shame.

There were more members in the family now. When Alex called Patrice about his entanglement with Sabrina, memories came rushing, slyly reminding Patrice this was her golden chance to visit retribution on the Sheppards. She could demand Alex abandon Ryan Sheppard's daughter the same way—

Patrice couldn't do it. The baby would be her grandchild. Her flesh and blood. And while her sons usually did what she asked, an order of such magnitude would require explanations, something she wasn't prepared to give. There was also the business alliance to consider. Besides, the Sheppards didn't give Patrice a chance to cause trouble. They insisted on a quick wedding in New York City even if none of Alex's family could attend. Patrice would never have agreed to be part of the celebration, anyway. Years ago, she swore to never again cross the threshold of a Sheppard home, and she refused to entertain the idea even for the sake of her youngest and his bride.

Sabrina was a lovely young lady, though. As soon as she exited the car, she ran into Lilah's arms, nearly knocking her over. When Lilah teased the girl about wearing the same blue color she favored since girlhood, Sabrina did a little jig, showing off. She even brought the wedding album with her for Lilah and Patrice to drool over. The Sheppards clearly spared no expense for their daughter's big day from the blue and purple orchids spilling over the tables in the Grand Ballroom at The Plaza to the very real pearls sewn onto the bodice and sleeves of Sabrina's Eve of Milady gown. With her blonde waves arranged in careful disarray under the fingertip veil, she looked like a tiny angel next to Patrice's tall, dark, and handsome son.

Feeling sentimental tears threaten, Patrice sat up, admonishing herself. She might have missed the mother-son dance at Alex's wedding, but Victor and Brad were yet to be married.

Glasses resting on her nose, Lilah was scribbling furiously on a sheet. Patrice liked Brad's fiancée despite the unfortunate fact she was a Sheppard. She should've been a Kingsley by now. One year, and Lilah apparently couldn't find a convenient date! First, law school, then business... there was always something more important. And the couple hardly did anything together. Not on their own, anyway. When Lilah visited the waterfalls of Boquete, she did invite Brad along—and Victor. She appeared unaware of the increasing irritation in her fiancé's eyes.

Perhaps *she* could go to the mountains, Patrice daydreamed. It seemed so long since she got time to herself. From the day Peter walked out, her life revolved around her sons. *All* her sons, not simply the three the world knew about.

Her eyes suddenly snagged on Harry. The young man wasn't even looking in her direction, but Patrice sat up, bizarrely worried he might know what she was thinking. She reminded herself of the promises she made so long ago, the secrets she swore to take to her grave. Harry couldn't be allowed to find out. Nor could her boys.

Chapter 44

Setting her pen aside, Lilah flexed her fingers and struggled with the urge to toss the Kingsley oil scout out on his ear. Oh, Masou clearly knew enough about the energy sector, but—

"Mr. Kingsley," Masou said to Brad, smiling and nodding near-constantly. "Our engineers estimate there are *billions* of cubic feet of gas in Vaca Muerta. All waiting for a driller brave enough to risk it. America was built by such bold pioneers. Rockefeller, Carnegie, Gould, Hearst... your name will soon be added to that list. Ms. Barrons, a shrewd businesswoman like you must know how much cash the project would add to the balance sheet."

Masou was part Native American, his father a member of the tribe who lived in the locality under discussion. Straight, black hair cut ruthlessly short, Masou wore a cap with Kingsley Corp insignia. His khaki overalls were immaculate, not an oil stain to be seen. All very professional. Except, his entire manner was getting on Lilah's nerves.

In a way, she *was* glad Masou came down to Colón with Harry and Alex. She needed the break from her personal messes.

After Alex left Panama, Lilah had finally approached a psychiatrist. Secretly... since it wouldn't do for the CFO of the newly formed company to be spotted in a shrink's office. The market would react badly to the news. All she said to the doctor was she was suffering from flashbacks to her abduction. Every day, she looked at the bottle of anti-anxiety medicine he prescribed. *A tool,* she told herself. Pills were merely tools to help patients. She still couldn't take one. To admit she wasn't strong enough to control her own mind... she just couldn't do it.

Muttering over and over that Brad was a nice man didn't get her brain to cooperate with even an iota of attraction toward him. If he didn't need her as much, politically speaking, she doubted he'd have let *status quo* go on this long without a showdown. As it was, he was pushing harder and harder. The hand on her knee, the arm thrown around her waist, fingers rubbing circles on her belly... it was all she could do to keep herself from shoving him to the floor and running. If they were lovers, *true* lovers... neither Alex nor Harry caused her to escape to the restroom to retch into the sink.

Alex... married to Harry's sister. The undercurrents when Sabrina arrived at the hotel were almost comical. The wariness on Alex's face changed to abject horror when his wife announced she would be Lilah's assistant in the company, and there was a question in Harry's eyes when he glanced from her to Alex. Lilah refused to acknowledge either man except in the vaguest way, resolutely ignoring the heaviness in her heart. Fortunately for all of them, Sabrina didn't notice anything untoward. She was taking a nap while the rest gathered to listen to Masou.

"What do you think, Lilah?" Victor asked, drawing her attention back to the present. "You're the engineer."

"Masou is going to have to do better than telling me there's gas in Vaca Muerta," Lilah stated. "He should already know that the oil and gas there can't be extracted by conventional means. Even Sanders is not doing any drilling on the land. So why bring this up with *us* when we don't have the capital to expand into long-term projects?"

"Fantastic question," said Masou, shaking his index finger in her direction. "The tribes who live in the region are called the Puelche. The military dictatorship in Argentina keeps a close eye on the Puelche because they provide shelter to trade unionists and dissidents, but the government can't touch the tribe because of Sanders. He has his people both in the administration and among the dissidents in the village. Sanders doesn't do any drilling there, but while he's waiting for technology to evolve, he's using the dissidents to convince the tribe to keep other companies away. Logically speaking, the tribe should welcome the idea of other businesses since it would give them more bargaining power."

Lilah countered, "You didn't answer the question I asked. Also, decisions such as these are not always based on cold logic. Sanders's henchmen might be fomenting resentment against other oil drillers, but as long as the tribe feels that way, there's nothing much we can do."

Masou tucked his hands into his pockets and bounced lightly on his feet. "I think the Peter Kingsley Company should at least talk to the tribe. There's hunger for more fuel, and it's only going to get worse in the coming decades. If your business is positioned to take advantage of it, what harm could there be?"

"Sir," Lilah said, voice firm. "You're continuing to evade my question."

Flushing, the oil scout glanced around. "Right... the funding... Kingsley Corp offered—"

She tossed a folder to the center of the table. "As the person in charge of the finances of this company, I must vote against the plan. Even if we ignore the ethical aspects of the idea—which we will not—there's no cash for diversification into long-term projects."

"We already discussed Kingsley Corp's offer of money," Harry said, his tone mild.

Masou nodded vigorously.

C'mon, Harry, Lilah scoffed in her mind. He couldn't possibly be mulling the same plan they once rejected. "There was no discussion," she said. "Masou merely stated Kingsley Corp would make sure we have the financial resources we need. We have yet to ask him the questions we should."

"Ms. Barrons," said Masou. "Mr. Kingsley—Mr. *Godwin* Kingsley—appreciates how careful you are of the company's money. He has authorized the release of *whatever* funds you might need for this project. You won't be risking a penny."

"What does Godwin gain from this?" asked Lilah.

"Grandfather's actually been a father to the three of us," said Brad. "Is it unthinkable he may simply want to help?"

Alex spoke up, "Grandfather and the president believe this will be a first strike against Sanders. It's worth a try."

Lilah asked, "If Godwin feels so strongly about Sanders, why doesn't he have Kingsley Corp do it? Also, we *might* succeed in annoying Sanders, but it's not going to bring him down. I'm sure Godwin knows all this, so why is he trying to maneuver us in this direction? I don't like it."

"I understand your concerns, but anything we do will reflect on Grandfather and the entire Kingsley family," Brad reminded her. "He's not going to push us into something that will damage his reputation."

"We're not going to merely 'annoy' Sanders," Harry contributed. "We're going to demonstrate to the rest of the sector he's not invincible. It's an important first step. Waiting until the Peter Kingsley Company got big enough made sense when there was no outside funding, but it's not the case now. Buying Vaca Muerta will also help us lay groundwork for future expansion of the alliance... again, without spending a penny. As for the ethical aspects... we'll make sure the tribe is taken care of. Part of the cash from Kingsley Corp can be used to provide incentive for the tribespeople to move."

Lilah huffed in exasperation, not at all comfortable with any of it.

"So our plan is to use Kingsley Corp money and maybe bribe the tribal leaders into evacuation?" Victor asked.

Brad responded, "I want to meet the leaders. Lilah, we shouldn't reject Grandfather's help without doing at least as much. Let's take a trip to Vaca Muerta."

"Neuquén," supplied Masou, "is the name of the town. There's a lake, too. Lago Los Barreales."

Alex rolled his chair back, wheels squeaking. "Excuse me, but *I'm* in charge of business development, and I'll need Lilah to discuss the finances."

What?

Brad demurred, "You just got married. I hate to ask you…"

A scouting trip with her and Alex? Bad, bad, bad idea. Lilah opened her mouth to put the kibosh on the thought.

Closing the folder in front of him with a snap, Harry stood. "I'd like to join the team if it's all right with you. Mr. Temple asked me to."

Lilah tossed a glare at Harry. Brad's eyes darted between Alex and Harry, mouth tightening.

"The president wants Mr. Sheppard to take the lead because he has experience dealing with the Argentines," said Masou.

"A couple of small oil companies in the region might put in a good word for us," explained Harry. "I helped them when they had a run-in with one of Sanders's men—a general in the Argentine army."

Masou nodded in Brad's direction. "Also, forgive me, sir, but I'd recommend you stay away from the preliminary negotiations. It leaves us the option of the CEO coming in with a more generous deal if the first offer is rejected. Mr. Temple did mention Mr. Alex Kingsley could represent the company along with Ms. Barrons."

"So Harry and Alex and Lilah?" Victor asked.

With a trace of a frown on his face, Brad nodded. "I suppose. It's a bit unfair to Sabrina. I mean, they're newlyweds. But—"

"Sabrina doesn't have to stay here alone," Harry interjected, tone casual. "She can go along." Inclining his head toward Lilah, he added, "Please reconsider your vote. What would be the harm in at least talking it over with the tribe?"

Part XV

Chapter 45

A week or so later, October 1982

Argentina

The need to limit the number of people who knew about the project meant Lilah couldn't bring her bodyguards. Harry and Alex would be adequate protection for the two women with them, anyway. Also, thanks to President Temple's repeated threats to use the military and financial might of the U.S. on anyone who dared attack Americans anywhere in the world, Lilah was thought to be safe from Sanders and his henchmen for the time being.

After landing in Buenos Aires, the scouting group opted to travel to Neuquén by road. Masou was journeying separately and would join the rest in town. Harry had arranged to have a motorbike waiting for him—a Harley, of course—planning to take advantage of the warm spring weather in the country.

In the airport parking lot, Lilah grimaced against the cramping in her lower abdomen. The jeans and cotton tee and sneakers she and the rest of the group wore weren't exactly comfortable during the time of the month. Traveling in the car would leave her less sore, but the idea of being stuck with the newlyweds for more than twelve hours... nope. Riding pillion on Harry's bike it would be. They would meet up with Alex and Sabrina at the restaurant they picked for lunch, and from there, they'd head to Neuquén and Lago Los Barreales.

Alex jogged to them, announcing with enthusiasm he'd rented a Suzuki Katana, a bike which looked like something James Bond might ride. Their luggage went with the driver who showed up at the airport. Naturally, it meant Harry and Alex would race.

Knowing what was about to happen, Lilah rolled her eyes. Harry losing a poker game or a bike race? Nuh-uh. No way. Not unless he were up to something.

As soon as Lilah swung her leg over the Harley, bass notes boomed from the exhaust. She threw her arms around Harry's waist. With a twist of the hand-throttle, he launched the bike onto the road. Air whooshed by. Her body jerked back. With a shriek of excitement, she held on tight.

"Eat dirt, sucker," Harry shouted, taking off before Alex got a chance to turn his own bike on.

Lilah threw her head back and laughed, trying to picture the dismay on Alex's face.

Harry zigged and zagged through the traffic in the city, the pounding roar of the bike threatening to reduce the buildings to rubble. Cars honked from every direction. Thick, gray smoke chugged out from every vehicle, piercing her nostrils. As crowded as the streets were, it wasn't long before Alex and Sabrina caught up. Alex shouted something, the words drowned by the sounds from the bikes.

It took them almost an hour to get out of the city. The route cut through grasslands stretching into the blue horizon. The smells of pollution and city life were replaced by those of vegetation and dust. Laughing in giddy pleasure, the four of them raced along the highway. Wind whistling around them, hearts hammering in the adrenaline rush, they hurtled down the tarred road and threw juvenile taunts at each other.

Harry took a curve, leaning so far into it they nearly touched the ground. Engines roared. Rubber burned. Sparks flew from the asphalt. Perfect. For a second, it seemed as though the universe had righted itself.

When Alex took the lead for the nth time, Harry swore. Lilah laughed again, resting her chin on Harry's shoulder.

Another hour along the countryside, and the Harley accelerated yet again. "Whoooaaa," Lilah screamed as they shot past the Suzuki. She pumped her fist in the air at Alex and Sabrina.

"Hold on," bellowed Harry. They jumped over the shoulder and nearly flew down the steep grassy bank of the highway to land on a parallel road ten feet below.

Lilah bounced on the seat, her head jerking around to where they left their companions. Alex had slowed, watching them disappear. He wouldn't dare try the same stunt as Harry... not with a pregnant wife in tow. "What did you do that for?" Lilah shouted.

"We need to talk," Harry shouted back.

Yes, they did. Lilah was growing more uncomfortable by the minute about this project. The tribe's wishes... Godwin's meddling... she didn't like any of it. "Here?" she asked, straining to be heard above the roar of the bike.

"Let's find a better spot."

They went a while without finding a convenient place. Lush green meadows spread far into the distance on both sides of the road, barns and large granaries dotting the landscape. Sheep and fat cattle grazed gently, protesting the presence of the loud vehicle with an occasional bleat or moo. The stink of cow pies saturated the air.

Loud, continuous honking blasted around them, startling her. The bike wobbled for a second. A couple of hundred feet in front, a truck raced onto the road from behind a granary and headed straight for them. Harry swerved out of the way, tires screeching. Someone yelled *"la chica"* from the truck. The chick?

Harry fought for control. The bike shimmied on loose gravel

before bouncing its way across grassy field. Lilah clung tightly to him, the world around nearly tumbling to one side before they regained balance. The Harley came to a halt next to an astounded goat.

Breathing sharp and rapid, Harry asked, "Are you all right?"

Her insides were still sloshing about, and she could barely nod. "You?"

"Yeah." He shook his fist and flung curses at the truck, which was by now a speck on the horizon. The goat bleated its agreement.

The town of Pehaujo was only minutes away. When they parked outside the restaurant, Harry said, "Feels like old times. You and me on a road trip."

Lilah locked her helmet to the handlebar. "Be glad no one's *trying* to kill us this time." Scanning the parking lot, she said, "Alex and Sabrina are not here yet."

"*We* took a shortcut. Like I said, we need to talk. It was damned difficult to get you alone in Panama."

Walking through the large doorway into the restaurant, Lilah halted to take a deep breath of pure pleasure at the gorgeousness of their surroundings. Pristine whitewashed walls were festooned with pictures of celebrities who'd dined there. Through the row of wooden, square-paned windows, they could see into the vineyard where workers in overalls and straw hats were pushing wheelbarrows.

The *maître d'* showed Harry and Lilah to a table not far from the piano, but there was no music at the moment, only the clatter of plates and cutlery and the muffled chatter of the other diners. With glasses of malbec, Harry and Lilah sank into companionable silence. They did need to discuss her misgivings about the Vaca Muerta project, but she hated to break the pleasant stillness.

Lilah shot a glance through the window below which there were wooden crates overflowing with purple grapes. A few of the guests were strolling through the vineyard.

A female shriek rent the air, followed by a guffaw. A running woman—Hispanic, from the looks of her—came into view, her playful attempts to evade the young man behind impeded by her helpless laughter. When he caught her around the waist and twirled her to face him, she laced her fingers through his hair and dragged his head down in a deep kiss.

"Honeymooners," Lilah commented, somehow unable to look away from their public display of affection. The universe seemed intent on thrusting newlyweds into her path.

"Lovers, anyway," Harry corrected. "On vacation. They can't keep their hands off each other." His voice was thick, as though... with a cough, he turned in a different direction and raised his hand. "Where's our server? I need something to go along with the wine."

On cue, the waiter appeared with olives in a large silver bowl.

Determinedly averting her eyes from the scene outside, Lilah bit into an olive. Its briny sourness exploded in her mouth. "I don't have a good feeling about this evacuation deal."

"I'm more worried about the idea of Steven and Sabrina. I've been thinking since then... someone was clearly trying to divide the Sheppard family loyalties." Harry took a sip of the wine. "Who? And why?"

"This Vaca Muerta project is more concerning, Harry. The easiest explanation for the Steven idea is Steven himself. He might have suggested it to Hector. Maybe they thought it would make the Sheppards ditch Brad and support *Steven,* instead?"

"Once again, why?" Harry shook his head. "It's not as though my family's support would be enough to form the network. Only *you* have access to shares of all three companies, and you're engaged to Brad. As far as the evacuation is concerned... Temple wants us to take care of Sanders sooner rather than later, and my guess is Godwin was persuaded to part with some cash for the purpose."

Lilah sighed. "Harry, you saw for yourself how Godwin keeps poking his nose into our business. He calls Brad every Saturday like clockwork. Brad's grateful for the support, but thanks to you, he goes by what I say."

"Brad values Gateway, not me," corrected Harry.

Lilah murmured noncommittally. The Kingsley brothers seemed genuinely in awe of Harry. She continued, "Now, this free money offer. I mean, if Godwin wanted to have a say in the network, all he needed to do was cut Steven loose and keep Brad. So why didn't he?"

"Hmm," Harry mused. "All of them are Godwin's grandchildren, but he couldn't trust Steven to run his own outfit after what happened. I bet Temple and the rest were worried about repercussions if word got out about Steven's criminal tendencies. Then there's the fact Kingsley Corp is their original business. Ain't surprising for someone like Godwin to stick to the old while trying to control how other people live their lives. You know..." Sitting up, Harry grabbed an olive and popped it into his mouth. "...it might be the answer to our first question. Actually, to both questions. Godwin wanted to keep Kingsley Corp *and* control the Peter Kingsley Company. He might have thought the Sheppards would promote *him* with Brad if my sister were married into the other half of the family."

Lilah considered the idea. "Go on."

"When the alliance was first suggested, Temple very likely didn't imagine you and I would remain friends. He and Godwin probably thought I'd be limited to being Gateway's representative. Maybe not even that. Godwin would be running the show through Brad. Now... you and your fiancé allow my involvement in the day-to-day operations of the company, and Gateway's clout makes sure Brad listens to you. I'm sure he thinks Godwin will understand his reasoning. A seasoned businessman would, and Godwin is certainly that."

"Ahh," said Lilah, realization dawning. "Godwin can't even ask his grandsons to pick between you and him. Gateway's potential reaction... they're going to want to know why you're suddenly being kicked to the curb. *I* would object. The whole network scheme could collapse before it gets off the ground."

"Right," said Harry. "It's impossible to close one of us out without the other raising hell. So Godwin starts cultivating Hector. The Sabrina proposal would've sounded better coming from Godwin rather than directly from Steven. Maybe not blatantly enough to alert Hector something was up. A hint from the Kingsleys... a casual remark which got my brother thinking. Imagine if they succeeded... I still couldn't be kept out because you'd protest... you could even quit. But the *Sheppards* wouldn't complain because Hector would be the one parroting Godwin's words... no one would see Godwin Kingsley pulling the puppet strings. If Hector and I clashed over some proposal... imagine all the different ways Godwin and Temple could use the chaos to take control. Temple clearly knew about the matchmaking scheme, so perhaps he suggested it to Godwin. In fact, I am certain Temple was involved in it. The network is his brainchild."

After a few seconds, Lilah nodded. "What *does* Mr. Temple gain from this? I know you think he's trying to crush political opposition, but I have a hard time believing that's all there is to it."

Harry set the glass down, his long fingers tapping the rim of the goblet. "Power is one helluva motive. The network in its final form will unquestionably be powerful. Marrying Runt to Steven was meant to be the first step in seizing control." Smiling in satisfaction, Harry added, "Thanks to Alex, their plot failed."

"Thanks to you is what you mean," Lilah retorted.

"Whatever. Lilah, even without the Steven problem, Alex needed a way to return. A split between Brad and his brothers is something we cannot afford. You simply couldn't keep Alex on an indefinite exile. Besides, he and Sabrina..." Harry sucked in a breath. "It's a good match."

"Worked out well for all concerned, I suppose," Lilah said, keeping her tone bland. She dragged her mind back to the puzzle of Harry's big brother and his involvement with the president and the Kingsleys. "Why is Hector so fond of Steven? And how does your theory explain Godwin and Temple's offer of money?"

"Nuh-huh. Not *their* offer. Only Godwin's signature is on the money transfer, but the documents don't specify what the cash is for. They're making sure there's no paper trail leading back to them in case someone kicks up a fuss. But yeah... both are involved. They're trying to bribe us. No question. Temple must have prodded Godwin into it after the failure of the original scheme. Does it matter? It does help us."

Lilah swirled the wine around the goblet, her eyes on the magenta stain around the rim. "No, Harry, there are too many loose ends. Something else is going on. I'm sure of it." Snippets of information drifted around in her brain—the enmity between Brad and Steven, conspiracies to change Harry's loyalties, an adversary within the Sheppard family, a tribe which refused to move, Temple, Godwin, Jared Sanders. She tried to study the chessboard to understand Temple's strategy, but pieces kept tumbling off.

Chapter 46

"I think—" started Lilah, stopping when she spied Alex and Sabrina at the entrance.

Both turned in circles, taking in their surroundings with exclamations of delight. Alex grabbed a grape leaf crown from the pile by the hostess station and popped it on his wife's bright-blonde hair, tucking a lock behind her ear. Mischief marking her grin, Sabrina nipped his finger.

Love... wild, crazy love... the olive in Lilah's mouth suddenly turned bitter. Pouring more wine, she took a healthy gulp as the couple joined the table.

Sabrina dragged the appetizer platter toward herself, claiming pregnancy gave her the right to gorge. Unfortunately, she ended up battling Harry for the cheese and Alex for chorizo. The ridiculous attention she paid to dividing the delicacies equally was enough to make a monk cackle. Sabrina might be a wife and would soon be a mom, but she was still the same spirited girl Lilah remembered. The same girl who always had the time to talk when Lilah visited the Sheppard home.

Tone even, Harry asked his sister how she ended up with a bit more cheese than him, a slice of sausage more than her husband, when it was all supposed to be... you know... equal. Lilah snickered and once again reached for her drink. Funny... it seemed to be all gone. Actually, so was the acidic taste. A pleasant warmth suffused her body, from the roots of her hair to the tips of her toes.

When the main course arrived, there were loud oohs and aahs from their table. Alex sniffed, a look of total bliss on his face at the smoky smell of sizzling meat.

There was a high-pitched scrape as a suit-clad man pulled out the stool by the piano. Settling down, he struck up, "That's Amore."

When Harry sang along, Alex joined him. Sabrina hummed a couple of lines as well, her strong, clear voice melding well with the men's. Lilah pursed her lips, resisting the impulse to lend her tune-free assistance to the three singers.

Harry playfully tugged at her braid. "You never used to mind singing with me," he teased, his tone sweetly tender. "C'mon, Lilah.

I promise to punch anyone who makes fun of you."

Memories. Sweet, silly memories of their friendship, of secret crushes and first kisses. Joy exploded within, spilling through her lips as laughter. Catching Alex's narrowed gaze on her, she stopped in a hurry. Harry let go of her hair and sat back, his face wiped clean of all traces of intimacy. Lilah focused her eyes on the lipstick smudge on her wine glass.

A sudden clatter. "Excuse me," gurgled Sabrina, spewing water onto the tablecloth.

All eyes turned to her. "Are you all right?" Alex asked, gently patting her between shoulder blades.

"The water... it went down the wrong way," she gasped, setting the glass aside. "Why did you stop singing?"

From then on, lunch turned surreal. Alex and Harry seemed determined to make the most of the trip, trading jokes and telling tall tales from their time in the military. Of course, each was a superhero in his own stories. Their exaggerated bragging kept Sabrina and Lilah in splits.

The musician continued to play Dean Martin songs on the piano, going from "Everybody Loves Somebody" to "La Vie En Rose" to other melodies Lilah didn't recognize. Dish after dish was brought to the table. They sampled a little of everything, pork ribs and beef stew and ravioli stuffed with ricotta and ham. Wine flowed. Even Sabrina took a couple of sips.

The men competed over who'd suffered the worst ever encounters with military bureaucracy. Sabrina nearly fell off her chair laughing at the account of the librarian who'd spent forty-some dollars tracking Alex down in Pakistan for a twenty-five-cent fine on a damaged book.

"Stop," Lilah gasped, laughing helplessly. She clutched her belly. "I can't take anymore."

That statement only prodded Harry into relating even more outrageous tales. Face twisted in an expression of comical disbelief, he told them about the call he'd taken from another unit, asking for help in finding a missing plane. Unfortunately, the person on the phone refused to give Harry the last known location of the aircraft, claiming it was classified.

"No," Sabrina exclaimed, eyes rounded in incredulity.

They spent a couple of hours in the restaurant, talking and laughing. From time to time, Alex would shoot speculative looks at Harry and Lilah. Harry would match him stare for stare. When Alex's eyes met Lilah's, he'd flush and look away. Irritated with herself for feeling guilty, Lilah would take a few evenly spaced breaths. Drunk with delight, Sabrina didn't seem to notice the undercurrents.

Licking the last of the *dulce de leche* off her spoon, Sabrina said she wanted a short stroll through the vineyard.

Harry stood, putting his napkin by his plate. "Let's go, kiddo. I want a few minutes to tease my baby sister one more time."

Lilah stifled a squawk. In a matter of moments, her wine-induced euphoria dissipated. *Oh, no. Harry.* He was *not* going to leave her alone to deal with Alex. Before she could say a word, Harry was at the door, Sabrina not too far behind.

Silence. Incredibly uncomfortable silence. Lilah watched Alex draw a pattern on the tablecloth with the tip of his butter knife.

Would five minutes be enough time before she could escape to the ladies' room without feeling like a coward? She recited the elements of the periodic table in her mind. *Hydrogen, helium, lithium, beryllium... don't bring up anything stupid,* she mentally pleaded with Alex. *Let's just pretend the whole thing never happened.*

"Lilah," he began, "I know I forced this trip on you, but I... it's difficult to get you alone in Panama, and I need to apologize."

Her head jerked up. "No need to apologize. Alex, it was only moonlight madness. A new woman in your life... when you tie a second knot on top of another, the first one always loosens, right? All the ladies who came before Sabrina..." Still blabbering, Lilah wiggled the fingers of both her hands. "...nothing to you now. Forget the stuff between us. I've known Sabrina since she was a baby. She's perfect for you. No wonder you fell for her."

Alex blushed, and eyes glowing with a soft heat, he glanced through the window where his wife was strolling with her brother. "Right. Sabrina... she's..."

The sniper was truly, madly in love. So was Sabrina. Lilah smiled. "Go to your wife and tell Harry to get lost. This is your *honeymoon. You* should be out there, walking with her."

"Wait. There's something I need to talk to you about." Lilah listened in bemusement as Alex poured out what went on in his life these last few months. A girl in Texas, the daughter of one of Alex's instructors at West Point... a marriage proposal he never thought through... his change of heart when they were in the judge's office. Raking his hair with his fingers, Alex continued, "Belle knew I was... ahh... holding a torch for someone when we got together in Austin. After I left, she saw some news reports from the shooting party last year and guessed who it was. Lilah, she's *craz*..." He flushed. "...*angry* about my marriage. She says she's going to call Sabrina and tell her *we're* having an affair."

What a comedy circus, Lilah thought in exasperation. *Harry's sister seeing me as a threat.* Aloud, she said, "Make sure Sabrina hears it from you first, or she *will* suspect the worst. Tell her Belle got it all wrong. You and I never had anything to do with each other."

"*Lie* to her?" Alex asked.

"Do you have another option?" Lilah snapped. "It's not only about you and Sabrina. If Brad gets to know, the whole arrangement could fall apart." It wasn't a lie, really, Lilah reassured herself. She and Alex ended things before they went too far.

Alex muttered, "I suppose."

The siblings walked in, a smirk on Harry's face at finding her in intense conversation with Alex. After lunch, Sabrina decided she was too tired to use the bike for the rest of the journey. Fortunately, the car and the driver from the airport met them at the restaurant as Alex arranged.

In the parking lot, Lilah settled her helmet back, ready to get on Harry's bike. "Don't you ever do that to me again," she hissed.

He didn't pretend not to know what she was talking about. "Alex is Brad's brother. You'd have had to make nice sooner or later. Better to get it over with."

"Over?" She snorted. "Not according to some girl in Texas."

Eyes narrowed, Harry asked, "What are you... he told you about Belle Archer? What did he have to say about the ladies from the strip club? Five of them! Good God!"

Harry *knew* about Belle? And strippers? One-two-three-four-*five*? Glancing from Harry to Alex, Lilah caught Sabrina looking in their direction. "Let's go," Lilah said. "We'll talk on the way."

A few minutes into their ride, the funny side of it suddenly struck her. The absurdity of it all... she started shaking with suppressed hilarity, and soon, both she and Harry were laughing so hard they needed to stop. "I'm sorry," she gasped as Harry reeled with mirth, pushing his visor up. "I love Sabrina, but this entire business is like a bad movie."

"I hope they survive this," Harry said, sobering.

"You hope?" Lilah's laughter sputtered to a stop. "Harry, you knew what Alex had been up to and still wanted him to marry Sabrina?"

Harry's eyes crinkled in a fleeting smile. "*You* saw something in him. Enough to confide in him about what happened in Libya."

The assault? The usual mix of dread and desperation surged. "I didn't 'confide.' Alex guessed something had happened. He doesn't know where or when, so how could he tell *you'd* already know? It was terribly bad of him to talk about it just because I turned him down."

"Nah," said Harry. "Alex simply wanted advice on how to sort out the mess. If he were after revenge, there are other ways... going to Brad, the media. Besides, I'd just told Alex we grew up together. He probably assumed I was aware... which I was. I did ask him not to repeat it to anyone else, but I know his type. He won't blab unless there's a gun to his head. The Texas girl, the strippers... he really *was* spiraling by the time we had our chat."

"What exactly did he say to you?"

"That he spotted something was off and asked you directly. He admitted you didn't offer specifics. But you... you would've put him back in his place in under ten seconds if you felt he was intruding. Instead, you even considered him for a... so I knew I couldn't go wrong."

"God, you—" Lilah exclaimed. On a rational level, she understood the urgency of the situation Harry faced. Still... Sabrina was his *sister!* "No more," Lilah said, voice hard. "Your scheming stops here."

Harry held his hands up in surrender. She nodded, noting grimly he didn't otherwise respond to her edict.

Her troubles were far from over. Later, at the restaurant they chose for dinner, Lilah sought the quiet of the ladies' room. She splashed cold water on her face and quickly swallowed a couple of pills from the Midol bottle, gritting her teeth against the spasms in her belly. A sniffle at the door broke the silence, and Lilah looked up.

Reflected in the mirror stood Sabrina, bright-green eyes puffy from tears. Voice unnaturally high, she asked, "That girl's an idiot, right, Lilah? You'd never..." Sabrina hiccupped. "Alex and you... you're engaged to his *brother*." When she held her knuckles to lips to muffle her sniffles, Lilah rushed to pull Sabrina into a hug and sat with her on the sofa. The sobs finally slowed to a stop, and Sabrina asked, her voice small, "Tell me, please."

"Gossip in the tabloids is all it was," assured Lilah.

Sabrina smiled in relief. "Thank God... you're like my sister."

Thank God, Lilah echoed in her thoughts. "Forget Belle and all the ridiculous rumors about me. Alex has clearly been terrified of hurting you. It shows how much he loves *you*."

Then, they were back on their way. When they stopped at the next gas station, Harry asked, "How did it go with Sabrina?"

Lilah sighed and came clean on her lies. "I had to, Harry. She was so upset, and I swear she will never have anything to fear from me."

He shook with laughter. "I already knew it."

The absolute trust in his words... Lilah closed her eyes in relief. "Besides, Alex chose *her*. Nothing else matters."

"I hope you're right," murmured Harry. "What *was* Belle trying to achieve? Where's the logic in what she did?"

"It's not about logic. When you're wounded badly, you lash out any which way you can, trying to injure the object of your affections." While Harry paid for the gas, Lilah pondered the foolish, self-destructive things people did for love.

Chapter 47

When Harry's bike rumbled to a stop at the waterfront villa on the northern bank of the lakes, Lilah spotted Alex and Sabrina's car in the yard. The couple stood next to the vehicle, eyeing the house.

Twilight painted the rippling clouds in hues of purple. Short shrubbery encircled the garden, and bright-orange daisies flitted about the green lawn in the mild breeze. Whitewashed railing bordered the second-floor terrace in front, complementing the peach hue of the walls.

"Beautiful," Lilah said, climbing off.

Sabrina sniffed, then covered her mouth and nose with a hand. "Oil."

There *was* a hint of tar in the air. Lilah smiled. Harry's sister spent a part of her childhood among oil rigs, but pregnancy did strange things to a woman, didn't it? "Go in and make sure the windows are closed," Lilah advised.

The next morning, Masou, the Kingsley Corp oil scout, met them in his customary garb of khaki coveralls and cap. "I talked to the tribe," he said. "Our meeting is tomorrow."

In the living room, Harry discussed plans with Masou and Alex. From the window seat, Lilah listened to the men while she examined a brochure listing climbing sites in the province, murmuring at appropriate intervals in response to Sabrina's chatter. Lilah had brought her rappelling gear with her, hoping to find some time to go climbing. It was irritating to have her period attack right when she needed to work up a sweat to clear her mind.

When Sabrina went to her room for a few minutes, Harry left Alex and Masou making calls and ambled over to Lilah. "Out with it," he said. "You're dying to nag."

"Harry, I'm afraid we're being played."

"This is our best chance to strike the first blow at Sanders. The perception of invincibility has to be stripped from him."

She stared at the picture on the flier showing brown cliff against blue sky. "Sometimes, I feel you're still trapped in Libya. Your mind is stuck on whatshisname."

Harry glanced out of the window for a second. "Sanders is not the only reason for the network—not even the *main* reason. Monsters exist, and he's one of them. You already understand it, so why are we having this argument?"

"Think, Harry! There's no moral argument to be made in favor of this plan. If it weren't for the loan promised by Godwin, there wouldn't even be any financial argument. He and Temple are pushing us into this scheme which makes little sense. Yeah, yeah... you think they're trying to bribe us. If that's the case, why not simply offer us money without tying it to the evacuation? We could certainly use the cash. No, those two know how you think, and they're playing you for reasons we're not going to like. And you... you're ready to sell your soul only to take a swipe at Sanders."

"Faust?" Harry scoffed as though goaded beyond control. "So be it. If I must sign away my soul to the devil to create a world where children aren't sold into slavery for political gain, I'll do it. I'll pay the price." Harry stalked away, leaving Lilah with her worries.

#

The meeting with the local tribe was set for the following morning. Lilah just stepped out through the front door of the villa to join the men when Masou deferentially inclined his head and claimed the tribal leaders wouldn't deal with women. She laughed, thinking of the distinctly female machi who led the tribe in the discussions with Barrons O & G. "No, not happening."

The Kingsley Corp man continued to smile, but lines of worry appeared on his forehead. And he kept insisting Lilah couldn't join the team. "My instructions were to take the two men." He turned to Harry. "I work for a salary! I have to do what I'm told."

"A minute, Lilah," Harry called. Standing by his rented Harley, he said, "Masou might be annoying, but he's right. Yeah... I know you were part of the Barrons team when they talked to the tribe, but they didn't get an agreement at the time, did they? So let's try what Masou says. Also, his father was one of the tribe. With him on our side, we have a better chance. We need Masou."

"He is *not* on our side," Lilah snapped, taking care to keep her voice low. Alex and Masou were still by the door. "He works for Godwin. I don't trust him."

Harry asked, "Will you at least give this a chance? If we drive Sanders from the area, there will be more businesses willing to join us. You *know* how it works."

Lilah rubbed her brow with a finger. "One chance," she finally agreed. "First sign of trouble, you get out, all right?"

Wordlessly, Harry held up his hand, backing away, and gestured at the other two men to join him.

Lilah called, "Harry?"

He turned. "What?"

Struck by a weird feeling of *déjà vu*, she shivered. "Nothing. Be careful, please?"

Masou was taking his Jeep. Harry climbed onto the bike with Alex, and turning the key in the ignition, he said to Lilah, "We expect to be in the village a couple of nights, but both Alex and I have guns. No one's going to take us down easily. You and Sabrina should be all right here, but just to be on the safe side, I've called Dante."

"You've called—" Lilah hissed. Sometime between getting to the villa and now, Masou already told Harry Lilah could not be part of the negotiations. That was the only reason he got Dante to join the party.

Before she could say anything further, a small car rumbled into the yard. Dante's head was poking out through the window. With a quick wave, Harry rode away, racing into danger he refused to acknowledge.

Part XVI

Chapter 48

An hour later

Puelche village, Vaca Muerta, Argentina

The machi was of indeterminate age with profuse wrinkles on her face but a sprightly gait. Harry noted she was the only one of the tribe dressed in traditional garb: a shapeless, ankle-length dress and silver jewelry. Walking barefoot alongside the Americans, she showed them around the Puelche village. Thatched huts called *rucas* stood among dilapidated sheds, with the *rehue*—standalone wooden steps—forming the spiritual center of the community. All very old world except for the smell of hot tar pervading the air.

A group of young boys chased each other across a small clearing, shouting in glee as they kicked a soccer ball around. Red dust flew. One of the boys ran sideways in the direction of the Americans, but his eyes were on the ball. *"Cuidado,"* yelled one of his teammates.

"Watch out," shouted Harry, echoing the Puelche boy.

A second later, the running boy collided with Alex, his head ramming into Alex's solar plexus. Alex grunted and staggered backward for a step or two before steadying the boy by the shoulder. "Whoa, buddy."

A couple of sharp words from the machi had the boy nodding. *"Perdóname, señor."*

Harry and Alex exchanged grins. The boy didn't look in the least bit sorry. He was hopping foot to foot, and his eyes kept darting toward his teammates. On his right wrist was a leather band with a crude rendition of the Hells Angels insignia—a budding motorcycle enthusiast, perhaps.

"Get back to the game," Alex said, giving the boy a little shove.

"Hey," Harry hollered.

The boy turned, running backward.

"We'll be back for a game," Harry said in Spanish.

"U.S.A. versus Argentina," the boy shouted back.

The machi laughed. "You'll never win," she promised Harry, a twinkle in her eye. "He's our golden child. Someday, he *will* be playing for Argentina."

However pleasant her welcome was, the machi wouldn't budge on the subject under negotiation. No matter how much money Harry and Alex put on the table, she refused to sell. The share they offered the entire tribe in future profits was not enough to tempt her or her council. She seemed amused by Harry's attempts to charm her, followed by Alex's. By evening, Harry was wondering why the lady agreed to talk.

He got his answer when the machi said she wanted to know what the business world thought the property was currently worth. She trusted Sanders but would verify his claims. If she did decide to sell the land at some point, he—or some other potential buyer—wouldn't get it for cheap.

The machi also expressed disappointment at Lilah's absence. The women had met when Barrons O & G attempted a deal with the tribe.

"Figures," Alex muttered to Harry.

Harry smothered a smile, knowing exactly what Alex meant. The stubborn old lady of course took a liking to Lilah. Probably saw her as a kindred spirit.

Masou's claim about the tribe not negotiating with women... Harry frowned.

A minute later, the oil scout squirmed in the quiet corner Harry pulled him to. "Ms. Barrons... ahh... some of the council members really didn't like her questions when she visited the first time. There's a way to deal with them, and she... you know. Mr. Kingsley—Mr. *Godwin* Kingsley—asked me to see if the council would be more receptive to men. Unfair, but what can we do?"

For a long moment, Harry contemplated the Kingsley scout. Catching the curious stares from the machi and her associates, Harry nodded and returned to the meeting.

The Americans called it a day after the sun set and given the late hour, were offered shelter for the night in one of the rucas.

"Look what I have," Harry said to Alex, bending to enter the thatched hut. Grinning, he held up a pot of the pungent drink. "It's *chichi*, their special wine. They say it makes them stronger than the other tribes."

Alex vaulted off the uncomfortable pallet. "Great! The day won't be a total waste." Holding the plastic cup to his lips, he asked, "You think it's okay to drink here? I mean... Sanders..." The tribespeople would have informed their protector about the meeting.

"Temple's not gonna let anyone hurt you," Harry said solemnly. At Alex's pithy curse, Harry let out a crack of laughter. "Sanders *will* think twice before trying anything with Lilah while Temple's president. I did get the chichi from the same pot the council was using... in case someone thought of poisons and such. Also, we have our guns." The holster holding Harry's weapon was still strapped to his thigh, just like Alex's. The lethally exquisite Ari B'Lilah—Harry's tactical knife—was tucked into his boot.

Alex took a healthy gulp of the drink and went into a string of coughs. "You couldn't have warned me?"

"Man up, soldier." Harry raised his cup. He, too, coughed, eyes tearing.

Alex snickered. The cousins sat on the pallets, drinking and swapping stories from their time in the service. "Political Action Group?" Alex asked when Harry declined to add to public information on the incidents which led to his Medal of Honor.

"Russians in Afghanistan?" Harry countered, remembering what the CIA director said about Captain Kingsley's exploits.

"I can neither confirm nor deny."

With a laugh, Harry said, "Gotcha."

An hour... maybe more... they continued chatting about the military, about their return to civilian life. Alex confessed to Harry about Belle Archer. And about Lupe, the woman who turned out to be the owner of the strip club.

Surprised, Harry asked, "You didn't recognize Lupe Valdez? *The* most influential businesswoman in DC?"

"Seriously?"

Harry guffawed. "C'mon! Didn't you notice any of the bigwigs waiting to make her acquaintance?"

Confusion on his face, Alex argued, "Liam seems to know everyone there, and he's no bigwig. *He* told me she doesn't usually... er... mix business and pleasure." Alex flushed.

With difficulty, Harry stopped his eyebrows from shooting up. "I've heard. Doesn't mean her employees don't, but it's not the whole story. Her club's a gathering place for rich and powerful men. Some ask for membership; some she invites. She introduces them to each other, helps oil the machinery. She has two more clubs... in LA and in Las Vegas."

"*You're* rich and famous. Have you met her?"

Harry grinned. "Sadly, Ms. Valdez has not yet deemed me worthy of a personal invitation." He waited a beat before adding, "Unlike you."

Concealing a burp with the back of his hand, Alex chuckled. "Some of us have it, and some of us don't. Something to be said for being tied up and at the complete mercy of a sexy and powerful woman."

"*What?*" Harry nearly choked on the wine. "Bet you didn't put it in your report... Lupe Valdez, then this... Belle Archer."

With a look of abject horror, Alex downed another mouthful.

Harry whooped. "What were you trying to do? Go through the entire female half of the United States?"

"*You* should talk. Half the women in New York claim to have slept with you."

"Oh, yeah?" Harry grinned absurdly. "How many are we talking?"

"The stupid tabloid—what's it called?"

"*The Big Apple Reporter?*"

"Bingo. It made a list." Alex made a show of trying to count. "Eight... no, a hundred... a thousand... *sixteen* thousand."

Harry howled. "How about sixteen thousand, one hundred, and eight?"

Alex bowed low, nearly toppling over. "You da man."

"How do these people think I find time?" Picking up the pot, Harry poured more chichi into his cup, some of the liquid splashing over the sides.

Alex snapped his fingers. "Magic." The men guffawed. Mirth

sputtering to a stop, Alex stared into his drink. "But never anything with Lilah, huh?"

Throwing Alex a sideways glance, Harry frowned. "Try to remember you're married to my sister."

Alex smirked. "*Lilah's* engaged to my brother." Seconds passed with him waiting in expectant silence.

Harry took a long swig of the drink.

"Don't tell me there's no story there," taunted Alex.

"I'm trying to figure out how much you can handle." Harry stared straight ahead. "You know what Sanders did to me... the abduction. I wasn't alone." It could've been the wine or the remote location which loosened his tongue, but Harry talked as he'd talked to no one else before. He slowed when he came to the part where he was separated from Lilah for a short time. "You're aware she has a... problem. It happened then. She was sixteen, a few months younger than me. A random criminal. Wrong place, wrong time."

Alex jerked back. "Tell me he's dead."

"Not yet, but I've been searching for him." In his mind, Harry saw the man walking the garden, whistling as he turned. *Colonel Sheffield Parker, I will find you.*

Perfect understanding in his eyes, Alex nodded.

"She says I'm still stuck in Libya," Harry said abruptly.

"So? It's only natural. Until you do what you gotta do."

"Exactly!" Harry wiped his mouth with the back of his hand and delved into other stories, revealing memories keeping him up at night. He talked about his trip to India, slowing again as he remembered the charred forms of the children.

Horror and anger in his eyes, Alex said, "We need to stop it."

It wasn't long before Alex collapsed onto his pallet to grab some shuteye. Alternately keeping watch, they made it to daybreak.

Sounds of the morning were only just starting outside as Harry gargled lukewarm water to clear the cottony taste in his mouth. "What I told you last night?"

Alex stopped stretching and dropped to the ground to do a couple of pushups. "Yeah?" he grunted.

"It stays between us."

"Absolutely."

"Thanks." Harry inclined his head. "No one knows exactly what... *Lilah* will decide if and when she wants to divulge any of it."

"I get it."

"And... uhh..." Harry took a deep breath. "Lilah's a good friend... beyond it... she and I decided a long time ago we weren't gonna go there. Your brother has nothing to fear."

Eyes crinkling in a sympathetic smile, Alex got to his feet. "I gathered as much."

Chapter 49

An hour later

Neuquén, Argentina

Alex ignored Masou's mild clucking when he saw the bleary eyes and unkempt hair on the Americans. "We have people from the government to talk to today," said the khaki-clad oil scout, adding he knew some other way of getting the tribe to agree.

As the Harley sped behind Masou's Jeep, Harry shouted over the wind to Alex, "If this works, we all benefit." They parked in front of a nondescript building. "Beyond some people's personal demons, there are good reasons to proceed. Are you in?"

"Count on it."

The Argentine man—El Gato as Masou called him—sported well-trimmed black hair, snapping, black eyes, and a neat mustache under his nose. He was no low-level government official no matter what the oil scout claimed. Alex had been a soldier for far too long not to recognize an officer. Alex was also certain El Gato understood them when they spoke in English even though he chose to use Spanish. He explained to the Americans the tribe was protecting dissidents—unionists and students from the local university suspected of being communists.

"As of now, they're sheltering with the Puelche, and because of Sanders's protection of the tribe, I haven't been able to touch them," El Gato said, venom in his voice. "If I can get those commies evicted from the village, I can get them arrested. *You* want the land, but the machi won't oblige. In both our cases, the tribe stands in the way. If you're willing to cooperate, I have the perfect solution for both of us."

Taking them to a windowless room in the building, El Gato showed them photographs pinned to a notice board. Alex commented, "Young."

"They grow up fast in this part of the world," El Gato said. The group stopped at the last picture. "This one," he said, eyes burning, "I want her captured unharmed."

The girl in the picture looked about seventeen. Alex shifted, uncomfortable at the near-maniacal fervor in the official's tone. He glanced sideways at Harry.

"Who is she?" Harry asked.

"Isabel—my wife, my *pregnant* wife. The commies brainwashed her, and she decided to leave me and live with the Puelche. She can do what she wants, but no one's going to keep me from my own child."

Alex tried to picture himself in the same situation. He, too, had a pregnant wife at home. How would he react if he were not allowed to see his child?

A few hours later, Masou and El Gato took them to the top of a small hill to the east, where the smell of burning tar was intense. Alex and Harry scanned the valley below. Vegetation was sparse. At a distance of about a couple of miles, they could see the village—shacks and thatched huts among the few trees. A rufous-tailed hawk circled the sky above, powerful wings slapping the air.

El Gato spread a map of the area on the hood of the Jeep. They crowded around to study it, Harry digging out a pen from his pocket to make his own notations on the paper. The village was to the north of Lago Los Barreales, between the lake and Neuquén River. The villa where Lilah and Sabrina were staying was to the east of the village.

Masou's map, with Harry's markings on it.

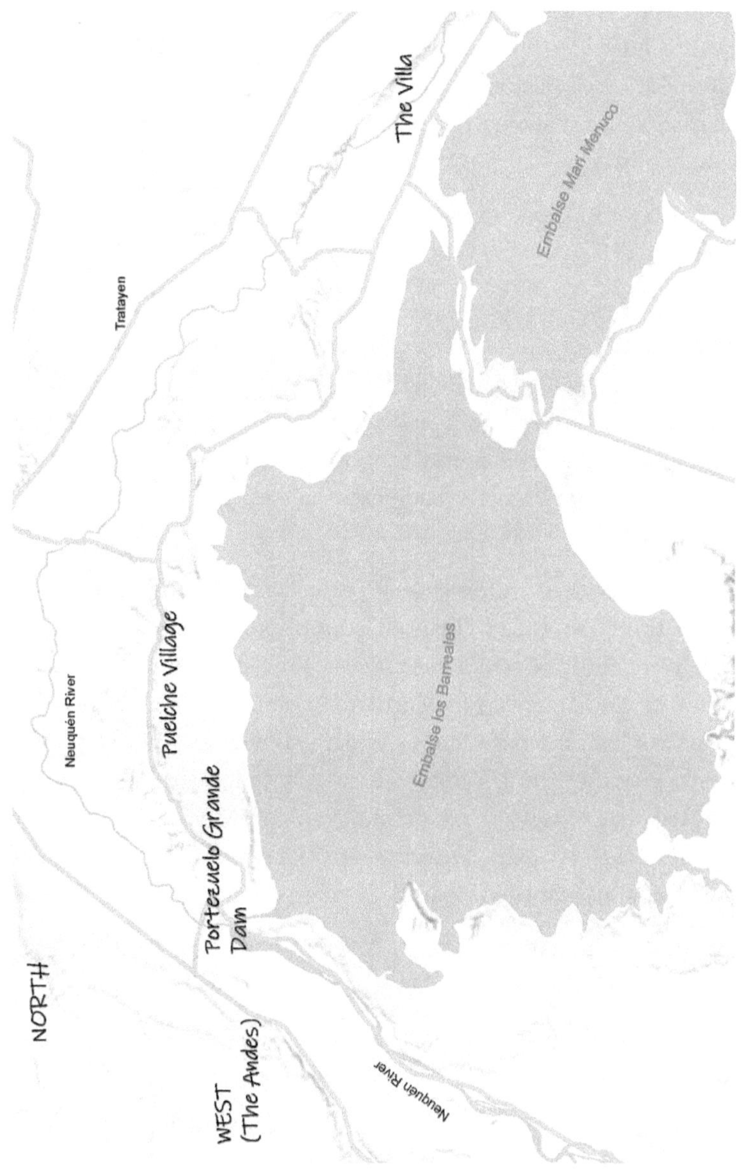

"We can smoke the tribe out from the north and the west," El Gato said. "The only logical place for them to flee would be to the east, or they'd have to jump into the lake. My men will cover both these sides and will know who to arrest. The rest of the villagers will be directed to a shelter in the next town. They'll be resettled in a couple of weeks."

"Why do you need us?" Alex asked. "Me and Harry, specifically?"

Masou was the one who replied. "A few reasons. There are people in the Argentine government who can be persuaded to turn a blind eye only if big names like Temple and Kingsley are involved... protection from Sanders. You two, specifically... because a sensitive operation of this kind simply cannot be delegated to anyone lower in the hierarchy. Plus, the equipment needed can only come from the military."

Alex nodded, understanding perfectly. The equipment would come from the *U.S.* military. The tools to do the job and the involvement of the senior executives of the alliance would serve as proof of the American president's commitment to the operation without which the Argentines wouldn't cooperate. Even if news of the evacuation spread, Temple's name was unlikely to appear in any investigative reports. Enough palms would've been greased to ensure it. The Kingsley patriarch's official contribution was limited to floating his grandsons a loan.

El Gato rolled up the map. "I won't bother the Puelche, but I want the unionists—and Isabel, my faithless wife."

"Wouldn't the tribe just return after everything's done?" objected Alex.

"Once the village is vacated, our people will move in and bulldoze everything," said Masou. "The authorities will then declare the land uninhabitable and lease it to you."

Harry's brow furrowed. "If we okay this mission, I want extra monitoring arranged for Sanders. We can't risk him flying to the rescue of his allies in the village. Also, may I have the map, please? I want to memorize the landmarks."

Handing over the rolled-up sheet of paper, Masou said, "Sanders protects the tribe but for his own purposes. *He* is also after the land."

"His motives won't matter," Harry snapped. "It will end up being seen as Sanders protecting the Puelche against greedy businessmen."

Masou said, "Mr. Sanders is in New York, and he's under constant surveillance. I assure you he doesn't have a clue what's going on here."

Harry shook his head. "*I* assure *you* he already knows we're here."

"Won't make a difference if he does," said Masou. "Negotiations happen all the time. It doesn't mean he's expecting us to try anything else."

"What about the general?" questioned Harry. Turning to Alex, Harry explained, "He's Sanders's go-to man in Argentina. I broke up his protection racket a couple of years ago, and he's been waiting for a chance to get back at me."

Masou waved a hand. "Isn't he in Córdoba? Too far to give us trouble."

"Make sure he stays there," Harry ordered.

Chapter 50

Not wanting to return to the villa and battle Lilah over the plan, Harry asked Masou to get them a room in the cheap hotel not too far from the lake.

As the three of them sat around the small coffee table, trying to reach a decision, Alex glanced worriedly at Harry. "According to our plan, we're going to leave the southern and eastern fronts open for the tribe to escape. But the villa is on the east."

Masou interjected, "El Gato's men will make sure—"

"Harry and I are also going to be on the eastern side," Alex muttered. "Still, there's no guarantee one or two dissidents won't get through. What if they attack the women and the staff? We should ask them to leave."

"We can't," Harry said. "Lilah will know something's up. Maybe we should call in her guards before doing anything else." He walked to the window and stared in the direction of the villa. "No, same problem," he mused. "She'd smell a rat." There was also the chance Sanders would hear of the elaborate security arrangements being made and would investigate.

"What about Dante?" Alex asked.

Not turning around, Harry nodded. "He can't be in on the plan, but I'll ask him to watch for problems. When he sees smoke, he'll insist on evacuating."

"Is it a go, then?" asked Masou.

"Yes," Harry said, annoyed at the sudden uncertainty in his mind. Lilah's dire warnings were getting to him. He blinked hard, trying to shake loose the ambivalence.

"Don't know, dude," Alex said from behind Harry. "What we're going to do... I really don't know."

Harry assured him, "The tribe will have to leave their homes, but you heard El Gato... they'll be resettled in a matter of days. We'll give them every assistance." They would get a new piece of land to call their own *and* be paid handsomely for the property they were forced to give up.

Alex asked, "The tribe will be fine, but what about the dissidents?"

"If not for us, *Señor* El Gato would've gotten the job done some other way."

"Reality is *we're* going to get them arrested," pointed out Alex. "I mean, we're vets... we're supposed to *defend* freedoms... exactly what the dissidents are fighting for."

Harry spun to face his cousin. Flickering light bulbs threw shadows across their faces. "What's reality, Alex?" Harry asked. "Your reality is created by your imperfect perceptions, your preconceptions, and your uncertainties. You're letting your limitations control you."

"So enlighten me," Alex challenged.

"Do you know how many wars oil has caused?" Harry asked. "How entire nations have been destroyed over it? How many millions have died? On a narrower level, do you know how many small companies have been ruined by rogue businessmen like Sanders? How many thousands have been left without a living? We need a control structure to stop it all. Without bringing down Jared Sanders, the Peter Kingsley Company will not be able to build it. With him in place, humanity has no hope for justice. There, my friend, is our first reality."

Alex shoved his fingers into his hair. "What happens if Sanders wins even after our shitty trick on the tribe? You don't think what we did will become public? I can't imagine the army's reaction."

"What we have here is a chance to change the destiny of mankind." Harry accused, "You won't cooperate because you perceive this world as one directed by a code of conduct. You've been taught to follow it to the letter by the military, and you apply it all through your life. An attempt at unorthodoxy might not lead to the positive outcome you want. You fear failure... dishonor. Therefore, you fear to act. But you forget one thing. Neither action nor inaction can guarantee the results you wish for. All you have control over are your own deeds. Here *you* are, giving up even marginal control because you fear an aftermath definitely out of your control. In other words, you're letting your doubts control you, thus almost guaranteeing failure. What sense does it make?"

Shifting on his feet, Alex stayed silent.

Voice ringing with increasing conviction, Harry asked, "What is it to be? Force the dissidents to surrender? Or let the dreams of a glorious future die?"

Alex stood still for a few seconds, eyes on the stars winking outside the window before turning to his cousin. "We build the future."

At a cough from Masou, the two men looked at him. "Weapons and transportation will be ready for you by tomorrow. I'll leave the pictures of the dissidents here." Tossing a few photographs onto the coffee table, he departed.

When the door closed behind the oil scout, Alex remarked, "Masou knew the tribe wouldn't agree, didn't he? He and his buddy planned this all along. How did they get Grandfather to cooperate?"

Harry grunted noncommittally. "Everyone knows Sanders needs to go."

The cousins spent the night there, sleeping little and talking even less. They went through the pictures of the dissidents, memorizing faces. Sometime before sunrise, Alex leaned on the railing of what passed for a balcony in the small hotel room, sipping coffee from a chipped mug.

Next to him was Harry, staring in the direction of the villa. "She keeps herself armed. I *know* she can protect herself and Runt." He was barely aware of who he was talking to. "They will be safe."

#

From the terrace overlooking the lake, Lilah tried to locate the village, but the sky was too dark. She took a gulp of the coffee. Grimacing at the bitter taste, she set her mug on the small table and wondered for the hundredth time what was going on at the negotiations. Harry had called but spoke only to Dante. Alex never bothered to come on the phone. She didn't like it.

Returning inside, Lilah hurried down the stairs. The small rental car would take her to the Puelche village in a matter of minutes. If the tribe objected to her presence... well, they could simply put up with her.

At the bottom of the steps, she collided with a shadowed form. "Oof! Dante! Sorry. I'm going to go over to the village. I want to know what's happening."

"Hold on, Lilah," said Dante. "Harry told us there are rumors of dangerous criminals roaming around."

No, Harry said it to only Dante, not the rest of them. "You believe it?" she asked dubiously.

"Why wouldn't I? In any case, they're not in the village any longer. The two of them are camped out a little to the west, closer to the site of the proposed wells."

A sudden tremor ran through Lilah's body... a feeling of being on edge. Like slides on a carousel, memories sped through her mind.

"An individual for a nation," Temple quoted over the chessboard. *"You've left the black king unprotected."*

"...murder potential threats..." Brad shouted at Steven at the conference where they split the company.

"Neither of you is running it..." Aaron Kingsley, Brad's uncle, chastised his nephews.

Harry's voice came over the phone, *"...trying to set her up with*

Steven."

"*The president wants Mr. Sheppard to take the lead,*" the oil scout said to Brad.

A hint of carefully crafted strategy. An opening gambit. But when she reached for the chessboard, the pieces vanished.

Part XVII

Chapter 51

Masou had asked the American men to return to the hill by late morning. El Gato was also around. Two black helicopters waited not far from the oil scout's Jeep.

"Hueys," Harry shouted over the thundering of the Harley as it bumped its way across the austere and uneven landscape. SEALs didn't always get to learn how to fly the utility choppers, and he'd asked to be taught. The skill served him well on his missions.

"How did Masou manage to get two whirlybirds over here without anyone noticing?" Alex asked.

"The Argentine government has been cracking down on left-wing guerillas," Harry said, bringing the Harley to a stop. "People have gotten used to military aircraft flying over towns and villages."

When the Americans jogged toward the Jeep, Masou opened the trunk and picked up a rifle. "It's a Galatz," he said, handing it to Alex. "Israeli make, Kalashnikov style. You'll have better performance at longer ranges. Only semi-automatic, but precision's better. You can use the main and additional sights at once. It's yours to keep." Masou opened a large box. "High-quality, 7.62X51 mm NATO ammo. You'll also have M79 grenade launchers."

The reverential expression on Alex's face at the sight of the sniper rifle... Harry bit back a grin.

El Gato stayed silent.

Alex picked up something else from the collection in the trunk. "FIM-92B Stinger... personal portable surface-to-air missile. How did you manage to get these? They just came out this year."

Without answering, Masou dragged out another of the tactical rifles. He waved a hand at Harry's thigh holster. "This is better protection than your revolver."

"You seem to know a lot about military weapons," Harry commented.

"I was in the army a few years before realizing it wasn't for me," Masou responded. "Glad I got the training, though. The kind of places I need to visit in my job..." He shuddered.

Harry nodded. Testing the weight of the weapon he was given, he charged a round. The suppressor was already attached. Looking through the scope at a distant tree stump, he pulled the trigger. The piece of wood exploded.

"It works very well," Masou said, voice eager. He'd also brought gas masks and protective gear. Masou told Alex, "I'll be your pilot, and I'm told Mr. Sheppard can pilot one of these, too. They are equipped with the M5 armament subsystem for XM574 white phosphorous cartridges."

"WPs," stated Alex, using military shorthand. An ugly substance used in smoke bombs and incendiary munitions as well as in other, more benign devices. On this mission, the WP bombs would be used only to smoke out the tribe, not burn.

Masou nodded.

El Gato muttered in Spanish about hurrying up.

"Sanders?" asked Harry.

"Safely home in New York," Masou said.

"So why the heavy artillery?" Harry asked. Each chopper could hold several Stingers.

"We won't have to use any of it," Masou assured him. "But better to be over-prepared."

Dressed in coveralls, Alex and Masou walked to their chopper with Harry keeping narrowed eyes on the oil scout's back. Surely, Masou knew what he was doing, or Temple and Godwin would never have allowed him to fly a Kingsley grandson around. Pivoting to his own helicopter, Harry placed both his gun and the sniper rifle on the co-pilot's seat. The map he got from El Gato followed. After a second or two, Harry picked up his Colt and strapped the holster back onto his thigh before climbing in. Rolling up his pant leg, he nodded, somehow reassured by the sight of the curved handle of the Ari B'Lilah, his tactical knife.

Chapter 52

October 1982

Vaca Muerta, Argentina

Seating himself in the Jeep, El Gato shouted orders into the radio in rapid-fire Spanish. In the distance, troops dressed in camouflage and armed with AKS assault rifles marched to the northern bank of Lago Los Barreales.

Harry glanced at the other chopper. Climbing in, Alex turned to look at Harry. When Harry made a "V" sign, Alex held his thumb up.

Harry snapped on his aviator helmet. Systems checked. Gages, green. Fuel tank, full. Lights, off. Area, clear. A bit of pedal and a bit of cyclic. Keeping his hand on the collective, he twisted the throttle. Engines roared, and rotor blades whirled. Hot air blasted from jet pipes.

Wobbling a little, the chopper rose to a hover. The ground fell away. One meter, ten meters, more. Inertia forced Harry's torso into his seat. He pushed the cyclic ahead, then further when he felt lift transition to forward motion. Finally, the aircraft was raised to maximum continuous power.

Harry looked down toward the other chopper. Brown dust swirled as it lifted off. Harry turned his chopper and flew it to the northern side of the village while Masou flew west with Alex. Harry checked the clock, and on cue, the radio crackled.

Alex's voice said, "Huey five-dash-fifty-six, it's eleven-twenty-eight. We're almost in position. Five-dash-fifty-five... over."

Harry responded, "I'm getting there. Five-dash-fifty-six... over."

#

The ground skimmed rapidly by as they flew, and suddenly, they were on the western border of the target. The Andes ranges loomed on Alex's left. Checking his watch, he said, "Five-dash-fifty-six, I have a visual on you. Five-dash-fifty-five... over."

Harry's voice responded through mild static. "Roger. It's eleven-thirty. On the count of three. Five-dash-fifty-six... over."

"Wilco," said Alex. "Five-dash-fifty-five... over."

Through the radio, Harry said, "One, two, three." He and Masou launched the ordnance. "Five-dash-fifty-six... out."

The WP bombs exploded at the northern and western borders, rapidly forming long, white lines of smoke. The spreading fumes would drive the tribe out.

Masou took the chopper down, the contraption landing with a bump before settling. Snapping his hood on, Alex jumped out, bending almost double to avoid the whirling blades, and waited for the other aircraft to settle on the eastern side. The oil scout soon joined him, and El Gato's soldiers were already patrolling both open borders. Harry emerged from his helicopter and jogged out from under the blades.

They stood at the edge of the region, watching for the dissidents whose faces they'd memorized. White smoke swirled, blocking their view of the village. It seemed... Alex frowned. Was it just the fumes? The fire itself wasn't supposed to spread over the village.

Something flew out of the fog, emitting guttural screeches. Alex leaped back, heart pounding, and a gray-yellow bird brushed past his face mask. Other birds flew out from the trees, followed by animals, filling the air with growls, squawks, and shrieks. Some met with flames at the border and dropped to the ground; some fell mid-flight from inhaling smoke. The strong, garlicky odor of the white phosphorous made Alex cough even under the protective hood.

Shadows ran out of the chemical fog. Human-shaped shadows. Alex couldn't make out their faces. "Harry," he said. "I can't see worth a damn. Let me back away and scan the perimeter."

Harry nodded. "Right."

Alex positioned himself a few feet behind, rifle ready. Masou accompanied him. It didn't do much good. People kept rushing by, coughing hard with their faces covered.

A murderous scream came from the dense smoke. A huge form rushed at Alex. The face was grotesque with the left eye a mass of burnt flesh and the cheekbone visible through a deep wound. Its arms were raised, and it was yowling in rage. Fear slammed into Alex; he raised his weapon and shot the thing. It dropped to the ground, skin still sizzling from chemical burns.

More screams came from the fog. Sweating profusely, Alex looked up from the corpse. Other human-looking forms were running out, some burnt. "What's happening?" Alex bellowed. "We're only supposed to smoke them out. Why are they getting burned?"

Masou didn't respond, grappling with a teenager armed with a kitchen knife.

Alex hefted the boy by his collar and tossed him aside. "Run,"

Alex said. The boy scampered away, sobbing and screeching.

Families were fleeing the village, some holding babies too young to walk. One man limped on a leg charred to the bone. A woman ran, clutching the burned corpse of a child in her arms. The woman halted when she saw Alex, her eyes wild with panic. She turned and ran in the other direction, stopping again when she saw Harry. Her head swiveled between the men in protective suits. *"Demons,"* she screamed. The limping man grabbed her elbow and dragged her along as he attempted to escape. He swung his free arm toward Alex, something metallic glinting in his grip.

Masou yelled when the limping man caught him in the arm with a blade.

"We're not going to hurt you," shouted Alex, tugging Masou back. Except for dissidents, all villagers were free to leave. Alex saw the weapon in the limping man's hand. A pair of scissors. *"Leave,"* Alex ordered the man and the woman. More tribespeople came at them. More scissors, more knives, even a screwdriver—the Puelche fought back with every weapon they possessed. "We're not here to hurt you," Alex shouted repeatedly, trying to push them away. Harry was also fending off attacks with his hands and yelling at the tribespeople to run to safety. Alex couldn't see what the government soldiers were up to, but the gunshot sounds behind him couldn't mean anything good.

For each wave they beat back, more and more of the tribespeople came at them. When one of the Puelche rushed Alex with a raised knife, he fired his second shot of the day. The man fell to the ground, his limbs seizing in the throes of death. Sounds of panic filled the area. The fleeing crowd turned toward Alex, thundering in fear and fury.

Alex fired indiscriminately. Damn it to hell, it was either them or him. Bodies dropped. Unearthly screams ricocheted from every direction, and the stench of blood and burnt flesh soaked the air.

Even the lake seemed to boil from the heat.

The carcass of a bird plummeted from the sky, seared featherless. "*Why* are they getting burned?" Alex hollered at Masou.

"How would I know?" the oil scout screamed, pushing an enraged tribeswoman away.

"This way," shrieked someone, and the escaping Puelche turned toward the lake. The government soldiers would be there, too, watching for dissidents.

"Captain Kingsley," shouted a dark form, emerging from the smoke. "Don't shoot."

The voice sounded familiar. Keeping his weapon trained, Alex held fire. El Gato materialized out of the fog, a gas mask strapped to his face. "Isabel," he huffed. "She's pregnant. Make sure you get her out alive."

Alex swore. "How the hell? The smoke's too thick here."

Masou said, "The chopper."

Firing their weapons for cover, Alex and Masou ran to the helicopter. They whirled off in a few minutes. Alex wished he'd warned Harry before liftoff, but if they were to take Isabel prisoner, he needed to quickly get a clearer view of the terrain.

#

Yellow flames and smoke soared high in front of Harry, the southwest wind bending the fire in a macabre tango. Loud crackles from the burning brush mingled with screams. The sharp odor of phosphorus pervaded the air.

Nothing was making sense. The tribespeople weren't supposed to get burned. The chemical was only supposed to smoke them out. Why was the village on fire? Sweat drenching him, Harry looked for Alex but couldn't find him. Masou wasn't anywhere to be found, either, but El Gato came running, pointing upward.

Sounds of chopper blades came to Harry above the screams. Alex and Masou were flying low enough for Harry to see Alex pointing his rifle at someone on the ground—a pregnant woman. Isabel. Rocks exploded in her path, and dust swirled. Alex was firing a barrage, preventing her escape. Nor could she run back into the chemical fire.

She turned frantically, gasping when she saw El Gato, her husband. He snarled with demonic glee as she recognized there was no place else to run.

Harry saw her decision on her face a split second before she made it. The anger, the determination not to give in either to the fire or the enemy.

Arm raised, he shouted, "Don't—"

Eyes screwed shut, she took one step, right into the path of the bullets from Alex's rifle. Isabel pitched forward, hit in the back. In an instant, the shots from the chopper ceased.

"No," Harry screamed.

Running to Isabel, he picked her up in his arms. She fought like a wild animal even with blood streaming down her shoulder. Weak punches landed on his chest as he ran with her to the chopper and placed her on the bench. Her blood stained his clothes.

Isabel moaned and curled her arms around her swollen belly. *"Mi bebé."* Her eyes fluttered shut. Her body slumped into itself.

With shaking fingers, Harry checked her neck for a pulse. Still there, thank God. She'd only fainted.

Kicking aside the box of ammunition in his way, he lunged at the radio, intending to signal Alex to abort the mission. The number of casualties had crossed acceptable limits, and Isabel needed immediate medical help. *The dam,* Harry thought. There was a dam on the river. If Alex could destroy the barrier, water would flood the village and neutralize the white phosphorous. Harry could take

Isabel to the nearest hospital in the meantime.

A young man sprang through the open side hatch, thundering in anguish. The machete in his hand hissed as it slashed the air mere inches from Harry's neck. *"La mató, bastardo!"* the boy screamed, accusing Harry of having killed the girl.

Harry held up his arm, trying to deflect the steel blade. The fabric on his coverall ripped. "She's not dead," he told the Puelche youth. "I'm trying to help."

In pain-fueled rage, the boy didn't hear. Harry grabbed the kid's weapon arm and wrenched it behind him. There was a sickening crunch before the knife dropped. With his good arm, the young man gripped Harry's neck in an awkward headlock around the hood.

Holding his rifle with one hand, Harry struggled to free himself. "She needs help, you idiot. Let me go."

They tumbled out of the helicopter's open door. Pain shot up Harry's ankle. Regaining his balance, he pivoted and slammed the skinny youth against the fuselage. Forcing the boy's elbow away, Harry underhooked the thin arm to break the clinch. He needed to get to the radio and have Alex destroy the dam... water... the village would stop burning. But more figures ran in Harry's direction, wielding weapons and screaming with murderous wrath. Letting go of the boy, Harry raised his rifle and fired.

El Gato raised his weapon, aiming at the boy.

"No," Harry screamed, diving to tug the boy behind him.

Blood gushed from the boy's throat. His eyes glazed over. Through the screams, through the crackling flames, through the thundering in his own head, Harry heard the sound of the bullet. The boy fell, face down. Breathing in gasps, Harry dropped to his knees and flipped the lad over. The boy's mouth twitched, then stilled. His body shrank into itself.

Bellowing in rage, Harry leaped. Before he could confront El

Gato, a heavy form landed on his back. Harry heaved the man aside, but more panicked tribesmen kept coming. Harry swiveled in a circle, shooting at anyone daring to get close. He tried to aim, to point his weapon where it wouldn't kill, but there was no way. There were too many villagers, too many knives, too many pitchforks and shovels.

Isabel... he needed to get help for her. Again, he tried to get back to the chopper to signal Alex, but more escapees kept coming. At his side, El Gato puffed. "The machi didn't die. She wasn't there. My informants didn't know."

"We're not here to kill the Puelche, you son of a—"

"You don't understand," El Gato said frantically. "She's Isabel's grandmother!"

#

In the other chopper, Alex fell back into his seat in shock. He never meant to shoot Isabel, only to stop her from escaping her husband.

She was still alive. She'd been struggling with Harry when he was taking her to his helicopter. Harry would get her out. He *had* to. If she died... Alex didn't know what he'd... Sabrina... she was pregnant, too.

Over the sounds of the monster chemical fire and the screams of the tribespeople, Alex heard a dull roar. A giant black shadow advanced from the mountains in the west. The dark form splintered into three choppers spreading out over the village. In his guilt and horror, they appeared to be the denizens of hell, approaching to visit retribution.

"The general," said Masou.

There were rough terrain vehicles on the ground, following the aircraft. "Who?" Alex shouted over the racket.

"Sanders's man in the area. Someone must have called him."

"What the hell?" Alex hollered. "*You* were supposed to keep an eye on him!"

Masou shrugged. "Didn't think he was close enough."

"Didn't think—" Alex cursed hard. "We were relying on you—of all the incompetent—" But there was no time for reprimands. Harry needed to be notified. Grabbing the radio, Alex shouted, "Five-dash-fifty-six, respond!" There was no answer.

Alex scanned the terrain. Next to the chopper, Harry was fighting off attackers with his revolver and a knife, the rifle given by Masou nowhere in sight. Enemy choppers were getting closer, but the angry tribesmen were preventing Harry from getting to his own helicopter. On the ground and armed only with a blade and a gun, he stood no chance against aerial strikes. He needed cover to get himself airborne.

Alex ran to the rack to pick up the grenade launcher. He felt the chopper tilt, change direction—Masou had turned northwest, leaving Harry alone to fend off his attackers. "What the hell!" shouted Alex. "Get back over there."

"We have other things to worry about. The general's men are headed for the dam," said Masou. Sure enough, there were two armed birds heading toward Portezuelo Grande Dam. "They're going to destroy the gate. It will flood the Neuquén River on the northern side. The water will neutralize the phosphorus."

Maybe it would save at least a few of the villagers. Alex cursed himself for not thinking about it earlier, but he didn't have the time to worry about it now. He needed to get to Harry. Switching to his rifle, Alex took aim at Masou. "Back," Alex ordered. "Make another move without my say-so, you're a dead man. *Capiche?*"

Masou flicked a glance at Alex, and whatever he saw was apparently enough to guarantee immediate compliance. He did as charged.

At the sudden turn, Alex felt the morning's coffee come up his throat. He leaned forward to clear the open door, his body tugged in opposite directions by the howling wind and the safety line. With the rifle, he shot at the enemy below and provided air cover for Harry so he could get to the Huey.

A lightning bolt of pain shot up Alex's left arm. His vision grayed. He looked down to see blood staining his shoulder. There was an enemy chopper not far away, a thick-necked man at the door. No way did he get his bullet into Alex from a chopper in flight. The fellow would have to either be damned lucky or a magician with a firearm. It was certainly someone on the ground.

"The general," stated Masou. "The chap in the helicopter."

Alex gritted his teeth at Masou's negligent tone. If the oil scout were a soldier under Alex's command, he'd be facing charges.

The general's aircraft was moving away. The fellow wasn't even trying to take a shot at Alex. No grenades, either. He was headed straight for Harry. The other two choppers were also ignoring Alex and were busy with the dam. "Why are they—" Alex hissed. He was the one in air and the bigger threat. But the general had a history with Harry. What better chance to get rid of an enemy? "We'll see about that," muttered Alex.

He grabbed the grenade launcher. Grimacing against the electric pain on his left side, Alex fired from his right shoulder. Almost at the same moment, the general's gunship released an array of antimissile flares. Alex's shot ran into one, detonating a few feet from his target.

"You almost hit him," Masou exclaimed. "With your weak side!"

"Evasive maneuvers," Alex snapped, not bothering to explain he didn't have a weak side. He was ambidextrous.

Reloading after each shot, he relentlessly targeted the general's chopper and the ground troops in the vehicles following. The general's pilot whirled the aircraft out of effective reach, but Alex kept them occupied, shielding Harry with a volley of charges. Gunfire roared back and forth across the skies, but Masou was also adept at dodging enemy explosives.

Even with his left arm feeling like it was exploding from the inside, Alex couldn't stop. Sweat beaded his lip as he watched Harry fight every inch of the way back to the helicopter. Still firing his gun, the former SEAL slid the cabin door shut. "Stay put," Alex warned Masou, continuing to shoot warheads at the general.

It seemed to take eons, but Alex finally saw Harry's chopper lift off. The general gave chase through air. But Harry was his own pilot, and the only weapons in the aircraft he could actually use were the WP bombs. The rest were useless to him at the moment. All he could do was try and evade the enemy.

"Get to the dam," Alex ordered. The embankment was already destroyed by the general's men, and water was flooding the village. Unfortunately, it was too late for the inhabitants. The enemy choppers were still there, though. "Let's give the general a distraction."

Alex shifted the grenade launcher on his shoulder. Pain shot all the way down to the fingers of his left arm. A quick glance at the wound showed the fabric of his coverall sticking to the skin and preventing further bleeding. "Get me as close as you can without drawing fire," he said.

Masou moved above the enemy aircraft. Taking aim, Alex fired. One of the choppers spun to the ground, black fumes gushing from the engine. Before the second gunship could retaliate, he sent more charges. It exploded in mid-air, debris scattering over the smoldering remains of the village. "Two down, one to go," Alex muttered. The command helicopter.

The general's craft continued to dog Harry, ignoring the carnage Alex was inflicting on his troops.

"Bastard!" Alex exclaimed. "He really is here to kill Harry, not save the tribe. Let's get him."

"Sheppard can take care of himself," Masou said, voice flat.

"Now!" roared Alex.

Masou grunted and obeyed. Alex turned his fire on the general's aircraft, but the pilot saved the day each time. The general continued to chase Harry.

As Alex took aim at the general for the umpteenth time, Masou advised, "Don't kill him. We don't want an international incident. It won't be like smoking out the tribe. The general has friends in the government. Plus, Sanders. The government won't side with him over a small tribe, but over a general of its army... it will be a big problem."

As soon as this was done, he'd deal with Masou, Alex promised himself. For the sheer incompetence, the nonchalant attitude, everything! For now, there was the general, but he had already moved away. "Get close to him," Alex ordered.

The radio crackled. "Go east," said Harry. "The troops shouldn't get to the villa. Runt and Lilah—"

"Understood," said Alex. "Move east," he snapped at Masou.

Alex's left arm was turning numb. He shook it, trying to return some feeling to the limb. Pain zig-zagged across his nerves. He muttered a prayer of thanks. Pain was good. It meant blood flow.

On the eastern front, Alex shot as many ground vehicles as he could with the grenade launcher. A Jeep spun out of control, crashing into another. Both burst into flames. But there were just too many enemy vehicles. Already, some of the general's men had gotten through and were moving toward the villa.

Alex cursed. "Launch the rest of the WPs," he ordered.

"What?" exclaimed Masou. "It will leave the tribe with only one escape route."

"The lake," Alex said. Unless they were dissidents, the government soldiers would do nothing to the escapees. Everyone else would be escorted to the shelter. "We have no choice. Can't let anyone get to the villa."

The bombs dropped. White fog bloomed. Chemical fire spread to engulf the eastern front.

The two Hueys circled the area, the general still chasing Harry. Alex fired at the enemy troops brave enough to break through the fire on the east. The injured girl was in Harry's aircraft, but Harry and Alex couldn't leave as long as the general and his men stayed. They couldn't let anyone get to the villa.

Alex saw the general circling around. While he was busy blocking the ground troops, the general's helicopter had gotten close to Harry. There was a weapon on the general's shoulder—a grenade launcher.

"Sheppard can't outrun it," Masou said. "Too close."

Alex took aim, huffing desperately.

#

Behind the gas mask, Harry took in short, sharp puffs of hot air, the smell from the chemical fog mixing unpleasantly with the stench of sweat and blood. There were no sounds from the wounded girl. He prayed like hell she was still alive.

Thick white smoke enveloped the terrain beneath. Through the side glass, Harry saw Alex leaning, pointing his weapon at the enemy chopper. Hood ripped off, he was screaming something, but the roar of the engines and the whipping of blades from the aircraft drowned out other sounds. Jerking his head to the side, Harry saw the grenade launcher in the general's hands.

Harry snarled. The bastard wasn't going to win this easily. Muttering another prayer, Harry pitched up the nose of the chopper and lowered the collective before stomping on the right pedal. The helicopter stalled in mid-air. Blood thrummed hard through his veins. The heat of battle enveloped him. Harry held flare and waited until the weapon launched. When the grenade was barely seconds away, he dropped.

The aircraft shuddered. He lost altitude. The helicopter entered vortex ring, a pilot's nightmare of uncontrolled descent. As the chopper dropped several hundred feet in seconds, Harry's insides sloshed within his body. There were thuds and crashes from the cabin as unsecured objects were tossed about, but the sounds were barely audible over the thundering explosion rattling the windows of the helicopter. The rocket had caromed nose-high off one of Harry's rotor blades, catching the tip and detonating between them as they whirled. The dropping aircraft escaped destruction by scant inches.

Rocky ground rushed up, the burnt corpses of human and animal victims waiting for him to join them. Swirls of white smoke swathed the chopper like a shroud. The vibrations inside the chopper increased, and his stomach clenched hard, sending sour fluid surging into his mouth.

Time slowed; every raspy breath was long and drawn out. In the window, in place of violent death, he saw anxious hazel eyes. "I'm not going to die," he assured her. "Not today."

Harry gritted his teeth and kept his gaze away from the smoke rushing by the plunging chopper. Sweat soaking his body, he lowered the collective and increased air speed. With a violent jerk, the machine stopped descent. Forces of inertia yanked Harry's body down into the seat. His head swam. The chopper moved forward, breaking out of the fog.

#

From above, Alex watched the helicopter falling as though sucked into the whirlpool of smoke and fire. "Harry!" he bellowed. All sound seemed to recede from Alex's ears. The valley fell silent. He somehow couldn't hear a single bird move, nor an animal. "Harry!" he roared again, but there was no answer.

A black shape burst out of the white cloud. Blades thwacked the fog; the engine thundered. Harry had returned, ready for battle. Alex collapsed into his seat, swearing in relief.

"Mad," muttered Masou.

The general, too, was hanging out of his door, expression one of shock.

Alex grabbed the radio. "Five-dash-fifty-six! Ground is now almost clear of the enemy."

"Got it," came Harry's voice.

While Alex again used grenades to keep the general busy, Harry landed. The few remaining villagers and enemy troops on the eastern and southern fronts were being handled by El Gato's soldiers. In minutes, the general became the target of both Alex and Harry. The enemy chopper teetered in mid-air and turned westward to alight clumsily away from the fire and smoke. There was no one on that side to capture him.

"Let him go," insisted Masou. "Too much trouble."

Alex spat to the side, muttering curses. On his instruction, Masou veered east. They landed a dozen yards from Harry's chopper. He was now helping El Gato's soldiers prevent the tribespeople who were still alive from charging the villa. Alex and Masou jogged to join Harry.

Soot and dust mingled with the red stains on the former SEAL's coverall. He stood with his revolver drawn, shooting at every being venturing east. At each sound, Harry turned and sent a bullet. Alex shot down those creatures escaping his cousin's wrath.

El Gato soon told his soldiers their work was done, but Alex and Harry refused to budge until they were sure the danger to Lilah and Sabrina had passed. Nor would Harry let El Gato get to Isabel. She wasn't going anywhere with anyone until a doctor checked her out. Face red with anger and frustration, the Argentine fellow snarled he would wait until he got what he wanted.

None of them noticed Masou standing behind, taking aim with his weapon.

Chapter 53

A few hours earlier

At the villa

"I don't like it, Dante," Lilah said for the hundredth time. "Harry and Alex should've called by now. I need to go to the Puelche village and see what's happening." A sharp smell tickled her nose, and she sneezed. Lilah opened her mouth to firmly tell Dante she was going whether he liked it or not, and she sneezed again. "What's this—garlic?"

"What?" He, too, sniffed the air. "Yeah, it reeks."

"Is something burning?" she asked. They ran to the kitchen to check. The staff looked up in surprise as the pair burst in. The cook was stirring simmering liquid in a pan on the stove, a maid was chopping vegetables, and another stood at the sink, washing dishes. Muttering apologies, Lilah and Dante ran back to the living room windows. A distant white fog blocked their view of the village.

"What's that?" asked Dante.

"Don't know." Lilah grabbed the keys from him and hurried to the door. "But I'm going to find out."

"I'm going with you."

Sabrina came down the stairs, disturbed awake by the commotion. She watched worriedly from the doorway as the other two ran to the car. When they reversed and turned to drive through the gate, an armored vehicle vroomed in, blocking their way. Gunmen jumped out, pointing weapons at the people in the car.

Lilah slammed the brakes, heart pounding. With hands raised, she exited the driver's side. The commanding officer ordered her into the house, gesturing with his muzzle. As she complied, she noted the insignia he wore proclaiming his high rank in the army. *Sanders's man?* Her belly knotted in fear.

"*Señor*, we have two men caught inside the village," Dante said. "We want to get them out."

"*No está permitido*," the commander said, waving his troops to a corner of the garden.

"Sir, why are you detaining us?" asked Lilah. "On what charges?"

"No charges, miss," the man responded in English. "For your protection."

"From what? We have family there. We need to get them out."

"*No está permitido*," he repeated, pointing the rifle at her. "You're safe in the house. I will not let anything happen to friends of the American president within Argentinian borders. Once things settle down, my soldiers will escort you to Buenos Aires."

Dante grabbed her arm, dragging her into the house.

"Harry and Alex... they're both there!" she shrieked. "If these are Sanders's men, they're in trouble."

"*You* could get into serious trouble if you try to leave." Dante closed the door. "Maybe not from the soldiers, but from criminals... Harry said something about it. Please, don't risk it. You heard what the fellow outside said. He knows our connection to the president. Temple wouldn't like it if anything happened to us. We'll be all right."

"Probably, but I'm not sure about Alex and Harry." Lilah looked around, thinking furiously. "The phones. Check the phones. The president may be able to help."

When Dante dialed out, Mr. Temple's private line was busy. The secretary promised to get him to call back as soon as he was free.

Lilah hissed. "That may be too late. Let's try Harry's father."

Sabrina said, "I'll call him." She took the receiver from Dante. Tone surprised, she said, "It's dead."

Lilah marched to the door and flung it open. "Commander, why did you cut our phone lines?"

"The town is under martial law. Communications are blocked except through military personnel." He pushed her back in and closed the door.

"Lilah, the staff have all been asked to leave," Sabrina said.

Lilah went to the door again to talk to the commander. It was locked. She ran to the kitchen exit. The last of the staff had left, and that door was locked, too. She returned to the living room. The three of them looked at each other. They were prisoners.

Lilah told herself over and over the soldiers wouldn't hurt them when Temple was the president, ready to retaliate with the might of the American military. But Harry... Alex... what was going on?

Hours went by, and they remained locked in. Lilah sat at the window and peered outside. Dante coaxed them, especially Sabrina, to eat a little, but no one managed to choke down more than a bite or two. Choppers battled it out in the skies, flame and fumes turning the air sooty.

Shoving gruesome images out of her brain, Lilah struggled to focus on the motive behind the proposed evacuation. Again and again, Lilah's mind returned to Temple. *"The president's busy,"* the secretary had informed her. Too busy to take a call about the mission he'd personally arranged?

"Why doesn't he have Kingsley Corp try it?" Her own question echoed in Lilah's ears.

Temple proclaimed in her memories, *"One man for a nation."*

"La chica," yelled the driver of the truck which drove Harry's bike off the road. Why had it mattered there was a woman on the bike?

Harry, what's happening there? Lilah asked.

Outside, there was an explosion in mid-air, and a chopper went tail first into descent. Her stomach dropped. She clapped a hand to her mouth, stifling a cry. The helicopter disappeared into the white fog. It would crash on the rocks below, tearing to pieces the body of the unfortunate pilot. Lilah froze in position. Heartbeat slowed; vision blurred.

The helicopter burst through, ripping apart the curtain of smoke. Horrified, Lilah watched the pilot cheat death with seconds to spare. In the clarity of that one moment, she saw the president's plan. *Harry!* she screamed in her mind.

Lilah was barely aware of turning and sprinting upstairs, the shocked voices of Dante and Sabrina following. She dashed to the terrace. The government vehicles were still parked outside, men leaning carelessly against them and chatting. One of them sketched a casual salute in her direction. Eyes darting across the compound, she counted the soldiers. Eight, the same number of men who'd blocked her way when she tried to drive out. They were all there, making sure Dante and the women stayed inside.

Footsteps sounded at the door behind, and Dante poked his head through. "Are you all right?"

Wiping sweat from her lip, she went over options. Dante would never let her leave on her own. "Trying to see what's happening."

As soon as he left, Lilah went to her room and gathered her climbing equipment, thanking God for her need to jump off cliffs when under stress. She picked up her gun from the nightstand and tucked it into her belt before sneaking into Harry's room. The bay windows faced away from the lake. Peering through the glass panes, she found no soldiers on that side. Maybe no one told them she was capable of escaping through upper-story windows.

As quietly as she possibly could, Lilah dragged the desk close to the window. She looped slings around two of the wooden legs, anchoring her rope to it. It wasn't the safest of the options, but she didn't have the time to search out a better one. At least she didn't need to use bedsheets.

Lilah raised the bottom sash and tossed the rope out. Climbing all the way to the ground, she left the rope hanging and ran to the hedge bordering the garden to crawl on hands and knees behind the tall shrubbery.

Someone laughed, and a male voice called out something in Spanish.

Lilah halted, waiting for footsteps to get closer. Fear squeezed itself into a tight little ball in the center of her chest. Her hand clenched around the pistol grip protruding from her belt. When the men continued chatting, she let out her breath.

"Shh!"

She swallowed a panicked gasp and looked up, heart thudding painfully. The wrinkled face of the machi from the village put a finger to her lips. The machi was crouched on the ground and beckoned Lilah to follow. Still on all fours, Lilah did as she was bid.

The hedge shielded them from the soldiers. When they got to the other side of the road, a tarp-covered ox cart waited, something frequently used by the tribespeople. Lilah clambered in after the machi.

"What's going on?" Lilah asked but found a knife at her throat. She froze, eyes on the sharp blade.

"You," the woman hissed. "You brought the demons to our doorstep."

"Demons?" Lilah croaked.

"The Americans." The machi spat to the side, the edge of the knife pricking the skin on Lilah's neck.

Sweating profusely, Lilah leaned back against the side of the wagon as it rocked forward. "Ma'am, let me talk to them."

"What's left to talk about?" the machi snarled. "My tribe's dead. My granddaughter, my precious Isabel, she was shot. Eight months pregnant, and the demons shot her."

"No!" Not Harry, never Harry.

"Yes." The woman's face crumpled. "They told me one of them put her in his helicopter. To give her over to that bastard husband who beat her—El Gato."

Lilah shook her head. The pointed tip of the knife nicked her skin, but she barely noticed the sharp sting or the wet warmth trickling down her neck. "There must be some mistake. Harry wouldn't do that."

"Get her out, or I'll kill you."

Lilah saw Dante and Sabrina at the upper window, waving frantically as they watched the wagon pull away. They would be safe enough inside, she consoled herself.

It took the cart only a few minutes to get to what remained of the village. Lilah stood at the top of the slope and viewed the horrifying scene below. Human remains littered the ground. Some were still alive and moaning, begging for help.

"She's there," the machi tugged at her arm, pointing toward a helicopter. "I saw the American take her inside."

The smell of garlic was strong here, mixing with the odor of burning flesh. Lilah gagged. A hand covering her mouth, she walked in a daze, the machi leading the way.

Flames had burned every living thing in the village. In the distance, two dark forms monitored the periphery. Dully, Lilah recognized the monsters as her own.

Masou stood behind them, weapon aimed at Harry's back.

She raised her handgun.

The machi screamed. "That's him. *El Gato. El bastardo.*"

At the machi's shout, Masou turned, his weapon no longer pointed at his unwitting target. Lilah jerked her head to the side and saw a man she didn't recognize running toward them, the pistol in his hand aimed at the machi. Lilah swiveled and shot him through the heart. He looked disbelievingly at the red color blossoming across his shirt. Then, he crumpled and died.

Lilah turned the smoking muzzle on Masou.

Chapter 54

The sun was on its way down, painting the sky orange red. Amid the smoke, all Harry could see was the blurry silhouette of a woman facing off with Masou. "Drop your weapon," Harry shouted.

Alex sighted through the scope. "Harry," he said in a choked voice, lowering the rifle. Harry looked at his cousin in puzzlement. Alex shook his head. "Lilah."

Blood drained out of Harry's brain. They both ran forward to tell her what happened, to try to make sense of it all. The fury in her eyes stopped them in their tracks.

Dante and Sabrina came running to them, panting as they struggled to reach Lilah. "What happened?" asked Dante, expression horrified at the death and destruction.

"Harry?" Sabrina asked, her voice trembling. "Alex?" She took a step toward her husband.

"No," Lilah snapped, still holding her pistol on Masou. The oil scout's rifle was pointed at Lilah.

Sabrina stumbled at the abrupt command.

Rage reverberating in her voice, Lilah said, "They... they did this."

Sabrina's face turned ashen, her lips pale.

The machi tugged at Lilah. "My granddaughter is in the helicopter. We must take her to the hospital. She's *shot*."

Lilah didn't look at the machi, her gaze whizzing between the men responsible for the carnage. Finally, she asked Masou, "Can you fly this?"

Masou nodded, his firearm still trained on her.

"Put your rifle down," she ordered, eyes steely.

Masou looked from her to the two men next to him, quietly dropping the weapon when he found no support. She gestured him into the chopper with her gun.

Sabrina was crying openly, glancing between her husband and her brother. Dante ushered her into the helicopter behind the machi.

Gesturing at Masou with her head, Lilah said to Dante, "If he tries anything, I'll have to shoot him. We'll all go down."

"We're going with you," Dante said. "What choice do we have? The soldiers are at the villa. And these two... these two..." He stopped, unable to vocalize the contempt in his eyes for Harry and Alex.

Harry tried to speak, but words wouldn't come. He extended a hand, but Lilah looked at him with loathing. She followed Dante in and slid the cabin door shut.

When they flew away, Alex staggered forward a few steps. Harry stared mutely into the sky, not having the strength to move. The chopper disappeared into the dark horizon.

Smoke hung over the village. Among the human remains, a shadow moved. The breeze carried to them the sound of a muffled whimper. Something crawled along the ground toward the river. "Who?" shouted Harry, raising his gun.

A young man got to his knees, hands together in supplication. "Don't shoot," the boy sobbed in Spanish. Wild eyes darted between Harry and Alex.

"Who are you?" barked Alex.

Eighteen years old and an architecture student at the local university—younger than Sabrina. "Don't kill me," he wept.

Vaguely, Harry heard Alex asking the boy to tag along.

Harry's foot struck something, and he glanced down to see a skinny arm tumble along the ground. On the wrist was a leather band with the Hells Angels insignia etched on it.

The boy with the soccer ball... his friends... Harry had said he'd return for a game.

Ripping off his gas mask, he fell to his knees. Fingers digging into blood-stained earth, Harry retched.

Part XVIII

Chapter 55

In the cabin, Lilah forced herself not to look through the window and kept her gun trained on Masou in the pilot's seat. Dante sat next to her, hugging a tearful Sabrina to his other side. At the back, the machi sat on the edge of the bench next to her granddaughter's head, chanting prayers.

Dante asked, "What happened in the village?"

Biting her lip hard, Lilah shook her head. She couldn't bring herself to explain the blackened corpses, the empty village, the image of Masou's rifle pointed at Harry's back. If the machi hadn't startled her by screaming, Lilah would have killed Masou. Then, she'd have beaten Harry to death, strangled him with her bare hands. *How could you?* she whispered in her mind, pain tearing through her heart.

"Let me," Dante said, taking the weapon from her sweaty fingers.

"Keep your eyes on him," Lilah warned, nodding toward Masou. If it weren't for their need for transportation, he *would* have been dead by now. Harry was their other option for a pilot, but Lilah didn't want him anywhere near the machi or her pregnant granddaughter.

Lilah was a witness to Masou's treachery. If he got a chance... once she was dead, he wouldn't let the other passengers live to give evidence against him. Lilah said none of this out loud. She needed to put the puzzle together first.

Willing every thought out of her mind, Lilah staggered to the bench where the machi's granddaughter lay and knelt by it. Beneath the girl's shoulder, blood had gelled on the seat. There was so much of it. She was so pale. *"Ayúdame, por favor,"* Isabel whispered, pleading for help.

Lilah took the girl's cold, clammy fingers between hers and mutely nodded. Sabrina crouched next to her, hands reaching for Isabel's swollen belly. "The baby's still moving," Sabrina whispered.

Closing her eyes, Lilah thanked God. She never thought to check.

A small health center was the first hospital they found. There was barely any equipment, but Isabel's treatment couldn't be delayed further. As they waited outside the operating room, Lilah asked Dante, "How did you get out?"

"We used your rope," Dante said.

She threw a quick glance at him, shocked eyes then going to Sabrina's middle. The pregnant girl had climbed down a building?

"What made you think," Dante asked, voice furious, "we'd let you walk into a battle on your own?"

Batting away the wetness in her eyes, Lilah nodded.

When the door to the operating room opened, it was a nurse with a bundle in her arms. Her face was somber. Isabel had gone into cardiac arrest before they could start surgery. It was all they could do to save her baby. Holding her great-grandson to her breast, the machi wailed.

An icy pain squeezed Lilah's heart. She couldn't offer comfort. She couldn't bring her arms to envelop the old woman. Isabel's blood was on her hands. The machi had trusted Lilah, and she'd brought death to their village.

At Lilah's side, Sabrina sobbed, helpless grief in her eyes. They watched as Dante folded the machi and the baby into an embrace, leading them to a chair. It was Dante who contacted another Puelche tribe at the machi's request. It was Dante who made arrangements to transport the body to their village for burial.

It took hours for the van to arrive. Lilah watched in silence as Isabel's body was loaded into the vehicle. Just before the machi climbed in with the baby, Lilah said, "Please—"

The machi barely glanced at her.

Hurrying forward in desperation, Lilah gripped the machi's elbow. "I'll send help, I swear. Every month. Whatever I have."

The machi spat. "Blood money!"

Lilah stumbled back.

Harsh fury in her eyes, the old woman said, "You can't buy your way out of hell. Live in fear, Delilah Barrons. I'll come for you."

As she watched the van leave the hospital grounds, Dante said, "Masou escaped."

She should've expected it. Once he got a chance to think over things, Masou would've realized killing President Temple's chosen linchpin for the network was not worth the risk. He'd have decided to skip when her back was turned.

Lilah called her twin to arrange the trip home, knowing he was the one person who wouldn't insist on answers. The flight from Buenos Aires to Panama was made in absolute silence. She didn't look toward Sabrina, but Lilah knew the younger girl would also be remembering their arrival in Argentina. The bike race, the wine, the happy laughter... the warmth of love, the joy of friendship... all of it lay shattered, every illusion now ripped away. Only death and loss remained.

Dante called Brad from the Colón airport. It seemed Alex and Harry had not yet returned. The Kingsleys met Dante and the women at the door of Brad's hotel suite, their eyes anxious.

Leaving all explanations to Dante, Lilah took Sabrina to a local doctor. "Just to be on the safe side," she said. Who knew what kind of harmful effects the chemical smoke could have? The doctor said she'd get back to them after checking with a toxicologist.

When they returned to the hotel, Lilah took one look at Brad's pale face and knew Dante had already divulged whatever he figured out. She didn't vocalize her own deductions, didn't reveal what she'd seen Masou about to do. She couldn't throw around accusations until she was sure. Perhaps not even then. Brad was not likely to believe what she had to say about his grandfather and the president. In the end, Lilah merely told her fiancé if he wanted her cooperation in any plans to come, he'd have to donate the land back to the tribe. Her threats weren't needed. Brad was equally horrified by the genocide and wanted to make amends any way he could.

Lilah emptied her personal bank account to start on reparations and called the machi to promise full payment soon. The machi didn't refuse the money, but she hung up without a response.

Chapter 56

The villa was dark when Harry and Alex returned, the architecture student sniffling behind them. The car they'd rented stood abandoned in the middle of the driveway. In silence, they gathered their things.

Harry noticed the hole with charred edges on Alex's coverall. A bullet wound. The blood on his arm was his own. "The general's men, I think," Alex said.

They couldn't go to any of the local hospitals for fear of authorities. Nor was it safe to use the rented vehicles, but they had no option. "We can go to Rio Negro," offered the student.

Driving the car to a town twenty miles away, they abandoned it there to rent a taxi. In Buenos Aires, Harry hunted down a surgeon willing to treat a gunshot wound off the books in return for a hefty bribe. He inspected the injury and told them there was no bullet embedded. Just a flesh wound already in the process of scabbing over.

It took even more cash to get a contact of Harry's to quickly make a fake passport for the student. Somehow, the fact the kid survived seemed to give Alex some peace, so Harry didn't object. He couldn't even bring himself to care about the possibility the boy could be a plant.

When they got to Panama, Victor met them at the door. Dismissing the boy to the care of Patrice Kingsley, Victor led Harry and Alex to the small conference room. Both Dante and Brad were there, as was Lilah. Rigid and ice-cold, she turned away. Damning the culprits with her silence, she strode out of the room.

When Brad asked them for accounting, Harry listened to Alex speak and stared straight ahead, fixing his gaze on the wall.

"The situation got out of control," Alex reported tonelessly. They never expected fire to spread across the village and burn everything down. They didn't anticipate the attack by Sanders's man, the general. They didn't expect to have to block off one of the escape routes to make sure no one got to the villa and the women. "We had no reason to doubt El Gato. He was introduced to us by Masou." According to Godwin Kingsley, Masou had gone off the radar. They assumed he'd been working with El Gato, intending to kill the tribe as revenge for protecting Isabel.

Harry interjected, "Alex did have concerns, but I talked him into it. Once things escalated, we had no choice but to continue. If we hadn't, the general's troops would have gotten to the villa."

Brad refused to be mollified. "Alex, I don't understand. I get how you and Harry are best friends, but why would you... how could you *both* have been so stupid?"

At Brad's side, Dante stayed quiet, but there was compassion in his eyes.

"How could you let Masou drag you into this... this *mass murder?*" Brad continued. Sounding bewildered, he added, "I'm sure this isn't what the president and Grandfather meant to happen."

Alex looked down, saying nothing.

Harry started, "I'll explain everything to Mr. Temp—"

"No," snapped Brad. "As CEO, I okayed this. It's damned hard to believe what you two..." Shaking his head, he pushed his glasses up his nose. "Harry, Lilah and I agree it's best if you return to New York. Permanently, I mean. It's the only way to assure all concerned this won't happen again. She's asked me to talk to Mr. Temple. In any case, I doubt the president will want to hear from you ever again. My God! If word gets out, we'll all be done for... maybe even Mr. Temple."

Part XIX

Chapter 57

Months later, December 1982

City Island, New York City

"Book up every appointment slot," Harry told his secretary after he returned from Panama. Evenings were spent in the boxing ring at the gym—bout after bout after bout until muscles screamed for mercy.

He couldn't allow himself even a few free minutes, or terrible memories would attack. Memories of fire and death and the dull horror in Lilah's eyes. But he welcomed the nights and the terrifying visions they brought with them. In his nightmares, Harry would stare unblinkingly at the blood on his hands, at the severed arm with the leather wristband. He'd sinned, and there was no way to atone for his sins. He couldn't even turn himself in without dragging Lilah and the Kingsleys into it.

Other than those present in Argentina, only Alex's family knew what happened. And of course, Temple and Godwin. As Brad Kingsley ordered, Harry made no attempt to connect with Temple, and the president didn't bother to demand a personal debriefing. Harry Sheppard was political poison at the moment.

A couple of weeks later, Dante delivered news about the president persuading the Argentinians to arrange a cover-up. There were rumors, but confusion was created by including the names of Jared Sanders and his general, and no one knew with any degree of certainty what happened. The general was both bribed and threatened into staying silent. The few surviving tribespeople were in a desperate enough state to accept financial incentives and stay mum. Even Sanders couldn't protest without potentially prompting international inquiries into his involvement, and the one thread might be enough to lead investigators to the rest of his crimes.

Since there was no longer any danger of legal repercussions, Dante suggested Harry put the incident out of his mind. After all, the oil scout tricked Harry and Alex into it. But Harry couldn't forget. He ventured on this mission to rid the world of monsters only to discover *he* was the worst of them all. Harry Sheppard was a mass murderer, and everyone who knew about the Argentine episode realized it. Oh, some still showed compassion he didn't deserve. Sabrina called him like clockwork. Alex called, too, even though he was drowning in his own guilt. The rest gave Harry a wide berth as they would to any psychopath. And Lilah... she refused all phone calls from him.

The only news he'd gotten of her was that she'd flown to Israel for the funeral of the former first lady she met at the White House event so long ago. One more loss to add to Lilah's too-long list. Harry didn't know where she found the strength to carry on after all the blows. Whom did she turn to for support? Brad? Sabrina?

Fortunately for Harry, the growing demand for Gateway's services kept his mind occupied during waking hours. Phones rang incessantly in the office in Brooklyn. On weekends, he used his parents' home as workspace since it was easy to connect with Hector, who'd bought the house next door. That meant dealing with Sophia Sheppard's obvious attempts to find him a wife.

"I like this girl," his mother said, moving around the office room, tidying papers which were already tidy. "Harry?"

"Hmm?" He needed to review the notes from his negotiations with airlines.

"Are you listening?" his mother snapped.

"Yes, I am. You like someone... a girl. Is Father aware?" The silly joke got him a sharp smack on the back of his head.

"I'm talking about Verity." Alex Kingsley's friend and daughter of Gateway's biggest outside investor, Will Luce. "She's visited quite often since you returned. Didn't you notice?"

Harry finally put the papers down and gave his mother what she wanted—his undivided attention. "Yes, Mother. I know she's been a frequent guest here. Yes, I'm aware she's given every sign of wanting to get to know me better. I've been trying to ignore it."

"Why? She's nice."

"Because she's too young is why."

"She's twenty-one. Barely five years younger than you." Firmly, his mother continued, "Harry, you've played around long enough. I invited Verity to dinner tonight. I told her you asked me to."

"What?" He stood. "Mother!"

"Your father and I've been talking to Will Luce. Hector gave him a job in the accounting division—he needed it after losing the stock. He likes you."

"Why? Because his property is under my control?"

"Because you showed spine and responsibility—his words, not mine," Harry's mother said. Luce was lucky it was Harry who triumphed at the game in the Catskills. The stock was safe, held in trust for Luce's children by Gateway's board. "He's hinted heavily he wouldn't mind you for a son-in-law."

"Great, my life's now complete." Throwing his hands in the air, Harry stalked out.

Not wanting to annoy his mother, he showed up at dinner but left most of the conversation to her. Harry wondered why he couldn't work up any enthusiasm for Verity. She was pretty, with an hourglass figure and platinum-blonde hair. Her feathered shag, she assured them, was the handiwork of the most in-demand stylist in Manhattan.

Harry grinned and managed not to roll his eyes at his mother's rather obvious hints toward the end of dinner. Finally, succumbing to a heavy maternal glare, he invited Verity for a stroll.

It was an unusually warm winter, and New York City had yet to see the first snowfall. Full moon night already passed, but what was left was bright enough to cast a warm glow over City Island. All in all, a pleasant evening for a romantic walk. When they got to the street, Verity turned to Harry. "Here, hold my hand. Quick."

"Excuse me?"

Verity said, "They're all at the front window. Take my hand if you don't want to be nagged when we return."

Surprised at this obvious ploy, Harry stared. Her gray eyes were so hopeful he laughed in honest amusement. He took her fingers and tucked them into his elbow as they walked past the window. "Tell me about yourself," he invited.

City Island Avenue was well lit. The shops were still open, but traffic was dying down. Only a few headlights went up and down the tarred road. Commuters, returning home after a late day at work. Even the Atlantic appeared to have settled for the night, its roar dulled to a mild grumble.

Verity talked almost nonstop, chatting about her work in interior design, unabashedly admitting she'd barely done anything before quitting. "It was just something I thought I could do," she said. "Actually, I wasn't too bad at it."

"Why didn't you continue?" Harry took a deep breath, enjoying the familiar salty smell of the sea.

She shrugged. "Too much work. Picking out fabric, watching budgets, and all that. I'm entitled to a life, right? There were other people who needed the job. Girls without money, you know."

Harry stared, unsure if he were meant to be amused by the virtuous tone. The shrill sound of a bicycle bell interrupted their conversation. Two kids skidded to a stop next to them. "Hi, Harry," sang a voice from under the helmet. The girls lived in the neighborhood, both not yet into their teens. One of them had ice cream smeared across her cheek.

"Hi to you, too," said Harry. He pulled out his handkerchief from inside the blazer and offered it to the girl.

She stared in incomprehension.

"Here," he said, wiping the smudge off her face.

Her friend giggled.

Harry cursed mentally. He should've remembered. All of twelve, they'd started practicing their wiles, fluttering eyelashes when they encountered him and striking poses probably meant to be enticing. "I saw your mother on the porch," he said to one of them. "Get home before you get into trouble."

They paid his admonition no mind. The girl closest to him twirled a strand of her hair around her finger.

Verity twined her arm around his elbow, leaning possessively against him. The kids straightened and exchanged not-very-subtle glances. "Right," one of the girls said. "Goodnight." They rode off.

He was about to thank Verity for rescuing him when he saw the triumphant smile she threw at the departing kids. Even if they'd only been children, she was quite pleased with herself for having gotten rid of competition. Harry was confused to find himself mildly flattered by the juvenile display.

"Let's talk about you now," she said. "Tell me why they gave you the Medal of Honor."

He smiled. "For knowing how to keep my mouth shut."

She pushed out her lower lip. "All my friends want to hear the story. They were very impressed by you. I mean, by what you did at the get-together. Liam told me Papa lost all our money. If you hadn't been there... I'd have had to ask for my job back." Her eyes shone.

Harry laughed in bemusement. He couldn't remember ever running into this level of candid superficiality before.

They walked the length of the island before returning. Standing in front of the short flight of stairs leading to his parents' home, Harry realized with surprise he hadn't thought about Neuquén for the entirety of the time. He'd been too focused on dodging Verity's unapologetic and unrelenting curiosity about what she believed to be his glamorous past. He hadn't even needed to fix his attention on her as he usually did with people. Verity was quite content to talk about herself without any prompts, subliminal or otherwise.

"Verity," he called. "Have you been to Lutéce?"

"The French restaurant?" she asked, pouting. "It's hard to get in."

It would be. Lutéce was one of New York City's finest dining places. "There's a Christmas party there I'm supposed to attend," Harry said. "Will you go with me?"

"Yes!" she squealed, clapping her hands.

#

It was a gathering of New York's top business executives and their significant others. Wine flowed liberally at such events, market tips were shared, and deals proposed. Afterward, Harry dropped Verity off at her Fifth Avenue condo, feeling mildly penitent for mostly ignoring her. He inquired if she'd been bored.

"No," she exclaimed. "I saw Brooke Shields! And Calvin Klein!"

Harry and Verity continued to meet over the next few weeks and spent New Year's Eve at Regine's, the night club on Park

Avenue. The place was packed with celebrities, sending Verity into high-pitched excitement. There were more than a few men—and women—eyeing her back with equal interest. The pink, spangled cocktail dress she wore was *haute couture*, designed to show off her tanned legs and curvy figure. The club had a dress code, and all the men, including Harry, were in formal evening wear.

Close to midnight, the crowd chanted numbers along with the CBS anchor, counting down to zero. The apple-shaped ball dropped. Wild cheers erupted, welcoming 1983. The band struck up "Auld Lang Syne."

Amid the other couples sharing their first embrace of the year, Harry and Verity kissed. Her arms curled around his neck, drawing his head down. Rounded hips were firm under his hands. Warm and eager lips, champagne on her tongue, jittery breaths, the scent of arousal...

It was nearly dawn when they got to her condo. "Stay," Verity said, peeling the tuxedo jacket off his shoulders.

Kissing, nipping, stroking, kneading, they staggered into the bedroom. Dirty whispers in her ear, searching fingers on her thigh, probing mouth on her body—Harry used every weapon in his arsenal, making her weep and thrash about, begging for more. Only when her eyes glazed over with delirious lust did he seek release.

The moment he withdrew from her arms, the spirits haunting him returned. They were with him when he dressed himself, when he covered her sleeping form with blankets. They were with him when he locked her front door behind him and slipped the key in through the crack at the bottom. They followed him all the way home, taunting him over his belief he was any better than the tyrants he battled.

Chapter 58

"And she was the last of them," Harry said to Verity, closing the office door behind his secretary. "Also, the most important."

He and Verity were spending nearly every evening at her place, but he'd been skeptical when she asked to visit his work. Surprise, surprise. She showed up at Gateway's headquarters in Brooklyn and spent the entire morning being introduced to the key members of Harry's team.

Over lunch at Junior's, they talked about Alex and other people both knew. "He taught me how to shoot, you know," Verity said. "He's good."

Harry merely smiled, remembering the skill and tenacity he witnessed in Neuquén. He owed his life to Alex Kingsley.

"What about Lilah?" Verity asked, daintily nibbling at cheesecake. "Brad's fiancée?"

Harry grabbed the napkin, wiping the corner of his mouth with it. "What about her?"

"You're friends, right?"

With extreme effort, Harry kept his face pleasant. "Yeah… Verity, I'm meeting someone in Dubai next week… a new oil field we're both interested in. I was wondering…"

The rest of the meal passed in a congenial discussion of Middle Eastern celebrities.

Much later the same day, the janitor whistled a jaunty tune as he mopped the empty hallways of Gateway's office. Tossing his pen aside, Harry leaned back in his chair. He'd skipped his gym session to catch up on work, but Verity's mention of Lilah had emboldened the ghosts. The memories refused to wait until he got home… not only of a love destroyed, but the fear on the face of the pregnant girl who'd bled in his arms, the children who'd burned to death, the boy with the—

The janitor's voice rose in a bawdy limerick, interrupting the parade of dark images through Harry's mind. He supposed he could return to his apartment and let the ghosts take over. He'd be alone, no protection from enemies, illusory or real. Well, except for his Colt and the Ari B'Lilah. Both proved handy in Neuquén, better than the sniper rifle provided by Masou.

After all, one bullet was all that was needed to take a life, including his own. He could put the barrel of the gun in his mouth... one slice of the blade across his throat and... would the guilt stop with death? Would the spirits be satisfied with his blood and leave his soul alone?

Snarling, Harry lunged off the chair and jogged out to the street to hail a cab. "Vet Center," he said, sliding in.

"Now?" asked the cabbie. "They're long closed, buddy."

"Right," said Harry, sweating despite the sub-zero temperature. "Let's get to the Brooklyn Bridge."

"You sure?" the cabbie asked, eyeing Harry's well-made suit. "There's no vet center there. Just some homeless old soldiers, smoking dope."

Harry was sure.

The next morning, while he was at work, he got a call from Alex. The conversation was short. Grayson Sheppard, whose many talents included being an ordained minister, had married Brad and Lilah in a surprise ceremony. Other than Brad's mother and his brothers, the only people present were Dan and Shawn and Sabrina. Oh, she and a couple of Lilah's old friends from school were her bridesmaids.

After Harry hung up, he told his secretary he was going home for the day. All the way there, he reviewed sailor's knots in his mind, blocking out the rest of the universe. When he got to his apartment, he locked his gun and knife in the desk and slipped the key into an envelope. With a shaky hand, he wrote his own name and address on it.

Harry jogged down the steps and out to the street. There were the usual drunks in front of the Palace Hotel. Drug dealers continued to conduct business. Those in Harry's way took one look and scurried off. When he got to the mailbox at the corner, Harry dropped the envelope in and walked to the local liquor store. Returning with 151 proof Bacardi rum to the fifth-floor walk-up, he flung his blazer on the couch. Methodically, he locked the front door and closed all the windows.

His next memory was waking up in his bed. Through bleary eyes, Harry scanned the room. The blinds were drawn, but there was sun filtering through the slats. The only sounds were those of traffic from the street. Strangely, the room stank of bleach disinfectant. He wondered how many days it had been. "You're up," said a voice.

Wincing at the sharp pain behind his eyes, Harry raised himself on his elbows. He was still in his dress shirt and pants, but the shoes were gone, and so was the tie. He turned his head toward the door where Dante stood, sipping from a cup. "Did I call you?" Harry finally asked.

"No, Alex did," said Dante. "The super let me in."

Harry's throat was dry. Coughing, he asked, "What day is it?"

"Saturday," Dante said. "You missed the inauguration."

Inaug—Temple's second term. Harry grimaced. The president had deigned to invite his former protégé probably to avoid gossip about Harry's continued absence in the power circle. He'd have to come up with a plausible excuse for not attending.

"You were down with the flu in case you were wondering," said Dante.

#

It had been a long week at work, but Harry couldn't break his promise to Verity. Reservations at Windows-on-the-World were not easy to get, and it was only thanks to his secretary's magic they were able to dine there. The restaurant on top of the World Trade Center's North Tower gave them a magnificent view of Manhattan. Verity was happy with the location and the food. After dinner, she told him two months of dating was enough to invite a girl home.

"This is my private kingdom," Harry told Verity, tucking aviator shades into his pocket. He swept his arm with dramatic flourish.

She giggled in delight and walked in, looking around the East Village apartment. "Beautiful."

"You think so?" he asked, absurdly pleased.

"Truly," she said.

Harry yawned. "Sorry," he mumbled. "Busy day."

Enjoying glasses of claret by the open window, Harry let the cold breeze wash away some of his fatigue. He watched the moon come up over the gritty neighborhood, painfully recalling an evening on a Brooklyn rooftop with his girl in his arms and the world at their feet. Neither of those young people knew at the time he would turn out to be a killer.

Harry blinked hard, struggling to yank his mind from the edge.

"Hey, I know her," said Verity. Waving, she shouted a greeting to someone on the street. When her friend waved back, Verity cuddled closer to Harry, her arms winding around his torso, her hand slipping inside his blazer. She'd become his refuge over the last few weeks.

Without giving himself another second to think, Harry called, "Verity?" She looked at him with a smile in her eyes, and he continued, "Will you marry me?"

Chapter 59

Fourteen days, Harry thought. Exactly fourteen days had passed since Lilah married Brad, and Harry was celebrating his betrothal to Verity. Even with the short notice, the Sheppards pulled off a grand event at their City Island residence. Harry thanked each and every person congratulating him, wondering how he could feel this detached about it... almost as though he were watching the party from a distance. At his side, Verity was glowing in excitement.

"Best choice you could've made, Harry," his father said for what had to be the hundredth time.

His mother nodded in agreement. "She's a sweet girl."

Dante walked in and headed straight for the engaged couple. Kissing the bride-to-be, he said, "Only a princess like you would've done for the Sheppard prince."

Verity preened. Her platinum hair and the sugared tangerine color of her mini dress did give her the appearance of a fairytale princess.

Later, as Dante stood on the deck, puffing on a cigar, Harry sought him and took the expensive stogie offered. His suit and tie were inadequate protection against the freezing weather, but the smoke would provide some warmth. It was also something to focus on.

"Your parents must be happy about the situation," Dante said, "Everything worked out, *and* Verity is a lovely girl."

Harry threw a half-glance at his boss. "Situation? Were they worried I'd change my mind about Lilah?"

"Huh?" Dante shook his head. "No, they know you well enough to realize it won't happen. I mean the Verity issue." When Harry frowned in confusion, Dante exclaimed, "Oh, c'mon. All your damned cousins were after the girl... after her father's stock. Whoever married her would've eventually inherited a chunk of Gateway."

"So?"

"What do you mean 'so'? Your father's in charge now, and he naturally wants control to stay in his own family. Er..." Dante cleared his throat. "There was some talk of setting her up with Hector. It was supposed to happen at the picnic."

Harry turned a sudden half-circle to stare at Dante.

Nodding, Dante said, "Then, the poker game. Your father was relieved you put the shares in trust for Luce's children. Believe me, there would've been knives out for you, otherwise. Your extended family would've seen it as an illegitimate power grab."

"I have to sign off on any attempted return of the stock even if the majority of the board agrees," Harry said. "Still, none of it will come to *me*. I don't get this about setting up Hector... wouldn't it also have been seen as a power grab?"

"You *know* a poker loss and a marriage would've been viewed differently," said Dante. "Hector gave Luce a job, but the girl made it clear to the whole world the only Sheppard she wanted to get to know was you."

"Hector got engaged to his old girlfriend soon after." With an inner huff, Harry stabbed the lit end of the cigar into the ashtray.

"Since Verity declared to everyone within hearing she wanted you and you alone, none of your cousins will be able to claim you're marrying her for the stock, either." Dante smiled in satisfaction. "I never liked the idea of pushing Hector toward someone he barely looked at. In your case... she was already interested." Placing his Habano on the ashtray, Dante continued, "Your parents have been worried. They're still upset about what happened with Sabrina, and Hector's been drinking a lot lately... your father told me. It's impossible to miss when they're living next door."

Harry frowned. "You're the COO. Any problems with Hector's work? Did his wife say something to my mother or father?"

"No and no, but it's not a good habit, especially when it's in the company of the likes of Charles Kingsley. Hector claims he's doing Steven a favor by keeping Charles out of trouble. Still... then there's you. Besides the problems with Gateway, there's the fact Ryan and Sophia do love you and want you to have a happy life." Dante glanced at his watch. "I need to head back. Virgil's visiting."

Dante's only child was an aeronautical engineer and worked in California. Virgil's rare stays in New York were much cherished by his widowed father.

"Harry, you need to... Verity will be good for you." Slapping him on the back, Dante left.

#

Verity chattered nonstop on their way back to Manhattan later in the night. If she noticed Harry's uncharacteristic silence, she didn't comment on it.

When they walked into the apartment, Harry kicked the door shut, spun her around, and caught her mouth in a deep kiss. Her lips were still cold from the wintry air, but they tasted of warm, plummy wine. The jasmine scent of Chanel N° 5 still clung to her skin. She twined her arms around his neck and plastered her body to his.

He unzipped her dress, his fingers strangely shaky. Stripping her naked, he carried her to bed. Harry undressed himself with unusual haste, tugging off shirt buttons which wouldn't cooperate. When he joined her on the mattress, he linked fingers with her and drew her arms above her head, looking down at the nude body beneath his.

As his mouth sank into hers, love-drenched hazel eyes filled his mind. Habibti, *his heart whispered, and he reached out to fist his hands in her dark hair. Muscles tautened in his shoulders. His body shook with need.*

Harry jerked up, eyes snapping open. He blinked, trying to focus on the platinum-blonde hair and stormy-blue irises of his fiancée. "Verity," he said, voice urgent. "Verity." He called her name again and again, desperate to keep his mind on her.

He ran his hands down her arms and sliding them under her back, lifted her body. His mouth traced its way across her cheek and neck to her breasts. Teeth tugging gently on delicate skin, his eyes drifted shut.

The intoxicating scent of warm woman mixed with the fragrance of blue lotus oil teased his memory. Longing for his beloved filled him. In his heart, Harry roared, seeking his mate. When she answered with a roar of her own, an animal desire seized his limbs—to claim her as she claimed him, to mark each other for eternity.

He reared with a suppressed snarl and raking his fingers through light-blonde hair, he called, "Verity," forcing her to open her eyes.

Breathing heavy, he kept his gaze pinned on her face. When he bent again to take her mouth with his, her hand went to the bedside switch. He caught her wrist in a gentle grip. "No. Lights on. I need to see... you."

He made love to her with desperate intensity, surprising both of them with an almost out-of-control passion.

Harry said sometime after, "Let's get married soon."

"What's the hurry?" she whispered, confusion in her voice.

"You're my only hope for holding on to reality."

Chapter 60

January 1983

Aruba

Except for the ceiling fan, the hotel room could've passed for any of the million such rooms back home in the U.S. with double beds and nightstands and a television. Nothing special for a honeymoon suite, but the beach view compensated for the lack of originality as far as Lilah was concerned. Plus, the fact Brad was a considerate husband *would* make their stay in the place special. Not many men would've so readily acquiesced to her request to wait the couple of weeks until their vacation before consummating the marriage.

At the sink in the restroom, Lilah poured herself a glass of water and swallowed the birth control pill. She turned over the second blister pack to read the label: "Ativan 1 mg." Still within expiration date, although it had been months after the psychiatrist prescribed it. Before she could change her mind, she popped one out and drank it down with water.

By the time she washed and changed into the blush-colored nightgown Sabrina gifted, Lilah could feel herself relaxing. When she heard the door open, the room was lit only by night lights, and she was at the window, watching the moon hanging over the Caribbean Sea. She turned to see Brad walking in, clad in tasteful silk pajamas.

Okay, Lilah thought in relief. It was good not to have to fight the urge to run from the greed in his eyes. *Okay*, she whispered in her mind. She didn't flinch when his fingertips brushed against the see-through bodice. "Nice," she murmured when he ran his hand along her inner thigh. The nightmares seemed to be staying away.

Neither talked. Tree frogs chirped outside the room's windows, but beyond that, there was silence. Brad took her hand and led her to the bed. He kissed her neck, his mouth leaving warm moisture on her skin. A musky odor joined the leathery smell of his aftershave. Without any fuss, he slid the nightgown and the panties off her, leaving her shivering under the breeze set up by the fan.

When he drew back the bed covers, Lilah lay down, staying perfectly still while he undressed. Watching the lights flickering on the ceiling, she fought a sudden urge to giggle. Her hilarity had nothing to do with Brad and everything to do with the funny pattern of the shadows she saw on the wall, but the book she read said men could be strange about laughter in the bedroom. She needed to be careful.

The mattress dipped when he joined her, his body blocking the moonlight. She felt his weight on top, his fingers parting her thighs, then a pressure in her womb. Her skin... it felt weird... numb. Lilah put up her hand, tentatively stroking Brad's back. She knew she was touching him, but she couldn't feel it.

Brad grunted and lunged against her body. When his tempo increased, there was mild friction inside her which was not entirely unappealing. She might have focused on it more, but she was worried about the lack of feeling in the rest of her body. Was the anxiety pill supposed to do that?

Within minutes, Brad groaned on a last thrust and collapsed on top of her. When she murmured in protest, he mumbled, "Sorry," and moved to the other side of the bed.

Must be the medicine, Lilah thought, her eyelids getting heavy. She yawned, feeling sleep taking over. She'd have to ask the doctor when they returned home.

#

Two weeks later, late January 1983

Panama

Lilah never realized a week in the Caribbean could be this never-ending. Long silences punctuated by stiff and awkward bursts of conversation... watching television and reading every English-language newspaper she could find... waiting for Brad to come back from the casinos. She took her pills every night, just about managing to stay awake until he was done. Even when they returned to Colón, she followed the same routine, taking Ativan promptly at 9 p.m., half an hour before she knew Brad would want to go to bed.

Lucky for her the workdays were packed. As she once predicted, their reputation for providing excellent services had spread. Now that the restrictive covenant limiting competition with Kingsley Corp in their territories was almost over, the number of oil drillers who wanted to hire the Peter Kingsley Company skyrocketed. Cash was pouring in.

Then there was the construction of the family mansion, which Patrice got started soon after the Argentina episode. Part of Brad's mother's reasoning was their finances were finally secure enough for it, the other part being the desperate need for distraction from recent happenings. The architecture firm she picked promised they could finish it within months.

"Seriously, Patrice," Lilah said over lunch at a seafood restaurant in the capital city. "I am perfectly comfortable with you and Sabrina making the decisions on the place."

"*My* requirements are simple," Sabrina said promptly, hands linked over her heavily pregnant belly. "Every luxury imaginable."

As they laughed, Lilah glanced sideways at Sabrina, thanking God for the one bright spot in it all. The younger woman was a constant presence at Lilah's elbow when she went about her job. The two of them discussed either routine business or pleasant personal things... funny thoughts and happy memories... nothing else.

"Ready to do your shopping?" Lilah asked. Baby clothes were not exactly her forte, but Sabrina had insisted on Lilah coming along.

For some reason, the smile vanished from Sabrina's face. "Yeah," she said.

There was complete silence from her for the rest of the meal, silence in the car, and silence in the store except for an occasional grunt or two.

Pregnancy hormones! Lilah decided in her mind. Even getting Sabrina to decide on the color of the onesies was proving difficult. "Yellow or green," Lilah eventually said. "And get three or four. Once you know if it's a boy or girl, you can always get more."

Sabrina was rubbing her thumb over a pair of dungarees with a cartoon mouse appliqued on the bib.

"Earth to Sabrina," Lilah called.

"Harry is engaged," Sabrina said abruptly.

"What are you—" Then, it registered. A sudden vacuum. A painful coldness in her soul. With fingers that shook only mildly, Lilah folded the yellow onesie. Voice almost calm, she asked, "Who's the lucky lady?"

Sabrina made a sudden gesture with her hands. "Verity Luce. Her father is a shareholder in Gateway. Have you met her?"

"No," Lilah said. "If you like those dungarees, let's get them. They're cute."

Chapter 61

A few days later

Upper East Side, New York City

The full moon cast a silvery glow on the grounds of the Kingsley mansion, giving it a magical appearance. The branches of the evergreens bopped up and down in the whistling wind. Every now and then, the windowpanes shuddered. Barely glancing at the scene outside Godwin's home office, Temple turned the large antique globe in one corner on its brass meridian. *Argentina. The*

Andes Mountains. Harry had left a map of the region with Brad, which was delivered to the president. The neat markings on the paper were surely made by Harry as part of his preparation for the mission.

From the leather chair across Godwin's desk, Noah commented, "I hope we're not in for another round of snow."

The blizzard which battered the eastern seaboard two weeks ago nearly shut down the city and delayed Temple's plans to visit. It didn't matter. Now, there was one more thing to celebrate besides Temple's new term in office: the unexpected success of their plan in an entirely inadvertent way. Shifting restlessly on his feet, Temple traced the border between Argentina and Chile with a finger. Almost the entire village perished… leaving the intended target still alive.

When Temple heard from Brad immediately after the events in Neuquén, he wasn't quite sure what to make of it. On one hand, Harry survived, but on the other, he was supposedly thrown out of the fold. Given what Masou said about Lilah's unexpected appearance in the village, Temple was worried she suspected treachery. Under the circumstances, he didn't dare mount another attack and confirm her suspicions, thus causing her withdrawal from the planned network. There had been no option but to wait and watch what happened. Godwin and Noah concurred.

Yet… this latest news… "Hard to believe it worked," Temple muttered.

"Believe it, dear brother," said Godwin, rocking back in his own chair. "Harry was not at Lilah's wedding, and she was not at his engagement celebration. You would've seen for yourself if you'd gone to Harry's party. Ryan did invite you."

Temple turned to face the other two men. "Security problems." If he'd accepted the invitation, the family would've needed to change venues to accommodate the safety demands of a sitting president. The Sheppards probably would've done it, but Temple wasn't quite ready to look any of them in the eye yet. Strange… this feeling of guilt and shame. Harry was a sailor, expected to follow the directives of his commander even into the arms of death.

"Time to focus on Sanders," Noah said.

"Right." Temple tried to shrug off the melancholy and bring his mind back to the enemy. "Brad tells me the company is doing extremely well now. The alliance is still not bigger than Sanders, but they'll need to get there in the next four years while I'm in office. One by one, we have to pick off his friends. Eventually, we'll destroy him, but we're once again going to have to wait a few months before we start."

"I agree," Godwin said. "Brad was really shaken by the Neuquén episode. He won't be in the mood to hear another word about Sanders or our plan for him."

More delays. Even waiting as long had been risky since reelection was never guaranteed, but there was nothing else they could do under the circumstances.

"By the time Sanders is out, we should be pulling all the strings in the alliance," said Godwin. "Afterward, if Lilah objects... the death beneficiary clause in the pre-nup is a problem, but there must be some way around it." The marriage contract specified her stock in the three companies would go to the person or persons she named in her will, who needed to be someone other than her husband and his family. Once she had children, she could name them beneficiaries, but the shares would be held in trust by an outside executor. Control of the network would thus pass to an outsider in the event of her death.

Temple shot a sharp look at the Kingsley patriarch. "We're *not* going to hurt Lilah." There was no reason left to go after Harry, either. He was already out of the Kingsley circle and no longer an influence on Brad and his brothers.

Godwin huffed in exasperation. "Lilah's ideas and attitude are what got us into this mess. If it weren't for her stubbornness, we wouldn't have been forced to... the tribe would've still been alive. Plus, Masou said she shot the Argentine character—El Gato—without blinking. She's a troublemaker, Temple. You're letting your fondness for her get in the way of facts. See, Andersen? This is what comes of ignoring your children when they're growing up. Now, mortality's staring at him, but his son won't give him the time of day. So he starts adopting random orphans."

Noah laughed.

Godwin was completely correct. Temple had been a miserable failure at fatherhood. But Lilah... it didn't mean Temple was blind to her faults. "There are better ways of getting her out," Temple snapped. "Lilah can't do anything if Brad isn't inclined to listen to her; *he's* the CEO. We simply have to make sure he always takes your word over hers."

"Starting trouble, huh?" Noah Andersen asked, a feline grin on his face. "It's easy enough, especially between spouses."

"Do it," Temple ordered. "I hope..." He glanced at the chessboard on Godwin's desk. "Damn it. This was too easy." A memory surfaced, one of Lilah's queen confronting Temple's king. Checkmate. "Maybe she did figure out what was going on."

"If she did..." Godwin leaned forward with his elbows on the desk. "...why would she have married Brad? Now, the network's set in stone."

"Hmm," said Temple, somehow unable to take his eyes off the chess pieces. Unable to shake the feeling defeat was merely one move away.

Part XX

Chapter 62

A week later, February 1983

Miami, Florida

"Do you not realize I don't have any kids?" Lilah asked, exiting the airport with Sabrina. Plopping large straw hats onto their heads, they waited while Alex thanked the crew of the private jet. As always, Lilah's bodyguards stayed merely a few feet away. "I don't know how to help you with childbirth."

"I want my friend with me," Sabrina insisted. "Not my mother or mother-in-law. And no doulas. There won't be much for you to do, anyway. Just give me company."

They would stay at a hotel not too far from Mount Sinai Medical Center and wait until either labor pains began or the prearranged date for cesarean section arrived. Sabrina explained the baby was big and in breech presentation, not expected to easily make it out the usual way. When Lilah humbly admitted to having no clue what breech meant, Sabrina explained the child was bottom down.

On the first day of their stay in the hotel, Lilah mostly avoided Alex, working in her room until it was time for Sabrina's walk in the afternoon. Then, the two women left him to his own devices and strolled barefoot on the seashore, dressed in one-piece bathing suits and sarongs.

The beach looked like a painting with aqua-colored ocean meeting the heavens at the horizon and white sand tickling Lilah's toes here on earth. The mild warmth of the sun settled on her bare shoulders. At her side, Sabrina lifted her face to the sky and sighed in satisfaction.

Weaving their way through the crowded shore, the women debated baby names. Sabrina wanted Michael for a boy. Alex apparently liked it, too, since Archangel Michael was the commander of God's army. Victor's son was called Gabriel, so the two boys would be a matching set. If the baby turned out to be a girl... "Angela," Sabrina said, giggling. "I once thought of using it as a handle."

"Huh?"

"Hacking," Sabrina explained.

"Hack—" Stopping abruptly, Lilah asked, "Are you *insane?*"

Sabrina laughed, a hand on the small of her back and the other resting on her swollen belly. "Oh, c'mon. There's no law against it."

"My God!" Lilah said. Hacking was not illegal, but there was legislation being pushed to make it so. "What if the FBI finds out? They'll put you on some kind of watch list. You have to stop!"

"Nah." Sabrina dismissed the concern with a wave of her hand. "I'd be miserable if I couldn't mess around with computers. I have very little fun these days." She batted her eyelashes, looking like a sad cherub with a slightly dented halo. A *pregnant* cherub. The entire effect was supremely innocent and utterly adorable.

Lilah nearly choked. Sabrina didn't remotely resemble Harry, but they were, clearly, siblings. "Oh, no, you manipulative, little—" Lilah said. "Save that trick for your husband." She narrowed her eyes. "Alex is okay with your idea of fun?"

Just a few months back, before the events in Neuquén, Lilah thought Alex Kingsley lived by the military code of conduct. Even in Argentina, he'd been following Harry's orders. She found it hard to believe he'd support Sabrina's insanity.

The smile on Sabrina's face vanished, and she stared into the ocean. "He doesn't know."

"Tell him," Lilah urged. "And work for the company. We could use a computer genius."

"No."

"Why not?"

"I don't know." Sabrina's fingers curled into a fist. "Some days, I feel I can talk to him about anything."

Lilah said, "Of course you can. You love each other."

"I love him, but does he love me? I'm not so sure."

"Sabrina," Lilah exclaimed. "He asked you to marry him."

"Because of the baby," Sabrina said, chin down, staring at the sand.

"He didn't ask you to consider other options, did he?" Lilah snapped. "The solution which occurred to him was marriage."

"Question is," Sabrina explained, "would it have occurred to him if I were not Harry's sister? Would he ever have—" She swallowed. "—bothered with me?"

Lilah's arms went around Sabrina. "Don't be silly." Talking to the top of Sabrina's blonde head, Lilah added, "Alex is lucky to have you, and he knows it."

"I hope so," came Sabrina's muffled voice. She shrugged loose from Lilah's embrace. "I wish it occurred to me to ask before I agreed to get married... before we jumped into bed."

After a few seconds, Lilah asked, "What brought this on *now*?"

"You, for one." Sabrina held up a hand, asking not to be interrupted. "Alex told me the truth a few weeks ago, Lilah. There *was* something between you."

Shock. Lilah's feet slipped on the sand. She staggered, clutching

Sabrina's arm for support. Panic. "I... oh, my God..." Lilah stammered, frantically wondering what exactly Alex said. "We never... I swear... oh, my God... I'd never..."

"Yeah, you never," Sabrina said, mouth drooping. "Because *you* kicked him out."

"Please, Sabrina," Lilah begged to be believed. "Even if I hadn't, nothing would have happened. I was already engaged to Brad, and Alex wouldn't—"

As Lilah's words came to an abrupt stop, Sabrina smiled, the glum look not leaving her eyes. "Alex wouldn't because his family was more important to him. You see? What would have happened if Alex hadn't asked me to marry him? I was already pregnant. Would the Sheppards have continued to support the Kingsleys? If he could give up one woman for his family, why not marry another one for the same reason?"

Lilah shook her head. "You can't honestly believe he's that calculating."

"I don't," Sabrina admitted, tone soft. "I know he was attracted to me. But was it Sabrina who attracted him, or was it Harry Sheppard's little sister?"

"C'mon," Lilah said. "You're asking for the impossible. You want him to prove he'd love you even if you weren't a Sheppard. He risked your anger by being honest with you about me. Now, take him at his word. He loves you."

"I might have," Sabrina said, brushing away a tear. "I *have* accepted your part in his past. I know both of you well enough to understand you've moved on. I could've moved on, too. But this is the same man who let himself be talked into a *genocide*. Again, for his family."

Lilah didn't know how to respond.

"He seems to like my company," Sabrina muttered. "You know,

he takes me out pretty much every evening? Says he wants to make up for not actually dating before marriage."

"See?" Lilah said. "He does love you."

"Yeah, he even goes to all my doctor's appointments."

"All that worry over nothing," Lilah scoffed, a flicker of relief in her chest.

"But he stopped wanting to get to *know* me after we got married," Sabrina said. "I was in my sophomore year... he could've said something... asked if I would like to continue. He hasn't bothered. This is the same man who calls Harry every week to make sure—"

"*You* could've said something to Alex about it, but you didn't," Lilah interrupted, "so he likely believes you don't want to continue. Don't overthink and drive yourself crazy. Either you intend to return to college, or you don't."

"Dunno," Sabrina muttered. "The pregnancy... the baby... plenty of things in the computer business I could do from home. I'll survive, I suppose."

"*Survive?* You can be our in-house computer expert."

"Nah," Sabrina said. "Not my kind of thing. I prefer working on my own." Rubbing her bump, she added, "The little angel just loves to stomp on my bladder. I feel like I have to pee." When they resumed their walk, she said, "You're gonna have to make it up to me. For lying to me, I mean."

Heat rushing into her face, Lilah mewled. "I'm so sorry. It was... God, I just didn't want to upset you."

"I might have been," Sabrina admitted, no real anger in her voice. "But all these things happened... so much to worry about..."

Lilah nodded, understanding perfectly. Like her, Sabrina was troubled by the meaning of their present, racked with anxiety about the future.

"Anyway, I don't want you telling Alex about my little hobby." Sabrina grinned. "He would insist I stop."

Playfully, Lilah accused, "You're keeping it a secret only because it makes you feel all mysterious and powerful."

Sabrina stuck her nose up in the air. "Yup, like a spy or something." Laughing and talking, they continued to trudge along the beach. The sun was on its way down, and the breeze was getting cool. Sabrina eyed the horizon. "Let's go back. It's getting late."

"All right," Lilah said. "I have to call Brad, anyway. A problem with one of the clients." She hesitated, then decided to blurt it out. "Sabrina, please don't say anything to anyone about what Alex told you. If Brad gets to know... it was before *I* made up my mind about the marriage, but he might not see it that way."

"I think you should tell him," Sabrina said. "Brad knows it started as a political alliance, and he wouldn't blame you for being a little confused, would he?"

Lilah shrugged. "Too risky. Family trouble, the business contracts... things will become an unholy mess. None of us can afford it. Not the Kingsleys, not Harry."

"Harr—" Sabrina started. "You know, I always thought... damn, I really do have to pee."

#

In a few days, Lilah watched from the door of the hospital waiting area as Alex paced, anxious about his wife. Family was not allowed in the operating room. Walking to him, Lilah offered one of the two cups. "Have some coffee."

They sat in awkward silence for more than ten minutes. Then, he asked, "You've been keeping track of the machi's grandchild, right?"

"Great-grandson... and yes."

Staring into his cup, Alex confessed, "I didn't have the nerve to ask you before how he's doing. Do you still hate me for it?"

"I don't hate you." Alex and Harry walked blindly into a trap, but their mistake cost the tribespeople their lives. Remembering the machi's vow of vengeance, Lilah whispered, "But I'm afraid it's going to follow you—follow us."

"I see her every night."

"Isabel?"

"All of them." For a while, both stayed mute, their minds on smoke and soot and violent death. "I'll do anything. Adopt the child, provide financial support... whatever."

"The machi won't accept it." The lady eventually took the cash Lilah offered, but from Alex, it would definitely be seen as blood money.

"Sabrina said the same." He groaned, rubbing his eyes. "God, I'm trying to... I want to go back to being the man she married... she deserves a partner who's..."

"You told her about me."

Alex flushed. "Not everything. I left out the part about what happened to you before... Harry said it was your decision not to make it public, and I swear I won't go against it. The rest... I needed to tell her. I *will not* keep secrets from her any longer."

"It's all right, Alex." Lilah smiled. "It was wrong of me to ask you to, and I'm grateful Sabrina still considers me a friend."

"If anyone deserves a friend like Sabrina, it's you."

The nurse entered, a bundle in the crook of her arm. Alex jumped up and hurried to her, leaving Lilah to follow. "How's my wife?" he asked.

"Doing fine," the nurse said. "She's getting stitched and cleaned. Congratulations, Mr. Kingsley. You have a son."

Alex glanced at the newborn swathed in hospital clothes. His eyes suddenly turned bright. "I have a son..." He laughed waterily. "My son... Michael."

Lilah was awed by the perfect form. "May I?" she requested. The nurse demonstrated the right way to hold the infant. Cradling the baby in her arms, Lilah laughed in joy. "Is he smiling?" she asked as the baby's lips puckered. When she touched the impossibly soft cheek with a gentle finger, the baby's small mouth followed her fingertip. "What's he doing now?" she whispered.

"Looking for his food," said the nurse. Alex stroked the soft downy hair on the baby's head. The nurse added, "I have to take him back to his mother."

While Lilah relinquished the baby to the woman, Alex asked, "When can I see Sabrina?"

"In a couple more minutes."

#

Next month, March 1983

Cerro Azul, Panama

Alex Kingsley was one lucky sonuvabitch. Michael's birth returned happiness to the lives of the Kingsleys, chasing away the censure in their eyes whenever they saw Alex. The tiny scrap of humanity drove the last of the shadows from their midst.

One beautiful day in spring, Alex stood before the large double doors of the newly built family mansion in Cerro Azul, a few miles from Panama City. They'd chosen the nation as base for the legal flexibility and the proximity to the U.S., but all of them had fallen in love with this part of Panama. The mountains, the waterfalls, the hiking trails, the birds... the place was astonishingly beautiful. There was also the year-round great weather.

The current political situation was a bit iffy. Problems with Noriega aside, there were his lieutenants and their drug dealer buddy, Jùn Wángzǐ. Victor told them in no uncertain terms he didn't want any of them investing with the company, but they kept bringing up the topic. Lilah suggested the prudent thing would be for the Kingsleys to relocate, and they'd already moved most of their assets back to the States, but even she hated the idea of completely abandoning Panama. The plan was to maintain enough physical presence in the country to keep calling it their headquarters. Also, to keep their new residence.

"A home of our own," Brad said, walking up with Patrice Kingsley.

It was built alongside an old fortress, almost as an extension. The castle itself was partly in ruins, which added to the dramatic appeal of the structure. Thick gray walls towered high, turrets projecting. There were cannons still mounted, pointing outward. The newly built portion boasted six wings, each a private residence, one for each of the brothers—including the half-brothers—and the sixth for Patrice Kingsley.

"What do you think?" Alex asked his mother. "Did Maya come through, or what?" The architecture student Alex rescued in Argentina had submitted a design to the firm hired by the Kingsleys. The firm, impressed by the student's talent, offered him a permanent job.

Alex still didn't know the boy's real name. When they got him the fake passport in Buenos Aires, he'd given his name as Maya. *"It means illusionist,"* he'd told them.

There was a good chance the fortuitous name was false, but Maya truly possessed the talent of a magician. His design was now the visual treat in front of them. An office complex was centrally located in the same compound. There was a massive guesthouse, as well, for visiting dignitaries and executives. The landscaping of the estate was also supervised by the young man. Orchids and tiger-lilies were planted as well as a number of species Alex couldn't name, their fragrances melding beautifully in the cool air from the mountains.

The front door swung open, and Lilah hurried out, Sabrina not far behind, holding the baby. "Victor just called," said Lilah. He was scheduled to stay behind in Colón for a couple of weeks, interviewing candidates for positions in their company. Dan Barrons was with Victor, having been assigned by Barrons O & G to help, and Shawn had come along. "Dan will take care of work while Victor goes to Monterey," continued Lilah. "Hilda's in the hospital with some kind of flu."

"Is Gabriel okay?" asked Patrice, her brows drawn in worry over Victor and Hilda's one-year-old son.

"Hilda's cousin is taking care of Gabe," said Lilah.

"*Señora* Garcia?" Alex asked, fondly remembering the family which sheltered the Kingsleys in San Diego.

"I think that was the name," said Lilah. "Shawn's going with Victor."

"Why?" asked Brad, frowning. "It's only the flu, right?"

Lilah said, "Sounds like it. I guess Shawn's feeling bored. He's into computers, not oil and gas."

Two days after moving into the mansion, Lilah got another call—from her brother Shawn. Hilda had died, leaving Victor the single father of one-year-old Gabriel.

Patrice prepared Victor's apartment for the arrival of the eldest Kingsley grandson, but a week later, Victor returned alone. Faced with the tearful baby boy he barely knew, Victor was relieved when Eduardo Garcia asked if they could foster the child.

When Victor got home, he broke down and wept. Alex didn't know what the sobs were for. Were his tears an outpouring of sorrow, or were they tears of guilt?

There was no time for prolonged grieving. Sabrina got news about Harry's wedding. He and Verity had moved up the date.

Chapter 63

A month later, April 1983

Paris, France

Harry looked on in amusement as Verity adjusted the chic crayon pink beret on her head, ignoring the chattering passersby swarming the foot of the Eiffel Tower. At her request, they'd come straight here from the Charles de Gaulle Airport, while their luggage was sent to the George V hotel.

She smoothed out the long sleeves of her matching mid-thigh dress and took a final look at her black, patent leather pumps before declaring, "Perfect." Paris was *her* choice for a honeymoon spot, and she wanted her first trip to be nothing less than absolute perfection, starting with the clothes she wore on their walk up the city's iconic landmark. Harry had declined her offer to *"outfit him"* and settled for his suit, telling her this was not *his* first visit to France. "Let's get to the observation deck," she said, shivering in the cool breeze. A bus raced by, blasting its horn at jaywalking pedestrians.

Honking cars and bicycle bells created their own music on the roads of Paris. The buttery aroma of freshly made croissants wafted down the street, courtesy of the bakery less than a block north. A few feet from the entrance was a peddler, selling souvenirs. There was a boy there—a teenager—buying a miniature Eiffel Tower on a silver chain for his companion, his words tripping over each other as he recited the stats on the engineering marvel. "...one thousand and sixty-three feet tall..." The girl was wearing a dark-blue varsity jacket. Too big for her… it was surely the boy's. She swept her hair to the side, inviting him to adorn her neck with the cheap souvenir. His nervous lecture faltered to a stop, the soft blush on the girl's cheeks apparently having stolen his powers of speech.

The trinket will turn green soon, Harry thought in exasperation. Dismissing the teenager and his girlfriend from his mind, Harry walked up the stairs with Verity and listened to her chatter about the wedding (beautiful) and the guests (strange).

The teenaged couple thundered up the stairs with the energy of the young, laughing in pure joy.

As they brushed past him, Harry staggered to the side, crowding Verity. She asked, "What's wrong?" He started to grouse about the young hooligans, but they'd disappeared around the corner.

Harry and Verity took the elevator from the second floor to the observation deck. Tourist season was already underway, and there were several visitors wandering around. Paris in April was as beautiful as the songs declared, complete with daffodils and cherry blossoms lining sun-kissed streets. The Seine flowed cheerily on. It felt as though the world had shaken itself awake from hibernation.

Harry wrapped his wife in his warm blazer as they stood looking at the city of lovers. He bent his head to hers, savoring the feel of her soft lips.

"A kiss on the Eiffel Tower," she said dreamily. "The perfect start to a honeymoon."

A giggle distracted Harry. Looking in the direction of the sound, he saw the same boy.

The kid stood with his back to the city, facing the girl leaning against one of the iron pillars. His hands were on the pillar, bracketing her face without touching it, imprisoning her there with his body. Teeth chattering in the nippy wind, she smiled at her companion with sweet longing. A jumble of emotion and desire was reflected in his eyes. Their unsteady breathing was audible to anyone within a few feet.

Oblivious to the rest of the world, he bent to kiss her. There was more youthful ferocity than finesse in his caresses, but the dazed look in the girl's hazel eyes said she didn't mind at all. When he came up for air, she yanked his head back to hers. The boy seemed as though he'd drown in her as he devoured her mouth, again and again.

The first kiss for both, Harry thought. He laughed and turned to Verity, but when she tried to see what he was laughing at, the young couple had already left.

He took Verity to the new restaurant on the second level of the tower, the Jules Verne. The server brought the finest of French cuisine to them. Sipping velvety Chardonnay and enjoying the delicate tang of seared turbot, Harry looked out the window.

The same teenaged couple walked along the street, holding hands and munching on baguette sandwiches. The boy had spent his last penny on her. At fifteen, his budget was limited, but he wanted to make the vacation memorable for both of them. Her parents were arriving that night, having sent her and her brother ahead with his family.

The *maître d'hôtel* wished the newlyweds a good stay in Paris as he waved them into the limousine. Harry listened indulgently as Verity listed the places she wanted to visit. The car slowed before Avenue Marceau. Looking right, Harry saw the Hôtel Marceau Champs Elysées.

In room twenty-four, the same boy and girl anxiously watched television late into the night. His parents had gone to the airport with the girl's brother to check on the passenger status of the flight which crashed into the mountain in Dubai that spring night in 1972. Her parents were on the flight. When the news anchor announced there were no survivors, she collapsed. The boy held her in his arms as he promised he'd be there for her until the end of time.

The valet at the George V showed Harry and Verity to the Royal Suite, entertaining them with the names of the famous people who'd stayed there. Chopin's "Piano Concerto Number 1" played softly in the background. The lights were just enough for them to see each other. A bottle of Dom Perignon rested in a bucket of ice on the table.

Past and present collided. Harry imagined the same young couple standing outside, staring at the window. There was accusation in their eyes.

Verity drew the blinds.

Chapter 64

The same afternoon

Cerro Azul, Panama

Gripping the newspapers and the magazines in one hand, Lilah locked the door to her bedroom suite behind her. There was complete silence, with not a honk or a chime or a chirping cricket, but she did a quick scan, making sure she was indeed alone. Her guards conducted inspections at random times every day before withdrawing to designated spots in the residence, and Brad was in the garden. But the household staff was always gliding in and out of rooms. Not that the employees hired by Patrice were anything but excellent. Unfortunately, their diligence meant Lilah got little privacy in the palatial home.

She sat on the king-sized bed which dominated the space. Sunlight filtered in through the gauzy curtains, throwing the vase of red roses on the console by the window into silhouette, but their presence was evident by the fragrance permeating the air. Lilah stared holes into the newspaper, reminding herself the wedding was over and done with.

The Sheppards had sent invitations to all the Kingsleys, but Patrice declined. Merely stating she would need company in the huge house, Lilah also stayed behind. The rest of the Kingsleys just returned from New York the night before and were enjoying another pleasant weekend in their new home.

Taking a deep breath, Lilah told herself to just rip off the bandage and face reality. Quickly, she flipped through the Sunday edition of *The New York Times*. There it was:

Rhea Verity Luce, daughter of William Luce, was married to Harry Ryan Sheppard, a commodities broker, last Saturday at the St. Thomas Church.

The bride's best friend from school, Beverly Newman, was matron of honor. Alexander Kingsley, married to the groom's sister, was best man for his brother-in-law.

The twenty-two-year-old bride is the daughter of Mr. and Mrs. William Luce of Greenwich, Connecticut. Mr. Luce has interests in many businesses, including Gateway, Incorporated, owned by the groom's family. Mrs. Luce has been deceased for two years.

Mr. Harry Sheppard, a former SEAL and Medal of Honor recipient, is currently working for the family company. The twenty-six-year-old groom is the son of Mr. and Mrs. Ryan Sheppard of New York City. The father is the President and Chief Executive Officer of Gateway, Incorporated. The bridegroom's mother, Sophia Sheppard, is a homemaker.

It is the first marriage for both bride and groom.

Tossing aside the *Times*, Lilah picked up *People*. She skipped the article and zeroed in on the photographs. There was one with the happy couple on the limestone steps in front of the church, laughing into each other's eyes. The bride's silk dress and tulle veil were reminiscent of Lady Diana's attire from the British royal wedding. The groom's charcoal gray suit was the perfect complement to the ivory-colored princess gown. Her arm interlocked with Harry's, Verity smiled proudly, proclaiming to the world this man was now hers. There was adoration in the gray gaze she directed at her new husband. "Fairy Tale Romance Ends in Dreamy Wedding," said the caption.

Lilah spent minutes staring at Verity's curvy figure and platinum-blonde hair before scouring the story for every detail of her life... learning how different Harry's choice of a wife was from her. Verity was fair while Lilah was dark, born into the lap of luxury and never expected to work for a living. Friends described Verity as an adorable child-woman, possessive but warm and loving. Quick to forgive. She was unlikely to insist on prolonged penitence over a silly lizard given as a birthday present. But she demanded commitment and received it from the same man who tossed Lilah aside.

Warm metal on her tongue... pain... there was blood in her mouth. Holding fingertips to her bitten lip, Lilah smoothed out the page with her other hand.

The periodicals went into one of the drawers in the spacious closet. Locked in the little safe at the back was a carved wooden box that held the few pieces of jewelry Lilah inherited. Her parents' wedding rings were inside, along with a chunky necklace of Indian design, a couple of dangling earrings, and a long silver chain with a locket in the shape of the Eiffel Tower.

The trinket had been locked in the box and out of sight since her wedding day. Lilah took it out and sat on the bed. Both the chain and the locket appeared dull. Holding it to her cheek, she let her mind drift to the joy of first love for a few moments. Something sharp and invisible pierced her chest. Lilah placed the jewelry back in the box and closed the lid.

There was one more thing for her to do. Tucked under her camisoles were the anxiety pills. One by one, she popped them out and tossed them in her palm. Lilah walked to the bathroom and flushed the pills down the toilet before wiping her palms on her skirt. She was as ready as she'd ever be.

When she went to the garden, she saw Brad seated on a bench, reading a book. Victor's wing was next door, and she could hear him in the living room, playing a desultory tune on the piano and talking to his mother. Lilah walked to Brad. "May I have this dance, please?"

Brad looked up with a puzzled expression.

"Trying to charm my husband." Nervously, she tried a flirtatious smile. "Is it working?"

Closing the book, he set it on the bench and stood to take her fingers in his. There was a pleased expression on his face. The explosion of mesmerizing colors in the garden, the potent fragrances of the flowers, the hum of fat bees drunk with honey... all formed the perfect backdrop for the couple waltzing under the bright-blue sky. Inside the house, Victor switched to a livelier song.

Chapter 65

Two months later, June 1983

Colón, Panama

In the summer, the Kingsleys held their first celebration in the family home. There was no particular reason for it except everyone was together under the same roof. Alex had returned from one of his frequent trips to New York, and the Barrons brothers were visiting.

Dan and Shawn were staying with Victor. It appeared Victor was now an unofficial fundraiser for an organization Shawn Barrons was part of, something to do with research into a new disease spreading through gay men. Victor was very enthusiastic about the project, wanting to respond in some way to the kindness Shawn showed after Hilda's death. All the legal formalities had been handled by Shawn, including the fostering of Victor's son with the Garcias.

The boy, Gabriel, was cajoled by Grandma Patrice to come to stay for a few weeks. At nearly two, he was giving the rest of the family a run for their money. Perhaps because his mother died, Gabriel seemed to take a special liking to Sabrina and spent a lot of time playing with her and baby Michael.

When everyone gathered in the family room in Brad's wing, Victor brought his boombox along and played Michael Jackson's "Beat It." Even the normally reserved Lilah was coaxed by Victor into trying breakdancing, much to the hilarity of her brothers.

Shawn told the Kingsleys about a conference he'd been to in Aspen. "Steve Jobs thinks electronic communication and radio networking are the future. He's a visionary."

"I forgot to ask," Lilah exclaimed. "Did you get the contract?"

"Yeah," Shawn said, smoothing back his hair with a smile. He explained to the rest, "Barrons wants to update digital systems, and I was one of the bidders. Dan put in a good word."

Dan waved a hand. "Nothing to do with me. You worked hard for it." He turned to Lilah. "Did he tell you he had a couple of offers for his consulting company? Big money, too."

"Oooh," said Lilah.

Shawn laughed. "I'm not selling. All I need is enough cash to keep me in food and boyfriends."

"You know," started Lilah. "There's an engineer we just hired. Shawn, I think you might like him."

"Oh, no," Shawn warned. "Not again."

Wildly waving her arms about, Lilah complained, "You have terrible taste—"

"My life, my choices," Shawn said firmly.

When Lilah turned her eye to Dan, he held up both hands. "I've taken a vow of celibacy."

As the rest laughed, Lilah pouted. "Fine, I won't nag."

"*I* will," said Shawn. "Lilah, I'm glad you've started computerizing your records, but I wish you'd involved me."

"The company will soon go digital," she soothed. "You can bid for the contract. The ones you saw were just *my* personal records."

"So?" Shawn asked. "It's always better to have an expert work on these things."

"Something wrong with the way it's been done?" Lilah asked, eyes flashing.

Examining his nails, Shawn said, "Like Victor can tell you, there's a difference between a cook and a chef. Although I've got to admit whoever you hired did a good job. If you were to put a gun to my head, I might even admit to being impressed."

Lilah asked, "How do you know I didn't do it myself?"

"Come on," Shawn teased. "You're a girl."

"Is that so?" Lilah arched an eyebrow, shooting a smug look at Sabrina.

Before she could say anything further, a maid walked in. "Excuse me, sir," she said, inclining her head slightly in Brad's direction. "There's a phone call for you from New York. It's Mr. Godwin Kingsley."

#

Brad stood in the office, smiling slightly as his grandfather talked.

"Perhaps for Christmas, we can have the entire clan in New

York," Godwin suggested over the line. He cleared his throat. "Brad, I meant to ask you about those tabloid items on Lilah."

With a small laugh, Brad said, "Her name sells copies. We don't expect the stories to stop."

"The latest one links her with Alex, complete with a photograph of them holding a baby together. The caption claims it's their love child. I'm assuming the picture was taken at Michael's birth, but it's easily misunderstood. As Mrs. Brad Kingsley, Lilah's going to be under constant scrutiny, and her actions—real or imagined—reflect poorly on you. Take advice from a man who knows a thing or two about strong-willed women. Rein her in before it's too late—at home *and* in the workplace. There can only be one boss, and everyone should know it's you."

After hanging up, Brad stayed in the office for a couple of minutes, drumming the desk with his knuckles. Then, he shrugged and returned to the family room.

#

Lilah chased Gabriel around the room, and when she finally caught him, the boy wriggled in her grasp, holding his football in a death grip. With an uproarious laugh, he elbowed her in the lower half of the breastbone. Breath whooshed out of her. Gabriel made his escape and whooped in triumph. For a couple of seconds, Lilah imagined she saw a star or two. She didn't know little elbows made such effective weapons.

"Gabe," Sabrina warned.

"Sowwy," Gabriel lisped, tone completely unapologetic.

Lilah sputtered. Out of the corner of her eye, she saw Brad walking in and settling on the couch, next to his mother.

"Little punk," said Shawn, ruffling Gabriel's hair.

Not paying any attention to the tussle over the football, Victor said to Shawn, "Can you please stop wearing those silly beads? You already run into enough trouble being gay, and people are going to call you a girl when they see a necklace."

Shawn twisted the amber jewelry around his neck. "Nah, I like it. I have nothing to prove."

Walking around the room, Lilah asked, "Did he ever tell you what's behind the necklace, Victor? I've been trying to pry the story from him for years, but he guards it like it's some state secret!"

The door opened, and the maid backed into the room, carrying refreshments. "Lilah," Victor called a warning, but it was too late.

"Oof," Lilah said as the maid bumped into her from behind. She went teetering and fell onto the couch, right into Brad's lap. Her arms went around his shoulders, holding on for balance. She laughed helplessly while the rest of the family made catcalls and whistles.

Brad pushed her off. "Stop, Lilah. This is not a strip club. Behave yourself."

She slid, nearly falling to the floor. With her flailing hand, she managed to find the edge of the couch and hauled herself upright.

Her face burned in mortified shock. Through her lashes, she saw Dan and Shawn, their expressions angry. Brad's mother and brothers were staring at him in confusion and embarrassment. Sabrina's eyes were flashing. Only the kids were unaffected, Michael sleeping in his bassinet and Gabriel trying to twirl the football. The maid set the snacks on the coffee table and left, mumbling apologies. An awkward hush fell.

With difficulty, Lilah tamped down on her anger and swallowed the retort springing to her lips. Abruptly, she said, "I have some work to do." She pivoted and strode out, calling to her brothers, "Dan, Shawn, I need your help."

When they were outside the door, she heard Victor say, "Bro, c'mon."

Brad snapped, "What?"

"Nothing," Victor responded after a pause. "Nothing at all."

Lilah stayed in her home office through the afternoon, even after her brothers left to rejoin the Kingsleys. She simply didn't know what to make of Brad's outburst... and right when their marriage seemed to be settling into a contented rhythm. She'd even been preparing to divulge the reason behind her prolonged hesitation about physical intimacy—the darkest chapter of her life. Massaging her temple with a fingertip, she decided confrontation was unavoidable.

The television was on in the living room. Brad was sitting on one end of the couch, pinching his lower lip with his thumb and forefinger while he perused the newspaper. The rest were cheering for the New York Yankees.

Lilah went to Brad. "Can we talk?"

The voices around sputtered to an awkward stop. Every eye was kept studiously averted from the couple. With a wary look on his face, Brad stood.

In the privacy of their bedroom, Lilah demanded, "I want an explanation."

"There's nothing new, Lilah." He sank heavily onto the love seat. "You need to learn how to act in public. I'm sick of seeing your name pop up in the tabloids every other week."

She narrowed her eyes. "We were not in public, and I was on my *husband's* lap."

Shaking his head, Brad said, "Actually, you're right. I'm not sure what came over me. I apologize."

Lilah wasn't certain what she should do next... if anything at all. In the end, she simply nodded.

Part XXI

Chapter 66

A few months later, November 1983

New York, New York

Harry walked into the garage beneath the World Trade Center. Gateway had relocated to shiny new digs in the South Tower where the Kingsleys and Barrons O & G also recently leased space. As far as he knew, Lilah hadn't been in the New York office yet. It didn't matter, anyway. She'd already put light-years between them.

There was a scuffling sound behind Harry. A muffled curse. Casually, he glanced at the window of the car next to him. Reflected in the glass at a distance was the same face he'd seen a couple of times over the last week.

Harry went to his bike and paused, patting his pockets as though he'd forgotten something, then returned to the lobby. Raising a hand in greeting at the security guards, he went into the men's room meant mainly for those who worked in the building. This late in the evening, it was usually empty. The janitor was yet to make his rounds, and an ammoniac smell overpowered the floral scent of the room freshener.

Retrieving his knife from his boot, Harry leaned against the wall on the hinge side of the door and waited with eyes fixed on the mirror above the row of sinks across the room. Thirty minutes was not a long wait for a former SEAL. When the door finally opened, the same face from the garage appeared in the mirror. The man inched forward into the room. In one quick move, Harry's arm circled the man's neck from behind and pressed the knife to his jugular.

A startled gasp.

Kicking the door shut behind them, Harry gripped the man's hair. "Talk."

"Don't kill me," the watcher gasped, his feet shuffling.

Harry yanked his hair back. "Who sent you?"

"Can't tell... *aahh*." The blade nicked the watcher's skin; blood trickled down his neck. "Please... please don't kill me. The oil lady. Delilah Kingsley."

Harry's fingers clenched hard around the grip of the knife. *Lilah?* Rage exploded first, illogical and unthinking. Then, confusion. Why a shadow? Perhaps a new enemy, using Lilah's name? Probabilities... odds... the man under the blade sobbed. With a growl, Harry flung the babbling idiot to the side and stalked out.

Returning to his office, Harry picked up the phone and methodically tracked his quarry. He ran down the cold stairwell half an hour later with white-hot fury heating his every hair follicle. Striding into the lobby at Hector's gym, one floor below Gateway, he demanded, "Where's Lilah?"

"I'm sorry, sir," the clerk stammered, "I'm not allowed to give out information on members."

Harry reached over the reception desk and grabbed the back-soon sign, which he set on top. "I bet you showed her to the VIP section. I'm going over there now. You can tell your manager I snuck back in when you went to the latrine."

The staff and the patrons darted out of Harry's path as he stormed through the gym. He was forced to stop outside the private area where Lilah's security guard was stationed. "You gonna be here a few minutes, man?" the guard asked. "I'm jonesing for a cigarette. She won't let me smoke around her."

Harry was too angry to laugh, but it appeared Lilah forgot to inform her crew he was *persona non grata*. Barely waiting for a nod, the guard left.

Flinging the door open, Harry exploded in. Tepid wind greeted him, tinged with the odor of sweat. *Of course* the air-conditioner was turned low. Lilah hated being cold.

Except for the red-and-white Nike cross-trainers on her feet, she was dressed in black exercise gear and boxing gloves, her hair held back in a high ponytail. She stood on the practice mat in standard defense position, elbows bent, fists in front of her chin, throwing forward jabs at the heavy bag. She pivoted and lifted her right leg to throw a side kick.

"You," he shouted, striding to the mat.

Startled, she spun to face him.

"You hired a thug to stalk me." With both his hands, Harry pushed her back by the shoulders, applying just enough force to make her stumble. "What the hell for?"

He was a big man, but Lilah didn't back down. Eyes sparking with fury, she spat, "To kill you of course. Punishment for a homicidal maniac."

So she *was* behind it. He pushed her again. "Oh, yeah? Wasn't it enough for *Her Majesty* to banish me from her kingdom? Did the arrogant *princess* decide to put a bullet in my head?"

"*Don't* call me that," she hissed.

Harry bared his teeth. "C'mon, Princess. Meet me man-to-man instead of attacking me from the back. After all, you know all my tricks. I taught you myself. Or are you too afraid? Huh? *Huh?*"

"Stop," she warned, her face aflame. "Get out. I don't want to talk to you."

"Princess, princess, *princess,*" he insisted. "C'mon, Your Royal

Highness," he taunted, gesturing at her with both hands. "I'll give you the first punch."

Lilah roared. Shaking wildly, she swiveled at her hips and socked him in the belly. Breath whooshed out of him. He doubled over, then straightened.

Grabbing her front hand by the wrist, he wrenched her arm behind her back. "Why..." he asked through clenched teeth. "Why did you send a tail?"

She gasped, eyes tearing. "Go away," she croaked.

"If you were trying to kill me..." he huffed. Their faces were so close their breaths mingled. "...you would've been the one pulling the trigger. You would've been looking me in the eye. He was too clumsy to be a spy. Confess, *Princess*. You sent me a *bodyguard*." They shuffled back and forth in an angry, awkward dance. "He was meant to be muscle. You told the loser to let me know right away who sent him, didn't you? In case I spotted him. Or I might've killed him. A guard... why? *Why?* I thought you never wanted to see me again."

Grunting, Lilah used her right hand to jab him under the chin, sending his head snapping back. Electric pain radiated up his jaw. He stumbled and let go of her arm. "I *don't* want you in my life," she said in a vicious whisper. "Get out, Harry."

She was lying; she had to be. She was only trying to hurt him. His body shook with the need to hurt her back. "Only a glutton for punishment would keep returning to you. Dunno why I bothered."

On an enraged sob, Lilah threw a wild punch, hitting him in the chest.

"This is all you have?" he mocked. They circled each other on the mat, fists raised, knees bent. Harry's lips curled into an unpleasant smile. He swiveled on his left foot, letting the right foot fly, walloping her on her left shoulder with just enough power to knock her off-balance. Lilah managed to stay on her feet. "Why did you hire the loser?" he asked, pleading and angry at the same time. "Didn't *Princess* Lilah already decide I was beneath her?"

She retaliated with a straight kick to his gut, but at the last moment, he caught her foot and twisted her leg, causing her to fall face down on the mat. She stayed prone, but when he stood next to her, she sprang. She caught his right elbow with both arms and rose. Using his body weight against him, she flipped him over her shoulder so he fell hard on his back.

Lilah snarled, breath coming in spurts. She circled the mat to look him in his face. "All my life, you've known me. You thought... I... you..." More droplets appeared on her lashes. "Go away," she said, voice hoarse. "Don't come back."

"Liar," he spat, leaping from the mat. When he delivered a straight punch to the same left shoulder, she went down. "Why did you hire the guard?"

"Figure it out yourself." Her hot, angry eyes followed him, muscles coiled to strike back the moment he got close enough.

Harry stayed at a safe distance, lifting his elbow to wipe the sweat from his upper lip on his sleeve. "Maybe the uptight little *princess* finally lost it," he taunted.

Growling in rage, she lifted her foot and aimed it at his crotch. He caught the foot with barely an inch to spare. She scooted around on the mat, struggling to free herself. Angry tears rolled down her cheeks, and she screamed, "They were trying to kill you, you... you... *dumbass*."

He staggered, trying to keep his plumbing from getting pulverized. "What?" Lifting her other leg, she hooked it around his thigh. He lost his balance and fell, letting go of her foot. She rolled to avoid being crushed. He landed next to her, face down. They both stayed put, breathing harshly. "*Who's* trying to kill me?" Harry asked.

For a long moment, he thought she wasn't going to answer. Then, she raised her head from the floor to look at him. "Temple and Godwin," she said, voice exhausted.

"Tell me."

They sat up on the mat, Lilah stripping her gloves off. "When I got to the village, Masou had his rifle aimed at your back."

"What?" Harry exclaimed. "Masou was sent by Godwin and Temple."

"Exactly," said Lilah. "They sent him to kill you."

"Elaborate."

Lilah gulped water from her bottle. "Did Sabrina tell you what happened at the villa while you were away?" When he nodded, Lilah continued, "As soon as the fire started, soldiers drove in and locked us inside, but the Argentine government supposedly didn't know what was taking place. They claimed later local officials noticed problems going on in the village and asked the military to quickly investigate. I don't believe it. The possible culprits in the illegal imprisonment are—" She held up successive fingers. "One, you and Alex. Two, Sanders. Three, the president."

Harry's brain worked as it hadn't in months. Taking the bottle from her, he said, "Alex and I wouldn't have locked you in the house—too risky. No matter what the official line is, someone on the Argentine side was definitely involved. Nothing else explains how the soldiers got there as quickly. They could've been in Sanders's pocket, but why would he simply order you kept there? Why not arrest you or kill you and use the massacre as excuse for your death? My money would be on Temple. He ordered it. The next question becomes why. At that point, you couldn't have stopped the evacuation, so there had to be another reason."

Lilah inclined her head in agreement. "I think it was to keep me from getting help for you but still to have me in the neighborhood as witness to the massacre. Also, the soldiers would've been protection in case someone reached the villa. The president wouldn't answer our call; then, the phone lines were cut. The whole thing was too convenient to be coincidence. Think, Harry. Alex told me the devices were meant only to smoke people out. So how come the entire village burned down? Were the bombs tampered with? Alex also said your rifle jammed."

Harry explained, "A squib load. It could've exploded in my hands if I continued to fire. But we had other weapons."

"Weapons *you* wouldn't have been able to use," Lilah reminded him. "You were flying your own helicopter. But *Alex* could."

Understanding dawned. "Temple and Godwin provided them for *Alex's* protection, not mine."

"Also, it would have given the impression you went there prepared to kill the Puelche." Lilah wrapped her arms around her knees. "More importantly, how come the general showed up? Isn't he Sanders's man? Alex said this general ignored him until he tried to give you cover to escape."

"Yeah," said Harry. "The general had a score to settle with me from one of our previous encounters. He was using Sanders's name to extort protection money from a couple of the oil drillers, and I put a stop to it."

Rocking lightly, Lilah said, "Sanders already wanted you dead. You have his general—this man with his own reasons to kill you— showing up at the exact moment when you were most vulnerable. He didn't care about Alex or anyone else. Only about you. Could Temple have tipped off Sanders?"

Harry dismissed the idea. "Temple and Godwin working with Sanders? I don't think so. As long as Sanders rules the oil sector, the Kingsleys will be vassals."

Lilah shook her head. "Then how did the general manage to

mobilize troops so fast? No, he was waiting for you to show up."

Harry's mind went over possibilities. "An anonymous tip. They could've sent word to Sanders with just enough time to intercept me but not to stop the evacuation. Sanders wouldn't have realized he was dancing to Temple's tune."

Lilah thought for a few seconds. "Temple and Godwin anonymously sent word to Sanders, knowing he could claim your death was more or less your own doing. The general could claim he killed you in defense of the tribe. I'm certain Godwin and the president tried to keep my presence in Neuquén a secret from Sanders since they need *me* alive. They were also relying on you and Alex to keep me safe. The president was the one who suggested the team, remember? The soldiers who were sent to the villa were added protection."

Harry stood and paced, leaving her sitting on the mat. "Go on."

"Also, the truck which almost ran us down... what if it was deliberate? The driver was yelling something about 'the girl.' Me, I presume. But I don't understand how he could've known where you were. We took a detour."

The impromptu bike race... the jump over the shoulder onto a different road to avoid Alex and Sabrina. "The Harley," Harry said.

"Huh?"

"It was rented. I'd arranged to have it waiting at the airport."

"So?"

"A tracking device," he explained. "The trucker must have been Temple's assassin. One last-ditch attempt at removing me from the picture without resorting to genocide. It would be easier for the president to arrange a hit-and-run outside the United States. The trucker didn't know what to do when he saw you with me. Masou probably told him you'd be in the car with Alex and Sabrina. It *was* the original plan."

Lilah shivered. "So when the trick with Sabrina didn't work, Temple and Godwin tried to have you run over. When you escaped that, they made sure your mission turned into butchery. They left you with a useless weapon. There was a good chance you'd get killed in Sanders's counterattack, and if the general failed, Masou was backup to kill you. Sanders could have been blamed for your death, either way. *I* was left there as a reliable witness to the genocide. They made one spectacular mistake, though."

"Alex," Harry stated.

"That's right," she concurred. "They didn't expect Alex to fight so hard to save you. Masou must have been desperate to get the job done for him to take the risk of shooting you while Alex was around to witness it. Then, I showed up before it was convenient."

Harry exclaimed, "My God, they set things up in such a way even my family wouldn't have been able to question any of it. *You* would've found it impossible to question. Alex might have been fed some story that I plotted it all. Sanders would've claimed he was trying to have me captured and brought to the U.S. to face justice for mass murder, but I was killed in the process. Temple would have the perfect excuse for not directly retaliating against Sanders. No president would take such political risk under the circumstances. My parents would've continued to cooperate with the Kingsleys because of Sabrina. You still would've called for Sanders's blood. You would continue to be CFO, and the alliance would also continue, but the power structure would've changed. Godwin would be calling the shots exactly as Temple wanted."

"At the expense of the lives of one whole tribe," Lilah said, voice breaking. "How could you, Harry?"

He dropped to his knees beside her. "I swear I didn't know." Taking her hands between his, he held them to his heart. "Or I'd have never gone along with the plan. Please, believe me."

"I do," she said, her hazel eyes full of pain and sadness. "But if you'd stopped to think..."

Harry closed his eyes for a second at the memory of the people he'd damned to a brutal death. "Did you decide you're better off without me?" he asked, telling himself he had no right to hope.

"I should," she said with a bitter laugh. "But you're like a bad habit, not easy to break." After a pause, she added, "My initial thought was if I kept you away, Temple and Godwin wouldn't have a reason to attack you. The guard was there as a precaution. If someone did try something, you'd have help. Plus, we needed time away from each other. You're being eaten up by your past, and I'm part of that. Look at you! You ignored every warning sign!"

"No more, please?" he begged, gaze pinned on the hands held secure within his grip. "I can't handle it."

Her fingers flexed. "*I* couldn't simply stand by and watch you turn into the thing you hate." Lilah looked around. "I was going to arrange a meeting. We need to brainstorm ideas, but I couldn't talk to you in public. My plan was to figure out from the staff here when you'd show up to work out. You beat me to it. When you ran in, my first instinct was to... I wanted to cut you with something sharp for what you did. I still do. The tribe..."

"There's no way to make it up," he said urgently. "I know, but I'll try. I swear."

"No, Harry. *I* will. The machi and the rest of the survivors won't want you anywhere near them. Stay away, please, and let *me* handle it. Trust me, she will kill you if she gets a chance. And God help me, I want you around even after all this."

With those words, strength started flowing back into Harry's limbs.

Lilah continued, "*You* need to help me figure out what to do with Temple and Godwin. Focus on them."

Slowly, Harry nodded. "I'll do as you ask." He stood and hauled her up by her elbows. Going to the back, he pulled two towels from the pile and threw one to her before wiping himself off with the other. "I'm not sure I understand Temple and Godwin's reasoning. You said it yourself... all Godwin has to do is leave Kingsley Corp and join the Peter Kingsley Company. If he were legitimately a part of the business, he'd have an *official* say in things... my presence notwithstanding."

"He can't... because of Sanders," Lilah said, settling into one of the chairs. "Harry, we initially believed Kingsley Corp would be the third partner in the alliance. We never expected Steven to try to kill Brad. We didn't know the parent company would be split into two. I kept wondering why Temple didn't insist they chuck Steven out and still do it the way we planned. I mean, with Kingsley Corp in the alliance, we would have been bigger than Sanders in no time at all. It would've been a quicker route to defeating him. I think there's good reason to suspect even the division of the company was pre-planned. So if the alliance failed to neutralize Sanders, Sanders would target the Peter Kingsley Company for retribution instead of Kingsley Corp and Godwin."

Harry objected, "A pre-planned division would mean Godwin somehow manipulated Steven into trying to kill Br—" He broke off, recognizing what Lilah was suggesting. "My God. You think Godwin plotted the murder attempt on his own grandsons."

"He made sure it wouldn't succeed," Lilah pointed out. "At least, Brad's Uncle Aaron did. Aaron informed Brad about Steven's plans."

Harry exclaimed, "There are no guarantees in such schemes. Also, Godwin could've simply split the company without going through all the drama. Steven and Brad were already fighting."

"Not possible," Lilah said. "If it had been a run-of-the-mill division of assets, what reason would Brad and his family have to cooperate with Temple's plan? Patrice would have put a stop to it as soon as she realized I was a Sheppard."

"So Godwin and Temple drove her to desperation," Harry muttered. With her sons' lives at risk, Patrice agreed to Temple's scheme without checking into who the intended bride was. "But it didn't have to be Brad. Things never needed to get to the point of attempted murder. If Godwin kicked Steven out with the prospect of a network later, I'm sure he wouldn't have objected. *He* has nothing against the Sheppards."

"Would Steven have been as ready as Brad to follow Godwin's lead?"

"No," said Harry, not needing to think twice. There was only one man the president had in mind for Lilah. Not Steven, not Alex. No one except Brad. Harry and Lilah played right into Temple's hands with their demands for a pre-nup and the CFO position, which meant the only Kingsley she could possibly marry was Brad. But if they didn't make those demands, Lilah would have remained a puppet leader. Temple would have won, either way.

"Temple likely believed Godwin could control Brad and have me sidelined," Lilah mused. "They didn't realize you'd end up being a bigger influence on my husband, and since my clout comes through you, Temple wants you out."

Harry didn't say it aloud, but Lilah had to know the death beneficiary clause in the pre-nup was one of the factors keeping *her* safe. If anything happened to her—death or some kind of incapacitation—control of her stock would pass to the outsider she named in her will. The agreement Harry forced on the Kingsleys was working as intended. Only, he never imagined Temple and Godwin would be the enemies it held at bay.

Lilah wrapped the small, damp towel around her shoulders. "Do you still believe Temple is doing this for political power?"

Harry snatched Lilah's gym bag off the floor and brought it to her. "The person in charge of the network *will* be more powerful than Sanders. More powerful than the president of the United States. Temple wants his family to have power."

"As president," Lilah argued, "Temple could easily get them there without all the scheming. I read Judge Bork's book on our antitrust laws. The federal government is considering adopting some of his ideas and stop prosecuting vertical integration. There's even talk he'll be appointed to the Supreme Court. So Temple didn't need any of this... this manipulation... no political marriage, just straightforward merger."

"One of the first companies to integrate vertically after the announcement of the new and improved antitrust regulations would be Kingsley Corp," Harry reminded her. "A political impossibility for Temple."

"True," she allowed. "Sanders would've had all of us in court, and Temple would've been asked to resign on corruption charges. But the Kingsleys could've waited a few years. Eight at the maximum. Afterward, very few would pay attention to what a former president's family company does."

"A simple vertical integration would mean sharing power more or less equally between the families. What we have now, on the other hand, is one person—you—representing two companies, with your husband representing the third. The Kingsleys—and Temple—rule. I think it's the whole point as far as they're concerned."

"Absolute control... unfortunately, it's become a tussle between me and Godwin Kingsley."

"Temple and Godwin believe I'm in their way. Hence, all the efforts to kill me."

"How are we going to stop them?" she asked. "We can't even put a hold on our plans for Sanders."

"I never even thought of Sanders the last few months," Harry murmured, dropping to the chair next to hers.

"I couldn't *stop* thinking about him, Temple, Godwin, everyone else..." said Lilah. "But there simply doesn't seem to be a way out of this trap. Temple got us the moment my engagement to Brad was announced."

Harry nodded. "Temple used his office to make sure Sanders stayed away from you after the car accident he arranged. But with the engagement announcement, Temple also telegraphed to the rest of the world the potential for trouble. If you showed any signs of backing out of the marriage agreement, he might've signaled Sanders he's withdrawing protection. Sanders would not have let the possibility of a problem—you—continue to exist. And he hates my guts. We would've both been done for."

"Temple tried hard to keep me from knowing who was behind the trouble in Argentina."

As soon as Lilah said it, Harry realized why she rushed her wedding to Brad after her return to Panama. "If I died, you might've decided to risk your own life and walk out on the marriage arrangement. You wouldn't let a vast structure like the network be created with Temple and Godwin essentially in charge. In one way, my being alive means they still have you trapped. It wouldn't matter to Temple you know about the double cross. At the first hint you were thinking of withdrawing from the arrangement, Temple would've alerted Sanders you and I no longer have the president's protection. You needed to get the wedding done without delay or risk further attacks on both of us. But the moment Temple realizes you do know what he did, *he'll* have to call a halt to his games with me... again, to avoid having you walk out after my death. Sanders or no Sanders, without you, there won't be the kind of worldwide network that was proposed. So we're at an impasse."

"But with another enemy waiting to get us," she pointed out. "Sanders will definitely send his thugs after us when Temple's presidency is over. That's our deadline, and Godwin and Temple know it."

"The Peter Kingsley Company is growing fast. In a couple of years, the alliance will be strong enough to beat Sanders in the business arena, after which we could make certain he does time for his crimes. Once he's done, we're back to the stalemate with—"

"The leader of the free world and a former supreme court justice want you dead, Harry! We could keep an eye out for dirty tricks *while* we deal with Sanders, but there's no way to cover all bases. Too many variables. Temple and Godwin Kingsley are the more immediate threats. First, we need something to make them back off. Then, we'll deal with Sanders."

The plastic chair was uncomfortable no matter which way Harry tried to adjust himself. "Recommendations?"

"I wish I had at least one." She unzipped her bag. "We need something on Godwin and Temple, but it's hard to track a president, and Godwin doesn't seem to care about anything other than the family name and his precious Kingsley Corp."

"Can you talk to Brad?"

"Are you kidding me? My husband thinks his grandfather walks on water. It's the reason I wanted to talk to you privately... without Brad getting even a hint of our suspicions. He might take your advice, but he'll never believe the murder attempt on him and his brothers was Godwin's plan even if *you* say so."

"Nor will Alex. If the Kingsleys brothers call off the alliance, we'll be back to Sanders being free to attack us." Harry went over possibilities. "Godwin built his company into what it is today. Given what we know of him, what are the chances he didn't do a shady deal here and there? Especially since he was also a justice at the Supreme Court for years." There was always a proxy for Godwin in the family business for the duration of his time as justice, but the company made no moves which didn't bear the patriarch's stamp of approval. "We'll hire someone to go through every single one of his cases. Bring him down, and Temple will fall, too, given their close relationship."

"That investigation could take forever." Lilah pulled a deep-red sweater over her head. Voice muffled by the wool as her face poked through the turtleneck, she said, "I even thought about keeping on pretending we're enemies, but—"

Harry shook his head. "If Temple buys the act, he could again use Sanders against me just to be on the safe side. Why would anyone expect you to retaliate by walking out if we're not on talking terms?"

"Argh," she said in frustration. Her hair had come undone, and she pulled it back into a ponytail, snapping an elastic band around it. "This is what I said. We can't confront Sanders directly for fear of Temple somehow using the opportunity to kill you. Nor can we postpone dealing with Sanders, or he'll kill us himself after Temple's presidency is done."

Harry stretched out his legs and leaned back, tossing a couple of other ideas in his mind before discarding them as unworkable. "We'll come up with something." Glancing at the wall clock, he said, "The gym will close soon."

She walked to the mat to grab her boxing gloves.

"You didn't do too badly," he noted. "Been working on your technique?"

Ruefully, she said, "You were barely fighting, or you'd have broken my neck in the first thirty seconds."

They left the building together, Lilah's guard trailing. It was late in the night, and there was no one else in the garage, none of the tabloid fellows who frequently popped up around Lilah. "I didn't even know you were in New York," Harry said. "I called Uncle Gray in Panama after the loser bodyguard said you hired him. Finally tracked you to the gym."

Lilah arched an eyebrow. "Doesn't Alex keep you updated on my movements? I heard he calls you like clockwork."

"Yeah," Harry said. "Alex is a better friend than I deserve. I hope he sticks around."

Lilah smiled. "You like him."

"He's the only good thing to have happened to me with this mess," Harry stated.

"Ahem," Lilah said, tone teasing. "Aren't you forgetting something?"

Harry was confused until she flicked a glance in the direction of his wedding ring.

"Verity," he said. "She's..." he stopped, uncertain.

"I've seen pictures. She looks lovely."

"Yeah... Lilah..." He took her left hand and stood next to her car.

Harry scanned her face, studying every familiar feature. In her hazel eyes, he saw their story, now forever incomplete. Her lips curved up at his prolonged scrutiny. Reflected in her wistful smile, Harry saw every bittersweet moment from their shared past. Every whispered hope, every shattered dream. Every ardent vow, every broken promise. Everyone who'd walked in and out of their lives.

He hoped Brad realized what a lucky bastard he was. Harry hoped her husband drowned her in love every single day until the end of time. "Are you happy?" he asked, twisting her ring around.

"I'm content."

"It's not the same as happiness."

"No, but we're working on it."

With a small nod, he let go. "Does this mean you'll show up for Michael's christening? Runt says you haven't agreed to be godmother yet."

Lilah crinkled her nose. "Only because I wanted to make sure we talked before meeting in public. But the baby needs *one* sane godparent."

He laughed. "See you there."

When he got home, he found his wife dressed to go out. She glanced at the clock with a sharp frown.

"Sorry, Verity. I got used to keeping my own hours. I'll try to do better."

"We were supposed to meet my brother for dinner, remember? I called and canceled. I tried to reach you at the office, but there was no answer. What happened?"

Harry winced. "I had to meet Lilah about something."

Chapter 67

Some days later, December 1983

New York, New York

Seated as she was with Harry's parents, Verity needed to crane her neck even to see Lilah's back at the christening bowl, forget her face. Sabrina had wanted Harry and Lilah as godparents. Holding the baby in his arms, Harry stroked him under the chin with a fingertip. The baby caught Harry's finger in his tiny fist, grinning and rattling off gibberish. His parents and godparents stood around admiring young Michael Harry Kingsley.

Soon after the ceremony, Lilah vanished into the side room at the church, not even turning to glance toward Harry's wife. Verity almost growled in disappointment. First, Lilah didn't show up at the wedding, and now, this. Actually, Alex's mother wasn't around for the christening, either. None of the Kingsley elders were, with Godwin and his sons—Alex's uncles—off on some business trip.

The party at the Sheppard home in City Island in honor of the newest Kingsley was well underway when Lilah and Brad made their reentry. Verity turned at the mention of Lilah's name and looked in the direction of the doorway. Her jaw dropped. This was Lilah? Verity had seen pictures, of course, but they didn't prepare her for the woman's in-person impact. Lilah was breathtakingly lovely.

Her coloring was amazing, light brown with hints of peach. Tendrils of glossy blue-black hair escaped the braided chignon to tease her cheeks. Not a trace of roots showed. Her neatly lined hazel eyes were enormous with long, silky lashes. Coral-painted lips curved into a smile. No plastic surgeon in all of America could achieve nearly the level of perfection in female figure with a scalpel. Lilah was devastatingly, achingly beautiful.

Verity's eyes took in Lilah's attire. She was dressed in a wine red, one-shouldered Grecian goddess gown, cleverly draped to hint at the secrets beneath. Delicate gold sandals adorned her feet. Surreptitiously, Verity tried to place the designer. Whoever it was, such simplicity usually came with a high price tag.

Lilah waved her hands about as she talked to Alex, the tiny diamond on her finger glinting under the light. Eyeing the man next to her, Verity surmised him to be Brad Kingsley. He looked nice enough in an old-money way. There was annoyance on his face when his wife kissed Alex on the cheek, but Lilah seemed unaware of the tension. She said something to Alex, gesturing vaguely at a group of men across the room. He straightened. Nodding, Alex marched off to follow whatever instruction Lilah gave. She waved to someone else and moved forward to greet them, leaving Brad to trail along.

A guest walked across Verity's visual field, briefly blocking her view of Lilah. Where was she... there, talking to Dante and those Libyan friends of Harry's, the al-Obeidis. Saeed and his wife lived in Norway and did something in the oil sector. He'd been one of the groomsmen at Harry and Verity's wedding.

"This guy," Dante was saying to Saeed's wife. "I have a hard time believing he's an adult now. You won't believe the kind of stuff he and Harry used to—"

At a quick cough from Saeed, Dante stopped.

"What?" asked Saeed's wife, glancing between the men.

Dante cleared his throat. "They used to pray five times a day."

Huh?

"Huh?" echoed Saeed's wife.

"Yup," said Dante, tugging at his collar. "Excuse me. I see someone..." He hurried off, leaving the rest gaping after him.

"I have to talk to Harry," Saeed said, stroking his beard as he walked away.

His wife rolled her eyes, and holding Lilah by the arm, she marched toward the chocolate fountain.

No one had yet offered to introduce Verity to Lilah, so Verity kept an eye on the other woman, waiting for an opportunity to announce herself. When Lilah was talking to Sabrina, Verity sashayed to them, wondering which of the two women was wearing the unusual perfume. Sabrina presented Verity to Lilah.

"Harry's wife," Lilah murmured, enveloping Verity in a hug. Lilah's palms felt callused and rough on Verity's bare shoulders. The nails on Lilah's fingers were clipped short and unpainted but buffed to a smooth sheen. Anyone would believe the woman actually worked in the oil fields.

Catching Verity's expression, Sabrina said, "I know. Doesn't all that perfection make you want to hate her?"

Lilah pinched Sabrina's ear. "Just because you got to be a mommy first doesn't mean I'm not going to box your ears. Be respectful to your elders."

Sabrina responded with an irreverent snort.

Shortly before the party ended, Verity accompanied Lilah and Sabrina when they went to take another peek at the baby.

Watching Lilah rock him in the crook of her arm, Sabrina teased, "You want one of your own, don't you?"

Lilah placed the baby back in the crib. "Mikey should have cousins to grow up with."

The unguarded expression of immense sweetness on Lilah's face made Verity feel she'd intruded on something intensely private. Turning from the baby, Lilah's gaze collided with Verity's, and Lilah's lashes fell, shuttering her eyes.

"We should return," Lilah said.

Chapter 68

A week later

Upper East Side, New York City

"Come on in." Godwin invited his eldest grandson into his home office as a slender man with jet-black hair stood. "You've heard of Andersen, of course. Former attorney general. Andersen, this is my grandson, Brad."

Shaking hands with Andersen, Brad said, "An honor, sir."

"Andersen was our corporate attorney long before your time at Kingsley Corp," said the family patriarch. "He has some ideas for your proposed expansion."

After they'd taken their seats, Brad said, "I don't know, Grandfather. The Peter Kingsley Company has been doing well, and I'm comfortable with where we are. When we initially talked about the network, I was willing to go along, but the episode in Neuquén was unsettling."

Andersen asked, "What are your concerns? Godwin's given me the gist of what happened."

"Oh? Then you must know Peter Kingsley Company would've suffered considerable damage to its reputation had the incident become public. Thanks to Mr. Temple, we escaped."

Andersen said, "You can't let one event deter you from your rightful legacy." At Brad's puzzled look, he elaborated, "Your father was a good friend of mine. It was a dream of his to create a socially conscious oil conglomerate. You have the skeleton of one here; what you should do is gain enough clout so other companies will join in."

Godwin rocked back in his leather chair. "You still need Gateway for trading and retail, but if you're not comfortable with Harry, talk to Hector Sheppard."

Brad dismissed the concern with a wave of his hand. "I have full faith in Harry's judgment."

Godwin shifted in his chair. "I was under the impression you'd asked him to stay away."

"Yes, but the decision was taken from the shock of what happened. Harry contacted me before Michael's christening to apologize... what happened in Argentina was simply a terrible mistake. There's Harry's previous record... he's always been a good man. I discussed it with Alex. He also swears they didn't know what Masou and El Gato were up to in Neuquén. My entire family believes we need Harry's help. I do, too."

Andersen shot Godwin a glance before turning to Brad. "Congratulations on your marriage, by the way."

"She's a lovely girl," Godwin said. "Have you ever met her, Andersen?"

"No," said the former attorney general. "But I've heard plenty. MIT and Harvard Law, heh? And she's the CFO. You're a lucky young man, Brad. The papers were gushing over the engagement. A lot of them got it wrong, actually. I'd understood she was engaged to Alex, not you, until I heard about the wedding. All the pictures with the two of them..."

Clearing his throat, Brad said, "Yes... there was some confusion initially, but we got it sorted out. We're all happy Alex found his true love. His best friend's sister."

Andersen's eyes widened, then crinkled as though in amusement at the cliché romance, but he didn't say anything.

Brad left soon after, promising to call back with his decision.

Chapter 69

Same night

Elsewhere

Sabrina ran with a baby boy on her hip, breathing in gasps. Fire raged behind her. A few more steps, and she'd be inside the house. She stopped, screaming wildly as a large dark form appeared in front. She turned to escape, but the monster raised his weapon and shot her. As she fell, the baby dissolved. She was pregnant, holding her belly and moaning, "Mi bebé."

Harry woke with a start and lay on his bed, sweating and heart pounding. *Just a dream,* he told himself as he'd done for countless nights. He waited while his mind focused, then looked at the bedside clock—one in the morning. Leaving a note for his wife, he went out to the docks for his customary walk among the homeless and the junkies.

There had been some snowfall, and it was cold but not enough to make the street dwellers go into one of the city shelters. A fetid smell arose from the garbage bags piled high on one side to protect the row of sleeping men from the chilly breeze. Used needles, cigarette butts, broken bottles, even a lethal-looking knife... New York City was suffering from economic mismanagement magnified by poverty and drug use and violent crime. Harry kicked aside a soda can and walked to the makeshift camp right under the Brooklyn Bridge, his black overcoat flapping in the wind.

"Back again?" asked a raspy voice from under a pile of ratty blankets. With strong odor of cheap weed wafting around him, the former infantryman sat up and accepted the handful of cash Harry brought out of his pocket.

"Go back to sleep, sir. I don't need your shoulder tonight." Going into the nearby phone booth, Harry dialed a number. When Lilah's sleepy voice answered, he slid down the glass wall to sit on the floor.

Harry kept her on the line for hours, talking about this and that and everything. Both gushed about baby Michael. When she teased Harry about his pretty wife, he laughed and needled her over the latest story in the tabloids. It all started with the event at the Barrons mansion when Lilah's engagement to Brad was announced. The media spotted something off in her interaction with Alex Kingsley. A tragic romance, said the gossip rags. Alex later fell in love with his friend Harry's sister, leaving the ravishing heiress—his own sister-in-law—pining for him. And according to the most sensationalist rag of all, *The Big Apple Reporter*, Lilah was married to all of Peter Kingsley's sons, including Brad's two half-brothers.

"I've never even met them," she complained, voice wild.

Harry snickered. "Does it mean you're married to the three you *have* met?"

"Ha, ha."

"Are you sticking your tongue out by chance?" he teased.

Finally, he told her of his terrifying visions and the late-night walks to the pier and the homeless veterans who'd become his refuge. He talked about the months he'd vacillated between praying the nightmares would stop and accepting the pain they inflicted. "I think I... I *need* them."

"Why?"

"I can't let myself forget what I did. The voices call me a demon, and I... Lilah, what if they're right?"

"Will you go somewhere with me next week? There's a doctor I want you to see."

"The same genius we saw after Libya?"

She laughed. "Poor man. How was he to know we were both lying through our teeth? This is a different one, anyway. Harry, he gave me something to take. Marriage... everything in it... I *needed* help. I was feeling powerless. My choice was taken away, right? Like before... you know what I mean. I needed to put the past behind me to move on."

There was an ache in Harry's chest. He wanted to destroy the criminal who'd hurt her, wipe off all traces of him from this world. How could she possibly put it behind her? Humbly, he admitted, "You're a stronger woman than I."

She sputtered. "That's a relief. Since you're not a woman."

Harry smiled, memories of the silly bantering from their childhood flooding him. "Hey," he chided. "Bad jokes are *my* turf."

They continued talking. It was near dawn when she said, "Harry, there *is* one way."

"Hmm?" The sky over East River brightened. The pink morning light somehow added immeasurable energy to his being.

"To solve the problem we talked about at the gym." To stop Temple and Godwin from using Sanders as a weapon to kill Harry.

"Okay, shoot," Harry said.

"Give them another target."

Part XXII

Chapter 70

Three months later, February 1984

World Trade Center, New York City

Beyond the glass wall, there was a sheer drop into the busy streets of downtown Manhattan. The city stretching out at her feet, Lilah watched the solitary ship on the waters beyond the tiny island. Behind her, muted gray-blue chairs were set on the hardwood floor in a casually elegant arrangement. Glittering letters on an immense slate slab to one side declared the identity of the company, and below the quartz was the reception desk. It was all nearly perfect, including the pleasant seventy-two-degree temperature maintained round the clock.

Hearing her name, she turned. At the door to the inner offices stood her chief accountant. "I have all the papers ready. Do you want to go through them one final time before the conference?"

"I do. Give me a minute, though. Harry will be here soon." She wanted him to see what they achieved in the last few years. The Peter Kingsley Company had gone from a ragtag group run by beginners to being profiled in the latest edition of *Time*.

"Mr. Sheppard?" asked the accountant. "From Gateway?"

"Yes—"

Outside the glass-doored entrance, the elevator swished open, and three men walked out. "Welcome to our new home, Harry," said Brad. Spotting his wife, he nodded brusquely.

"Hello, Lilah," Harry said with a wide grin.

"Looking good," Alex said to her.

Lilah smiled in pleasure. The rose-colored shirt and side-slit black maxi took a big bite out of her fashion budget, but it was nice to be able to indulge herself.

Brad flicked a glance in her direction but didn't say anything. Gray and Victor came out to speak with Harry, too. All were in the mood to brag, including Brad. "Everyone says our father did a great job as CEO of Kingsley Corp," he said. "I mean, he was around only a few years. Still... you know some of his former employees contacted us? They want to work here. And some of the drillers... they think he was brilliant! Ethical *and* tough. I want to carry forward his legacy and build this business into something future generations can be proud of."

Lilah followed the men in, black heels clicking on the polished floor. The accountant was waiting at the door to her office. Her team had been through the reports several times over, calculated possible and probable outcomes. But she wanted to make sure nothing was missed.

"Hey," called Alex, following her into the office. "Not joining us?"

"I am," she said. "I just have to get the final figures."

Outside, Brad continued talking to Harry, their conversation carrying in muted tones.

"What's this?" Alex asked, gesturing at the equipment on her desk.

Lilah tucked her pen into her neat French braid. "Motorola's new mobile phone." Sabrina had said it wasn't on the market yet, but she got one for Lilah to use in her car. Lilah even tried hooking the device on her wide, black belt, but it was too heavy.

Clearly losing interest in the phone, Alex asked, "You were a big part of our triumphs, so why aren't you out there, enjoying the retelling? Marvin can bring along whatever papers you need, I'm sure."

"Certainly, Alex," Marvin, the chief accountant, said, clutching a thick folder to his chest.

"No excuses." Alex grinned, grabbing her hand.

She laughed in mild protest and let herself be led outside, the accountant following with a small smile.

Brad's frowning gaze went to their clasped hands. "Behave yourself, please," he snapped, "at least when staff's watching."

Lilah jerked in shock. The accountant backed into her office, red-faced and diffident. Growling in anger, Alex dropped her hand. She didn't dare meet Harry's eyes, but his sharp hiss added to her mortification.

Something inside her condensed into an intense ball of fury. She flexed her fingers, fighting the urge to toss every bit of paper in the place in Brad's face before walking out. "I'm sure you didn't mean to be offensive," Lilah warned him, barely keeping her tone even. "Perhaps you'd like to apologize?"

Victor stepped between, shooting a reproachful glance at Alex. "Brad was merely asking us all to remain professional." With that, he herded the group into the conference room.

A copy of *The New York Times* lay at the foot of the table where Lilah usually sat. "BELL SYSTEM BREAKUP OPENS ERA OF GREAT EXPECTATIONS AND GREAT CONCERN," announced the headline on the open page. Setting a pile of folders on top of the paper, Marvin excused himself.

Once everyone else was settled in their seats, Brad asked his secretary to get coffee and turned to Harry. "We talked about spreading out before... drilling, trading."

"Yes," said Harry. "Renewable fuels as well. It's cost-prohibitive at the moment, but technology will eventually get to a point where clean energy becomes achievable."

Brad nodded. "Right. I met with Grandfather last week. Former Attorney General Noah Andersen was also there. They offered to help us with the expansion plan. I wanted to get your thoughts."

Harry was already planning to talk to Brad about expansion, setting the stage for their takedown of Sanders, but the next day, Lilah heard about her husband's meeting with Godwin Kingsley. Not only did Temple and Godwin make their opening move, they were now aware Harry was back in the fold. As soon as the president heard about this new plan, he'd come to the realization he wouldn't be able to do a single thing to Harry until Sanders was done and dusted.

The black king will not lose, Mr. President, Lilah muttered in her mind. Her opponents thought themselves unbeatable, but she'd win the game. A lure... her rook would dupe the enemy, triumphing against all odds. Looking at the sunny winter sky through the conference room windows, Lilah smiled inwardly. *The Manhattan Swindle.*

The secretary wheeled in the beverage cart. Harry thanked her and waited until she left to respond to Brad. "Haven't you talked to your family and the rest of your senior staff? Uncle Gray is a former chairman of NYSE."

"They are for it, but my brothers are inclined to want the best for me," said Brad, "and Lilah can't see beyond numbers."

She was tapping a muffled rhythm on the top folder, and her fingers skipped a beat.

Brad swiveled the chair sideways, avoiding her eyes. "There's more to running a business than money."

What is wrong— Lilah blinked. *Did he... no way...* Brad couldn't have divined her concerns about the Kingsley family. If that were the case, they wouldn't be having this mostly civil conversation. Curling her fingers into a fist, Lilah tamped down annoyance. She couldn't confront Brad over his behavior, couldn't afford to have him withdraw from their plans in a fit of displeasure.

Brad played with a pen, twisting the cap with his fingers. "Who knows what the motives of the other executives are? Some tell me what they think I want to hear, and some have their own agenda. Harry, *you* have experience being responsible for a business. I can trust you to give me an unbiased opinion."

"An executive who won't give you an honest opinion regardless of relationships or personal prejudices isn't worth space at the table," Harry said before turning to Lilah. "Let's take a look at those numbers."

She'd sent him the info days ago, but they needed to play out the scene for the benefit of the Kingsley brothers. "There's enough capital to fund some operations in India as Alex wants," Lilah said. "Victor recommends we concentrate on Latin America. Alaska and the Arctic were never discussed with Kingsley Corp when we divided assets, and the restrictive covenant is over in any case. So it's entirely fair for us to look at those regions."

Victor cleared his throat. "We're family-owned and operated, so decision-making will be easy."

Harry said, "So we're all in agreement? Good. But first, you'll have to destroy Sanders."

Everyone in the room froze, listening to Harry's proclamation.

Chapter 71

Pausing, Harry reiterated, "Destroy... not merely get bigger at some point in the future and squeeze him out."

Brad cleared his throat. "Grandfather did say we'll have to deal with Sanders, but it's exactly the same thing everyone said before Neuquén. I mean, my grandfather had... *has* the right intentions, but things got out of control. I don't want another genocide on my hands. Is there a way to do this without attacking Sanders?"

Harry stood and walked around to the canvas map stretching across the wall behind the conference table. "Take a look, Brad. Sanders has created an empire which extends into every continent. Do you know how many politicians and dictators he keeps in his pocket? How many elections he's bought?"

Alex went to stand next to Harry and studied the markings on the map indicating oil operations around the world.

Harry continued, "Sanders already knows you're a danger to his business. The president is keeping him in check for now, but Temple won't be in office forever. Once Sanders feels he's safe enough, he'll respond in ways you won't see coming."

"There was an article about his *m.o.* a couple of years ago," Victor said. "One of the business magazines... the reporter got fired for it, I think."

"Yeah... the kind of strong-arming Sanders, Incorporated did in the 'seventies..." Pacing the length of the map, Harry elaborated, "Sanders's holding company owns large chunks of several pipeline operators. He would bump up transport charges, but his own refineries and drilling outfits didn't suffer. The small companies... each time there was a rate increase, Sanders's executives would quietly confront small businessmen who were given a choice between financial ruin and selling." Picking up pins, Harry jabbed them along the southern border of the United States. "There were... still are oil drillers and refineries which associate themselves with him. They use the services of his company ostensibly at market price but with unexplained fees at the receiving end. In turn, Sanders keeps competition away."

Harry paused to let his words sink in. Discomfort was clear on every face at the table.

"The companies which refused to play ball encountered further increases in pipeline rates or a mysterious lack of buyers," he said. "Or they found themselves dealing with unexplained accidents. Leaks, train derailments, you name it. Once, there was even an unfortunate fire involving an aviation fuel tank at a refinery. A school full of children died. If none of these methods worked, he would hire thugs to physically put the competing oilmen out of the way. His pals in various governments kept turning a blind eye. You can't build this network without taking him out, Brad."

Brad was not persuaded. "This makes me wonder if the expansion is worth the loss of peace. If all these companies couldn't stand up to Sanders, how will we?"

Alex snapped, "Sign up for priesthood if you want peace. As CEO, you must do what's best for the company."

Taking a pin, Harry placed it on the northern part of Africa. "Sirtica... during the crisis in the early nineteen-seventies, Sanders had some of the Libyan revolutionaries in his pocket. Libya nationalized drilling companies or negotiated more expensive contracts with them. Once the smaller, less influential companies were driven off, the fields were leased to Sanders."

Harry's thoughts drifted briefly to his idyllic childhood, those days of innocence which lasted until the deaths of Lilah's parents. Life had taken both her and Harry far from that cocoon. Remembering two headstrong youngsters, he smiled.

In a softer tone, Harry continued, "You're probably aware of my family's story. We used to own and operate a drilling outfit in Libya called Genesis. We weren't big, not in the league of Barrons O & G, but life was comfortable. My father refused to sell Genesis to Sanders... certainly not at the price offered. Fifteen attacks, we later counted. Sometimes, the Libyan government hauled my father in under the pretext of some violation. Fires broke out. We experienced spills, leakages, transport accidents. I was involved in a couple of them. Frankly, I'm lucky to be alive." Shaking his head, he continued, "Finally, the sixteenth attack. My parents were accused of spying for the United States." All softness left Harry's voice, and his eyes narrowed. "There was no one to help us, not even the Kingsleys. Andrew Barrons eventually got them out, but even he couldn't prevent what happened next."

"The kidnapping?" asked Victor.

"Yes," said Harry. "After I escaped Libya, Sanders developed a fixation. I became his elusive white whale... Moby Dick to his Captain Ahab. I remember I'd just been to the doctor's office. A car came out of nowhere and tried to run me down. I was lucky. Someone—a cop—got me out of the way. There was no proof, obviously. But it couldn't have been anyone else but Sanders. When the hit-and-run failed, he sent more thugs. They managed to corner me..."

Harry told the Kingsley brothers how he fended off one of the attackers with a broken bottle, sinking the sharp glass into the criminal's crotch.

Smiling grimly, he finished the tale. "Luckily, Hector saw me being chased by the two goons. He took care of the second mugger." In truth, the criminal got his neck snapped and died instantly. The one who got the unexpected surgery on his plumbing was interrogated by Harry and Hector before being hauled to the cops. They extracted a confession from the thug on who paid for the operation. The word of the criminal wouldn't have been enough to put Sanders away, but he stopped the attacks, perhaps concerned about the police investigation initiated by Mr. Temple. It wouldn't have been easy for even Sanders to buy his way out of it within American borders when Harry had the backing of some rich and powerful people. The surviving thug was held for the murder of his partner and killed himself in prison. He either found life without family jewels unappealing or thought death a better option than facing Sanders after failure.

Nervous murmurs rose.

Harry continued, "When Senator Temple became president, we thought Sanders would... I'm not sure what we thought he'd do, but he tried to get at me in other ways. He started targeting people I cared for. The FBI director eventually talked with him about the 'coincidences' of the attacks on the president's supporters adding up to a pattern if he weren't careful."

The car accident Lilah barely escaped...

Harry said to Brad, "You worry about the unintentional slaughter of innocents in Neuquén, but do you know how many Sanders has killed? There's nothing he won't do to hold on to power. Bring him down... if not for ambition, because it's the right thing to do."

There was a deep furrow between Brad's brows. "If what you're saying is true, I'm not certain I want to start trouble by trying to expand."

Harry said mildly, "Brad, you claim you want the proposed network to be a fair system. An honorable intention, to be sure. But honor—truth—without valor is useless, and valor without sacrifice is meaningless."

Alex added, "If we choose not to act out of fear, isn't it almost as much a crime against humanity as actively supporting Sanders?"

Harry spoke again, "Sanders is a patient man. He's waiting for Temple to leave office. Two years is all the time we have. Afterward... even if you don't do a single thing, Sanders will come after you in ways you can't imagine. What if he decides to ensure your cooperation through Michael or any other Kingsley children? What would you rather face? The consequences of action or the consequences of inaction?"

"Even *you* fear him," Brad said. "What kind of a man is he?"

"Like I said... patient. And ruthless. Sanders's father was an Austrian national living in Malta. When WWI started, he didn't want to be conscripted and showed up in the U.S. with Jared in tow. Daddy Sanders started drilling in Oklahoma, and those who knew the family say the old man never got the respect he felt he deserved from the townspeople or the other oil drillers. To them, he remained the German-speaking foreigner... an enemy. Jared took over the company in his mid-twenties, and he was cutthroat from the get-go. You're right. I do fear him. I'd be a fool not to fear an adversary who's more powerful and will go to any lengths. Regardless, we *must* get him."

Brad finally said, "All right, if you think we can do it, we can at least give it a try. I want your personal involvement in this."

Alex pumped his fist in satisfaction. Harry smiled.

Setting her glasses on top of the folders, Lilah said, "The least bloody way to beat Sanders would be a takeover of his holding company since it is publicly traded." She handed out papers. "These are the annual reports from Sanders, Incorporated for the last ten years. They include the records of the domestic and international oil and gas reserves of the company. I have the projected interest rates, as well. All the data was fed into the computer program my team designed. The stock's undervalued, no doubt, but it's still too high for us to make a substantial purchase. Also, Sanders holds fifty-one percent. How will we get *him* to sell? Not to mention the fact he has capital we can't match to counter our every step."

On cue, Harry pulled out a chair and sat. "A coup isn't necessary. Give us a market scenario, a decision which can bring down a big company like his."

"Debt," said Lilah. "Combine it with unreasonable expectations of profit, any business will be destroyed."

"I don't see it happening to Sanders," Victor objected. "He has little debt, and his properties are making hefty profits."

"The markets are fickle," Lilah reminded them. "There's an oil glut going on. Prices are falling. If it continues, even Sanders's profits will be wiped out. But you're right about the debt part; he doesn't have much."

Harry leaned forward with his elbows on the table. "Actually, if Sanders wanted to, he could whisper in a few ears, and the oil glut will become worse right now. The whole sector will suffer significant losses. If he keeps it up long enough, several companies will have to shut down. But he will make sure it's over before *his* business takes a substantial hit. The rest of us... the only thing stopping him is Temple's presence in the White House."

"Gateway has been doing hedging, right?" Victor asked. "Enough to help offset potential losses?"

"Yes," said Harry. "We learned our lesson from painful experience. But in our case, it's a defensive tactic against unpleasant surprises. Sanders *creates* such situations and keeps tight control over what happens, making sure he comes out the winner. What we need to do is take away that control."

"How?" asked Alex.

"There are rumblings within OPEC," said Harry. "The Saudis are unhappy about declining market share. It *will* come to a point where they increase production to compensate. When it happens, prices will be in freefall no matter what Sanders wants."

"Your friend?" Alex asked Harry. One of the Saudi princes played a big part in Harry securing his first deal with Aramco. "He could help us take control."

Twirling a pen on the table, Harry nodded. "Batten down the hatches, Brad. Protect the Peter Kingsley Company from the economic tsunami about to hit."

Brad frowned. "Our strategy is to create problems in the market to take care of Sanders?"

At Brad's skeptical tone, Harry guffawed. "Have more faith in me, cousin. We'll make sure Sanders is unprepared for the downturn. We'll drown him in debt."

"That would be..." Brad coughed. "...difficult. I mean, Sanders can see the market trends as clearly as us. Why would he take on debt under current circumstances?"

"If you know what someone hates and what he values," said Harry, "you can predict how he'll react. Sanders—the man—is inseparable from his business. And he hates my guts. If he fears I might get my hands on his company... use it against him... he'll go into debt to stop me no matter what the market looks like."

"He might just kill you," Victor said. "Right now, he thinks we're trying to get bigger than him before potentially squeezing him out. Openly threatening the company would be like putting a knife to his throat. Would he worry about the president's reaction at that point?"

The Kingsleys didn't know it, but Temple would be happy to have Sanders kill Harry.

"We'll make sure the threat to Sanders, Incorporated doesn't change even if I die," Harry said. "There will be ways to transfer powers between us. So Sanders won't waste time singling me out while he's trying to get things under control, but the idea it was me who started it should goad him enough to the point he makes mistakes."

In silence, the Kingsley brothers mulled the idea. "Bro," Victor said, voice unhappy. "If we leave him no option, he might just decide to kill the whole lot of us, Temple be damned."

Harry laughed, a grim sound. "Oh, we'll leave him an opening to beat us. A decoy."

"Decoy?" Alex asked.

With a nod, Harry said, "We'll give Sanders a shot at destroying the network itself. He will need to be goaded enough to do it despite Temple, despite the markets."

"The network—" Alex swung to Lilah, realization in his eyes. "The easiest way to destroy the network would be to kill you. Sanders will choose to attack you."

With the criminal oilman's attention on Lilah—the linchpin of the network—Temple and Godwin wouldn't dare try any of their tricks.

"Alex," Harry said. "Sanders can't merely 'attack' Lilah. He has to plan her assassination. At a time and place picked by *us*."

Part XXIII

Chapter 72

Months later, June 1984

Harlem, New York City

"Bills... more bills." The shrill ring of the black rotary telephone interrupted the irritated muttering of the occupant of the small office as he went over mail during lunch. The swivel chair squeaked loudly when pushed back, knocking over a stack of newspapers piled close behind. Dust rose in clouds, making the man sneeze. He spat out rubbery chicken to pick up the receiver. "Yeah?"

"Hello?" said a slightly husky feminine voice. "I'm looking for Eugene Bishop."

"You got him."

"Mr. Bishop, this is Lilah Kingsley. I understand your publication ran a story about me being married to all the Kingsley brothers?"

Gene Bishop sank deeper into his chair. He was used to threatening phone calls from the subjects of his articles. "It was only the headline, Mrs. Kingsley. You can't sue me over it."

"But most of your readers don't get past the headlines, *do they?*"

"I got the First Amendment behind me, lady, and the sleaziest lawyers a man can hire. You won't win if you take me to court. And look, lady, I'm trying to make a living here; I got a family to feed."

"Why don't you publish *that* hard-luck story?" the voice asked dryly.

Gene examined his nails. "I'm not going to stop writing about you, so you can stuff your lawsuit where the—"

"There's no lawsuit, Mr. Bishop. I'm only suggesting you write a genuine story for a change."

"Huh?"

"How would you like to visit the family home in Cerro Azul? That should give you some material, and it would be exclusive."

"Huh?"

The woman laughed, a sound strangely mellifluous even as it was husky.

#

Next week

Cerro Azul, Panama

Gene Bishop wasn't a stupid man. There was surely some reason this beautiful woman gave him the time of day. Not as if he was left alone with her at any point. There was a giant security guard following them everywhere, glowering at him.

A young fellow with longish black hair and a massive bowtie walked into the parlor, throwing his hands up and slapping his forehead alternately, sobbing and begging in a mix of English and Spanish for help from the Almighty. Gene looked on curiously as the boy ran to Mrs. Kingsley and knelt flamboyantly by her side. The kid spoke rapidly, but Gene thought he caught the name Sanders in the outburst as well as something about Satan and burning.

Lilah Kingsley soothed the supplicant with a few comforting words and a suggestion to wait until the evening when she'd be free to talk. Wiping his eyes, the boy left.

"That's Maya, the architect who designed this place," Lilah said.

"He's prone to melodrama, I'm afraid."

Prone? Hah! It was a full-blown theatrical production. "He seemed upset."

"Yes. Problems with his family in Argentina."

Problems involving Sanders? Gene's journalistic antennae twitched. He knew as well as anyone else in the media business Sanders was at loggerheads with the president, and the Kingsleys were related to Temple.

As he was escorted to the room assigned to him, Gene tucked a twenty-dollar bill into the hands of the maid and asked for Maya in slow Spanish. *"El joven. El arquitecto. ¿Dónde puedo encontrarlo?"*

She told Gene in precise English Maya was in the garden and gave him directions. Wiping the sweat off his overheated bald pate, Gene tracked down the boy.

An hour later, Gene was tucking the small spiral notebook into his pocket. As he turned, mind trying to unravel all the tangles, he saw Lilah Kingsley leaning on the doorjamb, watching him. "I see why you asked me here," he stated.

She inclined her head. "I wanted you to meet Maya and hear what he has to say. Tell me… is *The Big Apple Reporter* up to publishing this story on Jared Sanders?"

Gene smiled. "Mrs. Kingsley, you and I both know mine's the only paper you'd dare approach to print something unsubstantiated like this. What's in it for *me?*"

"A chance to get into the big leagues. Introductions to the movers and shakers of the oil sector and elite society. If you play it right, maybe even an interview with President Temple."

Chapter 73

"Bishop is an interesting character," Harry remarked. He leaned back in the swivel chair, ankles crossed at the edge of Lilah's desk in her home office.

"Yes," she agreed, watching from the window as the tabloid owner's car left the grounds. "Works fast. He actually demanded I recite nonstop what I knew. Even got annoyed when I paused to collect my thoughts." She laughed. "I didn't mind. After all, he's helping us bait our enemy."

"Let's hope Sanders bites," Harry said. "Make sure we're adequately prepared before the story hits the newsstands. Sanders shouldn't get near you, not until we choose to let him. Did Brad arrange extra security?"

"Of course," Lilah said, tone vague.

Harry once again stopped himself from asking about her marriage. Given their tumultuous history, any hint of concern would be soundly rebuffed.

She toasted him with a bottle of water. "To Harry Sheppard and his takedown of the first of the enemies on our list."

Brad Kingsley was skirting close to being on said list. He'd been staying away from the public part of the plan against Sanders on Harry's advice, thus leaving at least a slight possibility the CEO of the Peter Kingsley Company would escape the criminal's wrath in case the rebellion failed.

The Barronses and the Sheppards were also asked to maintain distance to limit fallout from potential failure. Dan objected vociferously once he realized Lilah was the bait, but she told her twin to keep himself out of it if he didn't want to add to her worries. In fact, the first thing she insisted on before embarking on this mission was the safety of her brother. She refused to involve him even peripherally and risk the last of the family she had left. Poor fellow called Harry several times a day, warning him to protect Lilah at whatever cost.

Brad, on the other hand, was a full participant behind the scenes. The way he was behaving with Lilah... he didn't seem to appreciate his wife showing even benign affection toward anyone, himself included. Any show of spirit goaded Brad into asserting his authority. What Harry couldn't understand was why Lilah wasn't putting a stop to the attitude, choosing instead to bury her warmth under layers of cool civility.

Lilah asked, "What about the other papers I sent you? The Godwin case?"

Harry turned his attention to the matter of the Kingsley patriarch. "I have people following up, but it's beginning to look like Godwin left us nothing to work with except this strange story about some girl his half-brother refused to marry—his *already married* half-brother."

"Believe it. I had one of my IT staff go through LexisNexis painstakingly. The entire episode seems so strange. To begin with, the girl in question was Andrew's cousin... Amber... Amber Barrons. We already know the Patrice-Peter marriage was planned as a business alliance, so I'll go out on a limb and bet the Amber deal was the same, but the groom wouldn't cooperate. Afterward, she killed herself under questionable circumstances. As far as I can tell, Andrew didn't kick up any fuss. Not in public, anyway. Godwin still made a settlement to the girl's parents. The family name is all important to Godwin. Why did he choose to settle rather than fight? Why didn't Andrew say a word? I think we should take a look."

"Oh, I agree it's worth investigating," said Harry. "It's a break in pattern for all concerned."

Chapter 74

A week later, copies of *The Big Apple Reporter* (All the News that Ain't Fit to Print) appeared on the stands. "The Emperor of Oil Patch Kills His Subjects," screamed the headline. There was a detailed account of how on a certain American businessman's orders, a grenade was exploded over a Native American village in retaliation for the tribe's cooperation with the Kingsleys.

It was with some trepidation Sanders's PR man reported to his employer. After the call, he gulped a glass of water, dribbling a little on his white button-down shirt, relieved the only reaction he got from his boss was mild ire at "wasting my time with such garbage."

Sanders could've retaliated with facts if he chose to, but evidence mattered more, and there was none. Temple's need to cover his backside and the Argentine government's complicity made sure of it.

Next week's headlines read: "Oil King Destroys Town." The first story had been vague, but this one featured a retired schoolteacher who'd invested money in a small oil exploration company which was later driven out of business by Sanders. The edition on the third week did a story on a refinery in a Midwestern town which paid exorbitant fees to Sanders's oil drilling outfit for the privilege of buying his crude, complete with pictures of tombstones of a couple who committed suicide after filing for bankruptcy. Every subsequent week, there was a new story, and true to his *m.o.,* the publisher of the sensationalist paper never made any actual claims of wrongdoing. It was always limited to heavy innuendo.

The PR man scrambled to find the publisher of *The Big Apple Reporter,* but Gene Bishop had gone underground. "The paper has a circulation of about two million, but no one takes their claims seriously," he ventured to his boss, sweating as he waited for further instructions. He'd been working for Sanders for a couple of decades and knew most of the tales contained a kernel of truth. There was surely a source feeding them to the muckraker. He also harbored suspicions about who the source was but couldn't see the endgame at this point.

Sanders's spies later spotted Bishop at the summer Olympics in Los Angeles, but he was next to a couple of world leaders and couldn't be cornered. How a small-time rumormonger managed to obtain access to VIPs was a mystery to the rest of the media.

The following February saw a story in Bishop's gossip rag which found its way into more respectable publications. The remains of a missing congressional intern were discovered in the woods next to her home. The last time the girl was seen was at a meeting with her boss and his supporter, Jared Sanders.

The police made it clear neither the congressman nor Sanders was considered a suspect at that point, but the relationship between the two men became the subject of intense speculation. Journalists smelling Pulitzers went to work and unearthed more connections between representatives of the people and Sanders. *The New York Times* wrote an editorial demanding a congressional investigation.

"...clear violation of the Sherman Antitrust Act..." droned one congresswoman on C-SPAN.

"I wouldn't call it corruption exactly, but it doesn't pass the smell test," said a freshman senator to the investigative journalist from ABC TV.

The stock market responded with a steep fall. The value of Sanders, Incorporated shares once stood at a hundred dollars, dropping to seventy during the oil glut. Now, it plummeted to twenty-eight. Sanders ordered his staff to watch for unusual activity involving the stock, especially if linked to certain names—Kingsley, Sheppard, Barrons, and Temple. Bank employees were bribed to keep an eye on transfers of unusually large sums of money from company accounts or accounts with any of those names on them.

Chapter 75

In the New York offices of the Peter Kingsley Company, Lilah made calls transferring money from seven small accounts around the country to Citadel Partners, an investment consortium from San Diego. She dropped to a chair at the conference table. Resting her forehead on folded hands, she said, "Sanders, Incorporated stock is still too pricey for us. We just don't have enough cash."

"Our purchase needs to be substantial," Harry stated. "Or we won't catch his attention. We want him to take on massive debt to buy us out."

Alex slid a folder toward her. "I told you... Grandfather is willing to help. So he made a mistake trusting the oil scout. Doesn't mean he's going to do the same this time. We all deserve a second chance."

Lilah eyed the two men across the table with a mild huff. Harry had called her before on her private line, insisting he would have no qualms about taking the new loan. In his mind, it would be poetic justice since they would ultimately use it to defeat Godwin and the president.

But more Kingsley Corp involvement in the network... opening the folder in front of her, Lilah once again reviewed the cash offer. There was a strict requirement that it not be made public. If the Peter Kingsley Company failed to oust Sanders, Godwin would want his part kept secret, just like with the Barronses and the Sheppards.

"All the banks refused our loan application," Harry reminded her. "They don't want to go up against Sanders."

"If we lose, we're finished," Alex said.

"Guess we don't have a choice," she muttered.

The door swung open, Victor backing into the room with an icebox. "Born in the U.S.A.," he belted out Bruce Springsteen's latest hit, setting his load on the table and rubbing his hands together. "Beer's here!"

"Great," said Alex, leaping from the chair. He tossed a can in Harry's direction, beads of cold water running down its sides. "What about you?" Alex asked Lilah.

She declined with a tepid smile, turning her attention to her notepad.

Tabs on the cans popped open, and pale, frothy drink fizzed. Around Lilah, the men continued to discuss their plan to lure the tiger from his lair. Setting her glasses on the table, she rubbed circles over her tired eyes.

"Starting phase two soon," said Alex.

The rest filed out of the conference room, leaving Lilah still working. Harry poked his head back in. "Not heading home yet?"

"In a few minutes." Usually, she spent her rare free hours with Sabrina, playing with Michael or simply listening to his mother natter on about her latest triumphs in hacking. Sabrina laughed at Lilah's worries about the feds catching on, telling her to focus on the coup attempt.

Tonight, Lilah didn't dare go to the Sheppard residence where Sabrina and Alex were staying. Brad was expected back at night after a trip to Panama. If he heard Lilah had seen Alex outside of work... it was so, so weird that Brad's jealousies were focused on his brother. Lilah spent day after day after day coordinating plans with Harry—sometimes with Alex around, as well—and it didn't bother Brad. Not just him. The tabloids seemed to speculate on her relationship with every male between sixteen and sixty, except for Harry. Alex was the hero in most of the stories.

It surely wasn't easy for Brad to hear the stupidity, but he didn't have to add to it. Five minutes after he walked through the doors, he'd start. Something would set him off. He always asked for updates on the Sanders project after his trips. Any mention of Alex—once even the sight of his signature in a document—and a quarrel ensued. She'd tried to tell Brad there was nothing between her and his brother. God, she tried!

He'd be remorseful for a good hour before getting triggered by a stray word or even by her absent-minded silences. Lilah barely stopped herself from clapping her hands over her ears and screeching in frustration. She *couldn't* screech... the Sanders project wouldn't work without her, and if Brad became peeved enough to somehow interfere in it... not a risk Lilah could take. Still, she preferred to avoid spending her evenings feeling trapped. She'd stay in the office until she was reasonably sure Brad would be in bed. There were genuine matters for her to worry about, anyway.

Yeah, she said to herself. And one of those matters happened to be the very much overdue discussion with Brad about what had happened to her in the past. But to share something so deeply personal, something which created aftershocks in her life years later... it required a level of trust. Maybe after the mission was over, they'd both have the time they needed to focus on their marriage.

Chapter 76

When Citadel Partners bought fourteen percent of the stock of Sanders, Incorporated, the CFO of the company made inquiries.

"An oilman from Norway," the CFO told Sanders. "Saeed al-Obeidi—*he's* legit. From what I could find out, he spent a few years working in the sector and invested his money in oil stock. This is the first time he's gotten together a venture of this size, though."

"The members of the group?"

"Mostly Latino Americans living in California. Twenty-five percent of it is held by three people. Victor Kingsley, Alex Kingsley, and Harry Sheppard."

"Not Delilah Kingsley?" Jared Sanders asked, voice sharp.

"She's not involved," said the CFO.

"She can't be, of course," Sanders growled. The leather chair rocked when he sat back. "The government could step in because of antitrust laws. But any shares they purchase will indirectly be placed under her control. They don't need majority vote in Sanders, Incorporated. Sheppard simply needs enough stock in the business *I* built. Add it to the shares she already owns in *their* companies, she would get bigger than me. That's their plan. Sheppard is going to use *my* business to get Mrs. Kingsley to the top. He imagines I'll simply be forced to watch him do it." Face an alarming red, Sanders spat, "Damned thief. Trying to steal my company."

The CFO nodded vigorously.

"Let me see how he's actually going to make it happen." Pinning the CFO with a hard stare, Sanders ordered, "Get me the folder on her. It has the details of the pre-nup. There's always one in such marriages. Also, I need more info on the investment group. Who can proxy-vote for whom, that sort of thing. Sheppard will have covered all bases, but there must be someone we can potentially influence, some loophole."

There always was.

Chapter 77

Months later, June 1985

The Plaza Hotel, New York City

The Terrace Room was packed and buzzing. Journalists from

every major newspaper in the country and beyond wanted access to the press conference.

Rumors were rife about an impending takeover, gossip started by *The Big Apple Reporter*. The proprietor—Eugene Bishop—didn't need Lilah's promised reward of introductions to the bigshots of industry and society. Not beyond the first few months, anyway. Circulation had skyrocketed. Celebrities wanted to have their say on the paper's pages. There was even talk of a Pulitzer. But Mr. Bishop was not in attendance today, having chosen to remain safely hidden.

Breakfast dishes were arrayed on buffet tables on either side. At one end of the hall was a platform, currently empty. Three men stood in one corner of the room, holding plates. Alex barely touched the food, but Victor continued scarfing down scrambled eggs and thick slices of ham. Harry enjoyed the warm chewiness of his glazed donut, following it with creamy coffee.

"Phase three," said Harry. "Time to let Sanders's hatred of me do our work for us."

"Businessmen like Sanders are usually careful around the media," Victor pointed out, voice muffled by the food. "He might not show up."

Harry set his coffee on the table. "Which is the whole point. We need him provoked to where he forgets to be careful. The worry about what we're up to should make him show up. If he doesn't, we'll know our plan won't work."

"He *has* to bite, or we're in trouble." Alex huffed. "When do we start?"

"When we're ready," Victor retorted. "Don't wait for me after the conference; I'm going to have a chat with the chef. The eggs could use more flavor."

"Is it why you haven't gone for a third round?" Alex asked, voice sardonic.

Out of the corner of his eyes, Harry saw the *maître d'* gliding through the main door, giving them an almost imperceptible nod. Dabbing lightly at his mouth with a pristine white napkin, Harry murmured, "Showtime."

Leaning against the wall, Victor stayed out of the limelight while the other two strode to the stage.

"Good morning, everyone, and thank you for coming," Harry's voice echoed from the lectern. "Most of you already know why we invited you here. Citadel Partners, of which the two Kingsley brothers and I are a part, is planning to bid for shares of Sanders, Incorporated. We believe the current leadership has lost sight of its fiduciary duty to increase stockholder value. We believe it's time for a new direction." Harry rustled the papers in front of him. "There have been stories about Sanders, Incorporated, going around this town and indeed, around all of United States. Unfair trade practices, strong-arming the competition, forcing rivals to bankruptcies, collusion with players in the chain, collusion with politicians and bureaucrats... you've heard about all this from the *Wall Street Journal* and *The New York Times*. Because of the stories, the value of the company's stock has dropped in the last few weeks."

A man yelled from the door to the conference hall, "Hey, Sheppard, you damned conman. You and your family cheated your way into oil trade. Now, you're trying to trick the rest of the world into thinking I'm some kind of monster. You're trying to steal the business *I* built. You're nothing more than a thief!"

The room turned as one toward the powerfully built, slightly balding man with piercing eyes and an energetic aura. A loud buzz started. Jared Sanders was there in person to confront the accusers.

Harry's lips curled into an unpleasant smile. His heart thundered the rhythm of war drums. *Yes!*

At his side, Alex hissed.

Sanders strode to the stage and bounded up the two steps, almost crowding Harry from the podium. "Most of you here are experienced reporters covering Wall Street. Y'all understand how business works. The man offering high-volume business to a company gets some breaks. How can anyone possibly call this anti-competitive? If a smaller company is inefficiently run, I give them the option to sell to Sanders, Incorporated. If they choose to be foolish and go bankrupt, how am I to blame? Yes, I deal with politicians who support causes dear to me. Yes, I have lobbyists working to generate support for legislation which will benefit my company. How are those things wrong? My shareholders are happy with my management."

Tone honeyed, Harry said, "Sanders, Incorporated stock prices fell fast after the stories broke, and some of your shareholders lost their life's savings. You still claim they're happy with your management? Surely, you're not as delusional as you sound."

Sanders spat, "The stories you planted to drive the price down."

"You think I plant stories in *The Big Apple Reporter*?" Harry gestured in Alex's direction. "The last one they ran about me claimed I'm Alex Kingsley's boyfriend, but according to the same writer, we both spend our time cavorting with women. Orgies, no less."

In his chair, Alex started. He covered his mouth with a hand, eyes darting murderously toward Harry. The collected pressmen laughed.

Facing his enemy on the dais, Harry said, "Mr. Sanders, there are shrewd business tactics, and there are unethical practices. I acknowledge your brilliance. You've built your company into the dominating force in the oil sector it is today, but your success has come on the backs of many men and women pursuing legitimate trade. You've crushed them. What's more, you got help from some of our elected leaders to do so. I don't condemn the practice of capitalism as you're implying. I condemn the unethical business practices you employ. I condemn the closet support for such tactics from our politicians. I condemn the lack of concern among the guardians of democracy. I condemn the cronyism which causes the lack of concern."

Nostrils flared and hands clenched, Sanders struggled to contain his response.

Harry snapped his fingers. "In fact, I have a suggestion for you. We'll withdraw from our plans for your company if you're willing to pledge changes to your management style... agree to compete on a level playing field with rivals. Create a royalty trust to direct more of the profits to shareholders than into acquiring more companies."

Incredulity oozing from every syllable, Sanders asked, "An effective royalty trust will require me to put ninety percent of my profits back in. How will the company fund expansion?"

"Mr. Sanders, does your business exist to expand power or to provide value to shareholders? A royalty trust will help them avoid double taxation and let them keep more of their profits."

Sanders pounded the pedestal with his fist. A pen rolled off and fell to the carpet. "This is a way to hamstring the activities of Sanders, Incorporated. If I don't agree, you'll steal my company. You and the Kingsleys... the entire sector knows why you're helping Brad Kingsley. Talk about strong-arming competition!"

Inclining his head, Harry said, "The sector should also know Brad is a good businessman... effective *and* ethical... a great partner... excellent boss by all accounts." As far as Harry could see, the friction between Lilah and her husband didn't change how either ran the business.

"I don't give a damn," bit out Sanders. "*You* deciding how I run my company... no damned way! I won't put up with it."

"It's time someone looked at the activities of your company."

Harry's tone changed. Concern gave way to deep anger. "How many of your opponents have conveniently ended up dead, Mr. Sanders?" he boomed, voice reverberating.

His words threw the conference room into an uneasy hush. Reporters scribbled. Camera personnel filmed the adversaries facing off.

Jared Sanders growled.

"How many of them?" Harry thundered. "From owners to rig workers, how many deaths?"

Save for an uneasy mutter from a corner, the hall was silent. No one moved. No one breathed.

Harry goaded Sanders with a raised eyebrow, almost daring him to bring up the tribal village in Argentina.

Silence... there was only silent anger from the tyrant. Harry was almost disappointed. *Speak up,* he urged. *Tell everyone* I *did it, not you.*

Of course no one would say a word. Certainly not Sanders because there was a good chance his protestations would be dismissed as lies and might even prompt international investigations. Not Harry nor the Kingsleys. Not even Temple or Godwin because they would also be implicated in the crime. Harry would live with the guilt, the bloodstains on his soul.

"Coward," Sanders finally bellowed, spit spraying. He shook an accusatory finger at Harry. "You wouldn't dare say this to me without all of them here. Just like the tabloids, you don't dare put it as a direct accusation... I'd have you in court in a heartbeat."

Harry moved in, looking his enemy in the eye. "What price tag would you hang on all the lives you crushed? The families you devastated?" Through clamped teeth, he asked, "To brutally conquer enemy territory, to decide who'd be a vassal and whose life was worth nothing—Mr. Sanders, who made you our emperor?"

With a finger, Sanders repeatedly stabbed at the air. "Who the hell are *you*, Sheppard, to pass judgment on me? I at least am faithful to my friends. *You*... your ethics are nonexistent. Everything you and your family achieved came from the sacrifice of the same people who trusted you."

A muscle jerked in Harry's jaw.

Sanders curled his lip. "All of it is justified in the name of some mythical greater good. To sacrifice someone's existence, their property... Sheppard, who made you *God*?"

"Those who dedicated their lives to this cause willingly did so. They knew you needed to be stopped."

Sanders snorted. "You and they can do your worst. But you will never get your hands on *my* business." The angry man walked off, ignoring the flashing bulbs and shoving aside the microphones pointed under his nose.

Harry announced, "I want the stockholders of Sanders, Incorporated to know Citadel Partners is willing to buy your shares at thirty dollars. As of this time, it's trading at twenty-eight dollars."

A rumble started in the conference room. Reporters rushed to the phones. Television crews called their teams back at the station with breaking news.

"What are you up to, Harry?" asked a journalist who hadn't bothered to join the horde running out of the room. The *Wall Street Journal* correspondent once profiled Harry's rise as a commodities broker. "You just made the share prices skyrocket. How are you going to arrange a takeover this way?"

Harry grinned, saying nothing.

Chapter 78

A day later

Verity curled up on the recliner, only half listening to the Kingsleys visiting the apartment. She wished she'd insisted on Harry moving into *her* condo after their wedding. His place wasn't bad, but this was *Bowery Street*. Back on Fifth Avenue, she was in her own milieu. Everyone she knew from her hometown of Greenwich, Connecticut, maintained an apartment on what was surely the most elegant street in Manhattan. Thank God her friends knew how much Harry was worth, or there would've been snickers about Verity slumming it.

She'd planned to show him off to her social circle, but Harry didn't have the time for it. Lately, he had no time for *her*. Harry spent months in Panama, and even when he returned to New York, his days were occupied with this... network.

Verity frowned, remembering their conversation from the night before. *"Harry, let's do something crazy together. Let's go on a trip."*

"Now?" he responded, voice incredulous.

"You were different before we got married." Her mouth drooped.

"I'm a working man, Verity. I can't spend the rest of my life going to parties and restaurants and vacations with you."

Harry was currently at the other end of the living room, talking on the phone with one of his business associates. Victor and Alex were sprawled on the couch, watching Larry King on CNN interviewing someone about the effects of stock market fluctuations on the state's economy. Lilah drew up one of the chairs from the small dining table and seated herself next to the couch, ankles crossed neatly below.

"Government bungling," remarked Alex. "Damned politicians

are bringing New York to its knees."

"The incompetence is unbelievable," Lilah agreed. "Bad financial management. Economy is getting worse... poverty, drug use..."

"...mob violence, robberies, murders," continued Alex. "Elites like us can live in our safe little bubbles, but the rest of the world is suffering."

"As of today, Citadel Partners owns twenty percent of Sanders's company," a reporter said, causing the Kingsleys to fall silent and sit up. "But shares have gone up to more than forty dollars. What do you think, Governor? Will this stop the takeover attempt on Sanders, Incorporated?"

Alex turned off the television.

"The media doesn't believe we have a prayer of winning," Victor commented.

"The prices *are* high," Lilah said, removing her glasses and setting them on her lap. "We have to stop buying for a while."

Alex said, "Oh, good. I could use the break. It's gotten to the point even Mike can tell you how the stock market is doing."

Alex's son, Mikey, was a cutie. When Verity asked him how old he was, he held up two pudgy fingers before turning to his mother with an interesting bug he found. The Kingsleys were still laughing and marveling over Mikey's antics when Harry returned from his phone conversation. "That was Saeed. Sanders asked for a meeting with the shareholders of Citadel Partners."

Victor whooped. "He bit!"

"This is it," said Alex.

What? Verity mumbled. At least, she thought she mumbled until Lilah turned to her and started explaining.

"This is Sanders's last chance at avoiding a loan to buy us out," Lilah said, putting her glasses on the side table. "He'll try to get Citadel for cheap. If he succeeds, our plan is finished."

"He's going to throw everything at us at the meeting," said Harry.

"Especially at Lilah," worried Alex.

"Yes," agreed Victor, voice somber. "From this moment on, Lilah can't be alone. Not for any reason."

"Not until we want her to be," added Harry.

"Bro," huffed Victor. "You know my opinion about the idea."

"You've told me," acknowledged Harry. "Several times. But it's the only way our plan will work."

Verity stifled a yawn. For the past few months, she'd been unable to leave the apartment without guards flanking her, and Harry traveled everywhere with a battalion. Verity had a hard time buying their fear of Sanders. People didn't kill each other over business in 1985!

"You stay safe, too, Harry," Lilah ordered. "There's no way for us to be certain of Sanders's strategy."

At her tone, Alex brought his hand up in a smart salute, and Harry responded, "Aye, aye, sir!"

Lilah grinned reluctantly, but her gaze remained firm.

Verity nearly rolled her eyes. She puzzled over the other woman and how everyone took her so seriously. As far as Verity could tell, Lilah's parents hadn't been rich. Her father was an ambassador, but he got there slogging his way up the ranks in the state department. Her mother worked as a lawyer for the United Nations. Lilah didn't have any *family* money... only what was deeded over by the Sheppards and the Barronses. She was CFO of the Peter Kingsley Company only because she managed to snag Brad Kingsley.

Despite this, the woman acted as though she were a princess, issuing commands and expecting obedience. The men around Lilah, including Harry, stopped to listen when she spoke. Even now, Harry was leaning toward her, listening as she explained to Alex the details of... *whatever.*

Lilah patted around herself, searching for something. Harry smiled as he picked up the glasses from the side table and slipped them onto her nose.

Verity frowned. Suddenly, and for some reason she didn't dare dwell on, she couldn't stand having Lilah in her home. Verity said to Alex, "Can we stop this for a while? Harry and I have plans for the evening."

A red tide washed into Lilah's face. Mumbling an apology, she stood and urged the Kingsley brothers out.

"Remember what I said, Victor," Harry called from the front door when the guests were at the stairs.

"I got it, bro," Victor Kingsley hollered before Lilah admonished him to keep moving.

Verity tried to recall Harry assigning Victor some specific task. Unfortunately, she hadn't paid much attention to the conversations of the evening.

When the door closed, Harry raised an eyebrow. "What plans?"

She waved away his question. "We need to talk." She told him bluntly, "I want to have a baby."

"What?" Harry laughed.

"Yes," she said, warming to her theme. "Everyone says it's different when you have kids. Priorities change."

"You believe my priorities need to change?" he asked absently. Sauntering to the small dining table, he flipped through the documents Lilah left.

Verity wanted to grab the folder from him and toss it in the garbage. "You spend so much time fixing other people's problems. I think you need something else to focus on. Like a child and... and *me*."

He continued to study the papers.

With an impatient huff, Verity flounced to him and slammed a hand on the folder. "Are you listening?"

"Now is not a good time." Harry moved her hand to the side, seating himself before returning to the list of numbers. There was no trace of anger on his face.

"Okay, is it a good time for this?" Plunking herself on his lap, she threaded her fingers through his hair and yanked him into a kiss.

Verity felt the warmth of his hands on her hips, sensed the arousal in his sudden tension. *Yes!* she exulted, clenching her fingers on his muscled shoulders. It took her a second to realize he was untwining her arms from his body, pushing her away as he stood.

"Why do we need a child when yo—" Harry stopped. His hands came up to cup her elbows. "Is there something wrong?"

Tears sprang to her eyes. "Something? How about *everything?* I never see you since you started working on this network. You stay with the Kingsleys for months, and even when you're in New York, you're never home." Desperately, she demanded, "I want us to take a vacation. Forget everyone else for a couple of weeks."

Harry tapped her chin with a finger. "I promise we will. I have to see this through first." At her frustrated growl, he continued, "I've spent many years working on the Sanders project. This is as much about me as about the Kingsleys' plans for expansion." He asked, "Why don't you join us? After all, Gateway's your family business, too."

"What am I supposed to do?" she snapped. "I'm not a petroleum engineer. I don't know anything about running a business.”

“You could work with Lilah for a while… or Alex. There’s no one better to learn from.”

Verity couldn’t *believe*… did Harry seriously expect his own wife to fetch and carry for Lilah and make coffee? “I’m not working for that woman,” Verity managed to spit out, humiliation thickening her tongue. At the sudden tautness on Harry’s face, she hastily added, “For Alex, either.”

“We all had to start somewhere,” Harry said.

Verity couldn’t. She just couldn’t. “I want a baby,” she repeated.

Harry pinched the bridge of his nose. “Verity,” he sighed. “You’re young. Maybe in another couple of years. Besides, now is not the time to consider starting a family. Do you understand things could blow up in our faces any minute? Didn’t you hear Lilah?”

Lilah, Lilah, Lilah. How could Verity possibly not hear when Harry practically chanted the name every single day? Hardly able to recognize the tear-clogged voice as hers, she said, “This is 1985. People don’t go around knocking off people they don’t like! Your Jack Sanders—”

“Jared.”

“Whatever. Lilah’s crazy. Sanders may be a bad man, but he’s not going to kill any of you. For God’s sake, it’s only business.”

Part XXIV

Chapter 79

In four months' time, 15th October 1985, 9:30 AM

San Diego, California

Hotel InterContinental gleamed under the summer sun. On the bay, squawking brown pelicans glided in effortless mimicry of the waves, occasionally plunging to scoop fish in their oversized bills. Boats were moored in the marina. Even on the twenty-fifth floor, warm breeze brought the stench of engine oil and sea lion droppings into the suite. Wrinkling her nose, Lilah slid shut the glass door to the balcony.

"I know, Victor," Alex said for the thousandth time. "You think it's a risky play, but we have more people here than the presidential entourage." Not quite. Nine security officers in all, safeguarding the rooms and the conference venue.

Drumming fingers on the armrest of his chair, Victor Kingsley brooded in silence.

"Pac-man defense," Harry explained to one of the guards. "The players try to devour each other. We're trying to buy Sanders's company, so he tries to buy ours, instead."

"Cool," said the guard. "A real-life game."

Harry continued, "Unlike Sanders, Incorporated, Citadel Partners is not publicly traded, so it's not easy for him. For our investors to sell, they must get permission from the consortium.

Hence, today's meeting. We'll be voting on his offer." They'd kept Gateway and the Peter Kingsley Company closely held for the same reason. Barrons was publicly traded but was too big a fish for even Sanders to swallow.

"We cannot afford to lose," Alex muttered.

"Sanders is going to throw everything he has into the meeting," Harry buttoned his shirt over the Kevlar vest. "He will try to make us vote the way *he* wants."

"He's not going to try something stupid, is he?" one of the guards asked. "Like shoot you?"

"Not likely... he'd have to kill all three of us," Harry said, indicating the Kingsley brothers and himself. "There's the fact three major shareholders conveniently dying at the same time would create legal trouble for Sanders. And even if one of us remains alive, he can vote all our shares. But we'll play it safe. Get your vest on, Victor. You, too, Lilah... if you leave the room, I mean."

"It will be safer if she attends the meeting, too," said the guard, jerking his head toward Lilah.

Victor interjected, "Exactly what I keep telling them."

"No," said Alex, straightening the lapels of his blazer. "The meeting is for shareholders only. And Sanders."

He didn't mention the reason they'd agreed to a shareholders-only event, the real reason Sanders never tried to have Harry, Victor, and Alex killed when the takeover attempt started. There was another target in the enemy's sights. Delilah Kingsley—she would either be leverage for Sanders to make sure Harry and the Kingsley brothers voted to sell, or she would be killed, destroying the network itself. Sanders would time it exactly right. Today was the day. This was the place. If they didn't give Sanders this opening, he'd have ordered Lilah assassinated months back, regardless of the president's wrath.

"Her three guards will remain with her at all times," Harry instructed. "She won't be left alone even for a second."

Lilah told the security officer, "I'll be in my room, catching up on reading."

"Harry," called the leader of the security team. "Your brother left a message for us. The local office of Gateway is sending its own man over." He grumbled, "You Sheppards should trust us to know what the hell we're doing."

"Hector did call me about it." In spite of everyone outside the core team maintaining distance from the coup attempt, all three families increased security. And of course, all of them worried about the safety of the four people directly involved. Soothingly, Harry added, "The California office doesn't want any untoward incidents in its territory. I was very clear the new fellow will be with us in the conference room. We cannot allow any strange faces around Lilah. Everyone... make sure you have your cell phones. You, too, Lilah."

All the security officers carried a bulky phone hooked to their belts. Lilah eyed hers, resting on the console next to the window. She nodded.

"Make sure you check in as planned," Alex said to her. Before the vote, they needed to confirm she was safe from Sanders.

When they were ready to leave, Lilah saw them out. "I'd take your place if I could," Harry murmured when they were at the door.

"Dumbass," she mumbled back. "I'll be all right. Now, go and beat Sanders."

#

9:55 AM

Hotel lobby

The elevator doors swished open. A man waited at the reception desk, hand tucked into his pocket. Smiling genially, he straightened and walked toward Harry. "Mr. Sheppard, I was sent by Gateway."

Harry stopped, contemplating the local security officer. Military buzz, alert despite the casual stance.

"Former Marine Corps," the guard said in answer to the unasked question. He showed his ID to Harry but addressed Alex. "Captain Kingsley, right?"

"Plain Kingsley will do," Alex said.

The man nodded. "I've checked the conference room. Everything's secure."

"My men already took care of it," said the leader of the New York security team. He, too, verified the newcomer's ID. "Know what... I think I'll do one last run-through. Meeting starts at ten, so let's not waste more time."

The former marine inclined his head.

"You guys go ahead," said Victor. "I'm going to the kitchen."

Alex groaned. "He'll get us thrown out. Remember what happened at the Plaza?"

Victor waved a hand. "Nah. The chef here's a friend from culinary school."

"Mr. Kingsley," admonished the local guard.

"Sanders is not going to do anything to me," Victor said. "If I die, Alex becomes my executor, so what's Sanders going to gain?"

"Voting closes at twelve-hundred," Harry warned.

"I got it, bro," said Victor, his wink barely perceptible.

As he sauntered toward the kitchen, whistling under his breath, a man rose from the plush sofa behind a low table, folding his newspaper and tossing it to the side. He walked briskly in the direction of the elevator. The two crossed paths, Victor inclining his head in greeting.

Bumping into a wall console, Victor knocked over the vase. Water spilled on the checkered carpet, and a dark stain spread across the fibers. The other man jumped to the side, but not before some of the water splashed onto his pants. Victor knelt, clumsily stuffing flowers into the amphora, and apologized.

A smiling hotel employee guided Harry and Alex toward the conference facilities. "This way, gentlemen." The guards—including the new fellow sent by Hector—followed.

They passed through the large arch and turned the corner, leaving Victor in the lobby.

#

10:05 AM

25th floor

Pet Sematary was gripping, but it was scary as heck, and Lilah's nerves were already jittery enough. Besides, the constant flickering of the bedside lamp was interrupting the flow of the story. She tossed the book aside. A sweaty workout was what she needed. Bulletproof vest concealed by her customary exercise gear of black tank-top and leggings, she exited the bedroom, meaning to ask her entourage to accompany her to the gym.

It was the silence which hit her first. "Hello?" she called into the empty sitting area. The low hum of the air-conditioner was the only response she got.

The fluorescent lighting seemed to be suffering from the same malfunction as the bedside lamp, but bright sunlight poured in through the glass sliding doors between the sitting room and the balcony. There was a plate left on the coffee table, a partially eaten slice of apple on it, and there were a couple of open cans of soda, but the three guards were missing. The one other person she'd expected to see wasn't around, either: Victor Kingsley.

Dropping the gym bag next to her feet, Lilah ran to the door, desperately hoping they were outside. A quick look showed only an empty hallway. Her heart pounded painfully.

Locking the door to the suite, she ran back to the bedroom to check the nightstand. The handgun was still there. She picked up the phone. Dead. So was the one in the bathroom.

She tamped down panic and took the gun with her to the sitting area. Her cell phone was still on the console where she left it. Nothing... no response to her attempts to dial out. Hoping for a miracle, she checked the phone on the side table. Complete silence.

If she missed check-in... she needed to get to a phone and report to Harry as planned before he could vote. Weapon in hand, she went to the door and took another look through the peephole. Now, there was a distorted image outside. A man, certainly not someone she recognized. An assassin?

Her insides quaking, Lilah glanced at the wall clock. Five minutes past the time Victor was supposed to return to the suite. He wouldn't dare be late, not when there was so much at stake. Her head swam. Had Sanders's assassin gotten to her guards *and* Victor?

The check-in... holding the gun behind her, she opened the door, leaving just enough space to poke her head through. A wide back blocked her view. "Excuse me, sir. You're in my way."

The man—only slightly taller than her but with the bulk of

muscle—turned. "Delilah Kingsley?"

"Yes."

He held up a photo ID. The headshot showed the same close-cropped brown hair and brown eyes as the man in front of her. "Special security, arranged by Gateway California."

"*Hector's* man?" asked Lilah, disbelief clear in her tone despite her best efforts.

"Yes."

But wasn't he supposed to join the team in the conference room? Victor... her own guards... "What happened to the men from New York?"

The fellow jiggled keys in his pocket, eyes darting around. Behind him, the door to the other suite was open, cleaning cart in front. Female voices jabbered away in another language. "I was told to come up here to make sure you're all right," said the man. "The rest of your guards were called to the conference room. Mr. Sheppard's orders."

#

10:15 AM

Citadel Partners stockholder meeting

The classroom-style hall was packed, and at the podium was Jared Sanders. Eyes blazing, he pointed to Harry. "This man's a fraud. He blames me for all his family's misfortunes and is using you good folks for his personal vendetta against me. You, too, Kingsley. You're a damned fool if you think his friendship is genuine."

Harry and Alex were at the table in the front, the empty seat next to them reserved for Victor. Their guards were scattered around the room, including Hector's new hire, who was close to the stage. Alex wasn't paying any mind to the room, staring hard as he was at their enemy.

Saeed al-Obeidi was also on the dais, seated behind the microphone on the desk. Flashing his friends a glance, he said, "Mr. Sanders, I promised you equal opportunity to speak. It doesn't mean you can insult one of us and get away with it. Stop with the name-calling and tell the shareholders what you want them to hear."

Sanders snarled. "All right, I'll tell you something you *should* be interested in. There's no way in hell this little campaign's going to succeed. Citadel Partners can't engineer a takeover when I hold fifty-one percent. I don't know what kind of snake oil scheme Sheppard's sold you, but he's aware of this."

Harry stood. "If that's the case, why are you here, Mr. Sanders?"

"Because I don't want you anywhere near my business. I refuse to deal with con artists."

"I'm only a minority stockholder in this venture. My aim here is to make sure Sanders, Incorporated plays by the same rules as the rest of the world. And of course, to make some money for Citadel. The offer I made at the press conference still stands. If you agree to a royalty trust and oversight of your company, we can work together. You're a brilliant businessman, so our stockholders will still see a profit. You can even have your choice of a liaison between our group and Sanders, Incorporated."

Cursing, Sanders said, "As though anyone I choose is going to be more than a puppet for you. You'll get to stay in the shadows and instruct them on how to tear my company apart."

The lights flickered.

#

10:25 AM

25ᵗʰ floor

Lights blinked off, leaving the hallway shrouded in complete darkness. Behind her back, Lilah tightened her sweaty grip on the gun and started to slide it out to the front. Without warning, brightness flooded the floor. Every lamp turned back on. Lilah yanked her hand, keeping the weapon hidden behind her hip.

In the suite across hers, an irate female voice said something in a language Lilah didn't recognize. "Power problems," said a second voice.

No way was the fellow blocking Lilah's door the guard arranged by Gateway, or Harry would've sent word. Or maybe he tried to call and couldn't get her because someone from Sanders's side managed to disable the phones. But why would Harry summon her regular guards to the conference room without giving them a chance to let her know? Why would he then allow a stranger to stay as her protection, a face she wouldn't recognize? "I want to ask Harry about this change," she said, desperation mounting. "Like I said a dozen times already... I was going to the gym, anyway. There must be a phone there I can use."

"It's not safe," the man repeated. "You're supposed to remain here."

Lilah glanced between the elevators on one side and the exit to the stairwell on the other... no, she wouldn't make it. This *assassin* wouldn't let her.

The gun... her fingers were slippery with sweat. By the time she took aim, there was a good chance the man would disarm her. Besides, she was sure he was wearing a bulletproof vest, the same as her. In a tussle, she would come off worse—with no protection against a shot to the head.

Calm. She *had* to remain calm, or she'd never make it out of the suite until the meeting was over and done with. Once she missed check-in, Harry would be forced to surrender. "I don't care what kind of threat you claim there is. I *am* going to the gym! You were sent to guard me, right? So do your job and go to the gym with me."

He urged her back into the room. "I've been advised to keep you here, Mrs. Kingsley."

A couple of maids in black-and-white uniforms exited the suite across the hallway, excusing themselves as they passed Lilah's door. One of them loaded dirty laundry into a bag while the other pushed cleaning supplies down the passageway.

Her stomach knotted, watching the maids wait for the service elevator. *Last chance.* "Excuse me," Lilah called in a loud and shaky voice. "I need my room cleaned."

"Unwise," the man hissed. "You just dragged two other people into it."

Not responding, she said to the hotel employees, "I'll be at the gym for a couple of hours."

When the maids got to Lilah's door, she tried to squeeze by the man, and he shot out a hand, gripping her firmly by the elbow. She gasped, heart hammering. The gun slipped from her fingers and fell to the carpet. At the dull thud, one of the maids glanced down and screamed. The man bent to pick up the weapon, Lilah's arm still in a painful hold. Her next thought was that the man was right, she'd condemned two innocent bystanders to death.

"Hey," called a voice, startling them. Victor Kingsley ambled toward the group. "Oh, hello again. Sorry about the vase and the water, bro. Didn't mean to get your pants wet."

#

10:35 AM

Citadel Partners stockholder meeting

Microphone in hand, Sanders walked among the audience. "I went through the list of investors in Citadel. Except for Sheppard and the Kingsleys, y'all are ordinary people like me... immigrants. When my father and I fled Malta, we had the clothes on our backs and a few bucks to buy food. Nothing more. We asked for asylum in the States. My father worked every job he could find to feed me. Eventually, he started the company with a small loan of two thousand dollars. It was still difficult for him. For me, too. It's tough for people like us to get acceptance with the rich folks in New York. They don't get how hard we had to work. How important every penny is for us."

Harry stayed silent, forced to let the enemy have his say. At his side, Alex huffed in disbelief, but the audience was muttering in support.

Sanders continued, "Fourteen, fifteen-hour days. You understand how it is. You don't get to see your wife and kids. You sleep at work some nights. There are days when you worry if you're going to have to let fine people go because you can't make payroll. I *know* you understand. You came up the hard way like me. No one handed anything to us. There was no wealthy grandfather waiting in the wings to loan us money."

It didn't matter Sanders was possibly the richest person in the world, how the people he drove to bankruptcy were ordinary. It didn't matter he never played by the rules unlike the crowd listening raptly to him. What the occupants of the hall saw now was a self-made man who went up against the system and won.

"I know you good folks have put a lot of cash into this," Sanders continued. "And I have no intention of letting you suffer. The shares of Citadel are valued at fifteen dollars. I'll offer you eighteen, so both our problems will be solved."

Saeed spoke vigorously against selling to Sanders. So did Eduardo Garcia, foster father to Victor's son, Gabriel. While they were putting their points forth, a young man strode to Sanders's side and whispered something in his ear. Sanders's eyes narrowed in satisfaction, lips curling into a smug smile.

A hotel employee came with a message for Alex. He scanned the piece of paper and cursed. "Damn it, none of the phone lines in the building are working. They think it's because of all the power problems. And no one can find Victor."

"The cell phones?" Harry asked. His was fully charged but somehow unable to place or receive calls, the same as Alex's. "Lilah's phone... her guards... ask our men to call someone in the suite."

"Again, not one is working," Alex said. The guards in the conference room were glancing from Harry and Alex to the exit as though waiting for the order to proceed to Lilah's suite. "What the hell is going on?"

The muscles in Harry's shoulders bunched. His hands tightened into fists. The pen in his fingers fractured, and dark, sticky ink dribbled out. "Sanders."

Alex leaped up. "I'm going up there." Gateway's new guard— the former marine—took one step forward from his position by the stage, responding to Alex's obvious alarm.

"No," Harry snapped, voice low, and held up a hand to stop the guards from doing anything. He signaled a hotel employee to bring him a new pen. "A rescue attempt will only get her killed."

"If Sanders's men have her—" Alex started.

"We'll admit defeat. The only way to save her life."

On the dais, Saeed announced, "We'll vote on Mr. Sanders's

offer."

Alex stiffened. "Sanders is coming our way."

Pulling out the chair next to Harry's, Jared Sanders sat. His eyes burned with cruel triumph. "What about you, Sheppard? How're you planning to vote?"

Accepting the replacement pen and a box of tissues from a uniformed young man, Harry stared at Sanders in silence.

Alex snorted, desperate defiance on his face. "What do you think?"

Sanders ignored him and focused on Harry. Once the hotel employee left, the oilman said, "You may win this battle, but you need your empress in place. Without her, you won't have your virtual merger. How will you win the war?"

Suspicion turned to certainty. Fear and anger jolted through Harry. Lilah. Sanders had Lilah. Pulling out a tissue, Harry wiped up the ink on the table, seeing crimson on the wad of paper in place of dark blue. "You're a dead man."

Alex rose from his chair, his shoulders visibly shaking.

"Sit down, Kingsley," Sanders ordered, taking care to keep the conversation muted. "Make a move, and Delilah Kingsley will be the one who dies."

Alex sat back. "President Temple," he threatened.

Hand slicing the air, Sanders said, "If I succeed, I'll let her go, and Temple will do nothing because he won't want to mess up future chances. If this vote goes against me, the easiest way to save my company would be to kill Mrs. Kingsley. Without her, you have no network. I'll keep my business and face Temple's wrath. There's the problem of who inherits her stock. Way I see it, it's gotta be either her brother or you, Sheppard. Andrew Barrons won't let his precious adopted son put himself in danger by tangling with me, so he won't be a problem. If *you* end up inheriting, well…" With a low laugh, Sanders added, "Even if you manage to beat me, you'll hate every minute of your life afterward, knowing you caused her death. I'll consider it a win."

#

10:55 AM

25th floor

"Come on, man, let her go," Victor wheedled.

The maids clung to each other, too frightened to help. One of them was reciting something. *"Ave Maria, gratia plena…"*

"Please," begged the other one.

"Try something, and she'll die," warned the assassin, jerking Lilah back. The gunman couldn't get all of them, but he didn't need to. Once Lilah was dead, the game would be over. She tugged, trying to free herself. The hold on her arm tightened. "Stay still, bitch."

"Victor, go to the conference room," she begged. "You've got to get there before they close."

The assassin laughed. "I don't give a damn what the retard does. All I've got to do is hold *you* here until the meeting's over. If your pals do what they're told, you'll be fine."

"I gotta talk to Harry," said Victor, mouth opening and closing in confusion. "But you…"

"*Now,* Victor," she said.

Victor turned toward the elevator, then pivoted. Lilah ducked. His fist rammed into the assassin's jaw. A gunshot echoed across the hallway. A piece of molding broke from the ceiling and fell to the floor, gray-white dust coating the carpet. One of the maids dropped in a dead faint, the other wide-eyed and paralyzed in panic.

Victor grasped the assassin's gun arm and twisted it behind him until the weapon fell. Gripping the back of his scalp, Victor hammered the thug's head against the wall until he slid to his knees, body limp.

Even so, Lilah needed to pry the assassin's fingers loose, the indentations on her skin already bruised and painful. "Is he dead?" she asked.

"Nope, but he's going to wish he were," Victor responded. "Why were you outside on your own? Where are the guards?"

"No idea what happened to the guards. I was outside because *you* were late. Where *were* you?"

"I—"

A whimper interrupted their argument. The maid who'd fainted was stirring, her friend weeping silent tears by her side.

Victor scooped up the semi-conscious woman and carried her into Lilah's suite, depositing her on the couch. He then turned to her crying friend. "Lock yourselves here until the cops arrive. Take care of your friend, okay? And shh," he warned, finger to his lips.

"Shh," sobbed the maid, head bobbing obediently.

#

11:10 AM

Citadel Partners stockholder meeting

The stockholders were conferring among themselves. In five minutes, they'd vote on Sanders's offer. Jared Sanders walked around, chatting affably with the attendees and answering questions.

Saeed called the meeting to order. One by one, the shareholders voted "Aye" to sell to Sanders. It was forty-seven percent for selling, and only Garcia and al-Obeidi voted against the proposal. The Kingsleys and Harry hadn't cast their votes yet.

Victor... somehow, he and Lilah needed to engineer a miracle before Harry could vote.

"What about you, Sheppard?" asked Sanders, voice businesslike. "You and your friends have twenty-five percent."

Alex interjected, "You'll know our decision once my brother—Victor—gets here. We have until twelve noon."

Harry glanced at the clock. The ticking echoed in his mind, accelerating, taking them closer to defeat.

#

11:25 AM

25th floor

Lilah hurried to Victor. "I checked the phones on the entire floor. All dead. We have to get to the conference room before voting closes."

Victor slung the unconscious assassin into a supply closet and locked the door. "Sanders's men are on every floor, even by the fire escape. It's the reason I was late. Had to check on our escape routes."

Urgently, Lilah asked, "Did you talk to the elevator operator?" He was in Harry's pay and would get them nonstop to the lobby.

Victor grimaced. "About him—"

"What?" she asked impatiently.

"He was not in the machine room," said Victor. "Coffee spilled all over the place. I think Sanders's team got to him."

"Oh, God. One of our guards was supposed to be up there."

"Time for route number two," Victor said. "I left the elevators stuck in the basement and turned off the switch."

"The shaft it is. Do you have the keys and the rest of your things?"

"Of course," said Victor, jangling what sounded like a bunch of keys in his pant pocket before bringing out a butcher knife and a handful of narrow steel rods from under his blazer. There were two guns strapped to his ankles, but he ignored them.

"Spit rods and a cleaver," she muttered. "I must have been insane to think this could work."

Victor exclaimed, "Hey, I'm a chef. These are *my* weapons of choice." Approaching the emergency exit, he thrust the rod through the keyhole, exerting force until it bent at an angle. After the lock was jammed, he said, "Let's go."

Lilah followed him. Every nook and corner of the building would be familiar to Victor. Harry had insisted the boxer study the floor plan of the place every single day of the last year and a half.

Victor wedged the blade between the door panels of the service elevator, forcing them apart. "We'll travel the deluxe way through the shaft, but there *is* one small problem."

"What?"

The veins in his temple bulged with effort as he pushed the opening wider. "I jammed the lock to the machine room, but sooner or later, someone's going to check the mainline switch."

"Huh?"

He explained, "We don't have our man in the machine room any longer. If another technician turns the elevator switch back on while we're in the shaft—"

"Oh, God."

"—you and I will be crushed to death," he concluded cheerfully. Discarding his jacket, Victor hooked the meat chopper back to his belt. He pulled out a pair of gloves from his pocket. "Ready?"

Leaning into the empty space, Lilah grabbed the thick steel rope, her own hands protected by gloves. She sprang, twining her legs around the cable. In a second, Victor joined her, hanging on to the cable next to hers.

Grease and grime coated the rope, and losing traction, she slid. The light from the open doors vanished as she plummeted. Her stomach came up to her throat, and she swung violently from side to side, colliding with the wall of the shaft. Electric bolts of pain shot up her spine and into her head.

"*Lilah!*" Victor's scream echoed.

She oscillated in the small space, ricocheting to the back wall. The rails scraped her hip and thigh. Pain burned all the way down her leg before her sneaker connected with a notch. The muscles in her arms screaming, she brought herself to a stop.

A large shadow descended rapidly, Victor halting next to her.

A violent pulse pounded at her temple. Lilah refused to check how far she'd dropped. "I'm good," she said, tamping down the queasiness.

They continued their trip through the inky darkness. Under the bulletproof vest, her skin itched from the heat and the sweat. The odor of machine oil was thick, and Lilah took in short, sharp gulps of air through her mouth.

Disembodied voices came to them at every floor, irate at the malfunctioning elevators. Some of them might have belonged to

Sanders's assassins, ignorant that their hostage was only inches beyond the steel doors. "Check the mainline switch," shouted someone.

"Hurry," mumbled Victor.

Heart thundering, Lilah strained to hear any sound that might suggest the elevators were starting up. It seemed to take an eternity, but her shoes hit something solid.

Victor landed with a thud. "Where's... ahh, got it."

Metal struck metal, sending a loud clang echoing up the shaft. Sparks flew, and Lilah jumped to the side. Unlocking the emergency hatch with the keys they copied the week before, Victor pried it open. Lilah swung her legs in and gripped the opposite edge. She dropped, knees bending with the force of the fall. "Victor," she called softly.

"Yup." He squeezed through. "Damn, this thing's small." The car shook when he dropped to the floor. "Stay to the side," he said and wielded his cleaver once more.

Bright light flooded the space as the doors opened into the kitchen. Her back to the control panel, Lilah stayed hidden.

"Mr. Kingsley, did you get stuck?" a surprised voice asked.

"Hey, Victor," shouted someone else.

"I need a phone," Victor said.

"They're not working," said the other man. "Sorry."

Lilah snarled in frustration.

"It's eleven-fifty-one!" Victor bellowed. "We need to go."

She rocketed out of the elevator, surprising the kitchen staff. Victor and Lilah ran between piles of vegetables being cleaned by gushing water on one side and trussed chicken lined up on stainless steel counters on the other. Victor snatched an empty food trolley from a startled young lady and swung Lilah onto it. She squeaked in surprise.

"It's faster," he said, grabbing a metal tray. They zipped through the service area and into the lobby. Screams and shouts and curses came from different directions. Somewhere behind, a gun thundered. "Stay down," Victor roared.

She crouched, holding the tray over her head, flimsy protection against bullets to the brain.

#

11:55 AM

Citadel Partners stockholder meeting

On the dais, Sanders rubbed his hands together. "Five more minutes... and Citadel Partners will be a part of Sanders, Incorporated."

Saeed was nearly in tears. "Harry, please vote. What are you doing? We have no more time to wait for Victor."

Hands in his pockets, Sanders rocked on his heels. "Mr. al-Obeidi, we're at forty-seven percent to sell and sixteen to hold. If Sheppard wanted to vote against selling, why wouldn't he have said so already?"

Harry closed his eyes. He couldn't bring himself to give up. If only five minutes remained, he'd give Victor and Lilah until the last second.

The door to the conference room exploded open. "Coming through," boomed the voice of Victor Kingsley. He backed into the hall at breakneck velocity and spun, whirling a trolley around.

The form on top soared into the astounded audience. Chairs tumbled; tables tipped over. Curses flew in a couple of languages. "Sorry," came a female voice. Hair hanging haphazardly around her face, blood seeping through shredded leggings, Lilah clambered up. "I'll leave right now."

Harry's heart thundered. His hand clenched into a fist. *Yes!*

"Yes," hissed Alex.

Smeared with grease, Victor limped forward, a meat cleaver swinging from his belt. "I vote nay for the shares held by the Kingsley brothers and Harry Sheppard amounting to twenty-five percent of the company... and for twelve percent of the shares owned by Gabriel Ramirez, my son."

Chapter 80

A week later

New York, New York

Loud commotion erupted at the door of the conference room of the Peter Kingsley Company, making Lilah look up.

"Sanders is taking out a loan," whooped Alex, exploding in. "He offered Citadel one hundred-and-twenty a share for the Sanders, Incorporated stock."

After the episode in San Diego, the losing side had been prodded into demanding the ability to sell their percentages of various stocks if they so wished. Saeed al-Obeidi demurred. But now... he would give in under the pretext that kind of cash was hard to say no to.

Harry strode in behind Alex, and he was greeted by cheers from Victor and Saeed. A great deal of backslapping and congratulations went around.

Lilah stayed quiet, watching them with a smile. One enemy nearly down, many more to go.

The bodies of two of Lilah's guards were found in a landfill, and the third seemed to have vanished. The assumption was he was bribed by Sanders into luring out the others. Some kind of jamming device was surely used on the phones in the entire building, but a diligent search failed to reveal any. Anyway, it didn't matter when there were more pressing concerns.

Lilah was still trying to figure out why the assassin who came to her room claimed he was sent by Hector, Harry's brother. The actual guard sent by Gateway—a former marine—was in the conference room when she and Victor made their dramatic entry. The assassin clearly knew the Sheppards were sending an extra guard and tried to use the info to fool Lilah. There was a leak in their alliance. Harry asked his brother about it, but Hector simply stated he didn't have a clue how it happened. Neither Harry nor Lilah wanted to believe Hector could have... what would he gain from helping Sanders kidnap Lilah? But Hector once wanted Sabrina to marry Steven Kingsley, even knowing of Steven's attempt to murder his cousins. Conspiracies loomed whichever way they turned. Friends, family— who could they trust?

It was a while before the men settled down around the table. Victor said, "Harry, gotta give it to you... still can't believe your insane plan worked. Where does it put our enemy?"

"Billions in debt," Harry said, chugging water from a chilled bottle.

Victor pumped his fists in the air, roaring, "Success!"

"Not quite," said Harry. "The market has to work its magic."

Lilah picked up the phone and gave her secretary the number written on a piece of paper—the private line of a certain prince in Saudi Arabia.

"Your Highness," Harry spoke. "You can go ahead."

Two months later—in December 1985—Saudi Arabia announced it would increase production to recapture market share. Oil prices plummeted as expected. "A lot of small businesses will go under," Lilah murmured, folding the newspaper and sliding it across Harry's desk.

"The Saudis were always going to increase production," he said, placing the paper on top of the pile of mail. The tone was casual, but his eyes remained troubled. The chair squeaked when he sat back. "Their decisions had nothing to do with us, and those companies would have folded, anyway."

"Right," she agreed. "All we did was postpone things to suit our convenience." Desperate to stop Harry and lulled by the Saudi delay in responding to falling revenue, Sanders committed to recapitalization. He was now in debt, his profits nonexistent... just like many small oil companies. Ignoring the niggle of unease in her chest, Lilah mused, "It needed to be done."

Harry nodded. "Rough choice... but big picture."

After the price collapse, unable to recover from the high debt incurred to repurchase shares from Citadel Partners, Sanders, Incorporated filed for Chapter Eleven bankruptcy. Newspapers spent barrels of ink profiling the new team in charge of the oil sector, all in their late twenties to early thirties. There was also plenty of mockery across the globe for the tale Sanders tried to tell about a chemical fire which obliterated an entire village in Argentina. His claims were dismissed as a hopeless attempt at revenge.

In January 1986, the space shuttle *Challenger* exploded seventy-three seconds into its flight, killing all seven crew members. The Kingsleys and the Sheppards and Jared Sanders disappeared from the headlines, and so did the oil glut. Crude oil prices continued to drop, reaching ten dollars a barrel in March. Sanders, Incorporated went from Chapter Eleven to Seven—liquidation. The auctioneer told Harry, "The equipment barely got pennies on the dollar." The business was finished, torn to pieces.

Within days, Jared Sanders was hauled off to prison, charged with multiple counts of murder in one of the tanker explosions documented by *The Big Apple Reporter*. The only people to show up in court to support him were his two daughters and the Sanders family lawyer. Mrs. Sanders passed on more than a year ago, and the daughters were both physicians, married to colleagues and able to support themselves without their father's money.

Neither Lilah nor Harry wanted to attend any of the legal proceedings against Sanders, although they could probably have found a way in if they so wished. All Lilah longed for was to put the painful memories behind her and move on, and Harry surprised himself with his reluctance to witness in person the fall of the giant enemy who haunted their lives since they were in their teens.

Chapter 81

March 1986

Top of the World Observation Deck

World Trade Center, New York City

The rain which began the night before didn't let up for more than a few minutes at a time, and disappointed tourists returned without taking in the panoramic view of Manhattan Island and the ocean beyond from the observation deck. Lilah didn't know how

Harry did it, but they'd been allowed on the rooftop despite the bad weather.

There were no guards, thankfully. Now that Sanders was not a threat, she got her security team reassigned. Yeah, there was still Temple. He and Godwin couldn't do anything to her or Harry without risking the network itself. There was also the pre-nup. Unless and until their remaining enemies found a way around the complications, Harry and Lilah were safe.

Lilah stepped out onto the roof, and as though in accompaniment to her entry, lightning flashed across the dark sky. Thunder rumbled. There was a break in the downpour, but the air was still damp. She grimaced. The claret-colored Chanel suit and black pumps would be total losses after this jaunt.

Harry was watching the sea, and a large package was on the floor, next to his shoes. He turned, eyes lighting up at the sight of her. Wind whipped his tie into his face. "Alex?" he asked.

"Picking up something for our little party," Lilah said. By tacit consent, the celebration would include only the three of them.

"I have something for you," Harry announced. Picking up the package, he ripped open the wet coverings and handed her the picture. "This hung on his office wall."

"You went to see Sanders?" Lilah asked. "I thought we both decided not to."

"Yeah," Harry said. "But I *had* to check the office... and I went to the prison to visit. I needed to know..." It was one more attempt to locate the daughter of the Indian refinery owner he failed to save. He offered Sanders a loan to retain the best possible legal counsel if he'd hand over the girl.

"What did he say?"

"That I could go to my grave wondering," Harry said, tone flat.

Inky-black clouds rolled over Manhattan. The fury of North Atlantic waves battered the tiny island. "We'll keep looking," Lilah said, her heart aching. "You won't give up. You're still looking for the... the..." The monster who attacked her in Libya. "Aren't you?"

"Yes," Harry said. "We'll make the bastard pay for what he did. Sanders was just the first... what he said to me when I visited... the girl... there was no remorse. None! If there were a way to rip him in two and burn the remains, I would have. This picture's the closest we'll get."

With a small prayer for the unfortunate child, Lilah returned her attention to the eight-by-ten photograph framed in black metal. The sepia-toned image showed a sea of oil derricks in the distance with Sanders leaning back against a car, watching the rigs. "Let's not waste time." Lilah removed the photograph from the casing and held it as Harry took out a lighter and put the blue flame to a corner. Dropping it to the floor, they watched until it burned into a pile of ashes.

"Finally, we're done with Jared Sanders." Depositing the soot and the empty metal frame into the garbage can, Harry dusted off his palms.

Alex burst onto the roof, holding a bottle of Dom Perignon and three glasses. "Champagne in the storm," he shouted, handing them the flutes. "Aren't you two glad you made up? Imagine if you didn't." Harry seemed about to respond when Alex continued, "Success and failure will come and go, but we can't lose sight of the things which really matter... family... friendship."

The skies opened again as though in roaring affirmation of the sentiment. Chilled by the needles of icy rain piercing the tweed suit, Lilah shivered. The men were in no better shape, their blazers plastered to their chests. At the railing, Harry stood next to her, facing the city. Alex joined Lilah on her other side, his eyes fixed on the furious waves of the Atlantic.

Lightning streaked through the clouds. The building swayed, and thunder rattled its glass panes. The wind was almost strong enough to sweep them off their feet and into the skies. Lilah was reminded of another moment, of the day she stood atop a cliff in India, making the fateful decision to be the linchpin of their network.

Alex shouted something, his words drowned by the noise of the downpour.

"What?" Harry hollered.

"We beat Sanders," Alex roared into the gale. "We're now *the masters of the universe.*"

With a shout of laughter, Harry gulped champagne, letting some of it spill on his face.

The declaration rang through the air, wind carrying the words across the skies. The icy squall suddenly seemed to invade Lilah's soul, and her trembles turned to violent quaking she couldn't suppress. The mistakes of those who went before could not be repeated. They could not permit power to corrupt them. What Alex said... only words, Lilah tried to assure herself. The excitement of having brought down a giant. Today, the storm might rage and thrill, but tomorrow, the city would smell fresh and clean. Spring awaited them. A new beginning. A new life. A new empire.

THE END of Book 2

For a sneak peek at the next book in the series, please head over to www.JayPerin.com

Afterword

By now, those who know *Mahabharata*, the Indian epic mythology, will have recognized the core story. Most of what I have to say about the original story up to the fall of Jarasandha will be on my website, www.JayPerin.com

A few comments relating to this book and the previous one:

1.   My thanks to the writers whose works on *Mahabharata* I've enjoyed and learned from and to fellow myth enthusiasts from various discussion groups. Thanks to my friends who have patiently sat through my arguments on various plot points, especially Amrita Talukdar and Preeti Gopal.

2.   For the purpose of this story, Temple was president from 1979 to 1986. Reagan-Bush (take your pick) from 1986 to 1992. Yes, I realize that doesn't make it eight years, but it can't be helped because I want to end the story the year I want it to end, so Temple's presidency had to come at this time. Also, I didn't want Temple identified with either a real president or with one of the political parties. Right now, he straddles Carter (D) and Reagan (R) administrations.

3.   I did not use real characters except peripherally. That, too, only for things they were actually accused/guilty of doing. For example, Gaddafi did nationalize a lot of oil operations. Noriega is mentioned; he was imprisoned for drug trade and was supposed to have worked with Pablo Escobar.

4.   I tried to stick to historical facts throughout the story,

including the minor details, but some changes were inevitable. From Book 1, I don't know if Qasr Libya's church was active at the time, but I gave it both Greek and Arabic services. Tribes named Obeidat and the Puelche exist, but the particular clans mentioned in the books are strictly fictional. Then there is the Saudi prince. He is imaginary. The oil glut of 1985 and the country's reaction are not, but the delay created by Harry is definitely my invention. If you find any other inconsistencies… hey, it happens to be true only in this universe.

5.   Masou (I'm told) is a Native American fire god.

6.   The big question – Why the rape in the first book?

The character of Lilah is based on Panchali, the empress of Aryavarta. She is someone who evokes extreme emotions in people. There are some like me who are in awe of her intellect, her steel will, her enormous capacity to give of herself for the betterment of her fellow humans. There are some who loathe her for what they see as sexual immorality, excessive pride, and warmongering. She was assaulted in what was an attempt to gain power without spending blood and wealth on a physical conflict between kingdoms. The disrobing in the dice hall was only a prelude to what would have happened had she not been freed. She *would* have been raped as a slave. Arguing with some fellow myth enthusiasts, I was told not to exaggerate what happened to Panchali. *Exaggerate?* Slaves had no rights, including over their own bodies. Then there are the euphemisms used to refer to the attack—insult, dishonor, and their ilk. These minimize what is a brutal and very physical *crime*.

I wanted to visually demonstrate how different rape is from verbal insults and dishonor. Plus, there is an incident that happens in Book 3, which is there in the original, but I cannot use the same justification in the modern era. You'll see.

I would like to think the original Panchali would not mind her name used this way if it ends up changing at least one mind about the crime of rape.

7.   LexisNexis - database of legal information

So that's it. See you again when *The Cuban Gambit* releases.

Sincerely,

Jay Perin

P.S. As always, if you liked the story, do tell others about it. Also, writers thrive on reviews. They help us figure out what worked and what fell flat. They help other readers make up their minds. Please do leave a comment on any of the sites.

Visit www.EastRiverBooks.com for a bunch of interesting stuff.